BREAK THE BOND. BREAK THE WORLD.

"Aiden Crisp, before he became a novelist, was a submarine officer, and in *The Constantine Covenant* he takes us deep into mystery, suspense, and an apocalyptic tale set around ancient secrets and deadly Nazi U-boats. A brilliant thriller."
—Bernard Cornwell, author of *The Fort*

POWER OVER LIFE AND DEATH

"The power of God is not yours to—"

Elam had been so entranced by Sabe's stare that he did not see the Egyptian's servant approaching him from behind, and he found he did not have the energy to resist as the servant's knife drove into his back and lodged in between his ribs.

Elam dropped to his knees, tasting blood in his mouth. He tried to cry out for help, but it was no use.

"You are a simple man, Elam," Sabe said, now only a few inches from Elam's straining face. "A simple man of a simple people. I will use your god's power to free my people from their Kushite yoke. Then I will become pharaoh, and all the world will bend to my will, starting with your pathetic little kingdom. I will make your king my personal footstool, and his soldiers my slaves."

Elam saw the reflection of torchlight on bronze as the Egyptian used both hands to raise his *khopesh* again.

Sabe then paused and gave Elam an evil grin.

"Think of this, Elam, as mercy, not murder."

A heartbeat later, the blade flashed through the air, and Elam felt no more.

THE
CONSTANTINE
COVENANT

Aiden Crisp

JOVE BOOKS, NEW YORK

THE BERKLEY PUBLISHING GROUP
Published by the Penguin Group
Penguin Group (USA) Inc.
375 Hudson Street, New York, New York 10014, USA
Penguin Group (Canada), 90 Eglinton Avenue East, Suite 700, Toronto, Ontario M4P 2Y3, Canada
(a division of Pearson Penguin Canada Inc.)
Penguin Books Ltd., 80 Strand, London WC2R 0RL, England
Penguin Group Ireland, 25 St. Stephen's Green, Dublin 2, Ireland (a division of Penguin Books Ltd.)
Penguin Group (Australia), 250 Camberwell Road, Camberwell, Victoria 3124, Australia
(a division of Pearson Australia Group Pty. Ltd.)
Penguin Books India Pvt. Ltd., 11 Community Centre, Panchsheel Park, New Delhi—110 017, India
Penguin Group (NZ), 67 Apollo Drive, Rosedale, Auckland 0632, New Zealand
(a division of Pearson New Zealand Ltd.)
Penguin Books (South Africa) (Pty.) Ltd., 24 Sturdee Avenue, Rosebank, Johannesburg 2196,
South Africa

Penguin Books Ltd., Registered Offices: 80 Strand, London WC2R 0RL, England

This is a work of fiction. Names, characters, places, and incidents either are the product of the author's imagination or are used fictitiously, and any resemblance to actual persons, living or dead, business establishments, events, or locales is entirely coincidental. The publisher does not have control over and does not have any responsibility for author or third-party websites or their content.

THE CONSTANTINE COVENANT

A Jove Book / published by arrangement with the author

PRINTING HISTORY
Jove premium edition / July 2011

Copyright © 2011 by R. Cameron Cooke.
Cover design and photo illustration by Jae Song.
Text design by Tiffany Estreicher.

ISBN: 978-0-515-14960-9

JOVE®
Jove Books are published by The Berkley Publishing Group,
a division of Penguin Group (USA) Inc.,
375 Hudson Street, New York, New York 10014.
JOVE® is a registered trademark of Penguin Group (USA) Inc.
The "J" design is a trademark of Penguin Group (USA) Inc.

PRINTED IN THE UNITED STATES OF AMERICA

10 9 8 7 6 5 4 3 2 1

For Carolyn and Aileen

I approached Ekron and slew the governors and nobles who had rebelled, and hung their bodies on stakes around the city . . . As for Hezekiah the Judahite . . . forty-six of his strong, walled cities . . . by leveling with battering-rams and by bringing up siege-engines, and by attacking and storming on foot, by mines, tunnels, and breeches, I besieged and took them . . . Like a caged bird I shut up Hezekiah in Jerusalem, his royal city . . .

Sennacherib, King of Assyria, 7th century B.C.

And Hezekiah prayed before the Lord, and said, . . . "O Lord our God, I beseech thee, save us from his hand, that all the kingdoms of the earth may know that thou art the Lord God" . . . And it came to pass that night, that the angel of the Lord went out, and smote in the camp of the Assyrians an hundred fourscore and five thousand; and when the people arose early in the morning, behold, there were all dead corpses. So Sennacherib, king of Assyria, departed . . .

II Kings, Chapter 19, Holy Bible

Lord Holmhurst knew that things were serious now.

The gray-haired man—the one Holmhurst had overheard his other captors refer to as the admiral—had come back into the room and closed the door, and Holmhurst suddenly got the feeling that his interrogation was about to shift into high gear. Not because he had been conveyed to this place—wherever it was—with a hood over his head by two of the admiral's goons. Nor because his hands were cuffed to the chair. Nor was it the grim expression on the admiral's face, nor the fact that he and the admiral were now alone in the room that had him unsettled. What genuinely had Holmhurst concerned at the moment was the blue-barreled, semiautomatic pistol that had appeared in the admiral's right hand.

"What is that for?" Holmhurst attempted to manage the same composure he had maintained during his earlier interrogations. "You don't need that."

"You have disappointed me, Lord Holmhurst," the admiral said as he produced a silencing muzzle from his trouser pocket and affixed it to the weapon.

"But I've agreed to talk. I've told you everything I know."

"I've been in this business a long time, young man," the admiral said with a tired sigh. "You and I both know that is not true."

"Admiral—may I call you that? Admiral, be reasonable, please. I don't know who you're working for, but whoever it is, they don't seriously intend for you to murder me over a two-thousand-year-old stone carving."

"No." The admiral shook his head, and then looked vehemently into Holmhurst's eyes. "But for the most powerful weapon known to man, I would slit my own mother's throat."

Holmhurst swallowed once and managed to utter, "Oh, well. Horses for courses, I suppose, old boy."

"I want you to tell me about your contact. I want to know about the man called Sturm. I want to know how much he paid you, how often you corresponded with him, and how—"

"Wait, Admiral, *please*!" Holmhurst pleaded, considering his options. The information in his head was all he had to bargain with now. He was fairly certain Sturm would come after him if he divulged what he knew about his operations, and he was not about to walk that tightrope without proper compensation. "Perhaps we could first discuss some sort of payment?"

The admiral gazed for a long moment at the gun in his hand before saying, "I had thought you might be able to help us, Holmhurst. I didn't believe that you were a traitor. I'm sorry to learn that everything I've heard about you is true. Now millions of innocent people will die." With a swift motion the admiral placed the cold muzzle against Holmhurst's perspiring left temple. *"And so will you."*

Holmhurst felt his skin go icy. He had learned to be a fairly good judge of people over the years, and now he recognized true intent in the admiral's eyes. He quickly searched his mind for an answer, for an out, for any way of heading off the next twitch of his captor's finger. What was all the fuss over this two-thousand-year-old relic, anyway? He was starting to think it worth more than the hundred thousand pounds he had been promised to steal it. Sure, it was covered with ancient cuneiform writing. Sure, it had some measure of significance to the Christian and Jewish faiths. But he could not understand the admiral's obsession over it. What had the admiral said? Millions will die? Holmhurst was trying to piece it all together, but he was distracted by the cold round steel jabbing his temple.

There were cars on the street outside, and he heard the muffled voices of pedestrians. It was the end of the workday out there, in the world of the ignorant, the world to which he had never belonged. People were heading home for the day. There were probably a hundred people within a stone's throw of his chair. None of them could know that a murder was about to take place only feet away from their daily commute. For a brief moment, Holmhurst considered shouting for help, but a quick glance at the admiral's penetrating eyes told him he would never get it out.

"It all now boils down to one question, Lord Holmhurst," the admiral said as he pressed the barrel into his skin with enough force to bruise. "Are you more afraid of Colonel Sturm—or *me*?"

PART ONE

PROLOGUE

Jerusalem, 701 B.C.

Angry clouds swirled high above the city as Captain Elam and his seven handpicked men clattered down the torchlit stone steps just inside Jerusalem's eastern wall. The steps led down to a large rectangular pool known as the Pool of Shiloah, which served as one of the few sources of water to the besieged city. Thus, it was no surprise when Elam and his men found the base of the stairs blocked by a troop of the king's own guard, posted there to keep Jerusalem's citizens from carrying off more than their allotted daily ration. But the guards quickly parted and saluted when a brilliant flash of lightning revealed Elam's familiar face to them.

Upon gaining entry to the pool, Elam found the Egyptian prince, Anok Sabe, standing beside the water's edge in full headdress and battle regalia. Elam was surprised to find him there, and even more surprised to see Sabe's bald servant standing a few paces behind, cradling his master's gleaming iron *khopesh*. The long, two-handed sickle-like sword was favored by the people of the Nile. Apparently, the Egyptian prince was preparing to go into battle.

"Are you coming with us, sire?" Elam asked hesitantly.

"Yes," Sabe replied simply.

Sabe was a true Egyptian, with the unrevealing dark eyes and bronze skin of the people of the Nile—unlike the pharaoh he served, who was a black-skinned Kushite.

"It could be dangerous, sire," Elam offered, in the hope that the Egyptian would change his mind. "Perhaps even a trap."

"I wish to see the power of your god for myself," replied Sabe, the corners of his mouth turning up ever so slightly, imparting a doubly sinister nature to his already chilling features. "I want to see if the rumors are indeed true."

"We shall see, sire."

Elam took care to display confidence in the presence of his men and the surly Egyptian, but even he had his doubts about the stories that had made their way to the king's ears, and had thus prompted this mission.

The battle-hardened army of the Assyrian king, Sennacherib, was encamped only a few leagues away. It had succeeded in bottling up the city, and for the last several days the Hebrew warriors atop Jerusalem's walls had listened to the dull rhythm of hammers and axes as soldiers in the distant camp prepared siege engines and assault ramps to be used in breaching the city's defenses. The Assyrians were unstoppable, and the fall of the city inevitable. Elam knew as well as anyone that any sortie beyond the walls by the remnants of Judah's pitiful militia army would only end in disaster. Jerusalem would fall. Her inhabitants would be slaughtered or enslaved, and the last surviving tribes of Israel—the descendants of Jacob, Isaac, and Abraham, the last vestiges of God's chosen people—would be eradicated from the face of the earth. It seemed the will of Yahweh.

That had been the dismal outlook hanging over the heads of the Judahites for the last several days. But now, whispers of hope were spreading through the city. It seemed that the long days of fasting and prayer, of tearing garments and donning sackcloth, of offering the best of their flocks for sacrifice had finally bent the ear of Yahweh, and his merciful hand had stretched out to deliver his people once again.

At least, those were the rumors. Tonight, Elam and his men had been ordered to find out whether they were true.

In the scant torchlight, Elam suddenly noticed that Sabe's servant had a large waterskin slung onto his back. The awkward vessel appeared full to bursting and must have been an extremely heavy burden for the poor man, since he still carried his master's sword in both hands. It was certainly more water than any two men could drink on such a short excursion, and considering the strict rationing imposed on the rest of the city, Elam thought it rather presumptuous.

"Your servant must dump most of that water back into the pool, sire," Elam said to Sabe with a small amount of pleasure, for he had never liked the aloof Egyptian.

A flash of apprehension passed across Sabe's normally composed face before his eyes resumed their natural expression of mild amusement. "I admire the spirit with which you enforce your king's orders, Captain Elam, but do not worry. My servant's bag does not contain water."

"Then what does it contain, sire?"

The Egyptian smiled with his dark eyes, holding Elam in an almost hypnotic stare. Elam forced himself to look away lest he fall under one of the Egyptian's spells, for he had heard that Anok Sabe was also a priest of Rah who worshipped statues of stone and concocted evil potions from the crushed bones of the dead. Elam did not fear the Egyptian's *khopesh* blade, but he was very much afraid of witchcraft—especially any conceived by this particular Egyptian. He quickly decided to let Anok Sabe have his water and let the matter drop.

No one in Jerusalem liked or trusted Anok Sabe. And who could blame them? What was there to like about this insidious-looking creature who had spent the last several weeks gliding around King Hezekiah's court, gazing contemptuously down his nose at everyone and everything Hebrew? In Elam's mind, Sabe had no reason for such snobbery, since he was, after all, a refugee, a survivor of a broken army.

Sabe had been part of a massive Egyptian-Kushite army sent north by the pharaoh to help his beleaguered Judean allies. But on the coastal plains near the town of Eltekah, Sennacherib's Assyrian army had made short work of them, annihilating the pharaoh's force as if it were a mere bothersome fly to be brushed away. Only a handful of the pharaoh's men survived, and those were scattered like chaff in the wind. Anok Sabe had been one of these, and he and his servant had made their way to Jerusalem, where they implored King Hezekiah to grant them refuge. Hezekiah had agreed, but Elam wished the king had turned the Egyptian away. Sabe seemed more of a nuisance than a help, and his mere presence served as a constant reminder to Jerusalem's frightened soldiers that the Assyrian army was unbeatable.

As Elam watched Sabe's servant grunting under the weight of the water that would have been better spent quenching the thirst of Jerusalem's children, he suddenly remembered the old Assyrian saying, "Egypt is like a reed that pierces your hand when you want it to support you." How right they were.

A flash of lightning revealed an inky veil of smoke floating up from the city to join the thunderous clouds overhead. The smoke came from the temple, where Hezekiah, along with the prophets and the priests, now tore their clothes, poured ashes on their heads, and offered sacrifices to the Lord and prayed that he had indeed saved Jerusalem this night.

Whether the Lord had obliged their prayers or not, Elam and his men were about to find out.

They stripped down at the edge of the pool, discarding bulky iron and bronze breastplates but keeping their spears and swords. Elam took only a short sword, while his shield-bearer held the massive iron-backed wooden shield that would protect them both. Elam glanced with disguised envy at Anok Sabe's *khopesh*. The torchlight danced along the curved blade's length, giving it a magical quality. It was a beautiful weapon, with the finesse of a sword and the hacking power of an ax. Elam mused to himself that the splendid weapon might end up in the corner of some Assyrian officer's tent as a spoil of war—if things went badly this evening.

"The men are ready, Captain," the shield-bearer reported confidently.

"Very good, Jahel."

Elam stepped into the knee-deep water of the pool and turned to face his men. They were warriors every one, but the doubt and fear were clear on their faces. Elam knew he would have to convince them they were not about to die. He knew he had to say something inspiring, as he had done so many times in the past.

"We are going outside the city walls. Undoubtedly you saw the enemy encampment from the wall today. Undoubtedly you saw the innumerable tents of the mighty Assyrian host. But there is one thing that you did not see. You did not see a single Assyrian! According to our watchtowers, there has been no movement in their camp all day. Not one of those ugly sons of Belial has shown his face all day long. What is more, they have no fires tonight. An encampment of several thousand men with no campfires can mean only one of two things. Either the bastards are up to something, or they are all dead. And we, my Benjaminite brethren"—Elam forced a ravenous grin—"we are honored above all other warriors this night, because the king has given us the honor of finding out." Elam gestured toward an immense dark cave in the sloping rock face at the pool's north edge. "We go through the tunnel, single file. Stay close together. We cannot use torches inside or we will all suffocate. There is only one way: straight ahead. If we encounter the enemy, kill them quickly, and kill them quietly."

The tunnel Elam and his men were now entering was a new addition to the City of David, the conception of King Hezekiah, who had spent the first years of his reign brooding over how he would defend his city should the Assyrians attack. More important, he had wondered how he would get water inside the city if the Assyrians ever laid siege. The tunnel into which Elam and his men now ventured had been the answer. A small engineering marvel in itself, it had been cut by workers and slaves in a matter of months. It wound nearly twelve hundred cubits through solid rock, running beneath the city's eastern wall to connect the Spring of Gihon, a subterranean spring lying just outside the city, to the Pool of Shiloah, just inside the city. The tunnel had been completed only a few months before the Assyrian army arrived, and Elam could remember how the people had praised God and their king for giving them an assured source of water. Now Elam and his men would use the tunnel for an entirely different purpose: to sneak outside the city unnoticed by the enemy.

Elam ran his fingers across an inscription just inside the tunnel's entrance. The inscription had been etched there by one of the workers as the tunnel had neared completion. Elam had seen it many times before, and he did not know why he paused to stare at it now. Perhaps he wondered if it was the last thing he would see inside the Holy City. But it quickly faded from view as the last torch fizzled into the water, and there was nothing left to do but press on.

The water's steady current pressed against their bellies as they felt their way through the tunnel's many twists and turns. In some places the jagged ceiling was low enough to keep their heads throbbing from constant collisions, and in others the walls were hardly wide enough to squeeze through. But eventually the water receded, the tunnel grew larger, and they reached the great circular cavern where the spring flowed out of the rock. Here, they left the water and followed a steep cave up to the surface, where they were greeted by a flash of lightning that clearly revealed Jerusalem's immense eastern wall with its enormous guard towers now behind them.

They were outside the city, and Elam took a few moments to collect his bearings. Although the Assyrians' camp was on the west side of the city, the enemy had plenty of patrols watching Jerusalem's eastern gates. They had not yet discovered the cave leading down to the spring, so they would not be watching this particular area. At least, Elam hoped they would not.

"I must go before you, Master," Jahel said firmly.

Elam started to protest, but then quietly acquiesced. It was the proper way, after all. Jahel was his shield-bearer, and the shield-bearer must go in front of the sword-bearer. The two were a team, and they had trained extensively to fight that way. Jahel had scarcely left Elam's side since they were boys, and though Elam was an officer and Jahel merely a soldier, in battle the two fought as one man.

The eight Hebrews began their long trek around the

city, assuming a line-abreast formation with the four shield-bearers a short arm's length in front of the four swordsmen and spearmen, while Anok Sabe and his servant walked a few paces behind the group. Their sandals crunched on the loose rock as they made their way up the Kidron Valley to skirt around Jerusalem's northern walls and head west along the slopes that would allow them to approach the enemy camp from an unguarded quarter. After what seemed like an eternity, moving yard by silent yard, presenting weapons and shields to the looming darkness before them, each man holding his breath at the rustle of the smallest desert creature, they finally reached their objective. Elam neither saw nor heard any sign of the enemy as he and his men approached the last low rise that hid them from the Assyrian camp. No voices, no drums, no lowing of cattle or sheep. Nothing.

They reached the top of the rise, and the distant enemy camp now came into view. In the poor lighting, the several thousand tents of the enemy appeared as a great mass of dark patches across the plain before them. Then, suddenly, as their eyes adjusted, Elam and his men noticed something much closer. Directly before them stood two dozen figures, blocking their path to the Assyrian camp. The figures were featureless in the darkness but appeared to be of enormous stature, at least two or three cubits above Elam's head. For a moment, Elam and his men stood still, facing off against what they assumed to be Assyrian giants, but Elam soon pressed them forward.

"Remember the songs of old," he said encouragingly.

"Remember how King David slew the Philistine giant from Gath. Trust in Yahweh!"

Jahel and the other shield-bearers moved ahead, holding their shields high, while Elam and the other three swordsmen and spearmen came up behind, crouching low, preparing to strike at the legs of the fearsome giants. But as Elam and his men drew closer, a flicker of lightning revealed the giants' true identity. Each man, in turn, lowered his guard as he realized the sullen horror of the sight before him.

"I hardly think they will give you any trouble, Captain," Sabe said from behind the ranks, his voice laced with amusement.

Elam resisted the urge to turn on the Egyptian bastard and cleave his head in two. For these were not Assyrian giants at all, but rather Hebrew men, flayed and impaled high upon Assyrian pikes. One of Elam's men vomited when another flash of lightning confirmed the ghastly spectacle, illuminating the glistening bodies like something out of a nightmare.

Elam cursed himself for not choosing another route, for he had witnessed the grisly executions from the city walls two days before and should have expected to come across this. These men were from Lachish, a Hebrew city that had fallen to the Assyrians a few weeks ago after a gallant defense in which the Assyrians suffered heavy casualties. Evidently, the Assyrians wished to avoid taking such casualties when they attacked Jerusalem, so they decided to try to frighten the inhabitants of Jerusalem into surrender. They marched the two dozen captives from Lachish to a prominent spot, in clear sight of

Jerusalem's eastern walls, and there they methodically skinned each prisoner alive, one at a time, finishing off each devilish procedure by impaling the victim on a pike and leaving him to die a slow agonizing death under the burning sun and the eyes of his countrymen. Now, two days later, Elam could still hear the screams of those men in his head. But the creatures upon those pikes hardly resembled anything Hebrew anymore, or human, for that matter. All were dead by now. All except one pathetic creature whose throat gurgled as he stared back at Elam from a bare skull containing large unprotected eyeballs. The man had to be senseless by now. His ripened flesh had been roasting in the sun for two days and had become a feast for flies.

Elam sheathed his sword and gestured to one of his men for a spear. He approached the dying man and, in a lightning quick movement, thrust the spear up into the impaled man's heart, ending his suffering in a matter of moments.

It was the only thing he could do, but when he handed the spear back to his soldier, he noticed that the man accepted it only with reluctance. Evidently the soldier was uncomfortable with the knowledge that his weapon had been used to kill a fellow Hebrew.

"Thou shalt not murder, Captain," Sabe said from the darkness. "Is not that what your Hebrew scriptures say?"

"It was mercy, not murder!" Elam replied as his soul quickly filled with rage. Not at Sabe. For not even the Egyptian's sarcasm could divert his longing for revenge against the Assyrians for what they had done. The mission no longer mattered. Now he wanted nothing more than to kill Assyrians, and he silently prayed that God had left a few Assyrian throats for him to cut.

"Sneaking and spying be damned!" Elam said to his men as he drew his sword and pointed it toward the dark shadows of the Assyrian camp. "The enemy is there, and we will have their blood tonight!"

Then, with a war cry loud enough to wake King David in his tomb, Elam charged off in the direction of the enemy camp. He did not need to look to know that his men were behind him. The sight of the tortured prisoners had incensed them too, and they were right on his heels, following their captain to a potentially glorious, bloody, and swift end. As Elam covered the distance to the Assyrian camp, he fully expected to be knocked down by a fusillade of arrows, but none came. When he reached the outer tents, his sword ready to deliver death to the first Assyrian to cross his path, a foul stench suddenly took hold of his nostrils, and his warrior's grimace was replaced by a dumbstruck stare.

Corpses were everywhere. Assyrian corpses. Hundreds upon thousands of dead Assyrians lay strewn throughout the camp, in every pathway, across the thresholds of the tents, some in clumps, some alone, some naked, others in full battle armor, all bleeding from the nose and mouth with their faces twisted into the most unsettling expressions. Their last moments had undoubtedly been filled with immense horror and unbearable pain. Not one Assyrian soldier, not one camp slave, not even the sheep and cattle were left alive, and the stench alone was almost enough to drive Elam and his men back down the hill. Elam instinctively covered his face with the slack of his headdress to keep from breathing the foul air.

"They're all dead!" Jahel exclaimed. "It's an act of Yahweh! The Almighty has saved us! Praise be to God! We're saved! We're saved!"

Elam could not help but share a small sense of relief, but he knew Jahel's elation might prove to be a bit too hasty.

"How marvelous!" Anok Sabe muttered as he and his servant also walked into the camp. "The great army of Sennacherib struck down by the Hebrew God. Such power!"

The Egyptian was surprised to be sure, Elam could see that much. But while Elam and his men were horrified at the spectacle, Sabe appeared to be in a moment of blissful wonder.

"We too may die from this pestilence," Elam said, "but we must tell the people in the city first. Jahel, take three men. Go to the western gate and tell the captain of the guard what has happened here. Hurry now."

As Jahel and his men trotted off in the direction of the city, Elam saw his other men light torches and scatter to ransack the Assyrian tents. No doubt they were resigned to their fates. If the pestilence killed them, too, they would die with their pockets full of coins and jewels. Elam considered rooting around as well for some valuables before the mass of looters from the city showed up, but his thought was interrupted when he saw Anok Sabe hovering over an Assyrian corpse, studying it intently.

The dead Assyrian lay halfway out of an overturned chariot affixed to dead horses. Beneath his tall conical helmet, the dead enemy warrior stared up at the sky with unseeing eyes. His beard was long and thin, but he appeared to be quite a young man.

"Look at his garments and armor," Sabe said, running a finger across the dead Assyrian's bronze breastplate, covered in the dust and grit intrinsic to a long desert campaign. "They must have been a fine sight when he left Nineveh a year ago. Judging from their quality, I would say the youth belonged to a wealthy family. Perhaps he was even a prince."

Then Sabe used his finger to draw a symbol on the Assyrian's breastplate. It was an odd symbol, a symbol that Elam had never seen before. It looked like the profiles of two perched birds facing in opposite directions.

"What's that?" Elam asked hesitantly.

Sabe did not answer but said simply, "He will make a fine treasure."

"Treasure? He is an Assyrian, and he is dead. That is all I need to know."

At that moment Elam was distracted by a great cheer coming from the city. Torches had appeared atop Jerusalem's walls, and the cheering quickly turned into a great roar as the wonderful news spread from street to street, waking the sleeping Judahites to their day of deliverance.

"Captain!" one of Elam's soldiers said, excitedly. "The people are coming out of the city. They're coming this way!"

"Keep them away from here!" Elam ordered, foreseeing the rush of looters. "And take our dead down from those pikes. Judah should not see such sights on this joyful day."

As the soldier hurried off with the rest of the men to stop the curious mob from approaching, Elam turned his attention back to the camp and was surprised to find that Sabe and his servant had vanished. He hurried over to the spot where he had seen them last, near the dead Assyrian officer's chariot, but when he got there he was shocked to find the Assyrian officer without a head. It had been chopped off at the neck in one clean strike, a feat that could only have been accomplished by Sabe's two-handed *khopesh*. Elam found two more headless bodies nearby, both Assyrians of some rank, both bearing the same odd bird symbol on their bloodstained breastplates, and both undoubtedly victims of the Egyptian's blade, which had neatly sliced through the necks in a single blow.

What could it mean? What purpose could it serve? Elam was confused but instantly suspected it had something to do with Sabe's witchcraft. Elam had been told by Bedouin traders of the Egyptians' obsession with death, and how they erected great stone houses in which to place the dissected and embalmed bodies of their dead kings. Perhaps the mutilation of these Assyrian bodies had something to do with that obsession. But this was God's victory, and Elam was not about to let that son of Belial, Sabe, turn it into a pagan ritual.

Elam noticed that the ground was damp near all three of the headless bodies, but it was not damp with water, nor was it blood. He grabbed up a clump of grass stained with the liquid, held it to his face, and smelled the familiar aroma of olive oil. So this was the substance that had filled Sabe's servant's waterskin to bursting. Undoubtedly, the Egyptian had placed the severed heads in the bag and some of the oil had splashed out onto the ground. But why olive oil? Was Sabe using it to preserve the grisly objects?

Then Elam heard a low murmuring. Its source had to be close for him to hear it above the noise coming from the city. It was a language he did not recognize, and it seemed more like a chant than conversation. There was a tent nearby with the light of a torch flickering inside. It was a rather large tent, much more colorful than the rest, and Elam assumed this had been the Assyrian general's tent. With trepidation he held his sword before him and approached the entrance. He peered inside and saw the dimly lit silhouette of Anok Sabe. The Egyptian had his back to him and appeared as if in a trance as he slowly raised his great curved sword above his head. This was the source of the chanting, and Sabe seemed to chant louder as he brought the sword down on something Elam could not see. But he heard a sickening crunch and suspected it was the neck of the dead Assyrian general parting.

Elam had been a warrior most of his life, but he could not help but let out an audible gasp, which seemed to snap Sabe out of his trance. The Egyptian turned slowly to face him, a broad smile spanning the breadth of his thin dark face, his piercing eyes instantly demanding Elam's full attention.

"What . . . what witchcraft is this?" Elam managed to say, and raised his sword as confidently as he could. "I will not allow you to defile the Lord's victory with your heathen sorcery."

"You cannot understand this, Captain," Sabe said, and dropped his sword, much to Elam's surprise. "You cannot comprehend the power that is at your very fingertips. Judah could have ruled the world with such power. But now"—Sabe sighed, and his eyes glanced once beyond Elam's shoulder—"now, Egypt will."

"The power of God is not yours to—"

Elam had been so entranced by Sabe's stare that he did not see the Egyptian's servant approaching him from behind, and he found he did not have the energy to resist as the servant's knife drove into his back and lodged in between his ribs.

As Elam dropped to his knees, he tasted blood in his mouth and found each breath more difficult than the last. He tried to cry out for help, but it was no use. He could manage little more than a small wheeze. He knew that he was dying.

"You are a simple man, Elam," Sabe said, now only a few inches from Elam's straining face. "A simple man of a simple people. I will use your god's power to free my people from their Kushite yoke. Then I will become pharaoh, and all the world will bend to my will, starting with your pathetic little kingdom. I will make your king my personal footstool, and his soldiers my slaves."

Elam saw the reflection of torchlight on bronze as the Egyptian used both hands to raise his *khopesh* again.

Elam knew that his head was about to be severed and said a silent prayer.

Sabe then paused and gave Elam an evil grin.

"Think of this, Elam, as mercy, not murder."

A heartbeat later, the blade flashed through the air, and Elam felt no more.

CHAPTER ONE

The V-1 rocket had come from out of nowhere, its droning engine sputtering out before the missile nosed over into a steep dive and came down in the Aldwych just between the Air Ministry building and Bush House where the BBC kept its offices. The lunchtime crowd filling the street on that sunny summer day did not know they were in danger, nor could they have seen the danger coming because the ten-story buildings on both sides of the street hid the flying bomb from view until the final moments of its deadly journey. In a flash of light, the eighteen-hundred-pound warhead detonated, and the scenic square disappeared in a cloud of smoke and dust that rose hundreds of feet above the city. When the smoke finally cleared, the terrifying effects of the blast were revealed. Windows were shattered, automobiles crushed, and bodies torn to pieces. In all, forty-six were dead and hundreds more seriously injured. The stalwart Londoners who now sifted through the wreckage had become accustomed to such scenes during the first dark years of the war. Only recently had they dared to hope that Allied mastery of the skies, along with the recent landings at Normandy, had put a final end to the nightmare of the Blitz. Now a new nightmare had replaced the old. Bombers had been replaced by unmanned killing machines that buzzed over the channel from their launch sleds in Belgium and Holland to turn entire city blocks into cauldrons of death and destruction.

Just one street over from the devastated Aldwych, on The Strand, hundreds of citizens heard the V-1 explode and immediately sought refuge in Aldwych Tube Station. The deep reinforced tunnels that had once conveyed passenger trains on the Piccadilly Line now served as bomb shelters and had proven quite invaluable during the mass bombings of the Blitz, perhaps saving thousands of lives. The Aldwych Station shelter, like so many others, often became a steamy sauna when it was crammed with so many Londoners, especially on hot and humid days like this one. There was another tube at Aldwych Station, the east tube, which might have alleviated some of the overcrowding had it been open to the public. At this point in the war, everyone knew about its existence, just as everyone knew that it was off-limits. The entrance was cordoned off twenty-four hours a day and guarded by an armed sentry who allowed no one to pass under any circumstance. Even new mothers looking for a private place to nurse their screaming babies were unceremoniously turned away.

When asked, the local policemen gave the same explanation every time—something about concerns over the tunnel's age and structural integrity in the event of a direct hit. But no one ever really believed that answer, and without any further information from official sources, Londoners conjured up their own wild theories. Some claimed the tunnel hid high government officials during the raids. Some said the prime minister himself took refuge there. Others claimed that the tunnel held a secret stockpile of weapons, left over from the days when a Nazi invasion seemed imminent. One wild story even purported that the tunnel housed captured German scientists who were working on a secret doomsday weapon.

The stories were plentiful and grew more fantastical at each telling, but none ever came close to the truth. The truth was a carefully protected secret, known only to a few in the government, to even fewer citizens—and also to the four men who now walked briskly through Aldwych's deserted east tube as chaos ensued on the streets above them.

The four men did not speak to each other, nor did they pause at any of the many doors and junctions in the mazelike underground, where gleaming rails trailed off into darkness. They had been waiting for a moment like this one for a very long time—a moment when the German V-1s hit especially close to the station, prompting the guards who normally patrolled the east tunnel to abandon their posts and assist emergency crews on the surface.

The four men were therefore not surprised to find the east tube crammed floor-to-ceiling with crates of all sizes. It was a staggering number of crates, stacked tightly into two rows that ran along both walls and stretched into the black unlit portion of the tunnel. The largest of the four men, a man holding a flashlight, led the way. The other three followed him with a quiet obedience that indicated who was the leader and who were the lackeys. The leader was searching for one crate in particular and seemed to have no trouble finding it. He halted beside one stack of crates and held his light such that the beam focused on a four-foot-by-four-foot crate that was sandwiched between two others. The crate had no identifying markings, other than a serial number and a large stamp that read PROPERTY OF THE BRITISH MUSEUM.

"Tommy." The leader gestured with his flashlight. "Get your arse up there and read off that number."

"Sure thing, Patty." Tommy stood on the rail to get a better look at the serial number and read, "1-3-1-G-9-5-6-6-F."

"That's it," Patrick said agreeably, folding and pocketing the paper that contained the same number. "That's the one we came for, boys. Now, Tommy, give me a hand with this top one."

The two took positions on opposite sides of the top crate, which was blocking their access to the one they had come for. But as they hefted the crate off the stack, Tommy lost his grip and the whole container crashed to the floor, landing on its side with an accompanying shatter that portended an ill fate for the contents inside.

Tommy looked at Patrick sheepishly. "Sorry, Patty."

"Congratulations, you bloody idiot!" Patrick snarled in a harsh, but hushed tone. "I'll wager you just broke something what's worth more than your bloody life." Then he shined his flashlight on the faces of each of the other men in turn. "Now you bloody bastards better take care with this next one. Take care, or I'll serve your bloody balls up to His Lordship on a platter!"

Adequately warned, all four men took up positions around the crate in question and carefully lifted it together. Then, carefully but swiftly, they moved back down the tunnel the same way they had come. Patrick had chosen each man for his strength, and this allowed them to move at a cautious but swift pace back down the tunnel the same way they had come without taking any breaks. In less than four minutes, they arrived at an abandoned equipment room streaked with dust-filled cobwebs. The room contained several panels of half-salvaged switchgear that had not been used in more than a decade. This room was situated eighty feet underground, directly beneath a basement utility room at King's College London, next door to the station. Several weeks ago, Patrick had paid off a housekeeper at the college who had admitted him and his men into the room each night, where they had spent the late hours digging out a shaft six feet in diameter, exactly large enough to convey the crate without touching the sides. A freshly made hole in the ceiling of the equipment room represented the culmination of three weeks of all-night digging. A steady stream of muddy water trickled from the hole, seepage from the Thames River, not one hundred meters away. It had proven to be their most difficult obstacle during the dig, but they had overcome it with portable pumps.

With the skill of professional burglars, which they were, two of the men rigged a harness around the crate while Patrick and Tommy ascended the shaft to operate the winch assembly set up in the utility room. They took their time hauling the weighty crate up the long shaft, since any one wrong move would cost them each the five thousand pounds apiece they had been promised to pull off this job.

"Well done, boys," Patrick said when the crate was safely in the King's College utility room, wrapped in canvas and strapped to a large dolly. "Now, all we have to do is wait for our ride."

CHAPTER TWO

U-2553, North Atlantic, in the vicinity of the
Hebrides Islands, Scotland

Captain-Lieutenant Wolfgang Traugott ducked through
the watertight door and into the tight passage separating
the sound operator's and radioman's nooks. He found his
second in command hunched over the radioman's shoulder, waiting patiently while the U-boat's VLF antenna
intercepted the long electromagnetic waves bending
around the cold northern regions of the earth. It took
upward of two minutes to receive the short three-line
message.

"What is it, Number One?" Traugott asked finally,
still yawning after the short sleep in his boothlike captain's cabin.

U-2553's first officer, First Lieutenant Joachim Spanzig, removed a smoldering cigarette from his mouth and
turned to face his captain. He wore a scraggly beard and
deflated blue officer's cap that made him look decades
older than his twenty-four years.

"Convoy report, Captain, from *U-377*. I've woken the cipher officer."

As if on cue, another officer, younger than Spanzig, emerged through the door while struggling to keep his eyes open. His reddish hair was a tousled mess.

"Good morning, Richyar!" Traugott greeted the young officer with a smile.

Richyar scratched his head, but said nothing, still in a half-conscious state.

Traugott exchanged an amused glance with Spanzig before adding in a lighthearted tone, "Rise and shine, Richyar. Quick, quick! I know you had the evening watch, but that's no excuse. This is a ship of war, my boy. Do you want us to miss that convoy because you need a few more minutes' beauty sleep? Hope you brought your enigma machine with you."

"I have it right here, Captain," the junior officer answered wearily, yawning once before setting the box-like unit on a small desk near the radio stand. He rubbed his eyes as the radioman passed him the sheet of paper containing the raw typed text of what had just come off the radio broadcast. The message appeared to be nothing more than a jumble of letters, but it was in fact an intricate code, decipherable only by an enigma machine containing the correct cipher key. Richyar's fingers moved swiftly, and it took him only a few minutes to decode the message.

An eager Spanzig examined the decoded message first, then, after an acknowledging nod from Traugott, read it out loud. *"To all U-boat commanders in vicinity of grid AM44 . . . Enemy convoy sighted. Nine transports, seven freighters. Two ships damaged. Escorts far behind. Position at 1642 local, fifty-five-fifty-five north by thirteen-thirty-seven west, base course zero five zero, speed six knots."*

Spanzig looked up from the message with disappointment. "That puts them only two hundred fifty kilometers from us, Captain! Too bad we will not get to join in the fun."

"Who says so?" Traugott smiled.

Spanzig looked confused. "Our orders, sir. We must make the rendezvous. That is our mission, is it not?"

"I'm getting tired of such missions, Joachim," Traugott said wearily.

"I am, too, Captain, but, nevertheless, we must follow our orders. And our orders say to avoid contact with the enemy at all costs."

"You know what I think, Joachim," Traugott said, glancing around him at the forlorn expressions worn by everyone in the room. "I think we have reached a sad state, when news of a convoy is received with faces like these. We are no longer the hunters of the deep. We are little more than delivery boys, ferrying baubles around the Atlantic, ducking the enemy at the slightest hint of danger. Our leaders have successfully purged the fight from our souls. No wonder the Allies are driving us on every front."

Spanzig knew his captain was right, but he tried his best to appear confident for the sake of the men. "What can we do about it, Captain?"

"It appears we can do nothing, Joachim, until we meet our rendezvous. For those are our orders, are they not? But after the rendezvous"—Traugott paused and eyed him with a look of mischief—"after the rendezvous, we will bring on all engines and make for that convoy with best speed."

"Yes, Captain," Spanzig answered, beaming, and completely satisfied with his captain's plan.

"Another message coming in now, sir," the radioman interrupted, holding up his hand. "It has our number."

Spanzig and Traugott exchanged hesitant glances. Somehow, both of them knew what the new message contained. Moments later Richyar had decoded it.

"From *BdU*, to *U-2553*"—Spanzig read the message aloud, his hands almost shaking with anger—"Upon successful completion of pickup, proceed directly to Trondheim. Avoid all contact with the enemy. Do not engage enemy if encountered."

"Shit!" Traugott beat the insulation on the submarine's curved pressure hull with a solid fist, causing the men around him to jolt. "It's as if the shithead of an admiral has crawled inside my skull! Norway again! Damn them to hell!"

Spanzig was much more subdued than his captain, especially in the presence of the three junior crewmen, but he too cursed under his breath.

"Alright, Number One," Traugott mumbled, after finally resuming some semblance of composure. "They think they can deprive me of my kill. They think I'll just roll over and let them use my new boat as a damn ferryboat for their precious artifacts. Well, they can damn well think again!"

Traugott looked at each man in the compartment, making eye contact with each one until each turned away under the power of his captain's incensed stare. Such a show of temper was rare in their usually good-natured captain. Captain-Lieutenant Traugott was not normally like this, but they all knew to steer clear of him whenever he was.

"Now listen, all of you," Traugott said in a low voice but firmly, glancing at the doors to the adjacent compartments to make sure no one else was within earshot. "This message was garbled. We did not receive it clearly. Understood? As far as you are concerned it was never received. And I want no mention of this made to any other member of the crew. Is that clear?"

Around the room they each mumbled a weak, "Yes, Captain." All except Spanzig, who looked more uncomfortable now than angry.

"What is it, Number One?" Traugott asked in a somewhat more amicable tone, evidently somewhat concerned that his second-in-command was not on board with his plans.

"We have orders, Captain." Spanzig hesitated. "I am as angry as you are about it, but we cannot disregard them. This is from *Befehlshaber der Unterseeboot*. It may seem trivial to us, but there must be a good reason they want us to transport these things. Perhaps these items are crucial to the war effort."

"I'll tell you what these items are, Joachim. They are postwar coffers. They are rare valuables intended to line the pockets of the ruling Nazis so that they can live out their lives in comfort under new names in quiet corners of the world when the war is over and Germany is a wasteland. You heed well my words!"

Traugott seemed to suddenly realize that he had said all of these things in front of the junior sailors in the room. Glancing around, he gave a forced smile, as if his comments had been in jest. But everyone in the room knew their captain enough to know better.

Traugott finally crossed the compartment and laid his hands on Spanzig's shoulders. "Joachim, when you have been in the boats as long as I have, you will understand that there is seldom a good reason for our orders. To Admiral Dönitz and the *Führer* our U-boats are nothing more than model ships on a table—bathtub toys for them to play with. They know nothing of the human flesh that crawls inside these steel tubes, that sails them, that rides them down to crush depth under a barrage of *Wasserbomben*. They know nothing of what it takes to hold a crew together when they've been battling ten-meter seas for weeks on end, living off foul meat kept in foul water, sleeping in their own stink. They know little of our business." Traugott paused, evidently to let his point sink in. "I am a U-boat captain, Number One, not a merchant marine. You and I, and all of these men, are U-boat sailors! *U-2553* is a ship of war. She is *our* ship! And she is going to attack this convoy, whether the bloody admiral likes it or not. Are you with me?"

Spanzig considered for a moment while all eyes in the room were on him. Often in the past, he had had disagreements with Traugott, mostly stemming from the dichotomy of their characters—one man still hopeful in the dream of an eternal Reich, another whose faith in the admiralty and the *Führer* died long ago. But despite their differences, Spanzig held immense respect for his

captain. It was hard not to. Captain-Lieutenant Wolfgang Traugott was a U-boat ace several times over and
was idolized by most other captains in the flotilla, not to
mention his own crew. His exploits were renowned
throughout the fleet: twenty-eight ships sunk over the
course of the war, totaling 130,000 tons. Traugott's legendary status was one of the reasons he had been handed
command of an advanced vessel like *U-2553*. Perhaps it
was that legendary status that made it so hard for Spanzig to defy him. Spanzig came from a different generation, a different caste of U-boat officers, a generation
that did not break the rules. Though Spanzig often did
not agree with his captain, Traugott had an uncanny
ability to talk him into just about anything. Traugott
always knew just the right thing to say at just the right
moment, and men would follow him—*anywhere*.

"And after we've attacked this convoy, Captain,"
Spanzig said carefully, "then might we proceed to Trondheim as ordered?"

"Of course, Number One!" Traugott grinned, apparently pleased at Spanzig's conversion.

At that moment, Viktor Lehmann, the navigation
officer, ducked his head through the watertight door
from the operations compartment. "Captain, we hold
Islay off the port bow. That puts us exactly on schedule,
sir. We should enter the North Channel in just under two
hours, and then reach the pickup point just after sun-
down. Would you like to come up and take a look, sir?"

Though he had said it in an offhanded fashion, by
"North Channel" Lehmann meant the narrow, twenty-
kilometer-wide stretch of water, bristling with mines and

antisubmarine defenses, that separated the land masses of Ireland and Scotland.

"Any contacts, Viktor?"

"One picket boat well to the west of us, sir. That's it. But I'm sure there will be more. A few aircraft every now and then, but nothing close yet."

Traugott nodded. "Thank you, Viktor. I will be there presently. Pass the word to all hands, silent routine."

"Silent routine, aye, sir."

After Viktor had left the room, Traugott clasped Spanzig's shoulders with both hands again and looked him in the eyes. "I always knew I could count on you, Joachim. And do not worry. This is not the first time Admiral Dönitz has tried to manage my boat from Berlin."

Spanzig gave a defeated smile and said, "I only hope that after this, he does not take it from you, Captain."

CHAPTER THREE

Papago POW Camp, near Phoenix, Arizona

Captain-Lieutenant Gerd Schroeder lay awake in his bunk casually watching a brown striped scorpion scale the wall above his head in the moonlight. The sinister creatures liked the night. They made their way into prisoners' bunks at night and lay in wait. Schroeder himself had been stung on three occasions during his first few months here, before he had gotten into the habit of checking beneath his sheets before climbing into bed. It was a nuisance of life in the desert that took some getting used to, especially among the new prisoners.

But he was not new anymore.

He had been here for two years—two long years—ever since July 1942. Was it really that long ago? Had it really been that long since the American destroyer sank his U-boat off the coast of Virginia and fished him and the few other survivors out of the water? Had it been that long since he and his men were loaded onto a train in beautiful, green Virginia and not let off again for seven days—seven days spent traversing two thousand miles of North American countryside that had grown bleaker with each passing mile, and bleakest of all when they finally reached the hot deserts of Arizona and the dreary prison camp nestled between the wind-carved Papago Mountains east of Phoenix?

All told, he had spent more time in this desert prison than he had spent fighting at sea. But, perhaps, that was about to change.

Schroeder continued to watch the scorpion as its spindly legs made the transition from the wall to the frame of the bunk above him. The creature's sinister tail with its poised stinger was now only inches away from the head of the man sleeping in the top bunk.

Schroeder quickly rose from his bunk, picked up a shoe, and knocked the scorpion off the frame. Then, using the same shoe, he smashed the scorpion flat on the concrete floor before it could scramble away.

"Scorpion, Captain?" asked a blond man lying in the next bunk over. Like Schroeder, the man wore a plain khaki U.S. Army-issue shirt and pair of trousers, indicating that he was a prisoner of war.

"Yes, Heinrich." Schroeder nodded. "The little devil almost got Ludwig."

"I doubt he could handle a sting in his current condition, Captain."

"Agreed."

Both men turned their attention to the sleeping Ludwig, who broke into a coughing fit lasting several minutes. Heinrich joined Schroeder beside the bunk of their ill comrade and produced a damp towel with which he wiped Ludwig's feverish brow.

"He has been this way for three days now, Captain," Heinrich said. "I'm afraid he will die soon if he does not see a doctor."

"And he would have seen the doctor by now!" Schroeder said tetchily. "If it were not for that damn fool of a sergeant!"

Heinrich looked gloomily back at him. "I do not think Ludwig will be able to come with us, sir."

Schroeder sighed and nodded, knowing all too well that Heinrich was right. The journey they were about to embark on was not for the sick. Ludwig would never make it in his condition. He would have to stay behind in this hellhole.

Schroeder's thoughts were broken by a sudden clamor outside. Many footfalls crunched on the desert shale. A large group of men was approaching the barracks. Moments later, the door flew open and half a dozen U.S. Army military police entered the room in a flurry of white batons and crossbelts. Their leader, a tall sergeant with a large neck, a small forehead, and a lazy eye, flicked on the interior lights, instantly blinding every prisoner who had been feigning sleep.

"Atten-hut!" the sergeant bellowed with a scowl. "Atten-hut! Get out of the rack, you stinking krauts! This is an inspection! Get your asses out of the rack!"

All twenty-five Germans slid out of their bunks and stood at attention in bare feet, lining both sides of the narrow aisle that ran the length of the room—all except for Ludwig, who remained prostrate and coughing, even more vigorously than he had before.

Flanked by his men, the American sergeant strutted

down the aisle, repeatedly slapping the baton into his white-gloved hand as he stared down each prisoner. Some of the Germans flinched at the sound of the baton, and their fear seemed to give the sergeant a great deal of amused satisfaction, which only made Schroeder hate him that much more.

"So, what have we here?" the sergeant said when he noticed Ludwig, still in the bunk.

"The man is ill, Sergeant Foley," Schroeder said in heavily accented English while standing at attention at the foot of the bunk. "He has the camp fever."

"Bullshit!" the sergeant shouted into Schroeder's ear, then struck the post of Ludwig's bunk with his baton with such force that every prisoner in the room jolted. "Get up, you lazy kraut!"

"Sergeant Foley." Schroeder spoke up, doing his best to hide his contempt for the man. "Ludwig is ill. I have made several requests over the past few days that you take him to the camp doctor."

"So you did." The sergeant turned a wily gaze onto Schroeder. "Pity. I must've had better things to do at the time. Like now."

"He needs *ein* doctor, Sergeant!" Heinrich suddenly interjected, standing at attention at the foot of the next bunk over. His English was far inferior to Schroeder's. "He needs one *jetzt*, or he vill die!"

"Nobody asked you, kraut!" Foley barked, taking two steps and feigning a baton lunge at Heinrich's midsection, but the six-foot-one, firmly built German did not flinch. Foley seemed disappointed that he was unable to make Heinrich cringe like the others and abruptly moved in close to the defiant German's face.

"You think you're some kind of fucking hero, kraut?"

"*Nein*, Sergeant," Heinrich answered stoically.

"Yes, you do, asshole," Foley growled. "What kind of fool do you think I am? Don't you think I know the minute I walk out of here, you and your kraut buddies are gonna laugh it up? Think you can pull the wool over old Foley's eyes, do you? Well, I've got news for you, kraut. I'm not your fucking laughingstock! This is not a damn sick call, it's a damn inspection! And it's high time you Huns learned how to follow orders."

Foley turned his attention back to Ludwig, still lying in his bunk. The sergeant made a gesture to two of his guards, and both men converged on the bunk and grabbed the prostrate Ludwig's hands and ankles.

"Sergeant Foley," Schroeder said in an attempt to stop what was about to happen. "I must protest this treatment! I will report this to the camp commandant!"

Without warning Foley jabbed the end of his baton into Schroeder's belly, knocking the wind out of him and sending him crumpling to the floor.

"You won't report nothing, kraut!"

After somewhat recovering, Schroeder looked up in time to see the two guards yank Ludwig out of the bunk and let his limp body fall the five feet to the floor with a loud thud. Ludwig groaned from the sharp impact, but he was too weakened by illness to do anything about it. The two guards then backed away, allowing their sergeant full access to the prisoner in the confined space.

Still coughing from the blow to his gut, Schroeder made an attempt to go to his beleaguered comrade's assistance, but the extended batons of two more of Foley's men kept him away.

"Now that you're out of your rack," Foley said, grinning, as he hovered over Ludwig's crumpled body, "I'm going to give you to the count of three to stand at attention." Foley rapped the baton into his free hand, glancing back at his men and brandishing an ugly grin. "In fact, I'll tell you what I'm going to do. I'm going to count to three in that godforsaken language of yours, so there won't be any misunderstanding between us."

Again Foley looked over his shoulder at his men, and they all began to laugh uncontrollably, obviously amused at some kind of inside joke between them.

The feeble Ludwig must have sensed he was in danger, because he began groping for the nearest bunk post, anything that could help him stand up. He was obviously trying his utmost to comply with the sergeant's order, but every move seemed to deprive him of more energy.

"Okay," Foley said in a phony courteous voice after he and his men had regained control of themselves. "I'm going to count to three in German, and if you're not at attention by the time I get to three, . . . well, may God help you. Okay, here it goes."

A long pause filled the room, interlaced with the guards' continued snickering.

"Oh, wait!" Foley said suddenly, scratching his head in exaggeration. "I forgot. I can't speak a damn word of kraut!"

Without another moment's hesitation, Foley's face twisted into a snarl and he brought the baton down with great force on the kidneys of the prostrate Ludwig. Ludwig writhed in pain from the blow, stirring a roar of laughter from the guards. And the guards continued to laugh as their sergeant proceeded to beat the defenseless prisoner without mercy, his white baton moving like a flash of white lightning as blow after blow struck Ludwig on the back, the thighs, the buttocks. When Ludwig finally managed to roll over onto his back, Foley took the opportunity to plant the heel of his boot in the German's ribs, then proceeded to use the steel toe and heel of his boot on the prisoner's midsection just as enthusiastically as he had used the baton on his back.

Schroeder noticed that the guards around him were so entertained by the sickening spectacle that they had completely shifted their attention away from him. He was about to take advantage of the distraction when he saw Heinrich suddenly lurch past the guards.

Heinrich was on Foley in an instant, planting a knee in the surprised sergeant's gut, knocking the wind out of him and doubling him over. This was followed by a one-handed judo chop to Foley's back that so stunned the sergeant that Heinrich was able to easily swipe the baton away from his failing grip. Then, with the skill of an Olympic wrestler, Heinrich worked into a position behind the dazed Foley and held the baton with both hands firmly against the sergeant's neck, threatening to crush his throat if he continued the struggle.

For a moment, the other guards stood motionless, evidently confounded at how this unarmed German prisoner had managed to neutralize and disarm their sergeant so effortlessly. But they soon regained their senses and began to close in, their batons poised and ready to crush Heinrich's skull at the first opportunity.

"Zurückfallen!" Heinrich shouted with a look of suicidal determination in his eyes. *"Zurückfallen*, or I vill kill him!"

"Nein, Heinrich!" Schroeder pleaded. "Let the sergeant go. It is not worth it."

Prisoner or not, Schroeder was the senior officer present, and he knew it was his duty to defuse the situation. True, Heinrich's intervention had stopped the murderous beating, but now Heinrich himself might end up in front of a firing squad if Schroeder could not talk some sense into him.

"Heinrich!" Schroeder said again, this time in a more forceful tone. "Let the sergeant go! That is an order!"

But Heinrich seemed not to hear him. His face was set in an icy expression as he faced down the guards while holding their red-faced sergeant in a powerful vise grip. It was evident to all that Heinrich was not bluffing, and that one tight pull on the baton would mean certain death for Sergeant Foley.

"Atten-hut!" a loud voice suddenly boomed from the doorway.

Schroeder turned to see another group of Americans enter the barracks. These were officers, and one of them, a middle-aged man wearing the silver eagle of a full colonel on his collar, stopped just inside the doorway to take one disapproving look around the room before storming toward the melee with his entourage of captains and majors in tow.

"What the devil is going on here?" the colonel barked, first at the guards, then at Schroeder. "Captain Schroeder, what is the meaning of this? Why is your man holding my sergeant by the throat? I demand that you order him to release Sergeant Foley, immediately!"

"I apologize, Colonel Reardon," Schroeder said sincerely, with a sharp salute to the camp commandant. "Sub-Lieutenant Heinrich has acted hastily. I have already ordered him to release the sergeant, and I am sure that he will comply without delay."

"Heinrich?" the colonel said in an odd tone of surprise. "Did you say Heinrich?"

The colonel turned his attention toward the two struggling men, and Schroeder noticed a brief look of shock cross his face. It was a look Schroeder had never seen before on the camp commandant's face, and Schroeder could not tell if it was the sight of the veins protruding on Foley's face or something else that had startled him so. Whatever it was, the colonel quickly regained his composure and appeared satisfied when Heinrich finally released his grip on Foley and let the sergeant fall unceremoniously to the floor.

After a few moments, the red-faced Foley regained his breath and two of his guards helped him to his feet. His bloodshot eyes held Heinrich in a loathsome stare while one hand clawed at the abrasions left on his throat by his own baton.

"Seize him!" Foley ordered in a raspy voice.

The guards moved to comply, but were stopped instantly in their tracks by a single look from the colonel.

"You will apprehend no one, Sergeant Foley!" the colonel said in an irritated tone that transformed Foley's glare into a befuddled expression.

Ludwig still lay on the floor from the severe beating and coughed up several mouthfuls of blood and saliva as Colonel Reardon knelt down to examine him.

"I want an explanation for the condition of this man, Sergeant," the colonel demanded.

Foley appeared tongue-tied at the colonel's venomous look. The colonel was certainly no inexperienced fool and had undoubtedly deduced exactly what had transpired here.

"That kraut wouldn't obey orders, sir," Foley said indifferently, pointing at Ludwig's crumpled form on the floor. "Had to be shown his place."

"He was sick, Colonel," Schroeder offered. "We only wanted him to get treatment."

"Shut up, kraut!" Foley spat with venom in his voice, but was instantly squelched by a retort from the colonel.

"This man is an officer, *Sergeant*! And he will be treated as such!" The colonel then gestured to one of his officers. "Major, see to it this man receives swift medical attention."

"Yes, sir," the major replied, and then promptly selected two of Foley's own men to carry Ludwig to the infirmary.

After Ludwig had been gingerly removed from the barracks, Foley stepped up to the colonel, displaying an outward appearance of coolness, but obviously still fuming inside from the colonel's reprimand. "What about Heinrich, sir? What's going to happen to that krau—er, uh, that German, sir? He attacked me, sir. Can't let prisoners get away with that, can we, sir?"

"This is your barracks, Sergeant," the colonel said blandly, ignoring the question entirely. "You are responsible for the well-being of these prisoners! If I *ever* hear of you abusing prisoners again, I will personally see to it that you are transferred to a graves registration unit in Europe, *as a PFC*, for the rest of the war. And that's a promise. Is that clear?"

"Yes, sir."

"Now gather up the rest of your guards and get over to Compound Three, on the double. We've got a *real* problem over there. Move it! On the double!"

"Yes, sir!"

Once again every man in the room, guard and prisoner alike, came to attention as the colonel and his entourage stormed out the door. They were soon followed by Foley and his men, but not before Foley shot a poisonous glance at Heinrich. The last guard turned off the barracks lighting and bolted and locked the door from the outside. The camp was in lockdown.

As the footfalls faded in the distance, all of the prisoners in the room stared at Heinrich with amazement. Heinrich simply stared out the barred window near his bunk and appeared lost in thought.

"You saved Ludwig's life, Heinrich," Schroeder said as the rest of the prisoners eventually returned to their bunks.

"I hope so, Captain. Only time will tell, I suppose."

"It was quite impressive." Schroeder paused, then tried to hide the suspicion in his voice when he added, "I had no idea you were so skilled at hand-to-hand combat."

"I had an older brother who used to bully me as a child. I learned a lot of useful things."

Schroeder forced a small smile before continuing. "When I mentioned your name to Colonel Reardon, he seemed to recognize it. Any idea why?"

Heinrich shrugged. "Before today, I had only seen him from a distance. I do not know why he would know my name, unless he makes a point of knowing the names of all the officers in his camp. What is that look on your face, Captain?"

Schroeder had an inkling, and now he had to press it. After all, Heinrich *was* a relative newcomer to the barracks. What did they *really* know about him?

"It is strange, don't you think, Heinrich, that the colonel did not have you arrested for attacking the sergeant?"

"I suppose, Captain."

Schroeder looked intently into Heinrich's face, which was only partially lit by the camp lights through the window. If there was any indication of truth or deceit in the sub-lieutenant's eyes, it was hidden in long black shadows, and Schroeder cursed himself for being so paranoid again.

"Listen, Captain," Heinrich said, evidently seeing the uncertainty on his captain's face. "If I acted inappropriately, I am sorry. I know I might have put our plans at risk. But I could not stand by and watch that devil beat poor Ludwig to death. Perhaps I did the wrong thing. Perhaps I should stay behind with the others. After all, I have only been here for four months. It is shameful for me to go when there are so many others who have been here longer than I. Perhaps one of our comrades from the other barracks should take my place."

Schroeder stared at Heinrich for several long seconds before he finally made up his mind to trust him. From this point forward, he would banish from his mind any doubts about the sub-lieutenant's loyalty. After all, what choice did he have? Tomorrow night was the chosen night, and Heinrich was a key part of their plans.

"No, Heinrich!" Schroeder said, placing an encouraging hand on the sub-lieutenant's shoulder in an effort to restore confidence in the man whose loyalty he had just questioned. "Without you, we would be nowhere. You have been instrumental to our efforts, if not the guiding force behind them. Besides"—he smiled warmly—"you are my transportation officer, and I do not plan on walking all the way to Mexico. I'd rather ride on one of your rafts."

"Captain, you give me too much credit, I think."

"No, Heinrich. You do not know," Schroeder said solemnly, low enough so that the other men in the room could not hear. "Living out here in this hellhole for years on end, far from the sea, far from your family—it does things to you. Strips you of your spirit, your dignity. Makes you forget why you ever signed up to fight in the first place. As you well know, we get no news in here about the outside world. Just what the Americans tell us.

One Allied victory after another. Landings in Italy and Normandy. Our U-boats being scoured from the sea. It is laughable now, of course, but even I had begun to believe the American propaganda. But four months ago, Heinrich, when you arrived here, everything changed. You brought something with you that none of us had seen in a very long time. Not your pretty blond hair, Heinrich, or your boyish good looks." Schroeder grinned briefly at the jest, then his face turned earnest again. "No, Heinrich, you brought with you a fresh passion for the Fatherland and the *Führer* that most of us had forgotten. It was like a rebirth of our lost souls."

"I think you are still making fun of me, Captain."

"No, no, Heinrich. I am deadly serious. Perhaps because you were captured only a few months ago, you are not aware of how fervently the love of the Fatherland still burns in your heart, but it is evident to me, indeed to all of us who have been tainted by the American propaganda. You have given us a glimpse of the men we once were, and it has invigorated us to do things we never would have dreamed of before." Schroeder paused, then added, "If anyone goes tomorrow, Heinrich, it will be you. I will accept nothing less."

"Very well, Captain," the sub-lieutenant replied, appearing quite touched.

At that moment, the sound of distant voices filled the air. They were German voices coming from the direction of Compound Three, the compound at the northern end of the prison camp. They were singing in unison, belting out vibrant renditions of drinking songs, while the camp guards admonished them in tones equally as loud. The prisoners in Compound Three were defying curfew, and the guards were obviously having trouble getting control of the situation. This was undoubtedly the *real* problem the colonel had mentioned—the one that required every available guard to go to Compound Three *on the double*.

It was also exactly according to Schroeder's plan. The men in Compound Three were doing just as they had been told to do. But tonight was only a test, to see how the guards reacted to the small riot. Tomorrow night would be the real thing, and would involve several more compounds.

Schroeder stood next to the window checking his watch and verifying that all of the roving guards had indeed gone to Compound Three to help quell the chaos. When he finally turned around, all of the other twenty-three men in the room were staring back at him, anticipating his next words.

"Comrades! Be of good cheer, for tomorrow, we return to the war!"

CHAPTER FOUR

**Scottish west coast, sixty kilometers
southwest of Glasgow**

Several men stood near the shoreline, feeling the salty
wind on their faces as they stared out at the calm waters
of the Firth of Clyde. The last light of the setting sun
had just faded behind Ailsa Craig in the middle of the
expansive bay, and now the ominous round rock of an
island was nothing more than an eerie black smudge on
the dark seascape.

"Did anyone see you?" asked the best dressed man in
the group. He was elegantly adorned in a fashionable
black wool coat and tweed newsboy hat.

"No, my lord," Patrick answered, raising his voice to
speak over the crashing surf along the windswept, rocky
shore. "Well, of course they saw us, but I doubt they
figured out what we were doing. At least, I don't think
anyone did."

"You don't think?"

"Well, how can I say for certain, my lord? I had to
swipe the bloody thing in the middle of bleeding

London, in the middle of a bleeding air raid. It's not my fault the museum decided to hide their wares in a bleeding tube station."

The man whom Patrick had referred to as "my lord" smiled in genuine amusement as he stared at the truck that had just arrived at the isolated stretch of coastline. The truck had conveyed the stolen crate over the three-hundred-mile journey from London and had stopped once along the way to lose its white cross markings. Now it no longer looked like an ambulance, but rather a simple army vehicle, and its olive-green paint job blended well with the early-evening darkness.

Lord Holmhurst, the fifth Baron Holmhurst, was thirty-eight years old, handsome and refined. But like his father before him—and *his* father before him—Holmhurst had done nothing to achieve the honors and lands associated with his title but emerge from his mother's womb. Indeed, one would have to search back through five generations of Holmhursts to discover any strains of true nobility. The original Baron Holmhurst achieved his title from King George III as appreciation for valorous service under the future Duke of Wellington in the Indian campaigns of 1799. Along with the title went an impressive estate of six thousand acres, which had quickly turned into a small nightmare of mismanagement. Old General Holmhurst might have been a skilled leader of troops on the battlefield, but he had no skills for managing the needs of an agrarian community. His shortcomings were passed to his descendants such that each successive Holmhurst generation proved more incompetent than the last. Through one far-fetched scheme after another, the estate was mismanaged, and the holdings of the Holm-hursts dwindled. To make matters worse, the barons lived without regard for the future—or for anything but their own copious lifestyles of travel, drink, gambling, and debauchery. Each generation of Holmhursts resorted to selling giant sections of the great estate, until there was literally nothing left. Indeed, the present Holmhurst was a renter in his family's traditional mansion, since his father had sold the property to support his own retire-ment to the south of France, where he spent every last pound, and then some, before dying of alcohol poisoning at age sixty-two.

With none of the fortune of his ancestors, but with all of their appetite for lavish living, young Holmhurst had been forced to look for alternative means to support his own habits. He had, at least, inherited something from his great-great-great-grandfather—the old general—who was said to be an improvising genius on the battlefield. Young Holmhurst had inherited from his grandfather a gift for innovation—uninhibited innovation. He was an expert at exploiting what few assets he possessed, and at this point in time, the most valuable asset the Holmhurst family possessed was its connection to an untold number of high-class gambling establishments across the breadth of Europe. Over the generations, the Holmhursts had played with the wealthy and the powerful—the people who made million-pound deals before breakfast, the people who were running this war.

When the Germans invaded France in May 1940, a virtual wall had gone up between the Allied and Axis nations, and Holmhurst immediately saw it as an opportunity to recover his family's lost fortune. Using his wealthy connections, he set up an immense smuggling ring that quickly turned into a massive operation involving millions of pounds, deutschmarks, and American dollars. He had made an exorbitant amount of money, smuggling nearly everything: cartons of American cigarettes, priceless works of art, automatic weapons, fleeing Jews. If someone on either side was willing to pay the right price for an item, he would find a way to get his hands on it. Now, after five years of war, his operation had succeeded in putting his family's dwindling accounts back into the black, with hundreds of thousands of pounds to spare. His financial standing was so good, in fact, that he was planning on buying back the old ancestral home of the Holmhursts as soon as the war was over. Of course, once the war ended and the seas were open for free trade again, his operation would go out of business. Even now, with the end of the war in sight and the Allies firmly entrenched in Europe, he had already felt a crunch on his profit, losing some key customers in France and in the Mediterranean. Now only the biggest jobs paid off, the jobs for the highest-paying customers, the jobs that required a great deal of planning and security— like this one.

"Where the bloody hell is she?" Patrick muttered as he checked his watch between binocular searches of the white-capped seas. "It's bloody nightfall, already. Another hour and the damn moon will appear, and some bloody fisherman's going to nose over here and see us."

"Calm yourself, my dear Patrick," Holmhurst said with composure, his face smug despite the biting wind.

"Of all the people we've dealt with over the years, *this* client has always kept his appointments."

"Well, I bloody wish he'd hurry up. Being out in the open like this makes me nervous. Makes the lads nervous, too, my lord. I think they've an inkling of what'll happen to them if we're caught. And they're right. Their necks'll likely end up in a hangman's noose. Ours, too, I imagine."

"If they're nervous, my dear Patrick, then I suggest you remind them how much they have been paid. Or should I remind you how much I've paid *you*!"

"No need to get insulting, my lord," Patrick said with a shrug. "The lads are ready. They've done a fine job so far, and they'll do it again when the time comes. Everything's ready."

Holmhurst remained outwardly stoic. Everything was indeed ready. The small motor launch sat beached on the strip of sand below the parked truck. When the customer arrived, Patrick's five men, now huddled in a group on the beach, would move the cargo off the truck and into the launch, and the launch would shove off to meet the pickup vessel at sea. The item would be delivered and the launch would return to shore with twelve suitcases containing two hundred thousand freshly minted pounds— a true king's ransom. The whole handoff should take less than half an hour. But inwardly Holmhurst was beginning to worry, too. The moon would be up soon, and the pickup was late. In another fifteen minutes, he would have to call the whole thing off and order the truck and the launch to disperse. Until then, he had to keep the men's nerves under control, not to mention his own.

"Have the lads fetch some crowbars, Patrick," Holm-hurst said, staring gamely at the cargo space of the parked truck. "Let's take a look at this precious object before our customer removes it from our jolly isles."

"Forgive me, my lord," Patrick said, nearly stuttering, "but are you out of your bloody mind? We can't waste time with that!"

"I want to see it, Patrick! I want to touch it! That's no crate of sardines you've got there. It's a piece of history, a real relic of the ancient world."

"May as well be sardines to me, my lord."

"I know. But I have an appreciation for such things. God knows, my family had to sell enough of our own treasures to . . ." Holmhurst's voice trailed off, and he turned to look directly into Patrick's eyes. "Just do this one thing for me, Patrick, and I promise I'll make it up to you."

Patrick shook his head in bewilderment but eventually waved his men over, ordering them to bring their crowbars.

Holmhurst, Patrick, and two of the men mounted the enclosed truck bed and took up positions on each of the stolen crate's four sides. A few pounds of force on the crowbars popped off the top easily enough, revealing a bed of stuffing papers and padding wedges. When the paper and padding were removed, all that remained was an odd, almost cylindrically shaped item, about three feet tall and two feet in diameter, completely covered by a protective black canvas shroud. Patrick quickly pro-duced a knife that he used to slice through the canvas until it fell in a clump around the base of the object.

"What the bloody hell!" Patrick exclaimed.

Holmhurst said nothing but simply gasped in awe as his flashlight illuminated the smooth edges of what appeared to be a giant slab of stone. Further examination showed the object to be in the shape of a hexagonal cylinder with an abundance of markings etched into each of its six sides.

"You mean to tell me, we're risking our necks for this bloody bit of rock?" Patrick said with disgust.

"This bloody bit of rock, my dear Patrick, is over *twenty-five-hundred* years old."

"Seems like a whole lot of fuss over nothing to me, my lord."

"My dear Patrick, do you not know what this is?"

"Afraid not, my lord."

"Why, it's none other than Taylor's prism—the prism of Sennacherib."

Patrick shrugged. "You've lost me already, my lord."

"You know, Sennacherib? King of the Assyrian Empire? Seventh century B.C.?" Holmhurst's voice sounded uncharacteristically unsteady as he ran his fingers along the etched writing. "Just think, Patrick. This cuneiform was carved by a man's hand long before Christ walked the earth, before the Roman Empire, even before Alexander conquered Persia."

"So why's anyone give a damn about the bloody thing?"

"Because this *bloody thing*, as you put it, impacts the foundations of both Judaism and Christianity. You see, this ancient writing tells of Sennacherib's campaign into Palestine in the late eighth century B.C. It actually confirms that he laid siege to Jerusalem during the reign of Hezekiah, just as the Old Testament indicates in the books of Second Kings and Isaiah. Can you believe it, Patrick? We're actually touching an object that corroborates something written in the ancient Hebrew Scriptures."

"I never did pay much attention in Sunday school, my lord," Patrick said, obviously somewhat amused by his boss's obsession over the silly object. "Still, I can't see why our buyer would go to so much trouble for such a rare piece of shite."

Holmhurst shot an angry glance at Patrick as if he had just committed blasphemy. Then he looked back at the relic and sighed heavily.

"Nor can I, Patrick. Nor can I. But I know that it's of great consequence to him. And that this job is going to set us up for a very long time—a very long time, indeed."

At that moment, everything turned bright outside the truck. Holmhurst and Patrick looked at each other. Something was wrong.

Outside they could hear several men shouting, and one of the voices sounded amplified, as if through a loudspeaker. Through the open curtain, Holmhurst could see one of Patrick's men pull a pistol out of his coat, but before the man could even cock the hammer, the crack of gunfire broke through the whistling wind, and the man dropped to the sand, as limp as a rag doll.

"We've got you surrounded!" intoned the amplified voice. "In the name of the law, give yourselves up!"

"Buggers!" Patrick exclaimed, reaching for his own pistol.

"Don't be a fool!" Holmhurst said, clasping a hand over the weapon. "They'll riddle the truck if you make a fight of it, and I, for one, am not going to die like this!"

"Throw out your weapons, and leave the truck with your hands in the air!" the amplified voice commanded. "You won't get another warning, lads!"

Holmhurst, Patrick, and the two other men tossed their handguns out of the truck and exited the enclosed cargo space one at a time, joining their comrades outside, two of whom already had their hands on their heads, and one of whom lay glassy-eyed and motionless in a bloody patch of sand. Holmhurst could see that the truck was now surrounded by several vehicles, all with bright headlights directed with the intent to blind him and his men.

"Lord Holmhurst," a smug voice said, this time not amplified. "I've been waiting a long time for this."

A man soon emerged from the glare of the headlights, and Holmhurst instantly recognized him.

"Inspector Boggs. How good to see you again. Out for your evening roundup, I see."

"Oh, I've got you this time, Holmhurst. And you can wipe that bloody smile off your face, because there's no barrister in England that'll touch you now."

Boggs was flanked by several men, obviously constables, some holding sidearms, some holding Thompson submachine guns. The inspector approached Holmhurst while the constables hung back at a safe distance, ready to spray the outlaws with bullets at the first wrong move.

"Stealing from the British Museum," Boggs said, his face twisted into a scowl, "now that's a crime in itself,

Holmhurst. But aiding and abetting the enemy? I didn't think even you could stoop so low."

"For the life of me, Inspector, I have no idea what you are talking about."

Boggs sighed, then brushed past Holmhurst and walked a few paces down the beach where the boat sat waiting.

"Come now, Holmhurst. You've got a motor launch. Where else would you be taking your cargo, if not to some enemy shore?"

Holmhurst breathed a quiet sigh of relief. Boggs's statement proved that the overzealous inspector was still just as dense as he had always been. This was a fishing expedition. Boggs did not know anything. Boggs had simply gotten lucky this morning. Perhaps one of Patrick's new men was on the take and had tipped Boggs off. It only confirmed in Holmhurst's mind that he had made the right decision not to share the actual identity of his buyer with anyone else but Patrick.

Boggs came back up the beach and directed his attention now to Patrick and his men. "Maybe one of you others would like to tell us what you were doing here before we haul your bums before the magistrate. Sticking with Lord Holmhurst here can only lead you to trouble. Just look at your dead comrade, there. Now, if one of you was to help me out, I might put in a good word for you . . ."

As Boggs continued his fruitless fishing expedition, Holmhurst suddenly noticed something beyond the inspector's shoulder, something far out in the darkened sea. About a mile offshore, hugging close to the ocean's surface, a faint red light blinked twice before extinguishing itself altogether. Boggs had his back to the water, so he obviously had not noticed the light, and Holmhurst crossed his fingers in hopes that the constables had not seen it either.

In his head, Holmhurst began counting down two minutes.

"Now maybe one of you can tell me what you planned to do with this here boat," Boggs continued, turning to look at the beached craft. "Just look at it, all dandied up with that black paint. I bet it's all fueled up and ready to go somewhere, too. Now, if one of you was to tell me where that somewhere was . . ."

Holmhurst was still counting. Fifteen seconds left. He had to get Boggs's attention away from the water.

"Inspector," Holmhurst said, interrupting Boggs. "I'm curious. Are the rumors true?"

"What rumors?" Boggs said, irritated.

"That you let the chief inspector at Scotland Yard bugger you every day before afternoon tea?"

Patrick and two of his men chuckled at the remark, and it also had the intended effect on Boggs, who turned on Holmhurst in a rage. The inspector took two giant steps and brought the handle of his pistol down hard on top of Holmhurst's head. The blow put Holmhurst facedown into the sand, where he also received two swift kicks to the ribs before one of the constables managed to pull the incensed Boggs away.

"I will see you hanged, Holmhurst!" Boggs yelled. "Hanged! Do you hear?"

Holmhurst spat out a mouthful of sand and raised his

head slightly. He was seeing stars from the blow, but still managed to steady his eyes on the sea in time to see the red light flash two more times and then go away. Neither Boggs nor his men had seen it, and Holmhurst knew the light would not come back. It had been agreed upon with his buyer that the pickup would try to make contact twice, separated by a two-minute interval. If no response was received, the pickup was to go away and await further instructions. Now the pickup was gone, and it would not return.

Holmhurst could barely maintain consciousness from the throbbing in his head, but he managed a small smile secure in the knowledge that the identity of his secret buyer would never be known by Boggs, or by anyone else.

CHAPTER FIVE

Östersund, Sweden

Ulrich Adler, captain of engineers, had not been prepared for visitors this night. In fact, he had just made his final preparations for bed when the wire message arrived alerting him to the distinguished visitor's imminent arrival. Not knowing what to expect, he quickly threw on his field uniform, hastily assembled a platoon and a small convoy of two trucks and a staff car, and just barely made it to the Östersund airfield in time to receive the visitor.

Adler watched deferentially as the Siebel twin-engine plane descended from the night sky and touched down on the runway. It was a beautiful plane, painted gray with a red-and-white German cross emblem just discernible in the moonlight. Adler was an archaeologist by trade, and though his profession had always been to dig up the past, he had always been fascinated by planes, ever since he was a boy. He had kept up to date on the latest models being produced by the Reich, and he knew that this one was a rarity, with a range well over fifteen hundred kilometers.

There were not many of these around, and it lent some hint of his guest's importance.

As the plane rolled to a stop, Adler brought his platoon to attention and tried his best to look straight ahead and keep his admiring eyes from further examining the sleek craft. But when the side door opened and the visitor stepped out, all thoughts of the plane evaporated. The man descending the short stair was of medium build, dressed in the immaculate black uniform of a Waffen-SS colonel, complete with polished knee-high boots, black leather field coat, and gloves. But it was neither the man's uniform nor his rank that had drawn Adler's attention away so abruptly. Beneath the high, trimmed field cap, the colonel's face was completely hidden by an acrylic black mask that glimmered in the scant lighting of the airfield. Beneath the mask, a jet-black flash hood, or ski mask, extended downward in such a way that the colonel's head and neck were completely covered: not a single square inch of skin was visible. The mask somewhat conformed to the colonel's face and contained two small holes for the eyes, and an even smaller rectangular slit for the mouth, from which exuded a thin jet of vapor each time the colonel exhaled in the frigid air. The mask bore such an unsettlingly hollow expression that Adler felt compelled to tear his eyes away from it, and instead focused on the two SS sergeants who accompanied the colonel. Presumably, they were the colonel's bodyguard. Both wore empty expressions and each had an MP 40 machine gun slung under his arm.

The colonel stepped off the last stair and approached

Adler, who mustered a confident "*Heil* Hitler!" while thrusting out an arm.

"*Heil* Hitler." The colonel returned the salute, speaking in a raspy voice that was almost a whisper.

"Welcome to Sweden, Colonel Sturm," Adler said, now close enough to see the intense blue eyes staring back at him from beneath the mask. "It is a privilege to finally meet you in person, sir. I only wish I had had more time to prepare for your arrival."

"Unfortunately, Captain, time is a luxury we do not have," the colonel said firmly, waving a black-gloved hand in a dismissive gesture. "You were sent up here three months ago to accomplish a three-week task. Now we are behind schedule."

"Y-yes, Colonel," Adler stammered, suddenly put on the defensive. What did an SS officer know about such things? A proper excavation could not be rushed. He could not be blamed for the delays. A hundred obstacles had arisen since he had first received his orders to excavate the burial site—obstacles that he had successfully overcome. It had taken time, yes. There had been delays, but they were not his fault. Adler wanted to say all of these things, but he did not. This might have been his first time meeting with Colonel Sturm, but the SS officer had a reputation. Sturm was not one to be crossed.

"You know why I am here, Captain?" Sturm rasped.

"I . . . I assume you received my communiqué of yesterday, sir, and that you are here to see the artifact we uncovered at the dig site."

"Have you told anyone else about it?"

"No, Colonel, no one. My orders were to keep all

findings at the burial site confidential, and I have done that. Of course, my guards and work crew have seen it, but I doubt any of them know what it is."

"And the artifact? What is its condition?"

"Considering its age, I would say it is in fair condition, sir."

"Fair?"

"W-we have taken the utmost care with it, sir"— Adler fumbled over his speech—"but it did not stand up well to the removal process."

Adler suddenly noticed that one of the colonel's black-gloved hands was resting on the holstered Walther P38 at his belt, and he began to wonder if all of the stories about Colonel Sturm were true. Was he really the kind of SS officer who would order someone executed on the spot for saying the wrong thing? Adler was an archaeologist, not a professional soldier. He did not know how to play these games, but he did know that he had better say something to recover, and fast, or he himself might end up as an anecdote to Sturm's infamy.

"Wh-what I meant to say, Colonel, is that the artifact broke into several pieces. But it is all there, and every piece is accounted for. Nothing was destroyed by our excavation. Most of the runes are still there and quite visible to the naked eye. I am sure a much more thorough inspection, under laboratory conditions, will reveal more." Adler paused but could not stop himself from adding, "It is quite a remarkable find, sir."

Sturm's blue eyes stared hard at Adler, as if to search his soul. Perhaps the colonel sensed Adler's fear. Perhaps he was laughing beneath that mask. At any rate, Sturm finally broke the silence in a surprisingly genial tone—as genial as his hoarse voice would allow.

"I wish to go to the dig site at once, Captain."

"Certainly, sir." Adler breathed a sigh of relief. "Please, will you ride in my car?"

Without delay, the little convoy of two trucks and one staff car drove off in column formation, leaving the plane puttering on the runway. They drove to the outskirts of Östersund, then turned onto a dirt road leading into the low hills south of town. Adler rode in the backseat of the staff car along with Sturm and one of the SS sergeants. The other SS sergeant rode in the front seat with Adler's driver, and Adler overheard the two chatting. He heard the SS sergeant mention the word *Flammenwerfer* and could only assume that his nosy driver had posed a question about Colonel Sturm's mask. Perhaps the colonel had been burned by the terrible weapon and now wore the mask to cover up his disfigurement. The colonel gave no indication that he had overheard the conversation, nor did he utter a single word for the entire drive.

They drove for more than an hour on the rough road that snaked across the dark rocky plain. Aside from the dull glow of a few distant hamlets, the headlights of the staff car and the truck were the only sources of illumination on the dark road. The excavation site came into view long before they reached it—a giant burial mound lit up by dozens of suspended lights, like a great carnival in the middle of nowhere. Even though Adler had been living out here for three months, the remoteness of the place gave him a chill.

As the convoy finally rolled into the fenced compound

surrounding the burial mound, a formation of German engineer platoons and two dozen Scandinavian workers came to attention. Adler, Sturm, and the two SS sergeants stepped out of the vehicle and briefly reviewed the ranks of groggy-eyed troops, all roused out of their tents to greet the important visitor from Berlin. Sturm stopped abruptly when he came to the ranks of the Scandinavians, eyeing them with what Adler sensed as disapproval. The workers gawked back at the colonel, obviously captivated by the haunting black mask. A few in the back row chuckled, apparently amused at the masked man in the fancy SS uniform. Adler fully expected one of Sturm's sergeants to silence them but was surprised when Sturm turned his glaring eyes onto him.

"Your orders were explicit, Captain!" the colonel said in an irritated rasp. "You were not to use local laborers. That is why you were given an entire company of engineers!"

"I . . . I didn't think it was that important, sir," Adler stuttered. Again, he was a scientist, not a professional soldier. "My men broke their backs building the compound, sir. Since I had the funds, I thought I could ease their burden by hiring locals to—"

"You are a fool, Captain! A fool who cannot follow simple orders!" From his tone, the colonel might have been gritting his teeth beneath the mask. "We will make certain that you are not considered for any more positions of importance, either in the army or elsewhere in the Reich. Now, I suggest you take me to the artifact, before we decide to have you sent to the Eastern Front, as well."

Adler opened his mouth, stunned, but said nothing. What could he say? Sturm's use of the term *we* had an air of finality to it, as if Adler's name had just been added to the list of state enemies kept in some secret vault at SS headquarters. Whatever powers the colonel had, Adler got the feeling that his hitherto successful career in the Reich had just been terminated.

Still numbed from the abrupt end of his career, Adler mustered the fortitude to escort the three SS men to the entrance of the excavation, where a vast multilevel pit lay before them, carved out of the side of the burial mound. The mound had been stripped to form several levels, each connected by a spiraling earthen ramp. Adler took them down the ramp, passing each successive level where dozens of new wooden crates stamped with swastikas waited to be transferred to trucks for eventual shipment back to Germany. Each crate held neatly packed artifacts from various periods, progressing backward in time from one level to the next, from the nineteenth century to the Middle Ages. Like going on a trip through time, Adler and his men had removed the artifacts layer by layer, working back through the centuries, carefully cataloging and photographing every item discovered, no matter how small or how trivial in appearance. When they reached the bottom level, Adler led Sturm to a worktable on which sat a shallow wooden crate, much smaller than most of the others. The crate lay open, with the top removed, and two of Adler's own men guarded it, both snapping smartly to attention as the masked colonel approached.

Adler watched as Sturm's black-gloved hand fingered

the cloth covering the crate's contents. Adler thought he saw Sturm's fingers trembling just before the colonel threw back the cover to reveal the artifacts beneath. The box contained a chipped jar capped with the symbol of a double-headed eagle. By itself, the jar stirred the inquisitive juices within Adler, but the colonel paid it little attention. Instead he became instantly focused on the other items in the box—what appeared to be no more than a collection of metallic pieces, all severely corroded and twisted, but Adler knew better. So did Sturm, apparently, since the colonel audibly gasped at the sight.

There were nine pieces in all. They used to be one, until Adler's men broke it apart while prying it from the tomb wall where the weight of the earth above had collapsed the wooden box that had housed the artifact for the last few centuries. The pieces that the SS colonel now held in his hands had once made up a copper scroll of ancient origins. In its day, which Adler estimated to be anywhere from two thousand to three thousand years ago, the scroll must have been a shimmering object to behold, indeed a piece of ancient correspondence fit for a king's eyes. But now, it would hardly impress the lowliest beggar on the streets of Berlin, who would undoubtedly discard these torn shards as nothing more than scraps of metal.

Most of the scroll had turned green from the oxidation of two millennia, but with his trained eye, Adler had discerned writing on three of the pieces, which was by far the scroll's most astonishing feature. Clearly, the scroll contained etchings that looked very much like Egyptian hieratic, an early form of writing used mostly by priests in the ancient world. It was exactly what Adler had been sent to Sweden to find, much to Adler's own astonishment, since he had little confidence in the artifact's existence. Despite the delays, it really had not been all that difficult to find. Especially since Sturm had told him exactly where to dig and exactly where he would discover it—in the medieval tomb of a great Scandinavian warrior, marked with a double-eagle emblem. Judging from the swords, shields, and armor found during the excavation—all of which bore the double-eagle emblems—this grave had to be the right place.

But it was the double-eagle emblem that had Adler most curious, and he could not help but probe, even after Sturm's last outburst.

"It is curious, sir," he said carefully, while Sturm studied the objects, "that an Egyptian relic like that would be discovered in the grave of a *Rüs*."

Sturm shot him an intense blue-eyed glance that brought to mind the harshness of Russian winters, and Adler quickly repressed any more curious thoughts he might have had.

"I want everything from this particular grave loaded onto the trucks tonight, Captain."

"Tonight, sir?"

"And I want a platoon of your men to escort the trucks to the U-boat base at Trondheim. You will lead them personally."

"Yes, sir." Adler hesitated, but his scientific mind could not prevent him from asking, "Sir, could we not get these items to Germany faster if we simply took them back to Östersund and loaded them aboard your plane?"

"You are assuming these items are going back to Germany, Captain," Sturm said impatiently. "They are not. And air travel is far too risky for artifacts such as these. Planes have a tendency to crash."

If only I could be so lucky, Adler thought to himself.

"You will be responsible for getting these artifacts to Trondheim, Captain. I expect them there within twenty-four hours."

"It shall be arranged just as you command, Colonel."

"Now I wish to return to my plane."

Adler escorted the colonel back to the top level of the pit and out to the compound mustering ground, where the company of shivering engineers once again came to attention to see off the distinguished visitor. The Swedish workers had long since abandoned their jumble of a formation and, unlike the German troops, they did not resume it for the SS colonel's departure. Instead, they sat around a large fire sipping coffee and chuckling at the discipline of the German troops, whom they thought insane to stand in the cold for such pointless ceremony.

Passing in front of the formed-up troops, Adler walked a few steps ahead of the colonel as they crossed the yard to the idling staff car. He could hear the colonel's raspy voice behind him muttering something to the two SS sergeants, and Adler thought nothing of it, until he saw an expression of horror pass across the faces of his front rank of troops. Adler turned to look behind him and hardly had a moment to register what he saw before the staccato reports of the machine guns rang out across the compound. It was the two Waffen-SS sergeants. They had crossed the yard to within twenty feet of the lounging Scandinavians and were now proceeding to mow down the helpless workers with their MP 40s. The workers were taken completely by surprise as the near-continuous hail of nine-millimeter bullets filled the air around the bonfire. They did not have time to take cover. Some died where they sat, their heads bobbling in succession from the impacts as the sergeants rapidly swept their guns from left to right. Some tried in vain to rush their attackers only to be cut down by the dual stream of bullets. Three men fell wounded into the fire and were left to suffer slow shrieking deaths as the sergeants changed out their magazines and then riddled the backs of the fleeing survivors. When the sergeants' smoking guns finally fell silent, twenty-four bodies lay crumpled across the bloody ground.

"Are these all of the workers you employed?" Sturm asked.

Adler was so shocked by what had just taken place that he could not answer. Finally, an officer standing in the front of the formation of troops spoke up. It was Adler's lieutenant, a young man named Odeman.

"There are three others, Colonel," Lieutenant Odeman said evenly. "They are taking leave in Östersund this week."

Sturm stared briefly at the lieutenant, then turned back to face Adler, moving close enough so that the steamy breath shooting from the mask enveloped Adler's face.

"You will send someone to find them, Captain," Sturm said in his sinister voice. "Find them and make sure they are eliminated. This country is crawling with Allied sympathizers. That's why your orders specified to avoid using local workers. I have no doubt that one of these corpses here was an Allied spy."

"H-how am I to explain this?" Adler cried, visibly shaken and close to breaking down. "These people trusted me."

"Burn the bodies and bury them." Sturm shrugged. "It makes no difference to me. Then close up this operation and get your men back to Germany. Just make sure you get those last three locals, or you will answer to me."

Adler had recruited the workers from Östersund and had even met some of their families. The Swedish people were officially neutral in the war, but with Germany in control of both Norway and Denmark they had little choice but to allow German engineers to dig up the bones of their ancestors. To temper the resentment of the local population, Adler had come up with a cover story that the *Führer* wanted to collect archaeological evidence of Aryan ties between the Swedish and German people. Some of the Swedish workers seemed satisfied with it, others scoffed, but they seemed willing enough to accept Adler's deutschmarks in return for their labor. Adler thought he had been crafty in employing such a deception. Now he felt responsible for their deaths.

"You have much to do, Captain, so do not bother escorting me back to the airfield." Sturm climbed into the backseat of the waiting staff car, and added before closing the door, "Remember, Captain, I want those artifacts in Trondheim within twenty-four hours."

The staff car drove off, leaving Adler staring hollowly at the mangled corpses for several minutes while an icy-cold breeze plastered the long coats of the men in formation to their legs.

"Shall I dismiss the men, sir?" Odeman said from the front rank.

Adler could not answer. He simply nodded and then ducked his head into the wind and marched swiftly toward his own tent at the far end of the compound. Behind him, he heard the lieutenant give orders for the men to fall out, then heard the thump of several dozen boots as the troops rushed back to the warmth of their tents. But Adler's head was swimming, and he did not think clearly again until he was sitting at the desk in his tent, beside a warm stove filled with smoldering embers. He made himself some coffee, which he laced with a generous portion of rum, then thought about what he must do.

He had underestimated Colonel Sturm's desperation to keep the project a secret, and for that twenty-four civilians were now dead. He had underestimated the colonel's intentions. He had underestimated the colonel's cruelty, and now he could only imagine what Sturm and his associates would do with the copper scroll. Adler was not completely unaware of its importance or its potential to inflict great harm. He did not fully understand how it could do this, but he knew it was dangerous. He had not spent the last three months blindly digging in the cold tundra of Sweden. He was an archaeologist, not a soldier. The investigative life force within him could not help but probe further. Two weeks ago, when the excavation first unearthed the medieval grave and began to discover more and more ornate artifacts, he had felt the need to learn more about the burial site and, most important, to find out who was buried here, since none of the artifacts seemed to contain the name of their long-dead owner. He had taken a three-day furlough to Stockholm, under the auspices of needing a few days' rest in a warm bed. Once there, he contacted a prewar colleague at the university, who had managed, after some nudging, to get him access to the Swedish national archives.

Adler had had only three data points to start with. First, most of the objects dated to sometime in the late fifteenth century. Second, the excellent quality and vast number of objects found indicated that the person buried there had to be someone of importance, or at least someone who was very wealthy—perhaps someone of noble birth. And third, the double-eagle emblem, which resembled two eagles perched aside each other and facing outward. Adler knew of only one other such symbol from the period—the double-headed eagle of the House of Palaiologos, the last rulers of the Byzantine Empire, the heirs to the Roman Empire of the East, the part of the empire that had endured after the fall of Rome in the West. For a Scandinavian warrior to bear Byzantine markings on his armor was not all that strange, because for centuries the royal bodyguard of the Byzantine emperor had been composed of Norsemen—the famous Varangian Guard. But what Adler did find puzzling was the date of the objects. The Varangians disappeared as a functional unit sometime in the thirteenth century, two hundred years before this warrior was placed in the ground. So this warrior could not be a Varangian, Adler concluded. More likely, he was a Byzantine refugee, one of the many

Byzantine nobles who had sought refuge across Europe after the Muslim armies of Mehmet II captured Constantinople in 1453. But who was this man? Why would someone who was undoubtedly so important in his day be buried so far out in the country, far from any settlement or town? Most important, why did he have an ancient Egyptian scroll in his grave? For two full days, Adler pored over crinkled letters, manuscripts, and other royal correspondence from the late fifteenth century, focusing specifically on exchanges between the Swedish court and Constantinople. He looked for any mention of a deceased nobleman, assuming that this man might have left relatives or associates back in the Ottoman-occupied city— someone who would have been interested in news of his death. The information was sketchy and Adler hardly knew what to look for. Finally, late in the evening of the third day, just before he was about to give up, he happened across a letter from the Orthodox Patriarch of Constantinople to Charles VIII, king of Sweden. The letter was in Greek, as expected, and was dated August 14, A.D. 1470. It was exactly what Adler had been looking for.

The wind ruffled the side of the tent, startling Adler as he used shaky hands to unlock the top drawer of his small field desk. He removed a notebook from the drawer and opened it to a marked page that contained the notes he had taken in Stockholm. He had translated and copied the pertinent lines from the letter, and now he read over them again:

> *Excellency, we in the Church thank you for the kindness you have shown our late father in the waning years of*

his life. He has gone to his Eternal Father with all of the grace he deserves from a life spent serving his Master, Our Lord Jesus Christ. We trust that Your Excellency, in the spirit of the graciousness you have shown our late father, remember his desire that no person should desecrate his grave, nor have knowledge of his true identity, which is known only to Your Excellency and a select few of our brethren in the Church body. We also trust that, in keeping with our late father's wishes, you have laid him to rest with all of his accoutrements in an unmarked grave, in a place undisturbed by man. It is of the utmost necessity that his final request be arranged without deviation, as was agreed upon. As Your Excellency knows, our late father forewarned that, should the infidel discover his final resting place, an evil greater than any mankind has ever seen, even greater than that endured by the blessed martyrs of this city, will be unleashed upon all Christendom—Heavenly Father protect us from such a calamity. Please forgive this importune inquiry of Your Excellency and know that we send it only in keeping with the covenant we made with our late father, who, in life, implored us to ensure that his wishes would be fulfilled upon his death.

Adler's hands trembled as they held the notebook. He had drawn several conclusions in his own mind, all of which had seemed far-fetched only a few hours ago. Now he was not so sure. After witnessing firsthand the measures his superiors were willing to take to keep this grave a secret, nothing could be ruled out. Especially considering the new item he had found in the grave only yesterday—the item he had chosen not to tell the colonel about. Adler reached farther into the desk drawer but then withdrew his hand quickly when a voice suddenly spoke behind him.

"I have ordered a squad from the third platoon to dispose of the bodies, Captain."

Adler abruptly shut the drawer and wheeled around to see Lieutenant Odeman standing just inside the tent's entrance. Odeman had his helmet under one arm, revealing his square, chiseled features and a head of close-cropped, white-blond hair. There was no telling how long he had been standing there.

"Th-thank you, Lieutenant," Adler managed to say, uncomfortable at the way Odeman was eyeing his notebook, which Adler now closed instinctively.

Odeman appeared puzzled for a brief moment before speaking again. "I have also ordered the artifacts prepared for immediate transport, Captain."

"Good," Adler said as calmly as possible. He knew that his face was flushed and that his body was visibly trembling.

"Are you all right, Captain?"

"Yes . . . I mean, no, Lieutenant. I think I'm coming down with something. Influenza, I suspect."

"Shall I send for the physician, sir?"

"No . . . no, thank you. I'll be fine. I just need a few moments' rest."

Odeman smiled, almost in a condescending manner. "Never seen something like that before, have you, sir?"

Adler knew the lieutenant was referring to the massacre.

"No." Adler shook his head violently, then downed nearly half of the steaming coffee-rum mixture in one gulp.

"I thought so."

"You, Lieutenant? Have you?"

"I was in the Fourth Panzer Army in '42," Odeman said, as if that were answer enough. Evidently, he recognized the confusion on his commander's face, and then added, "In *Russia*."

"Oh . . . Oh, yes. I see."

"Shall I see to the remaining three workers now, Captain?" Odeman said forcefully, almost as if he were the one giving the orders. "Give me a platoon and three trucks, and I will be back before sunrise."

Adler stared blankly at the lieutenant, unable to speak. Adler was a scientist, not a soldier. He could not order the murder of three innocent men. He could see the disgust growing on Odeman's face as he stalled, and he was somewhat relieved when the rugged lieutenant took the initiative.

"I will see to it myself, Captain," Odeman said finally, putting his helmet back on and buttoning up his jacket.

Adler saw Odeman's eyes glance for the briefest moment at the closed notebook on the desk before the lieutenant lifted the tent flap, letting in a chilling gust of wind.

"Good evening, sir," Odeman said simply, then exited the tent, presumably to carry out the dreadful order.

As the flap closed and the tent returned to a livable temperature, Adler considered his predicament. For the first time in his life, he wished he had the fortitude of a soldier. He needed courage to do what he was considering. The war was over. Everyone with a brain knew it. The Americans and the British were driving across France, and the Russians were unstoppable in the East. This nightmare of murder and destruction, with which Adler had disagreed from the start, was almost over. Now Sturm and his associates wanted to add a new horror to the carnage—something more terrible than any weapon devised by either side.

Adler opened the desk drawer again and removed something flimsy—something resembling a crinkled and folded piece of paper. Adler turned the object over in his hands and unfolded it. It was a sheet of parchment—an ancient document, written on animal skin. He had found it yesterday not too far from the place where the box containing the scroll had been unearthed. It had spent the centuries sealed inside a simple glass jar, and, aside from a few cracks and warped edges, it was in excellent condition. On one side, it contained several lines of Greek text, divided into sections. Evidently, the document had been written by several people, because the handwriting was not consistent from section to section, but Adler had no trouble interpreting any of it. The document itself and the text written upon it were both rather plain, and perhaps that was why Adler's heart had stopped beating for several moments yesterday when he read it for the first time. What the text contained was truly remarkable—and truly frightening at the same time. It had sent chills running up his spine, and he felt the same chills again now, as he turned the document over in his hands, forcing himself to read it again in the faint light of his tent's swinging field lamp. He focused on the last and most recently inscribed text.

Where the Blessed Mother and Saint John the Baptist gaze upon the hands of Christ, Christ's Hands reveal where the sacraments were carried.

It was a riddle, and one that Adler had quickly solved. He opened the magazine on the desk in front of him. It was the March 1944 issue of the *Metropolitan Museum Bulletin.* He had obtained the American publication from a friend in Stockholm. He turned to the marked page containing an article about an American archaeology team's trip to Istanbul.

Adler stared at the parchment and then the photograph in the article, still not quite believing what he had discovered. As he stared at the two documents before him, he realized what he must do. He could not let Sturm and his cronies get their hands on the parchment, nor could he let them take the copper scroll. He had to stop them. Somehow, he had to stop them.

As he was considering what to do, he did not notice the sliverlike crack in the flap covering the entrance to his tent, on the other side of which Lieutenant Odeman spied on his captain with suspicious eyes. Having seen more than enough, Odeman retreated from his position with the delicate finesse of a veteran soldier who had sneaked up on many enemy positions during his career, his footfalls virtually silent in the howling wind. Odeman quickly marched to the radio tent.

"Get in touch with our field unit guarding the airfield

at Östersund!" he snapped to the half-sleeping trooper who was on duty. "And hurry!"

After several attempts to get through, the trooper finally reported, "I have Corporal Schmidt on the line, sir."

Odeman snatched the microphone from his hands.

"This is Lieutenant Odeman, Corporal. Has Colonel Sturm's plane taken off yet?"

"No, sir," the young voice said over the speaker. "The colonel's car has not yet arrived."

"Very good, Corporal." Odeman smiled, now breathing evenly. "Inform Colonel Sturm that I would like him to contact me before he departs. Tell him we have a problem."

CHAPTER SIX

"Torpedo impact!" A sailor's voice echoed up through
the control room's open hatch amid a flurry of cheers, as
the rumble of the distant detonation trembled through
U-2553's hull.

Above the control room, in the conning tower, inside
the small red-lit space known as the commander's control
room, Wolfgang Traugott smiled with satisfaction as he
looked through the attack periscope at the burning
freighter lighting up the night sky in the world above. The
type G7e torpedo's 280-kilogram warhead had blown a
hole in the ungainly vessel's starboard side, and several
secondary explosions now toppled her twin masts and
sent them crashing down into the sea, streaming piano-
wire-tight steel cables over her side. Traugott pulled his
eyes away from the scope to glance over his shoulder at
Spanzig, who was manning the torpedo calculator. Spanzig held up six fingers and brandished a wide grin,
undoubtedly amazed by his captain's incredible luck. All

six of *U-2553*'s torpedoes had run true, with no duds. And now, less than eight hundred meters ahead of the submerged submarine's six empty bow tubes, two Allied freighters and a tanker sat crippled inside a cauldron of burning oil, ablaze from stem to stern, and in various stages of breaking apart.

"Congratulations, Captain!" Spanzig said elatedly.

Traugott did not respond, but only smiled and returned his eye to the periscope lens. He could just make out the dozen dark shapes behind the burning ships quickly fading into the darkness beyond.

"The rest of the convoy has turned away to the south," Traugott announced. "They'll try to evade us, but the seas won't help them. I doubt they can make six knots in this gale. Still no sign of any escorts, either. Shut bow caps and reload all tubes. We'll go deep and sprint ahead of them."

Spanzig echoed the order down to the control room as Traugott took one last long look at the fleeing ships. Now that the enemy ships had completed their turn to the south, the waves were crashing against their bulky hulls and sending up white sheets of icy foam clearly visible even from this distance. It would not take long for *U-2553*'s enhanced battery system and twenty-five-hundred-horsepower electric motors to close the range. Once she was beneath the surface agitation layer, her seventy-six-meter cigar-shaped hull could easily make eleven knots and overtake them. Unlike previous U-boats, the new Type XXI—of which *U-2553* was the first and only one in service—had been designed without any external obstructions that might add water resistance when cruising submerged. She carried no deck guns, and her cleats, hatches, and masts had been designed to retract inside the hull so as not to disturb her streamlined shape. Even her conning tower was of revolutionary design. It more resembled a smooth rectangular fin than the odd, bulky tower found on earlier boats. Her twin two-centimeter antiaircraft guns were fully encased inside rotating turrets on the forward and aft upper edges of the conning tower, both perfectly contoured to retain the tower's smooth shape. And those were only a few of the remarkable innovations that characterized this new class of German U-boat—a U-boat that could turn the tide of the war in the Atlantic.

"Care to take a look before I lower the scope, Number One?" Traugott offered, rising from the small seat that revolved with the periscope.

Spanzig did not need to be asked twice and quickly changed places with Traugott. It was not often that a first officer got to look through the periscope during an attack.

"It is amazing, Captain," Spanzig said with unrestrained excitement as the firelight in the periscope lens danced across his eye.

"Still want to go straight back to Trondheim, Number One?"

Spanzig's eyes cut away from the lens for the briefest moment.

"Never in your life, sir."

Traugott chuckled and slapped Spanzig on the back, pleased that his second in command had come over to his line of thinking. There was nothing like a convoy

attack to invigorate the crew of a U-boat. The crew of
U-2553 had needed this attack, and Traugott had been a
U-boat commander long enough to know how to calm
the frazzled nerves of men at the breaking point.

Last night had been especially terrifying. *U-2553* had
spent several nerve-wracking hours sitting in the Firth
of Clyde—practically in the British prime minister's
bathtub—waiting for a signal from the shore that never
came. Then, as if sweating it out in a shallow enemy bay
were not bad enough, the U-boat had to slip past no
fewer than six destroyers and escorts as it crawled back
out of the North Channel, the narrow waterway between
Scotland and Ireland, skirting deadly minefields the
entire way. By the time *U-2553* had made it to the open
sea, the crewmen had reached their psychological limit.
Several simply shut down and went to their racks,
responding to no one.

Only now, after this torpedo attack, had they shown
signs of recovery.

"Rudder right fifteen," Traugott called down to the
control room. "Steady one-seven-five. Ahead standard."

The order was acknowledged by the helmsman below
and the U-boat slowly picked up speed, steering down to
a southerly heading. Traugott was about to take back the
periscope when he noticed Spanzig increase the lens
magnification and focus the scope down one bearing.
Something had grabbed Spanzig's attention, and now
his smile had transformed into a grave expression.

"What is it, Number One?"

"Survivors," Spanzig said quietly, in an obvious
attempt to keep his voice from being heard by the men

down in the control room. "Survivors in a boat. That fire is going to overtake them before they can reach open water. Very unfortunate."

Traugott quickly took the scope and found that all Spanzig had said was true. Twenty or more oil-soaked survivors, probably from one of the freighters, had taken to a small lifeboat and were desperately paddling in an attempt to get away from the lake of burning crude surrounding the gutted tanker and now enveloping the other two sinking ships. But the men in the lifeboat were fighting a losing battle. The six-foot seas and gale-force winds were setting them back two meters for every meter of gain. In less than fifteen minutes, they would be engulfed in flames.

"Very unfortunate indeed," Traugott muttered as he quickly scanned the horizon for any other Allied ships that might be coming to the rescue. There were none to be seen.

A wild thought suddenly formed in Traugott's mind, and he instantly knew what he had to do. He was a U-boat captain, not a murderer. His enemy was those ships with their stores of tanks, planes, bombs, and bullets—all implements of war that would have been used against the Reich. He had no hatred for these poor merchantmen, and he simply could not watch while fellow sailors died a horrible and fiery death.

"Prepare to surface!" Traugott shouted down the hatch. "Standby to man surface action stations! Assemble the small-boat-handling party!"

As several men in the compartment below donned helmets and broke open boxes of ammunition, a single uncertain expression from Spanzig was the only form of protest. Before he had even given the order, Traugott knew that his first officer would disapprove of the action. Admiral Dönitz's standing order concerning the treatment of survivors was quite clear. *No attempt must be made to rescue survivors of ships sunk . . . Remember, the enemy has no regard for women and children when he bombs our cities.* Anything that went against the grain of the naval high command made Spanzig nervous. Traugott was taking a great risk, but perhaps this would be yet another command lesson for the young first lieutenant.

A long shot of high-pressure air quickly pushed the water from *U-2553*'s main ballast tanks, and she shot to the surface like a leviathan. Traugott was the first one up the ladder, cracking the bridge hatch and climbing through a shower of ice-cold seawater. Within seconds, the lookouts were posted and the two antiaircraft turrets were manned.

It took a few moments for Traugott to get his bearings as he took in deep breaths of the frigid air. Moments before, his view of the world had been constricted to the small circle of light afforded by the periscope lens. Now he could see everything across the entire azimuth, and it was a little bit overwhelming, even to a veteran captain. Looking out over the top of the forward twin two-centimeter turret, beyond the white froth roiling around the U-boat's heaving bow, he could see the collection of burning ships. The two freighters were now little more than burning debris fields, and the tanker would soon be the same. It now stood on end, perpendicular to the water's surface with its blunt bow high in the air. Traugott could hear the groaning of its steel girders. A quick sweep of the horizon with his binoculars revealed no escorts in sight, and the rest of the convoy had already disappeared in the blackness to the south.

"The deck is clear now, Captain," Spanzig reported next to him. "But in this sea, I would recommend keeping the number of personnel topside to a minimum."

"Agreed, Number One. Three should be enough. Pass the word for the small-boat party to lay topside with their lines."

"Aye, sir."

No sooner had the word been passed than a hatch on the forward main deck opened and three sailors emerged toting several coils of hemp.

"I hold a lifeboat visibly, Captain," one of the lookouts reported. "One point off the starboard bow. Range two hundred meters."

"Very good." Traugott quickly found the small boat in his own binoculars. It was much closer to being swallowed up by the flames now, dipping in and out of the waves as it encountered each successive swell. Those in the boat who were not busy paddling had sighted the U-boat and were now waving frantically for assistance. Traugott leaned over to the bridge microphone. "Come right fifteen degrees. Ahead one third."

With the skill of an expert ship driver, Traugott conned the surfaced U-boat until it was within a stone's throw of the bobbing lifeboat, coming perilously close to the flaming oil. Traugott could hear the English sailors pleading for help as his own men on deck cast their lead lines in an effort to snag the small craft. It took three tries before one sailor's cast ran true and was caught by the men in the boat. Moments later the larger hemp line was played out until the eye reached the lifeboat and was securely fastened to its bow. As the U-boat backed off, slowly towing the beleaguered lifeboat out of danger, the relieved men in the small craft could be heard shouting, "Thank you!" across the turbulent space of water. Some even went so far as to shout, *"Danke schön!"*

"The *schweine!*" Spanzig muttered so that only Traugott could hear. "They firebomb our cities, they kill tens of thousands of our people, and now they thank us. We try to kill them, and now we save them. It does not make sense, Captain. Humanity makes no sense in such a war."

Traugott knew that Spanzig held nothing but hatred for the Americans and the British. He had a right to, because his parents and little brother had all been killed during an Allied bombing raid more than a year ago. An incendiary bomb had turned their quiet house into a raging inferno just as they were sitting down to dinner.

"Without humanity, Joachim, all that we fight for is meaningless."

Spanzig attempted a laugh, but Traugott knew it was only for his benefit.

With a good two kilometers of distance between the lifeboat and the burning field of oil and debris, Traugott finally ordered his sailors to cast the lifeboat loose. From here on, the men in the boat would have to fend for themselves against the waves and the elements. It was all

Traugott could do. He had already done much more than Dönitz's standing order allowed, and *U-2553* had lost precious time to pursue the remaining ships of the convoy.

"Let's get after that convoy, Number One," Traugott said. "Clear the decks and bridge, and prepare to dive."

"Aye, Captain."

As the lookouts and gunners filed down the ladder, Traugott took one last look through his binoculars at the Allied sailors in the lifeboat. He waved his arm high above his head to wish them fair winds and following seas but was surprised when they did not wave back. He had trouble making out their faces in the faint firelight, but he could tell they were no longer smiling at him. Then he noticed one of them holding something close to his ear and talking into it as he might talk into a telephone. A small secondary explosion among the debris field lit up the night long enough for Traugott to make out the whip antenna protruding from the boat.

They had a radio!

As he watched, one of the men in the lifeboat raised what looked like a pistol. The man aimed the pistol high in the sky and fired it. With painful slowness, a fireball shot up into the night sky, arcing until it was directly over the U-boat, where it burst into a glimmering flare. The blinding luminosity lit up everything within a five-kilometer radius, reflecting off *U-2553*'s hull as if she were painted snowy white.

"Alarm!" Traugott shouted into the intercom. "Fast dive! Fast dive!"

The alarm rang out in the compartments below, and

Traugott could hear the patter of feet as the off-watch hands ran forward to add weight to the U-boat's bow. The men on deck had already gone below, leaving Traugott and Spanzig as the only ones left outside the pressure hull. But before either man could reach the bridge hatch, the thundering rotors of a twin-engined aircraft blared over their heads, frighteningly close. For the plane to have gotten so close without being heard, it had to have been idling its engines, gliding in toward the U-boat under the guidance of the men in the lifeboat.

Two bombs, two enormous explosions, ripped apart the night, straddling the U-boat and shaking her to the keel as her knifing bow rapidly dipped beneath the surface. Shrapnel peppered the bridge on the starboard side, penetrating the thin walls of the fairwater, leading Traugott to conclude that one of the bombs must have been a fragmentation device, designed to kill men on the U-boat's decks.

Traugott felt a splash of warm fluid across his face and looked up to see that Spanzig no longer had a left arm. The stunned first lieutenant's face went white as he stared at the bloody mess of loose tissue and bone hanging from his mangled shoulder. Blood shot everywhere as Traugott unceremoniously shoved his wounded comrade down the hatch, then immediately followed him, dogging the hatch tightly shut as the first waves swept over the diving U-boat's conning tower.

"Take us deep!" Traugott shouted upon reaching the control room. "One hundred meters! Fast!"

"Yes, Captain," the officer behind the two planesmen

responded, his face grimacing slightly at the sight of Spanzig before he turned back to the planesmen and issued orders that would take the U-boat into the cold depths of the North Atlantic. The two planesmen turned their wheels, controlling the submarine's bow and stern planes, and the rate of descent increased.

Traugott helped two other sailors gently lay Spanzig's bleeding form onto the deck of the control room. Rivulets of blood instantly flowed down the angled deck plates, despite the fact that the medical petty officer had already applied a tourniquet to Spanzig's mangled shoulder. Spanzig did not cry out, he did not moan, he simply mumbled something about his mother as his eyes stared at the overhead and his face turned ashen. He was obviously in shock and suffering from loss of blood.

"Twenty meters . . . thirty meters . . . forty meters . . ." The diving officer called off the depth as the U-boat descended into the dark sea, and the control room fell deathly silent.

Traugott looked intently into Spanzig's face. "Joachim, look at me! Joachim, hold on! Don't let go. Hold on, damn it!"

For a brief moment Spanzig's glassy eyes focused on him and registered something like recognition.

"The ungrateful *schweine*," Spanzig gasped in a tone softer than a whisper. "There is no humanity . . . in war . . . Captain."

Then his eyes went blank, and all animation left his body. The medical petty officer reached over and gently closed the dead man's eyelids.

"High-speed screws, Captain!" the soundman reported

through the open door in the control room's forward bulkhead. "Escorts approaching fast, sir!"

A wave of guilt suddenly crashed over Traugott, and he found himself simply staring at Spanzig's still form, only half hearing the reports around him.

"Eighty meters . . . ninety meters . . ."

"Splashes above us, Captain! *Wasserbomben!*"

CHAPTER SEVEN

The brief knock was barely audible over the rain thrashing against the windows on the other side of the blackout curtains. Admiral McDonough, U.S. Navy, did not bother to look up from his desk when the door finally opened and a tall man dressed immaculately in clean white shirt, coffee-colored jacket, vest, and trousers entered his office.

"Admiral?"

"What do you have for me, Captain Ives?"

"Here's the data you requested, sir." Ives placed a folder on the desk in front of him. It was marked TOP SECRET: ULTRA. "We've heard from our listening posts in Belgium, sir. They've confirmed everything. *U-2553* is the boat we're looking for. We even think she was the boat tagged to pick up the prism last night in the Firth of Clyde."

"Very likely," the admiral said, studying the report through the glasses that had slid to the end of his nose.

"And I see here she's been ordered back to Trondheim, to pick up the artifact, presumably?"

Ives nodded. "It looks that way, sir. But she'll be there for a while, undergoing repairs. It seems she ran into one of our convoys last night and almost got herself sunk. Lost her executive officer and suffered pretty extensive damage. It was all in the broadcast the Dutch intercepted."

"Was it now?" McDonough looked up, suddenly animated and deep in thought, as if the machinery of his mind had been set suddenly in motion. "This presents us with a most fortunate opportunity."

"How do you mean, sir?"

"Has U-Boat Command already picked out a replacement for the dead XO?"

Ives picked up the folder and fingered through the report, settling on one page. "Yes, sir, here it is. A certain Lieutenant Helmut Rittenhaus. U-boat veteran. Served on the Mediterranean station. He's been on convalescent leave for the last few months. Took some shrapnel wounds off Tunisia last summer when a British gunboat caught his U-boat on the surface. He's set to return to active duty as *U-2553*'s second in command."

"Has he made it to Norway yet?"

"I doubt it, sir. I doubt his orders have even reached him." Ives flipped a page. "Says here his home is in Sonnberg, near Salzburg, Austria. That's probably where he's convalescing."

"Perfect!" the admiral exclaimed, jumping out of his chair with a vigor that defied his age. He pushed the intercom button on his desk. "Wendy, get me a channel back to the States. I want to talk with Assistant Director Wilkinson."

"Yes, sir," the secretary's elegant voice came back. "Right away, Admiral."

Ives's expression turned suddenly sour, an expression that was not lost on the admiral.

"What's wrong with you, Captain?"

"Let me guess, sir. Hart?"

McDonough nodded. "He's a shoo-in for this assignment, if ever there was one—especially considering his sub background. What's wrong, Will? You still harboring a grudge? I had hoped you and Matt buried the hatchet long ago."

"Honestly, Admiral, I think Hart would like to bury a hatchet about five inches into my skull—yours, too, sir."

The admiral smiled, waving his hand in a scoffing gesture as he struck a match to light a cigarette.

"What makes you believe he'll come back, sir?" Ives asked.

"Hart's a naval officer, isn't he? And an operative. He's got no choice. He follows orders, just like the rest of us. Besides," McDonough said with a sly smile, "you're the one that's going to go get him for me!"

Ives cleared his throat.

"Oh, don't worry," the admiral added, sanguinely, "I don't think you'll have any trouble persuading him, especially considering the *other* circumstances pertaining to this operation."

"If you say so, Admiral," Ives said halfheartedly.

"Right now, I'm more concerned about convincing the Bureau to give him back to us at the drop of a hat."

"I have the director on the line for you, Admiral," Wendy's voice intoned over the intercom speaker.

"Very good. Thank you, Wendy." Admiral McDonough picked up the phone and instantly assumed the voice of a refrigerator salesman. "Hello, Mister Director, how are you, sir? How's Mrs. Wilkinson . . . And the kids? . . . Oh, that's wonderful. Listen, Mister Director, I know your time is valuable, sir, so I'll get straight to the point. I'd like to talk with you about Special Agent Matt Hart . . ."

CHAPTER EIGHT

Papago POW Camp, near Phoenix, Arizona

Captain-Lieutenant Schroeder and his men worked swiftly inside their dark barracks. They kept the talking to a minimum, although such precautions were hardly necessary because nearly every guard in the camp had been diverted to suppress the riots now in progress in the other compounds. The German prisoners there were raising such a ruckus that the previous night's riot seemed like a birthday party.

It was all according to plan.

The prisoners in the other compounds were doing their jobs. Now it was time for Schroeder and his men to do theirs. They had gone over the plan so many times that any one of them could recite it in his sleep. Now they only needed to put it into action.

Within a matter of minutes, false panels were opened in the walls to reveal stockpiled tools and clothing. Mattresses were slit open and hidden stashes of U.S. currency retrieved. The wooden bunks were disassembled and their usable planks counted and stacked. Prisoner uniforms were exchanged for an assortment of civilian attire that had been procured over the last several months and carefully chosen to blend in with the local population. When all was ready, the twenty-four German U-boat men resembled a college fraternity more than they did a band of POWs.

"All ready?" Schroeder said, after calling them all together.

"Jawohl, Herr Kapitän!" they replied in unison.

"Auf English, *mein Herren,"* Schroeder reprimanded gently. "English from this moment on. Understood?"

The men smiled and replied again. "Yes, Captain."

"Heinrich will brief us on the plan one last time."

Heinrich produced a large paper map, which he laid out on the floor in the center of the group. A flashlight revealed a large-scale view of the southern half of Arizona with a stamped marking in one corner indicating it had been produced by the Arizona State Parks Association—yet another item *procured* by Heinrich. The prisoners knew the map by heart at this point, but all watched intently as Heinrich pointed out the series of conjoining rivers that crossed the breadth of the state from east to west and then ran down the Arizona-California border.

"We go in groups of two, at five-minute intervals," Heinrich said, then pointed to a thin blue line on the map. "Once outside the perimeter, you will head south along this canal. Move quickly and keep to the shadows. After you have traveled approximately one kilometer, you will be out of visual range of the eastern watch tower. Then it should be an easy run to the river, another three kilometers to the south."

Heinrich's finger stopped on a larger blue line, labeled SALT RIVER, running east to west.

"When you reach the north bank of the river, start assembling the rafts immediately." Heinrich gestured to the stack of wood in the corner, the remains of the bunks that were to be transformed into makeshift rafts. "We will wait until everyone is accounted for before shoving off. We cannot leave anyone behind. Once we are afloat, you all know the plan well enough. The Salt River will carry us to the Gila River; the Gila River to the Colorado River; the Colorado down to Mexico and the Gulf of California. In all, it is a three-hundred-fifty-kilometer journey. The dangers should be obvious to you all. We are deep inside a vast enemy territory with no prospect for assistance from the locals, who will undoubtedly be alerted to our escape. We float the rafts on the river by night, and hide out on the shore by day. If we encounter checkpoints, we carry the rafts overland to avoid them. The key is to stay together. We *must* stay together. Any questions?"

There were none, but the gravity of the plan and all of its potential pitfalls seemed to suddenly sink in, evident by the looks on their faces.

"Thank you, Heinrich," Schroeder said, taking charge of the briefing before his men thought about it too much longer. "Once we are safely across the Mexican border, we will make our way to Puerto Peñasco and contact one of the safe houses there. They will help us arrange

for passage to Argentina. Then—my comrades—we go
home."

A collective smile briefly passed across the grim faces
in the group.

"Viel glück . . . ," Schroeder started, and then checked
himself. "Or rather, *good luck*, my comrades." He nodded in the direction of two men. "Group number one, it
is time."

With that, the first pair of men shook hands with the
others, then shouldered their supplies and headed out
through a small trapdoor in the rear wall of the barracks.
The door had been hidden from the guards over the past
months by a locker. Two by two, at five-minute intervals,
the rest of the men exited in the same fashion until only
Schroeder and Heinrich remained.

"I keep thinking about the lake back home, *Hallstät-
ter See*, it is called," Schroeder said, as he waited for his
watch to count down five minutes. "You should see it,
Heinrich."

"I would like that, Captain."

"Cold water." Schroeder smiled as he stared out the
window, seeing the village of his youth through his
mind's eye. "Icy cold. Water that once lived atop
the Alps as virgin white snow. And I will never forget the
scent of those pines that surround the lake. How many
mornings did I push off from that pier with my father? I
could scarcely tell you. We went every Sunday. Always
had a boatload of trout by sunset. It was so cold, so very
cold. But, alas, so very beautiful." Schroeder felt a wave
of despair suddenly cross his thoughts. He stiffened as
the long-forgotten burden of command crept upon his

shoulders once again. Twenty-two men were now outside the prison walls, and soon he and Heinrich would follow. Whatever fate awaited each one of them, he bore the responsibility.

"It all seems so far away from this accursed place—this land of the devil," Schroeder added.

"Perhaps, you will see your home again soon, Captain," Heinrich offered optimistically.

"Perhaps. If all goes well tonight, my friend."

Schroeder finally mustered a weak grin and resigned himself to let the chips fall where they may. It was time. But before he and Heinrich could embark, he needed to gather one last item. Moving over to the discarded mattress that had been his bed for the past two years, Schroeder produced a small knife and carefully slit the mattress open on one side. He reached inside and pulled out an envelope that he knew was hidden there.

"What is that?" Heinrich inquired curiously. "A letter from your wife?"

"No. Nothing as important as that," Schroeder said evasively, and then placed the folded envelope into his shirt's left breast pocket. He chose not to disclose the contents of the letter to Heinrich. Such information would only place the sub-lieutenant in even more danger than both of them were already in.

Heinrich seemed unfazed and simply shrugged as he glanced at his watch. "Shall we go, Captain?"

"Yes, Heinrich. Lead the way."

Both men picked up their knapsacks and raft pieces and exited the barracks through the same trapdoor the others had used. They stepped outside onto the desert shale and waited a few moments for their eyes to adjust to the dull yellow tint cast upon the scene by the camp lights. They waited, but they hardly needed to see to know where they were going. The compound had been their prison for so long that they knew every square foot within its small perimeter. The compound was composed of several buildings, including nine more barracks like their own, four bathhouses, a laundry facility, and a mess hall. All of the buildings were constructed in neat rows across a flattened rectangle of desert, and the entire compound was surrounded by two layers of twenty-foot-high fences brimmed with barbed wire.

Schroeder could clearly see the guard tower near the eastern fence line and tried not to think about the searchlights and fifty-caliber machine guns hidden within its shadowy perch. On most nights, the searchlights in the towers ran continuous sweeps across the prison yard. But tonight, all beams were focused on the compounds to the north, where the prisoner riot was still in full swing.

Schroeder waved Heinrich onward, and they darted from the shadows of the barracks, making their way to the southern boundary of the compound within a few short sprints. They stopped near a bathhouse, a mere stone's throw from the fence line. This particular bathhouse was unique in that its southern side was always hidden from the towers, and thus it was hidden from the all-seeing searchlights.

Heinrich got on his knees and ran his fingers through the dirt until he came up with a small cord of rope that had been buried beneath a thin layer of gravel. He pulled on the cord, and the ground beneath it opened up to reveal a dark hole just wide enough to accommodate a man wearing a knapsack. The cord was attached to a shallow plywood box filled with gravel and made to look like the surrounding landscape, when in place. Over the course of the last few months it had hidden the tunnel from the camp guards, who often patrolled the area, and who had even walked over the spot on several occasions in the full light of day. The complete excavation had taken four months—four long months, with Schroeder's men working two at a time in shifts. They had disposed of the excess dirt in a nearby volleyball court, which had risen several inches over the past months without the guards taking notice of it. Many times Schroeder had bit his nails with certainty that the guards would discover their operation. But they never did, and the tunnel was finished without incident. Now, Schroeder and Heinrich dropped down into it for the last time, carefully replacing the camouflaged lid behind them.

The tunnel descended ten feet underground before curving off in the direction of the fence line. Schroeder had insisted on the extra depth to avoid the network of land mines that he knew pockmarked the space between the inner- and outer-perimeter fences. After a fifty-meter crawl on knees and elbows, Schroeder and Heinrich reached the other end of the tunnel, where another vertical shaft brought them up to the surface and to a similarly camouflaged covering.

As they emerged in the cold desert air once again, Schroeder breathed a small sigh of relief. So far, all was going according to plan. They had made it outside the prison camp, but they certainly were not yet out of danger.

From the tunnel, they emerged onto a patrol road that ran along the camp's eastern edge. The road was bordered by the camp's fence line on one side and by a deep canal on the other, with no cover at all. Had it been daytime, the guards in the eastern tower would surely have seen them, and soon afterward the packed dirt and gravel beneath Schroeder's and Heinrich's feet would have been ripped into mulch by a storm of fifty-caliber projectiles. The thought alone prompted them not to tarry. After a quick check of their equipment, the two headed south along the bank of the canal at a trot. Soon the watch tower was safely behind, and the sound of the rioting prisoners diminished with the distance. After they rounded a bend in the road, the looming dark shapes of the Papago Mountains became visible on their right, and the distinctive round mountains served as an adequate reference point to judge the speed of their advance.

"Not much farther now." Heinrich pointed to a long dirt embankment up ahead. "The river is just over that next rise."

Schroeder nodded and smiled. "The men should have the rafts assembled by now. I'm looking forward to a relaxing ride on the water."

They reached the top of the river's north embankment and peered eagerly over the crest of the dirt ridge. Schroeder fully expected to see his men on the river's shoreline, but the glare from the lights of Phoenix, now visible to the west, completely obscured his view into the chasm beyond. The river, and undoubtedly their comrades, were hidden down there in that black expanse that lay before them. But Schroeder did not hesitate. He gestured for Heinrich to follow, then headed down the steep embankment and into the darkness. As his eyes tried to adjust, he expected to either encounter one of his men or reach the water's edge. In the space of a few meters, he felt the ground beneath his feet turn from dirt, to sand, and finally to smooth rocks. But now he began to think that something was wrong. He had gone too far. He should be wading knee-deep in the Salt River by now, but his feet were high and dry and were still traversing smooth stones. At first, he dismissed the looming feeling inside his gut. Perhaps the river was low this time of year. Perhaps he had misjudged the distance. But when his eyes finally adjusted to the darkness, he stopped in his tracks and gasped in disbelief.

His men were nowhere in sight. The makeshift rafts were nowhere in sight. But more terrifying, the river was nowhere in sight. He stood upon a dry bed of rock and sand that stretched from the north embankment to the south embankment without even a puddle to indicate that water had flowed here anytime in the recent past. A few hundred yards to his right, a railroad bridge spanned the kilometer-wide riverbed. Even in the darkness, Schroeder could see that the bridge's concrete supports were not immersed in water, but were instead buried in dry dirt.

There was no river. No escape route.

As Schroeder tried to make sense of this unexpected turn of events, he suddenly detected, or more like felt,

Heinrich's eyes on him. The sub-lieutenant's shadowy form stood perfectly still only a few feet away and appeared to be staring back at him.

Something was terribly wrong.

"What the devil is going on, Heinrich?" Schroeder demanded. "Where is the river? Where are the men?"

"I am sorry, Captain."

At that moment, several powerful search beams switched on from both embankments and both men were suddenly illuminated in multiple concentric circles of light.

"Stop where you are!" an amplified voice intoned. "Put your hands in the air and lie down on the ground!"

Schroeder could hear American voices approaching. These men had dogs with them. There was no chance of escape. Schroeder could only assume that the rest of his men had been apprehended in a similar fashion. Heinrich's eyes were clearly visible now in the light of the search beams, and Schroeder was shaken to see that they contained no trace of shock or surprise; only, perhaps, a slight measure of remorse. It was at that moment that the cold realization sank into Schroeder's dazed mind.

Heinrich had betrayed them all.

"You knew!" Schroeder said in disbelief. "You led us to this!"

Heinrich nodded, somewhat contritely.

"You traitorous wretch!" Schroeder growled, holding back the impulse to attack the traitor before the Americans reached them. "For God's sake, why?"

Heinrich did not give an answer, and Schroeder did not wait for one. As much as he wanted to break Heinrich's neck, there was something more important that he had to do, and he had to do it before the Americans took him into custody. Groping for his shirt pocket, Schroeder swiftly removed the envelope he had taken from his mattress and ripped it open. He removed the folded paper from the envelope and quickly crumpled it into a tiny ball. He was about to toss it into his mouth and swallow it when a firm hand suddenly grabbed his wrist. It was Heinrich's, and Schroeder was amazed at the strength of the traitor's grip.

"I'll ask you not to harm that document in any way, Captain," Heinrich said through gritted teeth, this time in perfect English and without even the hint of a German accent.

Schroeder hesitated, still somewhat shocked by this sudden transformation in the man he had known and trusted only moments before. Briefly, Schroeder entertained the thought of fighting Heinrich, but then he quickly recalled how skillfully Heinrich had put the American sergeant on his knees only yesterday. Schroeder could see in Heinrich's face that he took no pleasure in what he was doing, but there was also something else in Heinrich's expression—something in his eyes—that told him he was dealing not with a simple informer, but rather a trained killer.

When Heinrich spoke again, his tone was surprisingly polite, but firm.

"Please, Captain Schroeder, I don't want to hurt you. I'm giving you the chance right now to hand over that paper peacefully. This is the only time I'll ask." Heinrich glanced once at the approaching guards. "If you hand it over to me now, you have my assurance that neither you nor your men will be punished, and no one in Germany will ever know about this."

"So, you are *Amerikaner*?" Schroeder said in an attempt to stall, though he did not know for what.

Heinrich did not answer. He simply held out his hand and said, "The paper, please, Captain."

"You ask me to betray the Fatherland?"

"I will have that paper, sir, one way or another. If I have to kill you for it, it will simply be another useless tragedy of this war."

CHAPTER NINE

Forty miles southeast of Phoenix
Two hours later

Sergeant Foley and another military police guard sat in the front seat of the 1942 Nash Ambassador 600 army staff car while Colonel Reardon and the German prisoner Heinrich rode in the backseat.

The car bounced along the rough lonely road at a steady pace, its headlights periodically illuminating families of javelina that scurried into the sagebrush whenever the beams of light touched their furry hides. Behind the car, a churning cloud of dust marked its path across the drought-ridden desert. Phoenix had been left behind, and now a dark desert plain stretched off in all directions, its vastness ever more apparent as the light of a new day outlined a jagged mountain ridge far to the east.

"I don't know what we're doing way out here, Colonel," Foley said for the hundredth time. "This prisoner should be locked in solitary confinement, like all the others."

"Just keep driving, Sergeant," Colonel Reardon said

irritably, "and keep your eyes on the road. We don't want to miss our turn."

"Yes, sir. But do you think it's wise to be out here, all alone, with this kraut? You saw what he did to me, sir. He's dangerous!"

"Keep your eyes on the road!"

"Yes, sir," Foley said, shooting a seething glance in the rearview mirror at Heinrich. The German prisoner was still in his escape attire, handcuffed and silent in the backseat. He stared out the window as if he had no interest in what Foley had to say. He had been silent for the entire trip—ever since being taken into custody along with Schroeder and the other escaped prisoners.

Foley had been with the guards who apprehended Heinrich and Schroeder, and while he was quite pleased that the insolent Nazi bastards were finally going to get a nice long dose of solitary confinement, he was somewhat confused when Colonel Reardon suddenly ordered him to separate Heinrich from the others. According to the colonel, Heinrich was to be taken to a "separate holding facility." Foley had grudgingly complied, and now, two hours later, he drove the car along the rough road, somewhat disappointed that he would not get to punish Heinrich properly. He would have very much liked to watch that bastard squirm under his baton. But it was no matter. There were still around two dozen German prisoners back at camp who needed to be taught a lesson, and he was looking forward to spending several long evenings with them, one at a time. He'd teach the bastards not to escape. His baton would teach them.

"Turn here, Sergeant," Colonel Reardon said suddenly from the backseat, startling Foley out of his daydream.

Foley turned the car onto another dirt road, still wondering where in the hell this other "holding facility" was. The colonel had taken them farther and farther into the desert, until now Foley was beginning to question the colonel's sanity. There was nothing out here, he thought, nothing but Palo Verde trees and tumbleweeds.

Half a mile down the new road, the car's headlights revealed something up ahead, and the guard sitting next to Foley in the front seat suddenly let out a gasp.

"What the hell is that?"

A towering structure appeared ahead of them. It was several stories tall, and had a large canopylike roof supported by four steel columns. It looked like a giant picnic veranda. As they drew closer, the headlights revealed another structure beneath the first—a boxlike, two-story building that appeared to be made out of dried mud. The canopy had obviously been constructed to protect the smaller mud structure from the elements, though Foley could not understand why anyone would want to save such a dilapidated building. He guessed that this mud building was another one of those protected sites he had heard about, scattered throughout the American Southwest. The ruins were probably built hundreds of years ago by some ancient people, and now the U.S. government protected them as a national monument.

Foley then noticed a solitary black Chrysler Airflow parked on the side of the road. It was the first car they had seen in more than an hour.

"Pull over right there, Sergeant," Reardon ordered.

Foley complied, bringing the car to a stop within feet of the Chrysler's rear bumper. Before he could put on the parking brake, two men got out of the Chrysler and approached the staff car. Both wore similar civilian attire—long coats, dark suits, and fedoras—but Foley could tell there was little else "civilian" about these two men. He noticed slight lumps in their coats, just beneath the armpit, and quickly concluded that both men were packing.

The colonel got out to greet them.

"You're quite late, Colonel Reardon," one of the men said from behind a smoldering red cigarette. "We've been here for nearly an hour."

"I'm sorry," Reardon answered, somewhat nervously, "but I was lucky to find this place at all. You couldn't have picked a more remote spot."

"We *didn't* pick it," the man said with slight irritation in his voice, then looked past the colonel's shoulder. "Where's our man?"

Reardon turned to Foley. "Sergeant, fetch the prisoner."

Foley, still somewhat perplexed, got out of the car and removed the handcuffed Heinrich from the backseat. Foley could not resist pushing Heinrich's head hard against the door frame while pretending to check that the handcuffs were secure.

"Sergeant!" Reardon snapped, apparently not fooled by Foley's brutal little trick. "You will treat that man with respect and courtesy! Do you hear? Go ahead and remove his cuffs."

"Sir?"

"Right now, Sergeant!"

Foley turned to see Heinrich wearing a smug smile.

You son of a bitch, Foley thought, as he took out the key and hesitantly released Heinrich from his shackles. The released prisoner instantly began massaging the red marks on his wrists and walked toward the two men in suits, paying no further attention to Foley.

"Good evening, sir," Foley heard Heinrich say evenly to the man with the cigarette.

A smile appeared for the first time on the smoking man's face. "Hello, Hart. How do you feel?"

"Like I need a vacation, sir."

"Do you have it for us?"

Foley watched with interest as Heinrich produced a crumpled sheet of paper from inside his shirt and handed it to the smoking man, who instantly tossed his cigarette to the ground. The smoking man perused the paper with a small flashlight, his face lighting up as he read, as if he were watching a high-stakes horse race.

"I've already checked it, sir," Heinrich said preemptively. "All the names and addresses are there. Should keep you and your boys busy the next few days, rounding them up."

"Indeed, Hart," the man said excitedly. "We will, indeed. And we have you to thank for it. You, too, Colonel."

"Well, I did very little—" The colonel began a modest reply but was abruptly cut off by Heinrich.

"The colonel never should have been brought into this! He almost blew my cover on several occasions, including yesterday. A day away from the escape and the fool came this close to bungling the whole damn thing!"

"Now, just a damn minute," Reardon stammered, "Heinrich, or Hart, or whatever the hell your name is. I watched over you. If it weren't for me, you'd have been locked in solitary, or worse, on numerous occasions."

"I'm a big boy, Colonel. I didn't need your help. I had the situation well under control." Heinrich then turned back to the man in the suit. "In future operations, sir, I recommend that no one—and I mean *no one*—on the camp staff be given knowledge of the mission or the identity of our agents. And that includes the camp commandant!"

"I'll not have secret agents running amok in my camp!" Reardon interjected hotly. "I don't care whose authority you're invoking, I'll not have it!"

"As if you had a choice," Heinrich said somewhat conceitedly.

Reardon's face turned red, but before he could respond, the man in the suit cut him off in an appeasing tone.

"Thank you, Colonel. You have performed admirably in this matter. You've far exceeded our expectations. We have the names we were looking for, and that is what is important. Our objective has been achieved. We appreciate all that you've done for us."

"Hrmpf!" Reardon snorted, evidently not feeling very appreciated.

"Special Agent Hart," the man in the suit added, "you have performed in an exemplary fashion throughout this entire mission. The Bureau owes you a debt of gratitude, and so do I."

"You could show your appreciation by giving me a few weeks' leave in San Francisco, sir," Hart said hopefully. "I'm sick of speaking German. I'm sick of stinking prison camps, and I'm sick of this whole damn desert. I need to get away."

"I wish I could, Matt. If it were my decision, I'd let you go right now, but . . ."

"But, what?"

The man in the suit hesitated. "There's someone here to see you."

"Someone *here*? Right now, sir?"

"That's the reason we had to meet way out here. He insisted that we meet away from populated areas. He says it's important no one finds out he's back in the States. From what I understand, this guy's a former associate of yours."

"Where is he?" Hart's tone indicated that he knew exactly who was there to see him.

"Over by the ruins." The man in the suit gestured toward the dark shape of the old mud structure. "We'll wait here for you."

Foley had been eavesdropping on the entire conversation and had managed to piece together enough to discern that Heinrich—or Hart, as the man in the suit called him—was some kind of undercover agent. Foley suddenly felt like a fool. But, more important, he felt afraid—afraid that Hart might now choose to retaliate for the past months of abuse. Foley swallowed in relief as he watched Hart walk toward the ruins and disappear into the darkness. He wondered if there were any more undercover agents back in the POW camp, and he suddenly had second thoughts about punishing the prisoners when he got back to camp.

CHAPTER TEN

"Hello, Matt. It's been a long time."

Hart saw the dark form of a man materialize near the outer wall of the ancient caliche structure. The man casually strolled toward him and lit a cigarette, the flaring match revealing a plain tweed suit and a face Hart had fully expected to see but had dreaded at the same time.

"I'd salute you, Captain Ives," Hart said abruptly, "but I'm afraid I'm out of uniform, sir."

It was a lie. Hart would not have saluted Ives, even in uniform, and Ives obviously knew it. His narrowing eyes in the dying matchlight revealed that Hart's impertinence had fully registered.

"Still harboring a grudge, eh, Matt?" Ives shook his head. "After all this time?"

"Pardon me, Captain Ives," Hart said sardonically. "I understood that I was expected to accept the fate of my men. It was not my understanding that I should forget them, as well."

"Of course not, Matt," Ives said in a somewhat conciliatory tone. Then, as if to change the subject entirely, he said, "So how have you been? Do you like it here?"

"You certainly didn't come all the way to Arizona to buy me a drink, Captain, so I suggest you get to the point. What's wrong? Have you and the admiral run out of junior officers to dispose of?"

"Always the cocky son of a bitch, aren't you, *Lieutenant*?" Ives's eyes squinted. "All right, I suppose I deserve that. I suppose the admiral does, too—even from a *junior* operative. But, for what it's worth, you should know that I went out on a limb to get your men out of there. I really did. It just wasn't in the cards." Ives paused, exhaling a cloud of smoke. "Maybe you'll understand, someday. Nobody could have saved them. Not with the stakes set as high as they were. Not even the admiral."

Hart said nothing but kept his face set as if it were made of stone. He had heard this same routine long ago. He did not believe it then, and he did not believe it now.

"The admiral would like to see you, Matt." Ives could obviously see that he was getting nowhere down the other course. "He'd like you to come to London with me."

"And if I refuse?"

"Perhaps you didn't hear me, *Lieutenant*! Admiral McDonough wants to see you."

"Do you have written orders for me, sir?"

"Of course not. You know we don't operate that way."

"Then I'm sorry, Captain. I take orders from the director of the Federal Bureau of Investigation now. If the admiral wants me, then I suggest that you go through official channels. Talk to my superiors at the Bureau."

"Of course we've done that." Ives was apparently growing annoyed. "Come on, Matt. Why don't you stop playing the dejected agent for just one minute and listen to what I have to say?"

"I'm not interested."

"How long are you going to brood over the past, Matt? It's been almost two years. A lot's happened in the world. Things have changed."

"My men are still dead. Their names disavowed. Their families left to live in shame without so much as a thank-you from their country."

"Oh, bullshit, Matt." Ives sighed heavily, then continued in a pandering tone. "You stand there and pretend to be some kind of grieving superhero, the loyal captain of a handful of doomed men who would have survived had 'other officers' not let them down. That's it, isn't it? You've shifted the blame away from yourself, leaving only the admiral and me with blood on our hands. Very convenient for you, I must say. And now you hide here, immersed in these meaningless missions—"

"What I do here is not meaningless, sir! It's vital to the war effort."

Ives chuckled at that, and it made Hart seethe inside.

"So, you like it here, Matt, working with the FBI? You like rotting in a filthy desert prison camp for months on end? You like taking beatings, and God knows what else, just to come up with a stupid list of Nazi safe houses in Mexico? I find that hardly instrumental in the grand scheme of things, Matt. Perhaps this is your way of paying penitence, a way of tempering your own guilty conscience?"

Hart shot Ives an evil glance, but it only seemed to amuse him.

"You and I both know the real reason you left, don't we, Matt?" Ives said complacently. "We both know how you felt about *Agent Sevilla*."

Hart took a step toward Ives and came close to knocking the cigarette out of his mouth, but he refrained. Ives was a son of a bitch, an asshole, and a man he had always loathed. But Ives was also a damn good field operative. One of the best in the OSS. He had a special knack for sizing up people, for changing tactics, for probing relentlessly until he discovered his opponent's soft underbelly. And he had just found Hart's.

"Don't ever say her name again in my presence," Hart said, in the most even tone he could manage.

"Is that an order, Lieutenant?" Ives replied, appearing delighted at Hart's sudden vehemence.

"Call it a warning, *sir*."

"Fair enough. Then I take it you wouldn't be interested in any information I might have about her? New information? Information that crossed the admiral's desk not four days ago?"

All of the rage on Hart's face melted away in less than a millisecond. "She . . . *she's alive?*"

Ives smiled. "Ah, ah, ah. Not so fast, my old friend."

"Damn you, Ives! Don't play games with me!" Hart felt suddenly weak in the knees. He could not think. He could not help but clasp Ives's shoulders in his hands and demand again, *"Is Isabelle alive?"*

"There is a chance," Ives said, suddenly solemn.

"What do you mean—?"

Ives held up a finger. "I can say no more. Not here. If you want to know more, you'll have to come back with me to London. I'm afraid this information is far too sensitive to share with anyone outside our program. I'm terribly sorry, but those are the rules. Come back to Odysseus, and you'll learn what we know about Agent Sevilla. Don't come back, and you can forget about her and get ready for your next mission inside that godawful POW camp."

Hart hated Ives, but the bastard had him. He had him hook, line, and sinker. The bastard could be lying about the new information. He could be making it all up, but Hart knew he would never sleep another sound night, if he did not try. There was a chance, just a chance, that Isabelle was still alive, and that was all he needed to jump off any cliff.

"And the mission, *sir*?" Hart asked hesitantly.

"Nothing much." Ives shrugged. "Just a little foray behind enemy lines. You see, the Nazis have gotten their hands on something. Something big. They're losing the war on all fronts, and they're looking for that one big superweapon that will turn the tide back in their favor. We think they may have found it."

"If it's just a simple little foray, then why do you need me?"

"Let's just say that foray involves infiltrating the crew of a German U-boat, stealing a handful of ancient artifacts, and finding out what the hell the Germans are planning to do with them." Ives shrugged. "That's all. Nothing to it. You'll be back in the States, fly-fishing in Montana, eight weeks from now."

"I guess I don't have much choice, Captain."

"No, you don't, Lieutenant." Ives rubbed his hands together and began walking toward the road. "My plane's at the airfield at Casa Grande, just a short drive from here. Those Bureau folks will take us there in their car."

"Just one thing, Captain." Hart stopped him with a hand on his forearm. "How the hell did you know about the list of safe houses? That mission was top secret. Only my handler and three other people knew about it."

Ives gave a disappointed smile. "Oh, Matt. You've been away far too long. In Odysseus, we know *everything*."

CHAPTER ELEVEN

Halifax, Nova Scotia, ten thousand feet
Fifteen hours later

"You're a clever one, Hart. That's good. And quick with the gun. That's better. You're better than most of the bloody Americans I've seen pass through here. That's not saying much, mind you. Still, you might turn out a first-rate spy—if you live long enough."

Hart could hear the words of his old instructor resounding in his head above the roaring engines of the C-47 Skytrain as the big transport climbed for altitude in the skies over Halifax before heading out across the Atlantic. He glanced out the window at the froth-ringed coastline below, watched it disappear into a shroud of mist, and then settled back in his seat for the long flight that would take him back to the life he had tried so hard to forget. Ives sat two seats away and had hardly said a word since the plane took off from Casa Grande fifteen hours ago. That suited Hart just fine, because he had nothing but disdain for the man and made few attempts to hide it. Years ago, he had sworn never to trust Ives again. And now, strangely, he was doing just that, and the words of his old instructor were emerging from his memories as if from his own conscience.

Even now, years after graduating from the top-secret spy school known as Camp X, and after numerous missions, Hart still felt like he had something to prove to his old instructor. The sergeant major of the British SIS, known only as "Jones" to the American spies in training, had never seemed satisfied with Hart's performance, and his words had proved all too prophetic.

"The problem with you, Hart, is that you can't separate your bloody devotion to your men from your bloody devotion to the mission. There may come a time when you have to let them die. Hell, you might even have to pull the trigger yourself. The mission comes first, second, and last, Hart. It's the way of the operative. You can throw all that boorish American nonsense about camaraderie out the window. You talk about esprit de corps? Never trust anything conceived by a bloody Frenchman, Hart. The mission, the mission. All that matters is the bloody mission!"

Camp X sat just thirty miles outside Toronto. Few in the Canadian government even knew the place existed. It had been set up by the British to train their inexperienced American allies in the fine arts of spy warfare, and it was there that Hart had met Sergeant Major Jones for the first time. Jones was just one of the many British instructors there, on loan from the SIS with orders to impart their veteran knowledge to the new agents of America's fledgling Office of the Coordinator of Information—later known as the Office of Strategic

Services, or OSS. Hart and his fellow operatives in training learned everything there was to know about espionage, subterfuge, and sabotage. They learned to be demolitions experts, small-arms marksmen, and down-and-dirty knife fighters. They had been recruited from all walks of life, from every background imaginable, some military, some civilian, each one bringing with him some unique skill from his former life. Hart had been chosen because of his naval intelligence background, or more precisely, because he had served under Admiral McDonough at the Office of Naval Intelligence. When Admiral McDonough left the ONI for a new position at the OSS, he had demanded that a few of his protégés come over with him—Hart being one, Ives being another.

Admiral McDonough had been an intelligence chief for the Office of Naval Intelligence during the peacetime years, but when war broke out, the OSS needed someone to head up a new division forming within its own Special Intelligence department, and McDonough was selected for the job. The new division, code-named Odysseus, would deal exclusively with naval matters. Its mission: espionage, subterfuge, and sabotage.

The admiral's transfer had sent sparks flying in the top brass of the Navy and War Departments because they were losing one of their top intelligence leads to a competitor organization over which they had absolutely no control. But they soon learned to be thankful for it, when a series of Odysseus missions ended up saving the Navy hundreds of ships and a whole lot of face.

The most successful of these occurred in October

1942, when Operation Torch—the Allied invasion of French North Africa—was just getting underway. As the vast armada of Allied ships carrying tens of thousands of British, American, and Free French troops crossed the Atlantic, the Germans sent a wolf pack of nearly a dozen U-boats to lie in wait for them just outside the Strait of Gibraltar, where the Allied ships would certainly encounter a traffic jam, making them perfect targets for German torpedoes. But before the Allied fleet arrived at the narrow waterway, the U-boats were suddenly and mysteriously ordered to another sector, allowing the troop-laden transports of Operation Torch to steam unmolested through the strait and successfully carry out their landings.

Odysseus had been responsible for diverting the U-boats, and Hart had been at the center of the operation. He had led the team of agents—three men and one woman—into France, where they infiltrated the operations staff at the German U-boat base in Saint Nazaire. They supplied the false information that prompted the German admiral in charge to order his U-boats away from the Strait of Gibraltar to attack another convoy cruising up the west coast of Africa. The U-boats pounced on the unlucky convoy, sinking thirteen ships. But the whole thing had been a carefully planned ruse. The convoy in question was on its way back to Britain after delivering goods to Sierra Leone and had been quite empty when it was attacked. In the six days the wolf pack spent harassing the relatively inconsequential targets, wasting time, fuel, and precious torpedoes, Operation Torch went off without a hitch. Allied troops landed in North Africa, and another front had been opened in the war. One small act by Hart and his four agents had saved thousands of lives, and Odysseus's future as the Allied center point for naval espionage seemed secure.

It was, without a doubt, the high point of Hart's career, and Admiral McDonough's, and no doubt promotion and honors would have awaited them both, had it not been for the mission's disastrous aftermath—the ultimate reason Hart left the OSS.

With Allied troops firmly grounded in Morocco and Algiers, Hart and his team executed their escape and extraction plan. They slipped away from the prowling German authorities in France and crossed the Pyrenees into neutral Spain. Once there, they moved into a safe house in Cartagena, where they planned to wait for extraction. Through circumstances that were still unclear to this day, the female agent—Isabelle Sevilla—went to the docks to make contact with the fisherman who would smuggle them out, and she was never seen or heard from again. That same morning, the safe house hiding the rest of Hart's team was raided by Spanish secret police and the team was captured. Hart alone escaped, and only because he was not at the safe house at the time of the raid. Not only was the capture of the team a personal embarrassment to Admiral McDonough, but it also sparked a national crisis, as the U.S. ambassador to Spain tried to explain to the Franco government why American agents carrying American-made weapons bearing American serial numbers were discovered hiding in their country. Of course, the U.S. government disavowed the agents without hesitation, claiming they were renegade soldiers of fortune operating entirely on their own. And, of course, the Spanish government did not believe it and promptly put the three men on trial for espionage.

For weeks, the whole thing played out on the world stage like a Greek tragedy, and Hart watched it all from the Odysseus office in London. He could not help his men. When you got caught, you were on your own. It was a chilling fact understood by all OSS operatives. But when the trial finally reached a guilty verdict and a sentence of death was handed down, with no sign of any intervention by the U.S. government, Hart felt it was time to act. He went to the admiral and demanded he be given a new team to launch a rescue mission, but McDonough flatly refused.

Hart remembered distinctly how cold and curt the admiral's response had been. He even remembered the bastard glancing impatiently at the clock on the wall as if he had to be somewhere, and Hart was just wasting his time.

"If you wanted them rescued, Lieutenant, you should have done it yourself, before you were extracted. This little debacle has already pushed Franco into Hitler's arms. I won't risk any further damage to our already icy relations with Spain, nor will my superiors. Not to save three men."

"These aren't just three men, Admiral," Hart had retorted hotly. "These are *our* men. They've put their lives on the line. They've saved thousands."

"And they'll save thousands more with their deaths, Lieutenant! They know the rules about getting captured.

It goes with the territory. Besides, they should have taken their L-pills long before the Spanish police ever got their hands on them. I'm sure the limeys are splitting their sides over this one."

An L-pill was a small rubber-coated capsule filled with a lethal dose of sodium cyanide. Every agent carried one and was expected to take it if capture appeared imminent. It was at that moment that Hart decided to leave Odysseus, when he realized that McDonough and all of his superiors were more concerned with showing up the British than they were with the lives of their own men.

Two weeks later, Hart's men were hanged, and the next day Hart submitted his request for transfer out of the OSS.

PART TWO

PART TWO

The streets of the city were crowded this morning, as worshippers headed to mosques for prayers. Avni Kasaba had already been to his that morning, a tradition he had kept every Saturday for the last twenty years. Normally, he would spend the rest of the day with his wife and children, perhaps with a few friends as well. They would get together, have an opulent feast to mark the end of the fast, and recite the Koran, as they did every Saturday, praising Allah for sparing their blessed nation from the death and destruction once again wrought on the world by the vicious Christian nations. But today, as happened from time to time, before Avni joined his family for the feast, he had an appointment to keep. He made his way along the bustling pathways between the tightly packed buildings that made up Istanbul's business district, walking past mosques, onetime churches that had been standing for a millennium and that would probably stand for another thousand years, wars and earthquakes providing. At least they would be spared the destruction of this war that now seemed to have touched every capital from Tokyo to London.

Avni was thankful. Thankful that his beautiful city would not see the bombs that now laid waste to so many other cities. Thankful that no Western army would have an excuse to occupy Istanbul. Thankful that his city would remain in Muslim hands. But most of all, he was thankful for his occupation and the business that had provided so comfortably for his family over the years, not to mention the prestige that went with it. He was not ashamed to admit that the fame was more satisfying than the business itself. Three years ago, when war broke out and the nations of Europe chose which side they would take in the slaughter, Avni had feared that his business would go under. He had even considered closing up shop. But he was surprised when the exact reverse happened. His revenues, if anything, increased as the war grew in intensity. With more and more of Europe choked off by advancing battle lines, Istanbul became a virtual gateway between the Allied and Axis worlds. Virtually overnight, it became a place teeming with refugees, diplomats, even tourists. As an upturned rock exposes a mass of writhing worms, the war revealed a whole new market of customers—high-paying customers. Customers willing to pay like never before for almost everything Avni had in his inventory.

Avni wove through the crowd. No doubt the customer he would meet with today was one of these faces flashing past him on all sides, observing him, watching him, verifying that he was indeed alone. Avni always made a point never to make eye contact with anyone on the street. He knew that his customers cherished their confidentiality, and he respected that. If word ever got out that he was too interested in his customers' identities, his business would certainly suffer for it. He waited for two cars to pass by and then crossed the street to a four-story office building where he kept offices on the second floor.

It was a nice building in the high-rent district. The great majority of the tenants were financial firms, trading in various commodities, making millionaires overnight in the demands brought on by this war, and quite often Avni's own customers were the customers of these same firms, so the location made sense. Today the offices were all closed, and, as expected, Avni found the double outer doors locked and sheathed in a sliding iron grating. He opened his jacket to remove two keys from his vest pocket, one to open the iron grating and the other to unlock the double door.

He checked his watch before proceeding inside.

Eleven fifty-eight.

His customer would arrive in two minutes, so he left the door unlocked and took the grand stairway up to the second floor. He came to the door of his office, the third door on the right, where he produced a third key and unlocked it. Before entering, he glanced with pride at the mahogany-framed brass plate on the door.

It read: A. KASABA, BOSPORUS INTERNATIONAL, INC.

Avni smiled at the Greek name that had prompted so much chastisement from his fellow countrymen. "Why couldn't you have used a Turkish name?" they often chided him. "Are you not proud of your heritage?"

Perhaps someday he would change the name of his company, but certainly not anytime in the near future. As long as most of his customers were Westerners, he would keep the name that resounded with their passion for antiquity. Because that passion was the source of Avni's livelihood.

As Avni entered, he stooped to pick up a scatter of mail on the floor, as he had not been there in several days. His office was small compared to the other offices in the building, consisting of only a single room, but it was large enough for Avni's purposes. Copies of Byzantine frescoes and Turkish vases adorned the walls, while two elaborate rugs covered the floor, each marking off a distinct area in which Avni conducted his business. One lay beneath a walnut coffee table surrounded by a set of upholstered chairs, while the other lay beneath a large desk near the office's only window.

Before Avni could take a seat at the desk, he heard footfalls in the hallway. He quickly dumped the stack of mail on his desk, gathered his thoughts, and approached the door just as it opened and his two visitors, a man and a woman, entered the room.

Avni dabbed his upper lip and forehead with a handkerchief. He had been sitting at his desk, pretending to be absorbed in his backlog of mail for the last hour as the antique clock on the wall ticked away. Truthfully, Avni had managed to open one piece of mail. But now, an hour later, he still held the unfolded piece of correspondence in his trembling hands, having read not a single word. Instead, he had been listening to every tick of the clock, every pulse of his heart, counting off every second of ominous silence that had descended on the room since the man and the woman had left.

A car horn on the street outside startled him. He was jumpy, and his heart raced. In all of his business dealings he had never felt so incredibly afraid. He had never before dealt with customers quite like the ones he had met with today.

The phone on his desk rang, and Avni's blood turned ice cold. He stared at the clamoring device, its cold and unfeeling face staring at him as if to challenge him to pick it up. The phone continued to ring. Avni made to answer it but drew his hand back at the last moment.

No. He must be calm. He must be brave. They could not force him to do this. They would never force him to do it. It had all been talk. The man and the woman, both Caucasian, both immaculately dressed, and both speaking English heavily influenced by German, had made curt demands. They had offered to pay an exorbitant amount of money for what they wanted from him. When Avni had refused, they had issued threats. But they were hollow threats—or, at least, that was what Avni kept telling himself. But it did not seem to help. With every ring of the phone he felt himself shaking with fear.

What if it stopped ringing? He had to answer it. He had no choice.

"This is Kasaba," Avni said as resolutely as he could into the receiver.

"Mister Kasaba, you have had one hour," a man's voice said tersely on the other end of the line. The voice had a thick German accent. "I will ask this only once, Mister Kasaba. If you do not give us the answer we are looking for, then—you know what will follow."

"Please," Avni said trembling, "I am not used to negotiating like this. Please, give me some time to evaluate its worth."

Avni was saying anything he could to stall. His head was spinning, and he needed some time to think, to contact people who could help him.

"Your hour is up, Mister Kasaba. My client cannot wait. He is offering twice the street value. You must give me an answer without delay."

Avni sucked in a breath and tried to hide the fear in his voice. "But, sir, I have told you. This item is a national treasure to the Turkish people. As a Turk and as a Muslim, I cannot simply sell off a piece of my heritage. Perhaps if we conducted joint negotiations with the national museum we could work out a loan agreement—"

"Your answer please, Mister Kasaba," the man's voice prompted, succinctly, dispassionately.

"Please, be reasonable, sir."

There was a long pause, and Avni thought he heard the sounds of movement on the other end of the line, as if a chair were being dragged across a wooden floor. Strangely, the sound was very familiar to him, but he could not place it—that is, until another voice came on the line, a voice wrought with distress and abject terror.

"Avni?" the trembling voice said. It was a woman's voice this time.

Avni's face turned white, and he felt suddenly nauseated as the cold realization came over him. "Leyla?"

"Avni, please help us," Avni's wife cried on the other end of the line, her voice barely intelligible. "They have the children. They have your mother and father. They are threatening me—"

The line suddenly went dead, and Avni found himself listening to dead air.

"Leyla! Leyla!" Avni shouted, mashing on the phone lever. "My God, Leyla! Please no!"

Avni immediately tried calling home. He tried several times, but the line simply rang and rang.

What had he done? He had underestimated these people. They had offered twice the street value, and he had not taken it. Now his family was paying the price for his greed. He had to get home.

With his mind reeling, Avni reached for his keys and bolted for the door. Just as he was about to close it behind him, the phone rang again.

He practically knocked over the walnut coffee table in his rush to answer it.

"Hello!" he said, breathing heavily.

"Mister Kasaba." It was the German man's voice again. A woman wailed in the background.

"Yes, yes. I am here. Please do not harm my family. I will give you what you want. Please, do not harm them."

"I am afraid it is too late for that, Mister Kasaba." The man paused, as if to let Kasaba's imagination run wild. "I am sorry to inform you that you are now an orphan."

"What?" Avni said crying, tears streaking down his face. "What did you do?"

"If you want to see the rest of your family again, Mister Kasaba, you will do exactly as I say."

"Yes." Avni sobbed uncontrollably, and found it hard to speak. "Please. Please don't hurt them any more. Please. I'll do whatever you say."

CHAPTER TWELVE

Glasgow, Scotland

Holmhurst was well aware of his situation. He had many hours of solitude to contemplate it. *As a man washed upon a shore*, the shore being cell A32 of Glasgow prison.

That was why he was surprised when, at six thirty A.M. on the fifth day of his imprisonment, he was awakened by the guard who had brought him breakfast each day. But it was too early for breakfast this morning, and instead of a tray of food, the guard now greeted him with a waiting pair of open handcuffs.

"Rise and shine, sir!" the guard said in a voice that was far too loud for the hour. "Better bring your coat and hat with you."

"Why?" Holmhurst rubbed his eyes. "Don't tell me. You've finally decided to be decent law-abiding officers and have contacted my lawyer."

The guard gave a courteous smile of crooked yellow teeth. "You're being transferred, sir. Come along. There's a good fellow."

"And to where am I being transferred?"

"Don't know, sir. Don't care, sir."

The handcuffs snapped shut on Holmhurst's wrists, a little too tight for comfort. He was led out into the hallway, where another guard stood by to assist.

"After you, sir."

Holmhurst was guided down the same passage he had traversed many times over the past few days—whenever he was taken to the prison's bleak interrogation room. He had spent hours on end there while one police official after another grilled him about his operation while the ever-derogatory Inspector Boggs looked on. They wanted to know everything. Who were his customers? Who were his foreign contacts? How many thefts had he organized? Who were the other members of his smuggling ring?

Of course, they were all barking up the wrong tree, just as Boggs had always done over the years. Despite being threatened with bodily harm on several occasions, even slapped twice by an enraged Boggs, Holmhurst gave them nothing. He responded to every question with a request to see his attorney, a request that appeared to fall on deaf ears. Holmhurst had to admit there were a few moments when they almost had him convinced they were willing to breach the limitations of the law to get him to talk. But now that he was being transferred, Holmhurst felt comfortably assured that Boggs had abandoned that scare tactic in favor of something else. Holmhurst hoped it meant he would get a proper arraignment. Of course, there was always the chance that Patrick had talked, though Holmhurst doubted it. Holmhurst had not seen his trusty cohort since the day they were both arrested on the beach, but he was sure Patrick had remained just as stalwart as he had under questioning, if not more so.

The two guards directed Holmhurst down several passages lined with cells much like his own. They went down a flight of stairs and finally reached a receiving area where a droopy-eyed clerk sat in a small office on the other side of a barred window. The clerk yawned as he passed a set of papers through the iron bars to the guard.

"Here. Inspector Boggs is in the antechamber. He's taking custody of the prisoner. Have him sign that and then bring it back here, will you?"

"Right!" said the guard. "I'll be glad to get rid of this one. Had a nice quiet place here until he showed up. Now we get more bigwigs passing through our gates than Scotland Yard. And all for such an insolent bastard!"

"Pardon me, *Ernie*," Holmhurst said in the most contemptuous tone he could manage. "I believe I have an appointment with the good inspector. Wouldn't want to keep him waiting now, would we? Chop-chop."

The guard's smile faded to a scowl. "Just pray they don't send you back here. We'll see how highbrowed you act when I get you in a cell alone."

"My lord!" Holmhurst said reprovingly. "You will address me as *my lord*."

"Why you . . ." The guard looked mad enough to rip Holmhurst's head off.

"Easy, Ernie," the clerk behind the window said. "Just take the gentleman to the inspector and be done with it."

Without further incident, Holmhurst was escorted to the antechamber where Boggs was waiting for him along with two well-built constables in blue uniforms. A pair of constables normally accompanied Boggs everywhere he went. Usually, it was the same two men, both of whom Holmhurst had come to recognize. But the two men who now flanked Boggs on both sides, wearing hollow faces, were new. Holmhurst had never seen them before.

"Here ya go, Inspector," the guard said, handing Boggs the transfer papers. "He's all yours now, sir. And good riddance."

Boggs said nothing but simply signed the papers and handed them back, not once making eye contact with either Holmhurst or the prison guards. This surprised Holmhurst, who fully anticipated a customary insult from the inspector. But Boggs did not appear to be himself this morning. He appeared flustered and somewhat out of breath, with his bulbous face a pale shade of red. Holmhurst could even make out a thin film of perspiration running along the inspector's balding forehead.

Something was not right.

Holmhurst was ushered into the backseat of a waiting police car. He sat next to the big constable—the one who looked like a six-foot-four kid with muscles—while Boggs sat in the front seat with the other constable, who was driving. None of the three said a word to him as the car pulled out of the prison yard. Boggs had to lean across the driver to flash his badge at the gatehouse. As the elderly guard manning the gate examined the badge and the transfer papers, Holmhurst could have sworn he saw Boggs's extended hand trembling.

What was going on?

The moment the car left the prison grounds, Holmhurst detected that something had sharply changed in the demeanor of his three custodians. After an insufferable silence, Boggs muttered something to the constable driving.

"Not now!" the constable retorted in a tone far too commanding for a uniformed policeman addressing one of Scotland Yard's chief inspectors.

Much to Holmhurst's surprise, Boggs complied. Both constables appeared a bit too confident to be a pair of Boggs's underlings. Boggs began to sweat more and to visibly squirm in his seat.

"Listen," Boggs pleaded to the constable driving. "I can get you cash if that's what you want. It will only take a few days."

"We don't want your cash, Inspector," the driver replied, sounding somewhat annoyed at the disturbance. The driver jabbed a thumb over his shoulder in Holmhurst's direction. "We just want him."

Something told Holmhurst that a London prison was not his destination, and that his luck had just taken another turn—whether for the worse or for the better was yet to be seen.

"All right, I'll bite," Holmhurst offered to the silent three. "Where are we going, Inspector?"

At first no one responded. Boggs scoffed as if it gave him pain to do so.

Finally the constable next to him said, "You're being transferred. Now keep your mouth shut."

The Scottish accent was thick—a bit too thick. Who were these chaps? More important, why did the inspector look like he was going to have a coronary at any moment?

"Where are the other two goons you usually tote around, Inspector?" Holmhurst asked blithely. "Who are these chaps?"

His question was answered by a blow to the side of the head, a hard blow that left him seeing stars for several seconds. When he finally came to his senses, a glimpse of the brass knuckles clinched in the right fist of the constable next to him was enough to explain why his jaw now throbbed and felt twice its normal size.

"This is brutality, Inspector," Holmhurst protested.

This was answered with yet another blow from the brass knuckles, this time harder, after which Holmhurst tasted blood in his mouth and felt his lower lip start to swell. He said no more, instead looking out the window to determine where the hell they were taking him. This wasn't the bloody way to London.

About twenty miles outside Glasgow, the car pulled off onto a muddy road that led to a glade hidden from the highway by a fold of rolling hills topped with ancient stone fences.

"Out of the car if you please, Inspector," the driver said when the car came to a stop. His Scottish accent was even worse than that of the first constable. "You, too, my lord."

The constable in the backseat opened Holmhurst's door and shoved him out onto the wet earth.

"Come on! Move it!" he said.

With his bound hands limiting his mobility, Holmhurst did his best to comply.

"Help him up, Inspector," Holmhurst heard the constable in charge order. After a few mumbling curses, Boggs relented and gave Holmhurst a hand to pull him up out of the mud. This assistance, however, was not without a certain measure of roughness. Boggs then wiped his hands on his jacket, as if coming into physical contact with Holmhurst had contaminated them.

All four men now stood outside the car, the two constables facing down a disgruntled Boggs and a perplexed Holmhurst.

"All right, you've got him," Boggs said disgustedly to the constables. "Now what about the photographs?"

The constable in charge smiled beneath his blue uniform hat, then nodded to his compatriot, who produced a manila envelope from the trunk of the car. With a small smile, the constable tossed the envelope to Boggs.

"There you go, Inspector. Now, you don't have to worry about the good Mrs. Boggs ever finding out."

Holmhurst watched somewhat amused as Boggs fumbled with the envelope, practically tearing it open to get at the contents inside. Holmhurst could see that it was full of large photographs. Boggs seemed to sense that Holmhurst was watching him and quickly thrust the stack of photos back into the envelope.

"How can I be sure they are all there?" Boggs asked

the constable. "How can I be sure that you don't have copies?"

"Oh, rest assured, if we ever require your services again, Inspector Boggs, you will hear from us," the constable answered smugly.

"Damn you to hell!" Boggs spat.

"I'm afraid we can't offer you a ride home, Inspector, so you'll have to walk."

"We're five bloody miles from the highway!" Boggs protested.

"I'm glad you mentioned that, Inspector. We can't have you getting home too early, now, can we? A man of your capabilities will be on our tails in no time flat," the constable said sarcastically, and then pointed at the inspector's feet. "Your shoes, Inspector. Off with them, please."

"My shoes?"

"You're a stout man, Inspector Boggs. I think five miles isn't enough to slow you down. So take off your shoes and toss them into the car, if you please."

"I will not!" Boggs said flatly.

"Don't make my friend there force you," the lead constable said while pointing to the other constable, who was smiling and smacking a baton into his open palm.

Boggs was obviously boiling with anger, but he complied, much to Holmhurst's amazement.

"Am I free to go now?" the shoeless Boggs asked.

"Just one more thing, Inspector." The constable produced a key and, much to Holmhurst's surprise, uncuffed him.

"Thank you," Holmhurst said, now convinced that Patrick had somehow escaped from the authorities and had arranged for all this.

"Hit the inspector," the lead constable ordered Holmhurst.

"I?" Holmhurst asked, somewhat stupefied. "Hit him?"

"You see, Mr. Boggs here must have a credible story to tell his chums back at the Yard when he explains your escape. Now haul off and hit him, and make sure you hit him hard."

Holmhurst met Boggs's hateful eyes. The baleful inspector was staring at him with a contemptuous expression.

"You'll be mine again, Holmhurst, I promise," Boggs snarled through gritted teeth. "Run wherever you like. I'll find you, and I'll see that you hang. You're nothing but a bloody piece of filth, an overblown boozing loser just like your father was—"

Boggs was abruptly cut off by a solid blow on the nose from Holmhurst's clenched fist. Boggs fell back into the sucking mud, his smashed face covered in streams of blood running from each nostril. Boggs did not move for several seconds afterward.

"That hard enough?" Holmhurst asked the lead constable.

The constable simply raised one eyebrow as if the ferocity of the blow had taken him by surprise, and then shrugged his shoulders. "I suppose."

Boggs clutched his bloody face now and rolled in the mud, moaning from the pain. As Holmhurst looked down on the pathetic, middle-aged, overweight inspector, he actually began to feel sorry for him. He thought of offering Boggs a hand out of the mud, but before he could the big constable slapped the pair of handcuffs on him again and made them just as snug as they had been before.

"Now, look here!" Holmhurst protested.

"Into the car please, my lord," the lead constable said bluntly while the big constable pushed Holmhurst's head into the backseat. Before Holmhurst could sit up straight in the seat, the car was speeding back toward the highway, leaving the wallowing inspector on the side of the road holding his now-bloody envelope to his face. It was at that moment that Holmhurst realized that the duplicitous constables were not Patrick's men at all. Patrick's men would have surely had a bit more fun with Boggs before leaving him. These men were an enigma. Holmhurst could not figure out who they were working for. He was not at all sure that his present situation was an improvement over Glasgow prison. At least there, the worst he had to face was a violent interrogation. Who knew what these desperate men wanted?

The car eventually reached the highway again and turned to head east, the opposite direction from Glasgow.

"Look here, chaps," he said. "I don't know what this is all about, but you two are the dog's bollocks. If you're looking for some kind of financial incentive for releasing me from that hellhole, I can certainly accommodate you."

Suddenly a hood went over Holmhurst's head. A set

of brass knuckles pressed into his ribs. It was a clear enough indication that his offer was not well received.

An hour later, the hood came off, and Holmhurst discerned that he was sitting in a simple chair in the parlor of what appeared to be a small deserted house. The dirty floors and scant furniture seemed to indicate that the house had been deserted for some time. A pair of dingy windows adorned with old curtains lined the front of the house and allowed only a blurry hue of light through. Apart from the fact that it was daytime and that an occasional car or truck puttered by on the street outside, he had few clues as to where he was. Judging by the time he had spent in the car and the relatively short but rough-handled transport from the car to the house, Holmhurst assumed he was in a row house somewhere in Edinburgh.

Now the same constable who had driven the car was in the room, along with a gang of three or four others. The younger men passed in and out of the room, constantly checking the windows and the doors. These were obviously the security of the operation. Only one man in the room appeared to be anything over forty years old. This was an older, gray-haired man who sat at a small table on the opposite side of the room sipping from a cup and puffing on a pipe. He nodded slowly as the constable whispered in his ear, all the while holding Holmhurst in a locked gaze. There was another man in the room, too, one whom Holmhurst did not notice at first. This one was tall and leaned casually against the wall in a dark corner, where he smoked and appeared to be staring back at Holmhurst. Holmhurst could not make out this man's features clearly, but he could discern that he was dressed like the older man. Both wore plain dark sweaters, trousers, and caps—the same kind of clothing one might see on any man walking the streets of Edinburgh. By all appearances they were locals, but Holmhurst suspected they were something different.

After the constable finished speaking, the older man rose and dragged his chair over to within a few feet of Holmhurst. There, he resumed his seat and greeted Holmhurst in the worst Scottish accent Holmhurst had ever heard.

"Good morning, Lord Holmhurst." The man's pipe filled the air with the sweet aroma of tobacco, reminding Holmhurst that he had not had a smoke all day.

"Good morning," Holmhurst answered politely.

"I trust your trip wasn't too uncomfortable."

Holmhurst shrugged. "If you consider a full hour wedged in the backseat of a car with a foul-smelling brute next to you, brass knuckles pressed into your side, and a hood over your head comfortable, then that's your business, old fellow."

The older man did not smile. "I suppose you're wondering who I am."

Holmhurst did not answer. Beyond the old man's shoulder, he could see the constable and the taller man studying him, each from opposite sides of the room.

"Lord Holmhurst," the older man continued, "I am a gentleman who appreciates fine objects, art, antiquities, and the like. I covet them with a passion."

"Good for you, old boy. And who are these other two gentlemen who gawk at me as though I were Nelson atop his column?"

The older man took a puff on his pipe before continuing, completely ignoring the question. "Unfortunately, my little pastime has been frustratingly interrupted by this war. The war has made it extremely difficult to obtain such objects. From what I understand you have a unique talent for acquiring special items from, shall we say, inaccessible markets."

"A moment, if I may. You are saying that you helped me to escape from that prison so I could act as your broker?" Holmhurst asked, not believing it for a minute. "Why is it you have never contacted me before? Surely, if you are in the right circles, you would have heard my name."

"I enjoy my privacy more than I do my collection."

"And now that I've been arrested, you suddenly decide to contact me by springing me from prison, risking discovery and exposure to yourself?" Holmhurst chided playfully. "And if I refuse to help?"

The gray-haired man raised his eyebrows. "You are wrong in your assertion that you have escaped, my lord. In spite of the courtesy I have extended, you are completely in my power. No one knows where you are or who abducted you."

"Abducted?"

"If you refuse, that would leave me with very few options. Now, Lord Holmhurst, I am sure you are a smart man."

"I suppose I'm smart enough to recognize a bunch of

Yanks trying to pass themselves off as Scotsmen," Holm-hurst retorted with great satisfaction.

The old man stared at him for a few moments, more a look of deep thought than of surprise. After a quick glance over his shoulder at his two compatriots, the old man spoke again, this time with an accent Holmhurst instantly identified as belonging to the northeastern United States. "All right, Holmhurst, have it your way. You're right. We're not Scottish."

"Obviously." Holmhurst chuckled, trying to seem cool and confident.

"My name is McDonough. That man over there in the corner is Ives." The tall man in the shadows nodded. "And this fellow, who got you out of prison, is called Hart." The man in the constable uniform gave a small smile, but it was obviously only out of courtesy.

Holmhurst concluded that these were all cover names.

"We work for the American government," McDonough said. "Good enough?"

Holmhurst nodded. "For now."

"We need your help," McDonough said gravely. "You may not know it, but you possess some information that is vital to the national security of our country, and yours. If you help us, lives will be saved, both British and American. Interested?"

"Not particularly."

"Really?" McDonough said with raised eyebrows. "With your family heritage, I would have thought other-wise. I hardly believed all those stories from Scotland Yard about you being a traitor."

"I thought my arrest hadn't been publicly announced."

"Oh, it hasn't, but I have access to certain information." This time it was McDonough who sounded smug.

"Even Mister Churchill doesn't know, or so Inspector Boggs told me time and again."

"I know what you had for breakfast this morning, I know how many times you've taken a leak. I know you've got a thing for cabaret girls in red lingerie, you like cheap drink, and you cheat at cards."

"No more than the next man." Holmhurst did his best not to sound surprised.

"The point is, I know you, Holmhurst, like your worst best friend. I know how to get to you. That's my job. So you might as well give me what I want." McDonough paused, then added, "Besides, I've a hunch you're not a traitor, and you want to see as few deaths as possible in this war, just as I do. The sooner the war is over, the sooner the killing will stop on both sides. That's what we all want."

"Is it really?" Holmhurst said slyly. "The war ensures that I have a lucrative business. Free trade again is the worst thing that could happen to me. And how about you, McDonough, and your pals back there? Each one of you could have stepped off the cover of *Stars and Stripes* magazine. It's quite obvious you all belong to some sort of military organization. The three of you are probably officers—probably professional officers, at that. Hasn't the war been lucrative for your business as well? What chance does a soldier have for promotion and reward when a war ends?"

"But we are getting off the subject, aren't we?" McDonough said with some measure of annoyance.

"So, I'll get to the point. What if I told you I know all about your little operation? About the different accounts you keep, the various banks you work with, the aliases you use?"

"I'd be impressed," Holmhurst admitted, and then added blithely, "if you indeed have such information."

"Mister Hart," McDonough said over his shoulder.

The man in the constable uniform, the one who had been introduced to him as Hart, stepped forward, producing a file folder. Hart seemed a very grim individual and appeared more annoyed with Holmhurst's delaying tactics than his older compatriot was. Hart opened the folder, flipped through a few pages, settled on one, and began to read.

"You have an account at Bromley's of London under the name Oliver Twistam. Another at Lloyd's under Jacob Marley. A third at Barclay's under Robinson Marner. Two accounts at Coutts Bank under the names Mycroft Jekyll and Sherlock Hyde." Hart looked up with amusement, meeting Holmhurst's eyes. "Shall I go on?"

Holmhurst could not help but shift slightly in his chair. "I don't think that will be necessary."

McDonough smiled triumphantly. "You see, Mister Holmhurst, that it is well within my power to ruin you."

"Yes, well, identifying accounts is one thing." Holmhurst had managed to regain his composure somewhat. "Seizing funds is quite something else."

"I have the power to do both."

"So you say." Holmhurst knew this was a poker game. How would he know what cards his opponent held if he did not call his bluff from time to time? He had to do something, and his mind was racing fast. Truthfully, he knew that the information in his head was now the only thing he had to bargain with, and he was not going to play that card unless he had to.

"Mister Hart," McDonough said. "Why don't you tell His Lordship what else we know about him."

Hart flipped to another page in the file. "For the past five years you've been the ringleader of a smuggling operation, trading with agents on both sides of the war, transporting just about anything, from priceless art to refugees. Your operations have dealt with both Nazis and—"

"I hope it says in there that I never once transported a single weapon across enemy lines," Holmhurst interjected. "Nor have I done anything that could be injurious to my country."

"No weapons, you say?" McDonough said. "We'll see about that. That can be added to the list, if need be."

"In the business of fabricating evidence, are you, McDonough?"

"I won't have to. The item you stole from the British Museum will certainly qualify."

"Allegedly stole, you mean," Holmhurst corrected. "And I really don't see how a twenty-five-hundred-year-old stone carving could ever be perceived as a weapon. Unless the Nazis were planning on dropping it on Monty's head."

McDonough did not appear amused. "Tell me what you know about it, Holmhurst."

"Sennacherib's Prism? Oh, only what every amateur student of antiquity knows, I suppose. The thing dates to around 690 B.C. It's thought to be written by Sennacherib, the king of the Assyrian Empire at the time—hence its name. It chronicles the king's conquests of Phoenicia and Judea in a very illustrative, if not self-gratifying, prose."

"And why is it so valuable?"

"Well, apart from being so old, it contains a few lines that seem to match up, for the most part, with the Hebrew Bible's description of the Assyrian siege of Jerusalem in 701 B.C. The two records agree with each other, right down to the amount of tribute paid to Sennacherib by Hezekiah, the Judean king at the time."

"But they don't match up perfectly?"

"No, they don't," Holmhurst said guardedly, suddenly feeling as though he were telling McDonough things he already knew.

"Where, specifically, do the records disagree?"

"Well, according to the prism, Sennacherib shut up Hezekiah in Jerusalem and forced the Judahites to pay the aforementioned tribute, something like eight hundred talents of silver and thirty talents of gold. After that he and his army marched happily back to Assyria."

"And how does that differ from the Bible's account?"

"If you go by the Hebrew Bible, you get a much different ending. The Bible claims that the tribute was paid, but the Assyrian king decided to lay siege to Jerusalem anyway. Well, of course, the Hebrews were a bit distraught by this treachery and prayed to God to save them from the Assyrians. So, on the second day of the siege . . ." Holmhurst felt a sudden chill come over him as he remembered McDonough's statement that the prism might qualify as a weapon.

"Go on."

Holmhurst swallowed. "On the second day of the siege, the Assyrian army outside the city was struck down by the hand of God. One hundred eighty-five thousand men killed over the course of one night. And Sennacherib went back to Nineveh with his tail between his legs."

"So, I ask you," McDonough said, as if establishing the prism's origin were enough to invoke a confession out of Holmhurst. "What do you know about the Nazis' interest in this artifact?"

Holmhurst looked back at McDonough defiantly and said nothing, holding on to the only playing card he had left. McDonough did not appear to be surprised at his silence.

"Let me tell you what we know, and maybe you can fill in the gaps for us," McDonough said. "We know that you were planning to deliver the prism to a U-boat, *U-2553* to be precise. You were to rendezvous with this U-boat in the Firth of Clyde. We know that you received an advance payment to make this delivery and that you were to receive the final payment during the exchange. That much is clear to us." McDonough paused and Holmhurst could feel his eyes scanning his face for any sign of treachery. "How am I doing, so far?"

"How should I know?"

"You know something, Holmhurst. To be very honest with you, I don't think you're a traitor. I've looked at your file. I've seen your portfolio and your financial situation. It's quite obvious to me that you're nothing more than a spoiled playboy with expensive habits you can't possibly support, and your little smuggling operation is the answer to that."

"I'm glad you see it that way."

"The Nazis are after something big here, and you're nothing more than the middleman, a minor link in a long chain of events."

It was a vindicating remark, but for some reason it made Holmhurst feel somewhat deflated.

"Have you ever heard of a man called Avni Kasaba?" McDonough suddenly asked.

"No," Holmhurst lied. He knew full well who Avni was. He had been one of his key clients in Turkey. That is, until a year ago, when the antiquities dealer had mysteriously vanished.

"Let me tell you about him," McDonough said in an almost patronizing voice. "Mister Kasaba had a business similar to yours, only his was legal. He was a rare-artifacts dealer for high-priced clients in Istanbul. Well, about a year ago, Mister Kasaba got his hands on something—something that was quite a little jewel. Oh, I'm not talking about some bauble that used to reside in the navel of some sultan's favorite whore. I'm talking about a piece of history, an old text, something that would have been of great importance as a national treasure to the Turkish government. Do you know what it was?"

"I haven't a clue," Holmhurst lied again.

"Mister Kasaba had got his hands on the secret memoirs of Mehmet the Second." McDonough paused, and then added as if to explain, "He was one of the Ottoman sultans during the fifteenth century."

"I'm well aware of who Mehmet the Second was,

Mister McDonough," Holmhurst answered, somewhat insulted by the implication. Of course he knew who the sultan was, and he had also been informed of Avni's remarkable find.

"You see, Mister Kasaba made a deal with the Nazis just like you did. At first he did not want to cooperate, but they threatened him and he gave in. He gave them the documents."

"How do you know all of this?" Holmhurst was incredulous.

"German agents are easy to follow in Istanbul, Mister Holmhurst. We have agents there, too."

"So you know what became of Avni—er, Mister Kasaba?"

McDonough smiled. "Shortly after his last known meeting with the Nazis, our people found his body floating in the Golden Horn. Someone had used a blunt object on him. He had been beaten to a pulp. Nearly every bone in his skull had been shattered. His face was so mutilated that we had to use fingerprints to identify him. Here, see for yourself."

Without warning, McDonough produced a large black-and-white photograph showing a wet and bloated body laid out on a concrete slab. When McDonough flipped to the next photo, showing a closeup of what used to be the man's face, Holmhurst almost vomited. Finally, after several excruciating seconds in which Holmhurst did his best to appear unfazed by the gruesome sight, McDonough put the photo down.

"I won't even tell you what they did to his wife," McDonough added.

"Poor fellow. But what does all of this have to do with me?"

"We know that Mister Kasaba had been dealing with a certain colonel of the Waffen-SS—a man called Sturm."

Holmhurst swallowed once and then shifted in his chair. The room suddenly felt stuffy.

"I believe this was the same man you were dealing with. Am I right, Mister Holmhurst?"

Holmhurst's mind reeled. He did not have the where-withal to answer.

"We believe the two objects are connected in some way, Mister Holmhurst. As you can see, these people aren't playing games. They're after something, and they will stop at nothing to get it. What I want to know is how does the story end for you. Do you help me, or do you someday end up like this?" McDonough held up the photograph again.

Holmhurst closed his eyes and shook his head. He could not look at it anymore. "Take it away!"

"Will you help me?" McDonough pressed.

"Alone!" Holmhurst gestured toward McDonough's two henchmen. He was having trouble getting his words out. "I will speak to you alone, McDonough. No one else."

Hart leaned against the short railing that lined one side of the steps leading up to the front of the row house where he had brought Holmhurst over an hour ago.

He had changed out of his constable jacket and

now wore a civilian coat and cap that blended appropriately with the other sidewalk loungers of this low-income neighborhood on the north side of Edinburgh, near the Leith Docks. Only Lord Holmhurst and Admiral McDonough remained inside the house now. McDonough had agreed to the private conference and had summarily excused everyone from the house, including Ives, who now sat on one of the concrete steps nearby smoking and appearing every bit the shipbuilder just gotten off shift. The rest of the team was around watching the back side of the house and trying to appear as casual as Hart and Ives were out front. Of course, they all drew glances from the passersby. They were, after all, new faces in the neighborhood. Not to mention, they were lounging in front of a house that most everyone knew to be empty. But thus far, curiosity had not yet won out over caution, and the locals seemed content to let the strange men be.

Hart caught Ives looking in his direction and quickly looked the other way. The last few days had done nothing to allay Hart's dislike for the man. True, Ives had changed a lot in the past two years. But any changes in the aloof, double-talking Ives had been for the worse, if that was possible. He was no longer just an asshole. Now he was arrogant and condescending. Now he had an air of self-assurance about him that Hart did not remember from before. Hart could only guess that Ives must have participated in multiple operations since their last meeting, and that the promotions and rewards obtained from that service had left his head somewhat inflated.

"Good work, Hart," Ives suddenly said. He was still

seated on the front step of the house and was lighting another cigarette.

"What?"

"I said good work. The prison break went off without a hitch. You planned it well. Not bad for two years away from the big show."

"Thanks," Hart said impassively. "So, don't you think it's time yet?"

"Time for what, Hart?"

"For you and the admiral to tell me about Isabelle."

"All in good time, Hart." Ives smiled. "All in good time."

Hart sneered, expecting no less from Ives. Ever since Hart's arrival in London three days ago, neither the admiral nor Ives had mentioned a word about Isabelle, and Hart was beginning to believe he had been lured into coming back into Odysseus by false bait.

The prison break had been a run-of-the-mill maneuver, but it had been enough to keep Hart busy from the moment he had arrived at Bletchley Park to meet with Admiral McDonough. The admiral had greeted him warmly, as though the years of silence between them had only been a dream.

"So good to have you back, Matt," McDonough had said quite familiarly, rising from his desk to shake Hart's hand vigorously, as he used to do during their days at the Office of Naval Intelligence together. "I'm so glad you could come. We're in dire need of some real operatives around here, Matt, like you. Not these adolescent schoolboys Ives keeps recruiting. Captain Ives and I have been lost without you for the past two years."

McDonough had immediately briefed him on the situation surrounding Holmhurst and the botched museum heist, and then, much to Hart's surprise, he placed Hart in charge of the operation to apprehend the English lord.

"Scotland Yard plans to move him in two days, so you've got twenty-four hours to plan it," McDonough had said, as if he were ordering a plate of fish and chips for lunch. "Consider this a refresher, Matt. Or you might call it a warmup. A small mission, before you embark on the big one."

Now that Holmhurst was securely in Odysseus custody, the mission would be considered a success. Of course, as the admiral had said, this was nothing compared to what lay ahead for him. A part of him felt very tired at the thought of what he must endure over the next few weeks, but another part felt invigorated. As much as he hated to admit it, he felt an inner euphoria after accomplishing the mission. The audacious spirit within him had awoken from its long slumber. It was almost enough to make him forget the true reason he had returned.

Hart glanced up at the house in which McDonough and Holmhurst now conversed. He would have given a month's pay to know what they were saying. He was certain Ives felt the same way. McDonough would certainly debrief them both afterward, but the admiral tended to pass on only select information, and Hart wanted to have everything on the table before the next phase of this operation.

"Excuse me, sir," a woman's voice said behind Hart.

Hart turned to see a woman in her midtwenties, with

pale skin, smiling up at him. She wore a black hat that accentuated her blue eyes and bright red hair.

"Could I trouble you for a light, sir?" she said frivolously, tossing back a stray red lock as she held a cigarette to her lips. She had a slight trace of freckles across her nose and exuded complete innocence. She was obviously a local who had been walking by and noticed him standing there at the moment she needed a light. She could have no idea what world-changing events were transpiring inside the house not thirty feet away from where she stood.

Hart smiled and struck a match for her. He said nothing, not wanting to risk his poor Scottish accent on a local. As her soft, cold hand touched his to hold it steady while she lit her cigarette, Hart's senses were awakened. Her feminine touch invoked the memory of the last time he had held a woman—the last time he had held Isabelle.

"Thanks, Yank," the red-haired woman said, winking once and flashing him a grin before sauntering off into the mix of pedestrians passing by on the sidewalk.

She had called him Yank. Was it that obvious that he was not a local, or was there something more to this innocent-looking young lady? Hart walked down to the sidewalk and looked after her, but to his surprise, he could not find her in the small crowd of shipyard workers heading home for the day. Her black hat was nowhere to be seen, and there were certainly too many redheads on the sidewalk to discern her from any other.

Perhaps she was Odysseus. Hart knew there were now many more agents in the organization than had been two years ago. He did not know all of them, but he thought he knew everyone who was working this particular assignment. On the other hand, Ives was here, and he had been known for bringing his own team along on operations, standing by and ready to pick up the pieces if another team fell apart. Perhaps this young lady was one of his underlings.

Hart glanced back at Ives, who was still seated on the step. Ives seemed somewhat amused. Hart was not sure what he found so humorous, but he was intent on never giving the bastard the satisfaction of an inquiry.

Ives looked as though he were about to make a comment, but at that moment the front door opened and Admiral McDonough appeared in the doorway.

"Please come inside, gentlemen," he said wearing an eager grin. "We have much to discuss."

CHAPTER THIRTEEN

Molesworth Airfield, England
One week later

The flight of Boeing B-17 Flying Fortress bombers roared down the airstrip in the fading light, taking to the skies one after the other. With each passing orbit, the circling armada swelled in numbers. It soon joined with other squadrons from other airfields, until the entire air wing had risen from the earth. When all was said and done, 118 B-17 Flying Fortress and B-24 Liberator bombers blotted the night sky over the Norfolk countryside. They formed up and headed due east at thirteen thousand feet, the drone of their nearly five hundred engines stirring the grazing farm animals far below.

The black mass of the British Isles rolled away beneath the formation, replaced by the moonlit North Sea. Machine guns cracked to life as foggy-eyed gunners blasted away at the whitecaps below to test their weapons. Navigators took final fixes on British landmarks. Bombardiers crawled along the narrow platform inside the bomb bays, running final checks on the instruments of terror that would be dropped on Germany this night—everything from incendiaries to antipersonnel mines.

The 40th Combat Bombardment Wing was flying a mission much like the fifty-two missions it had already flown this year. Proceed to such-and-such a place and drop on such-and-such a target with such-and-such weapons. These days, the targets bomber command chose were invariably infrastructure oriented, and that meant striking deep within populated areas, striking at the very heart of the German manufacturing and supply machine. And then there was the recompense, the give-and-take, the stark truth that hung over the head of every man riding in the rattling air machines. There were more than a thousand men in the 40th. One hundred of them would be dead within the hour, a statistical certainty outwardly shrugged off by most, but ever-present in the innermost thoughts of all.

But tonight, one plane was playing a different set of odds. It was an extra—a tagalong. It was one of those things the commanding general of the 40th Combat Bombardment Wing had learned not to ask questions about. This morning the general and his staff had planned a sortie for 117 aircraft, and not one plane more. But late in the afternoon—very late in the afternoon— he had received a rather abrupt phone call from the chief of staff at bomber command. There would be another plane joining tonight's mission. Radio communications with this new plane was to be kept at a minimum. Beyond providing a few navigational details, he was not to interact with the new plane's crew. Above all, he was not to ask questions. And, just like that, Plane 118 was added to the sortie.

Now, the general sat in the cockpit of his own plane. His aircraft was near the center of the armada, flying in one of the many defensive box formations the B-17s had assumed to ward off German night fighters. A thousand things were on the general's mind, not least of which was the deadly flak corridor up ahead through which he must soon lead his air wing. But he had the wherewithal to ponder Plane 118 and to wonder about her real mission. No doubt it involved some sort of covert insertion behind enemy lines. Looking out his own plane's side window, the general could make out the mass of black shapes off to the left. Plane 118 would be out there somewhere, hugging close to the trailing edge of the flanking squadron. Whatever her purpose, it had to be an important one. Soon she would be leaving the formation to depart on her own mission. The general could not help but wonder whether the 40th Combat Bombardment Wing with her mass of bombs or Plane 118 with her mysterious cargo would strike a more devastating blow to the enemy tonight.

"Navigator to pilot," a voice said in the headset. "We're over the Dutch coast now, sir. Five minutes to decision point."

The general sighed. It was a clear night over Holland. The weather was perfect. The skies over Hamburg would be the same. There would be no turning back tonight. The 40th would unleash her bombs, and people on the ground and in the air would die, like a Greek tragedy played out on the same stage every night.

"Good luck, 118," the general said quietly, and then keyed his microphone. "Pilot to navigator, roger. We're going in."

It had been more than an hour since Plane 118 had left the formation. When the rest of the air wing had turned east to start the bombing run to Hamburg, she had turned north, up the Danish coast, toward the Scandinavian peninsula. Now, from the plane's starboard side window, Hart could just make out the flashes on the southern horizon, the distant web of probing searchlights, the dull glow of a thousand fires marking the spot where a German city now burned and a great battle raged in the sky above it.

"Glad we're not with them," the man crouching next to him said. "They'll be catching it all the way home."

Hart nodded from behind his goggles and fingered the woolskin hat that made his scalp itch. The hat matched his woolskin-lined leather jacket and trousers, identical to those worn by the rest of the crew. The air in the northern regions could get cold, and tonight was no exception.

"Ever been on a bombing run, Commander?" The airman had to shout into his ear to be heard over the B-17's engines.

Hart simply shook his head, saying nothing. He disliked small talk, especially before a mission, and especially with someone who knew nothing about him.

"Hey, Newton!" the airman shouted back to his

compatriot manning the tail gun. "The commander here's never seen the big show!"

Newton turned and grinned at his compatriot, both seemingly satisfied that Hart was a greenhorn among hardy veterans. Hart did not care what they thought. The less they knew about him, the better. He only cared that their pilot got him to the drop point on time.

Plane 118 was a B-17—albeit a very special B-17. She carried no bombs and was painted completely black, and where most B-17s mounted two waist guns, she had a sliding cargo door, from which, along with her bomb bay, she could drop items or individuals into enemy lands. It was from such planes that the various teams of Jedburghs spread across occupied Europe often received their regular supply drops. The plane was owned by the OSS, and while every member of her crew had at one time belonged to the Army Air Force, they now flew for the secret air force of the fledgling spy agency.

The last several days had been a whirlwind of activity, with Hart spending every last hour either training for the mission or interrogating Holmhurst. He questioned Holmhurst for hours on end. He questioned him on his network, his contacts, his recent activities, anything that might help clear up the murky picture of his relationship with the Nazis and what their true intent was. Holmhurst had been somewhat helpful, but Hart had taken everything he said with a grain of salt, certain that he was not sharing all that he had shared with Admiral McDonough. This was, after all, a traitor to his country. How could he be trusted, with anything? Apparently Hart's disgust for the man had shone through.

"You don't like me, do you, Hart?" Holmhurst had said after one long session in which Hart had gotten frustrated with the Englishman's seemingly endless witty quips.

"My personal opinion of you doesn't matter. I have a job to do, and the admiral seems to think you can help us."

"And what do you think, Mr. Hart?"

"That you're a no-good, two-bit swindler. An opportunist. A traitor! That you've gotten caught and now you'll tell us anything to gain your freedom and set yourself up after the war."

"True." Holmhurst nodded. "I am all of those things. But come now, Hart, you're a spy. Surely you've done something unethical in the course of this war. Something you're ashamed of. No? Surely, there's a deep dark secret somewhere in your past you'd never tell your old mum about."

"Not treason."

"But what does that really mean, Hart? You call me a traitor, but a traitor to what? To king and country? The same king and country that sent so many of our chaps to slaughter in the first war, and who are now feeding another generation to the meat grinder. So many young men who had their lives and loves ripped away from them and now lie buried in shallow graves from Burma to Africa. You tell me who the traitor is."

Although Hart thought Holmhurst's logic irretrievably flawed, the mention of betrayal had brought the memory of his men in Spain to the surface.

"But then I forget," Holmhurst continued wryly. "You

Americans don't think in such terms, do you? You're all cowboys. Give me a gun and an Indian to shoot, right?"

"If it were up to me, you'd have gone before a firing squad."

Holmhurst had seemed amused at that. "Well, now, that would never do."

The two days spent with Holmhurst had seemed the longest of Hart's life. It was one thing to interrogate a prisoner; it was something entirely different to extract information from a self-professed con artist who knew he had the upper hand. If only Admiral McDonough had not given him specific orders not to harm Holmhurst in any way, he would have helped the haughty English bastard on to his new life, with a new face.

Hart was brought back to the present by a figure bundled in leather skins making his way down the plane's length to eventually kneel beside him. Hart recognized him as the copilot.

"We're approaching the Norwegian coast, sir. Twenty minutes to the drop site."

Hart gave a thumbs-up. The droning B-17 engines had almost put him to sleep. That and the low oxygen at nineteen thousand feet. The oxygen mask on Hart's face was uncomfortable, and he was sure he did not have a good seal. He gave it a good tug, but it was no use. The rubber was probably warped from prior use.

Why bother, he thought, glancing out the window at the dark forested coastline below. He would be returning to an oxygen-rich environment very soon, and this damn mask would be the least of his worries.

CHAPTER FOURTEEN

The two German Focke-Wulf 190 fighters flying at twenty-two thousand feet above the moonlit Scandinavian mountains banked sharply and headed south at two hundred knots. They were night fighters, specially equipped with thirty-millimeter Mark 108 machine cannons to blast from the sky any American and British bombers attempting to infiltrate German-controlled airspace.

The squadron these fighters belonged to normally spent its time protecting the U-boat pens at Trondheim. But on this particular evening, these planes had been given a special assignment. Both pilots had been briefed with secret orders.

Captain Hans Maier, the lead pilot and squadron leader, had been surprised when the orders arrived earlier that evening in a flurry of activity. The squadron had been on a twenty-four-hour stand-down to give his pilots a much-needed rest after taking on the Allied bombers for nearly twenty days straight. The orders had come in earlier that evening, just as the pilots were sitting down to supper. They had been hurriedly briefed by a sweaty and anxious-looking SS man whom none of them had ever seen before. Within minutes of the briefing the squadron had been thrown aloft, breaking up into pairs to cover a search area nearly a hundred miles wide. Each pair was to take station at such-and-such a location at such-and-such an altitude and wait. What they were waiting to intercept, neither Maier nor any of the rest of his men knew. Maier only assumed it would be obvious when he saw it. The SS man had not been any more specific than to say that they were to completely destroy whatever they came across this evening.

Maier checked his watch. The appointed time had come and gone. Still no sign of their prey. He was confident that the clear skies would not allow anything to get by him unseen. That coupled with the partial moon made this a night fighter's dream conditions.

It was a cold night, however, and the cockpit windows were beginning to fog. Without looking at his panel, Maier thumbed the dehumidifier and waited impatiently for the windows to clear, all the while cursing the lost moments of visibility.

"Plane Two, this is Plane One," the headset intoned in his ears. "I think I see something, sir. Three o'clock low."

Maier strained against the seat harness to see over the remaining moisture on his windshield. He had always had excellent eyes, a prerequisite for the night fighter squadrons, and he had no trouble picking out the small black shape floating by three thousand feet below him. It was heading north, just as the mysterious SS officer had said it would be.

Partly elated by the find, and partly unnerved at the accuracy of the intelligence, Maier took the control stick and banked his fighter sharply to the right, reversing direction to take up a position behind and above the unidentified aircraft. His wingman, who was trained to minimize radio communications in such circumstances, mimicked every move, staying with him through the turn until both fighters now rode up on the intruding aircraft, like a pair of wasps approaching a fluttering butterfly.

As the large black aircraft in front of him crept into his sights, Maier still could not identify it. But that did not matter. Someone important wanted that plane destroyed, and so tonight it would die, as would every man aboard. Whatever it was, Maier's orders were explicit. He must destroy it. He must strafe any parachutes that might deploy. He must strafe any flares or signal fires sighted on the ground. Those were his orders.

It was the dirty side of war. He did not feel good about it. But, then, orders were orders.

CHAPTER FIFTEEN

"Ten minutes!" the airman shouted into Hart's ear as Hart stepped through the final checks of his gear.

He would be landing in the heart of the Scandinavian mountains, where he was to meet up with the Norwegian resistance and a team of OSS Jedburghs. The two crates he now checked were for them, filled with radio equipment, medical supplies, and the latest "goodies" crafted by the OSS's special weapons unit.

The airman made similar checks on the same gear, giving Hart a thumbs-up that all looked in order. Hart was just beginning to climb into his own parachute when the airman next to him tapped the earpieces of his headset and keyed the microphone button at his collar.

"Roger, I'll tell him," the airman said, then turned to Hart. "The captain wants to see you on the flight deck, sir. Pronto."

"Right." Hart nodded, let the straps of his chute fall to the floor, and began making his way forward inside the cramped aircraft, crawling the last few feet. Reaching the cockpit, he poked his head up between the pilot and copilot. He expected this to be the usual well-wishes and good luck before he departed, but was surprised when the pilot turned to him wearing a stern expression.

"We've been spotted." The pilot had to shout the words over the din of the engines. "Tail gunner's reported a couple of Fws creeping up our tail."

Hart nodded in comprehension. A thousand possible scenarios ran through his mind, all leading to a single conclusion—betrayal. Someone had given away the mission. Only a handful of people were privy to it, so the list of suspects was relatively small. The pilot and crew of the bomber did not know the destination until Hart gave it to them after they were airborne. Thus, the treachery had to lie somewhere closer to the mark—within the very ranks of Odysseus itself.

"We can't escape," the pilot continued. "The best I can do is try to lure them in and let my tail gunner get off a few shots. That'll at least get us closer to the drop point and might give you time to make your jump. But I'm not giving any guarantees."

"Understood."

"One more thing, Hart." The pilot seemed to fumble with the words, like someone who knew he was about to enter the gates of hell, the struggle between duty and the instinct for survival flashing across his face for the briefest moment. "Make sure you grab the right chute. And if you ever get that goose-stepping Nazi bastard in your sights, give him a bullet in the balls for me."

Hart gave an appreciative nod. "Will do, Major."

The two shook hands, each with a duty to perform, each with a fate already sealed.

CHAPTER SIXTEEN

Maier and his wingman had now closed to within three hundred yards of the black aircraft. They guided their state-of-the-art German fighters with adroit precision, creeping up on the intruder with the proficiency of professional hunters. Their prey had not changed course or speed yet and by all appearances was completely oblivious to their presence.

Maier checked once to his left. His wingman was there, as expected, a hundred yards abreast. They were in the perfect position to launch a coordinated attack. No matter which way the enemy plane evaded, it would drive itself across the guns of one of the fighters. The plane was close enough now that Maier had identified it as an American B-17, an effective defender when in formation with other B-17s, but a lumbering pigeon when isolated and alone. The projectiles from the Fw's thirty-millimeter cannons would slice through the unwieldy bomber's engines and paper-thin fuselage like darts through a balloon.

The range was now two hundred yards. Maier looked down for a moment to check his speed and to arm his weapons. Suddenly, he heard a muffled staccato, and at the same moment a garbled voice crackled over the radio. Maier looked up just in time to see a lightning-fast stream of phosphorescent tracer projectiles erupting from the B-17's tail section and riddling his wingman's plane. One instant, a spark ignited near his comrade's right engine. The next, the engine burst into flames, severing the right wingtip and instantly sending the Fw into a billowing death spiral.

The screams of the young aviator rang out over the radio as his plane plummeted uncontrollably toward the earth, mercilessly rotating on the axis of the fuselage, undoubtedly pulling enough g's to prevent the young man from bailing out.

"Scheiss!" Maier cursed. He flicked off the radio to silence the screams. There was nothing he could do, and listening to his wingman's death throes would not help his shooting.

He pushed the throttle forward and rapidly accelerated toward an imaginary point off the B-17's starboard side. He was chased by tracer rounds from the tail gun but soon showed the bastard that German pilots could be unpredictable, too. Maier knew the maximum field of fire of a B-17's tail gun, and once he was beyond that limit he extended flaps and turned hard over to the left, sweeping past the bomber's tail in the blink of an eye while at the same time letting loose a three-second burst from his Fw's thirty-millimeter cannons. Even in the darkness he could see chunks of debris falling from the B-17's tail section as round after round hit home. The bomber's tail gun did not return fire as Maier swept past, but a spray of droplets spattered the fighter's windshield. In the darkness, the droplets appeared black as oil, but Maier knew they were blood, most likely from the tail gunner's pulverized body.

Maier had avenged his wingman, a college youth who had not yet reached his twenty-first birthday. But there was little time to savor the moment. The B-17 was banking to the right in an effort to get away, nearly a miracle with the tail section virtually shot away. Maier knew that he was facing a veteran opponent, and that the B-17 was by no means finished, as her top turret gun was still spewing tracer rounds in his direction. As he brought his Fw around in a tight arc for a second attack run, he saw the B-17 level out and then dive to gain speed. The maneuver was expertly executed, but futile in result. The powerful BMW engine allowed Maier to close the distance in less than a minute and to once again drive up on the bomber's tail. He squeezed the trigger, firing both thirty-millimeter cannons in a long, steady burst that swept across the width of the B-17 from one wingtip to the other. The B-17's starboard engines took direct hits and instantly began trailing great ribbons of black smoke. Several rounds had penetrated the fuselage, striking the tail and traveling along the bomber's length, undoubtedly turning the crew compartment into a cauldron of blood and death. One of these rounds must have killed the pilot, because the bomber now sagged to the right, arcing over in a slow spin that apparently no one attempted to correct. The Fw flew past, driving at a much greater speed now. By the time Maier brought his fighter around again, the B-17 was a ball of flame, hurtling to the earth wing over wing.

Maier instantly spotted two parachutes. Both were floating down at about eight thousand feet with the dark forest below providing the perfect backdrop for sighting the bulbous white circles. Maier put aside his rage for a moment to consider the bravery of these helpless men. They were aviators, simply doing their jobs, just as he was doing his. He wished he could leave their fates to providence, but he could not. He had orders not to let them reach the ground alive.

Maier descended and maneuvered to go after the first parachute. Shooting a parachute from the sky was not as easy as it might seem, but Maier did not attain his squadron command through average flying. He was a squadron leader, a top pilot, an ace, and an expert killer. In no time, he had the parachute in range and squarely in his sights. He drew close enough to see the dark figure suspended beneath it and then squeezed off a short burst. The straining chute instantly tore open, deflated, and plunged to the earth.

Maier mentally blocked the thought of the terrible death he had just consigned to that individual and moved on to the next chute. He dispatched this one in a similar manner, and watched as the white streak fell for several seconds to be swallowed up by the thick forest below. The spectacle left Maier feeling somewhat disgusted. Disgusted with his orders. Disgusted with the war.

He halfheartedly scanned the area but could see no more parachutes. Then, just for a moment, he thought he saw movement, a dark shape moving against the black backdrop of the forest below. He lost it and could not find it again. He thought of descending even farther for a low-level sweep, but the sick feeling in his stomach told him he had had enough of parachute hunting.

Maier took one last look and then turned his plane north, heading for his home airfield, comfortable in the knowledge that his mission had been accomplished and that he had done all he had been ordered to do.

PART THREE

PART THREE

Theophilus was used to the smell of burning flesh. As the bishop of Alexandria, he had witnessed nearly every cruel punishment Rome and the Church could enact. He had seen hangings, beheadings, crucifixions, and some other means of torture that would make the fattest of German butchers wince. There were always pagans to be cleansed—infidels who needed the pain of death in this life to purge them of their impurities so that they might have a chance at salvation when they faced the one true God on the Day of Judgment.

He contemplated this as he watched the prostrate man on the stone floor before him, struggling under the weight of the two soldiers holding him down. Once more, Theophilus's fine-skinned assistant approached the man with a fiery brand that glowed in the dimly lit room. The assistant looked once at Theophilus and, after receiving an approving nod, held the brand close to the struggling man's face.

"Please," the youthful assistant said, almost politely but without much concern, "tell His Grace what he wants to know, confess your errant ways, and the pain will stop."

The prisoner stared wildly at the burning brand and uttered something in the native language of the Egyptians. It was a language Theophilus had never taken the time to learn in all his years in Alexandria, instead choosing to stick to his native Greek, like most of the cultured nobles of Alexandria.

Whatever the pathetic creature had said, it did not satisfy Theophilus's assistant, and once again the elegant youth pressed the orange ember into the skin beneath the man's ear. What little hair the man had instantly caught fire and burned itself out within moments, and once again the room was filled with the aroma of burning flesh and screams of agony. The screaming was loud enough to drown out the commotion in the other chambers of this monstrous structure, which the pagans had the impertinence to call a temple, and in which at this very moment Roman soldiers under Theophilus's orders ransacked, looted, and slew those belonging to the accursed cult of Serapis.

Serapis—that was what these wretches called their god. A god that manifested itself in the form of a sacred bull every so many years. Worshipping a beast of the field, how far could their sacrilege go? How could the previous bishop have allowed this deep-rooted cult to go on for so long?

Another scream as the ember was once again pressed to the prisoner's face.

When would they learn? Theophilus wondered. How long would they resist the truth? Regardless, after tonight, the bull-god would never be worshipped in Alexandria again. This would be a Christian city. A thriving, teeming polis of Christians, and Theophilus would be the one who made it happen. News would travel quickly across the sea, and perhaps his achievements would even raise the eyebrows of the bishop of Rome. Perhaps, if he found what he had really come here for, he would garner the interest of the emperor himself. For Theophilus's concern for the souls of the pagans was only secondary to his chief reason for invading their temple.

"Again, I will ask you to tell me what His Grace wants to know," Theophilus's assistant said. "Tell me, and you will be free to go."

The man looked back at Theophilus and his assistant with disbelief, his nervous eyes darting to the headless corpses tossed into a heap on the far side of the room. These were the first priests of Serapis to face the youth's questioning. The prisoner knew full well that he was the last.

"Do not concern yourself with their fates," the evil youth said in a calming tone that seemed to have a chilling effect on the man. "They did not answer the question. If you tell me what I want to know, you will go free. Otherwise . . ." He gestured to the pile of bodies, causing the priest to cringe. "Now, it really is no use. We know it is here. We will find it eventually. Why must you suffer for such a futile cause?"

The Egyptian uttered a few words that were

unintelligible to Theophilus but quickly caught his young assistant's attention.

"Yes, that's right. Go on. What do you know about the legend?"

At this small amount of encouragement, the man sputtered a long, rambling explanation, which Theophilus's assistant devoured with much interest. The assistant even went so far as to put down the firebrand.

"A jar, you say?" the assistant led him on. "And a scroll? . . . two eagles? . . . No, a single eagle with two heads . . ." The assistant met eyes with Theophilus. This was exactly what they had come for.

"Can he take us there?" Theophilus asked.

The assistant looked at the prisoner, who responded with a short answer Theophilus knew was refusal. Why did these people think they could hide it from him?

"Does he understand Greek?" Theophilus prompted.

The assistant uttered something to the prisoner in the tongue of the Egyptians, and the man replied with a short answer and a nod.

"He understands it, Your Grace, but he cannot speak it."

"Excellent. Then tell him to sit down."

The prisoner was forced to sit on the floor while a chair was quickly produced for Theophilus. Theophilus slightly lifted the skirt of his robe before sitting, then folded his many-ringed hands in front of him to rest on his knee.

"Let me tell you a story," Theophilus said to the man in Greek. "Many centuries ago, there was a certain priest of your cult called Anok Sabe."

At the mention of the name the prisoner's eyes grew wide with fear.

"I see you have heard of him, too." Theophilus smiled. "How do I know this? Well, you would be amazed at what one of the members of your accursed order told me, under torture, of course, so it may not be reliable. He told me the plans that were in place in the event that Christianity ever threatened to snuff Serapis out. He told me the most amazing story, I must confess, about the priest Anok Sabe, and how this priest returned from Jerusalem many centuries ago bearing the power of God in his hands. He told me how this vile priest, how this pagan wretch concocted some kind of weapon that would unleash the power of the Almighty. He told me how Sabe started a cult that was hidden within Egypt's different religious orders. Eventually this cult made its way into the cult of Serapis, and the secret power was passed down through successive generations, only to be unleashed when the worship of Serapis was threatened."

The man did not respond, nor would he make eye contact with Theophilus.

"He told me how this power was used to destroy the army of Cambyses, that Persian ruler that once governed your land. Normally, I would dismiss such claims, but that man caught my attention, and—considering the wretched state of his body at that point—I am certain there was a ring of truth to it."

The man covered his ears and spat at the name of Cambyses. He was promptly thwacked on the back of the head by one of the soldiers, who undoubtedly thought

his behavior insolent. Theophilus, however, knew different. He knew that five hundred years before the time of
Christ, during the period that Egypt fell under Persian
control, the Persian governor Cambyses had become
enraged at the priests of Apis and had stabbed their sacred
bull. This affront to their god had never been forgotten
by the worshippers of Serapis, and the mere mention of
the name of that Persian overlord was considered blasphemy. That was how the story went, or at least how
Theophilus and every other educated Roman had learned
the story during their school years.

But could it be that Cambyses was punishing the cult
for the destruction of his army, that famous army of fifty
thousand men that marched into the desert and disappeared? Could it be that the priests of Apis had something to do with that army's destruction? What if it was
true that the cult had somehow managed to harness the
power of God? If so, then it was Theophilus's duty as a
Roman magistrate and a Christian to approbate such a
weapon for the empire. Such a weapon could be used to
contend with the seemingly incessant surge of barbarian
tribes that were appearing on Rome's borders more fre-
quently with each generation.

Theophilus drew close to the perspiring prisoner.

"Before he died, your wretched priest told me the
secret power was hidden here, inside this temple. Either
you help me find it, or you will die like your pagan
friends and I will wipe your accursed cult from the face
of the earth forever. The decision is yours."

The man's face twisted in nervous indecision, first
glancing at Theophilus and then at the pile of bodies in

the corner. He finally nodded and uttered something in Egyptian.

"He agrees, Your Grace," Theophilus's assistant said, a hint of disappointment in the young man's voice. Theophilus knew that he had a special obsession with pain and torture. "He says it is down in the catacombs, where the sacred bulls are entombed."

"Excellent. Tell him to take us there." Theophilus had heard of the great tomb beneath the temple where these foolish people kept dozens of sarcophagi enshrining the remains of their sacred bulls through the generations. How could they be so misguided to put their faith in a beast of the field? Yes, he would certainly have to burn this place to the ground. Emperor Theodosius was correct in his edict that all pagans must be either converted, put to the sword, or driven out of the empire. They were a pestilence that preyed on the weak-minded.

The prisoner was quickly tethered to a cord and led out of the room, with Theophilus and his entourage following. Outside, in the temple's courtyard, they were met by a black night disrupted by the flaming torches of several dozen Roman soldiers running to and fro. Screams exuded from every corner of the temple as the followers of Serapis were hunted down one by one and butchered. Some soldiers carried the temple's precious treasures of gold, silver, and jewels.

At the sight of all of this, the prisoner cast an anxious glance back at Theophilus.

Theophilus smiled reassuringly. "Simply show us the weapon, and I will order all of it to be stopped."

The prisoner's eyes were untrusting, but he had little choice. He led the bishop and his party through a dark passage that immediately descended into the earth, dropping through several flights of stairs, where the air turned to a cold foggy mist.

Theophilus could see his breath and pulled his cloak around him. The place smelled of ritual and sacrifice, and he could only imagine what practices the pagans undertook in the dark chambers that lined both sides of the passage. The great temple of Serapis in Alexandria was more than five hundred years old, though the cult of Apis had been around much longer than that. In fact, Theophilus knew of several Serapis temples that dotted the Nile valley. They all had fallen into ruin, neglected and abandoned to the winds and ravages of the desert as the Christian faith spread through the land. Only the temple in Alexandria remained, harboring the last vestiges of the ancient cult.

The prisoner led the Greeks and Romans down one dark passage after another, descending ramps and stairways, the entrances to which had been strategically placed in hidden corners of the vast structure. The air turned cold as they walked, and Theophilus was certain that they must have descended several levels below ground level. Eventually, the torchlight began to dance along great rectangular boxes made of stone, lining both sides of the passage. Theophilus did not need to be told that these were the sarcophagi of the sacred bulls, going back several hundred years. Eventually, the prisoner stopped at one sarcophagus in particular.

"This is the one?" Theophilus asked.

The prisoner responded in his gibberish.

"He says it is inside," the assistant interpreted.

The soldiers heaved and pushed the great stone. It would not budge until one soldier produced an iron bar that was used as a lever. The stone lid was pried to one side, exposing the dark cavity beneath it. A putrid odor filled the air, prompting Theophilus to hold his robe to his face. He peered over the edge of the giant sarcophagus while his assistant held a torch nearby. Theophilus saw what he fully expected to see—an elaborate casing shaped like a bull that no doubt contained the mummified remains of the sacred animal in question. That was not surprising. From all appearances it seemed like nothing more than an overly elaborate grave for a beast of the field. But there was something else. Theophilus took the torch and shone the light into the farthest and darkest corner of the container. He could not see the objects clearly.

"Where is it?" he asked the prisoner.

The man pointed to the dark corner of the sarcophagus, pointing to an elaborately ornate box that appeared to be made of solid gold. The prisoner uttered something.

"He says it is in there," Theophilus's assistant interpreted.

"Then tell him to get it for me!" Theophilus ordered somewhat impatiently.

The prisoner hesitated but eventually complied, climbing over the lip of the stone container and retrieving the box, which appeared to be quite heavy. He passed it out to the soldiers, who set it on the floor before the bishop.

"Open it!" Theophilus ordered the soldiers, who proceeded to knock away the crude bolt lock with a few blows from their *gladii*. When they opened the box, Theophilus's eyes widened and it was all he could do to keep his composure. He could not keep from kneeling and reaching into the box himself, pulling out its contents—a small canopic jar with a lid fashioned after a two-headed eagle, and a scroll made entirely of copper. These were the only two objects inside, and to Theophilus initially, they seemed somewhat anticlimactic.

"These items are the divine power your cult has protected all these ages?" Theophilus said, half believing it.

The man nodded and spoke a long rambling explanation that the assistant interpreted as fast as he could.

"Your Grace, he says the scroll contains the information you need to make the power, and the jar contains what you must use to make it."

Theophilus ran one hand over the imprints in the copper scroll. He could see that it was written in some old, pre–Ptolemaic Dynasty script. It would take several scholars months to decipher and analyze it. But the jar. It was here right now, and he felt an irretrievable impulse to open it and be the first Christian to set eyes on this ancient power.

"No, Your Grace!" the assistant called in warning.

But it was too late. Theophilus had already removed the lid and now stared down into a dark void filled with hundreds of small golden objects. They looked like gold nuggets. But upon extracting one from the jar and holding it up to the light, Theophilus saw that they were not nuggets at all, but human teeth, encased in gold.

Some kind of ancient witchcraft was going on here. It might all be hocus-pocus and all of the stories mere myths. But there was a chance that these ornate teeth were the key to a weapon that could defeat entire armies. As long as there was a chance, Theophilus was determined that Rome should have this power for itself.

The prisoner said something again.

"Your Grace, he says the teeth contain the pestilence, and the scroll contains instructions for unleashing it."

"Are these the only remains of this ancient power that he knows of?" Theophilus asked, now thinking of the future and dropping the gold tooth back into the jar with the rest.

The prisoner nodded.

"Tell him thank you," Theophilus said, with a courteous smile and nod to the nervous prisoner, who was still standing in the sarcophagus. Then Theophilus's eyes narrowed and his expression turned sinister as he motioned to the guards. "Close up the tomb."

The guards moved to the other side of the immense lid and began to put their backs to the stone. The prisoner instantly saw what they intended to do and desperately scrambled to get out, but he was struck down by Theophilus's assistant, who carried the bishop's gold-headed crosier. His screams were heard only momentarily as the stone lid rumbled back into place, and then were quite muffled altogether when the lid was shut.

"Ah. Those Egyptian builders," Theophilus commented, running a smooth hand across the top of the stone lid that had just sealed the unfortunate prisoner inside a pitch-black and airless tomb. "Such craftsman-ship!"

Theophilus carefully returned the implements to the gold box, and with a snap of his fingers he ordered the guards to bring the box along. Having retrieved what they had come for, the party of Romans exited the chamber, leaving behind the rows of silent graves containing the bulls of Serapis, and one grave from which the screams of a dying man would never be heard.

CHAPTER SEVENTEEN

U-2553, North Atlantic

Traugott peered through the periscope lens at the world above. It was a hazy day in this patch of ocean, somewhere between the Faroe Islands and the east coast of Iceland. The ocean surface was placid, as if a giant had smoothed it over with a great putty knife. There were no signs of life above—no ships, no aircraft, no birds. It was as if the sea had taken a day off from the war.

Traugott knew it was a rare moment that would not last for long. *U-2553* was only three days out of Trondheim and was still traversing waters normally teeming with Allied vessels.

He rotated the periscope until he could see *U-2553*'s snorkel mast, only a few feet displaced from the periscope and protruding from the water with about the same amount of freeboard. The snorkel mast brought in air for combustion, allowing *U-2553*'s massive diesel generators to operate while the U-boat was submerged, eliminating the often deadly time spent on the surface for charging batteries—the vulnerable time when most submarine sinkings occurred. The mast was another of the many remarkable feats of German engineering, a technology that was years ahead of other nations' submarine development efforts.

The glassy water swirled around the base of the mast as the U-boat moved along at a steady ten knots. It was the only disturbance on the glassy sea. Satisfied that the world above had not changed, Traugott slapped up the handles of the periscope and ordered it lowered.

"No contacts, Captain?" a sub-lieutenant asked from the navigator's stand.

Traugott shook his head. "None, as before. But we have a long voyage ahead of us, and I do not expect this lull to last for very long."

A collective sigh came from the men manning the giant handwheels at the rudder and planes control station. Traugott smiled inwardly. They might complain about their duty, but he knew each one of them would do his job admirably when called upon. They were that kind of crew, one that he and Spanzig had molded together. Spanzig's imprint was still on each one of them—so much so that Traugott half-expected to duck through the next compartment and see his late first officer standing there with another report for him to approve. He did not know why, but he felt Spanzig's loss much more deeply than he had felt other losses. He knew the crew felt the same way. God only knew how they would get through this deployment—how *he* would get through this deployment—without Spanzig's calming influence.

A man ducked through the forward watertight door,

carrying a clipboard, wearing the uniform of a naval sub-lieutenant.

He was younger than Traugott, in his thirties, but he had the tired eyes of an old man and several scars near the left temple that spoke of a recent war wound. Traugott studied the man as he approached. For this was Lieutenant Helmut Rittenhaus—Spanzig's replacement, and Traugott's new first officer.

"How are the levels, Number One?" Traugott asked, accepting the clipboard from the officer.

"Satisfactory, Captain," he answered simply, offering no more. Traugott had learned over the past few days not to expect much conversation from Rittenhaus. The young officer was the silent type, but he seemed very efficient at running the administration of the boat.

"Have you taken your tour of the boat yet?"

"Yes, sir. All is in order." Rittenhaus paused, and then added in a low voice, "The crew seem . . . complacent."

Traugott smiled. "Give them time, Number One. They will warm up to you. They are a good crew, and as such are a very tight-knit group. Remember, you are the newcomer."

Rittenhaus nodded unconvincingly and said, "Of course, you are right, Captain."

"You will see, Number One. Now, come have tea with me, in my nook."

"If you insist, sir."

Traugott ordered tea from one of the seamen and then motioned for Rittenhaus to follow him back to the captain's nook, a boothlike table in an isolated corner of the officer staterooms where both men could have a conversation without standing aside every few minutes to allow someone by.

Traugott had seldom had a chance to speak to his new first officer in the hustle of getting the ship repaired and then underway on time from Trondheim. He felt like he hardly knew the man. Now that *U-2553* was settled on a course into the North Atlantic and Allied air and naval power to this point had virtually been nonexistent, he thought this an opportune time to get to know his somewhat unsociable and withdrawn Number One. Rittenhaus always seemed uncomfortable. He was obviously a man battling his own personal demons. Traugott had seen it too many times before in other veteran U-boat men. There was a point at which the pressure of life and death in the boats simply broke you, and Traugott suspected that had happened at some point in Rittenhaus's not-too-distant past.

"So you were in the Med, Helmut?" Traugott asked in a friendly tone.

"Yes, sir."

"Which boat?"

Rittenhaus looked at him confused. "But you must surely know that, sir. You have no doubt reviewed my file."

"Of course I have read your file, Helmut. This is called conversation. I get to know you, and you get to know me. We are going to be working very closely together in the coming weeks. I have found that the better my first officer understands me, the better he can anticipate my decisions and act on his own initiative. The better we understand each other, the better chance we have of bringing these boys home safely."

Rittenhaus nodded, it seemed skeptically.

"You do not think so, Helmut?"

"It's not that, Captain. It just seems that getting to know someone in the boats only sets one up for a loss."

"Easier to just do your job and not worry about the consequences, is that what you mean? If you are not emotionally attached to the crew, all the easier to send them to their deaths, is that it?"

"I suppose." Rittenhaus shrugged. "Something like that."

"Well, then, you listen to me, Helmut. I have been in this stinking war a long time. I have lost men for the Fatherland, not for that perverted Nazi corporal, that maniac. God help me, I remember every one of them. Their names, their hometowns, their wives' and sweethearts' names, their hobbies, and their nuances. Call it a curse, but I remember it all. And God help me if I ever do anything less. Their memories will survive in me. I will remember them, even if no one else does. And if I survive this war I will visit each and every one of their loved ones. I will tell them how bravely their son met his end. That he was not just another number on Dönitz's wall, but a human being whose loss was felt and whose loss was grieved by his captain. I will give them closure to this tragedy in which we are all embroiled. I will tell them that, Helmut. It is my duty to tell them. It is a duty that is perhaps, at this point, more important than sinking enemy ships. War is emotional, my boy. It kills human beings. God help us if we ever drive the human toll from our conscience. It is that emotion that brings such wars to an end. And I hope the end of this one is not far off."

Rittenhaus only nodded, seemingly lost in his cup of tea, swirling a finger in the tepid drink, as if Traugott's sermon were as trivial as the latest film reviews from Paris.

"So, tell me about Sonnberg, in Austria, Helmut," Traugott said, trying another tack.

"What would you like to know, Captain?"

"Anything. Just tell me about it."

Rittenhaus sighed, as if the conversation were a struggle to him. "I come from Sonnberg, a little village near Rossleithen, in the Alps."

"I know where that is, Helmut."

"Then you know it is cold in the winter and hot in the summer."

"I once knew a man from that country. Schroeder was his name—Gerd Schroeder. Did you ever know him, Helmut?"

For a brief moment, Rittenhaus seemed somewhat startled. It was the first time Traugott had ever seen him so.

"The name is familiar," Rittenhaus finally said.

"He was a good friend, and a first-rate U-boat man." Traugott smiled and then frowned at the memory of his friend. "He served under me in my first boat out of Kiel and eventually commanded his own boat."

"What happened to him?" Rittenhaus asked with an uncharacteristic level of interest.

"His boat was sunk near the eastern seaboard of the United States—two years ago. There is a rumor that some of the crew were captured and sent to a POW camp in the American Southwest, but I do not know what to believe. U-Boat Command has a habit of quashing such stories, probably out of fear that our boats would surrender to the first Allied forces they came across." The thought of his lost friend suddenly filled Traugott with a hopeless feeling. "I am sure he is dead, like so many others."

Whatever had disturbed Rittenhaus before seemed to have subsided, and the first officer went back to observing his tea.

"Those scars," Traugott said, wanting to change the subject, "did you get them in your last action?"

Rittenhaus ran a finger over the rough skin and nodded.

"I trust your time in hospital was adequate? That your convalescence furlough allowed you enough time to recover?"

Rittenhaus did not have time to answer before they were interrupted by a short-haired, blond, rigid-looking young man in the uniform of an SS army lieutenant. The lieutenant promptly saluted Traugott in the usual Nazi fashion and issued a curt nod in Rittenhaus's direction.

Traugott sighed. He had little time for this imbecile.

"Captain Traugott," the young officer said, standing at attention as if on parade.

"I have already told you I do not know how many times, Lieutenant Odeman, we set ceremony aside in the U-boats. Especially when at sea."

Odeman appeared somewhat insulted, but after a short glance at Rittenhaus, he continued. "Permission to speak freely, Captain?"

"Of course."

"I must report, Captain, that I am somewhat shocked that certain members of your crew wish to impede an officer of the Reich in the execution of his duties."

Traugott saw Rittenhaus roll his eyes.

"To whom are you referring?" Traugott asked, knowing full well that tension existed between his passenger and his first officer.

"Forgive me, Captain, but I am referring to none other than your first officer, Herr Rittenhaus."

"Is this true, Number One?" Traugott casually asked Rittenhaus, who was in the middle of taking a long sip from his tea.

"I am an officer of the *Wehrmacht*!" Odeman snapped. "My word is not to be questioned! If I say it, it is true!"

This retort summoned the blood in Traugott, who had already grown weary of this Nazi fool's posturing. He shot Odeman a wrathful glare that seemed to have the desired effect, as the SS lieutenant's scowling face melted into an embarrassed blush.

"I . . . I am sorry, Captain," Odeman finally said, though it appeared to give him great strain to do so. "Please forgive my outburst. I am a panzer soldier by trade, and as such I am more suited to the plains of Russia than the swells of the North Atlantic. Since we got underway, I have not been eating properly, and I am afraid my disposition has affected my patience."

"Aboard a U-boat, Lieutenant Odeman," Traugott said quietly but firmly, "no one may lose his patience with the captain. Is that understood?"

Odeman nodded. "Perfectly, sir."

"Now, if you have a concern, please tell me about it."

"I think I can elaborate, sir," Rittenhaus spoke up. "I believe I know what has the lieutenant upset."

"Go ahead."

"I was conducting an inspection of the forward spaces this morning, as I do every morning. When I requested that the lieutenant and his men remove themselves from the torpedo room so that I could thoroughly inspect their cargo and verify that it was properly stowed for sea, the lieutenant refused. I then ordered him to leave the room, and he refused again. Then, I regret to say, our intercourse quickly devolved into a heated argument, with several of the crew and Lieutenant Odeman's men within earshot. I said a few things—which I now regret—and I believe I embarrassed the lieutenant."

The formerly subdued Odeman's face instantly turned red with anger. "I assure you, Herr Rittenhaus, that is something you could never achieve. I am a decorated veteran of the Twenty-fourth Panzer Division. I have seen action in Stalingrad, Leningrad, and Kursk. I have been wounded five times in combat—"

"I think your honor is not in question here, Lieutenant," Traugott interrupted before Odeman got out of hand again. Odeman was about to continue, but Traugott raised a hand. "Never fear, Lieutenant. You were quite right to contradict my first officer, and on that point I support you." Traugott turned to Rittenhaus, who appeared to expect a dressing-down. "Number One, you know my orders. Lieutenant Odeman and his men are our guests. Their cargo is of a special nature and is not to be disturbed or inspected. At least two of the lieutenant's men must be with the cargo at all times. Our orders are very clear on that, and you well know it."

"Yes, Captain," Rittenhaus said, appearing unfazed. "I was only performing my duty, sir. I would hate for one of those boxes to fall to the deck and bring a destroyer down on us."

"Yes, Number One, I understand your concern, and you are right to have it. So, I propose an agreement, gentlemen. Number One, you may inspect the torpedo room once a day, and Herr Odeman will accompany you. If you find any of the cargo improperly stowed for sea, you will inform Herr Odeman and advise him on how it may be corrected. Will that be satisfactory, Lieutenant Odeman?"

"Most satisfactory, sir," Odeman answered with a triumphant smile.

"Then I expect the rest of our voyage to be a peaceful one. Is that clear, gentlemen?"

"Yes, Captain," both men answered, and then nodded to each other in agreement.

Odeman then saluted smartly and left the compartment, while Rittenhaus seemed unaffected by the altercation and went back to his tea. Traugott sighed, holding his own cup with one hand to keep it from sliding across the table as the U-boat absorbed a deep North Atlantic swell. This was merely the latest rift between his new first officer and his unlikable passenger. Since *U-2553* had left Trondheim three days before, the two had been at it over one thing or another. They seemed diametrically opposed to each other from the start. Rittenhaus had displayed ill blood toward the SS lieutenant, and

Traugott assumed he was one of the many officers in the German navy who hated the Nazis.

Rittenhaus had seemed good-natured enough when he reported aboard, just before the U-boat embarked. He seemed a good addition to the crew, coming with good recommendations, a glowing record, and a temperament that seemed suited to the soul of this vessel. He had stepped right into his duties from day one, taking charge of the functions that had once been Spanzig's. Rittenhaus seemed well intentioned and devoted to the ship, so Traugott had not given a second thought to his apparent coldness toward the rest of the crew. He could learn to get along with the crew at sea, and Traugott had had few doubts that, given enough time, Rittenhaus would be accepted by the men just as Spanzig had been.

Then, the day before *U-2553* sailed, her special cargo arrived, accompanied by Lieutenant Odeman and a squad of soldiers. It was at that moment that all prospects of a happy cruise vanished. As had happened so many times before, *U-2553* was to carry a dozen crates of various sizes to the same secret destination she had taken other similar objects on her three previous cruises. Somehow, this batch of crates seemed more important than those *U-2553* had carried in the past. Each crate was sealed with a robust lock. Each was stamped with a swastika, and each one weighed so much that block and tackle had to be used to convey them through the torpedo room. They were so heavy, in fact, that the chief engineer had to pump a thousand gallons of water to the aft trim tanks to compensate.

Perhaps the problems between Odeman and Rittenhaus had started on that first day, when the crates were being loaded into the forward torpedo room. Odeman had watched the entire operation, never missing a single swing of the cargo net, and never failing to scold any sailor he felt was being too careless. One would have thought the crates contained Schliemann's gold of ancient Troy, judging by the way Odeman nursed them. At one point, Odeman went too far with a particularly harsh reprimand of the work detail, and Rittenhaus responded, lashing out at the meddling army officer who, in his opinion, should have been minding his own business. Traugott had been the eventual peacemaker in that altercation, too.

Traugott now sighed as he stretched out his arms in the cramped booth. Rittenhaus stared into his tea, his mind obviously elsewhere. Somehow, Traugott knew there would be many more altercations between Odeman and Rittenhaus before this voyage was over. It promised to be a long, arduous voyage, after all, and one that Traugott was not looking forward to.

CHAPTER EIGHTEEN

U-2553 had traveled down the seventeenth longitude, down past the Bay of Biscay, without incident. She reached the warmer waters off Portugal and Spain also without incident, diving to deeper depths only whenever a plane or a single escort was sighted. But now she had reached a crisis—a crisis that, more than anything else, indicated how Germany was faring in the war.

Traugott peered through the periscope one last time before giving the order that he dreaded issuing in full daylight.

"Surface the boat!"

"Surface the boat, aye, Captain," came the reply from the diving control station. Almost immediately the sibilant sound of high-pressure air blowing into the main ballast tanks filled the small space crammed with crewmen in helmets, holding belts of large-caliber ammunition for the two antiaircraft guns in the conning tower. *U-2553* was transformed from a neutrally buoyant vessel to a positively buoyant one in a matter of seconds, and her sudden lightness shot her to the surface like a cork. Traugott did not wait to see the water streaming from her decks before he handed off the periscope to a junior officer and headed up the ladder to the bridge. He almost collided with Rittenhaus, who was scrambling up the same ladder. Both men looked similar, having donned black bridge coats, U-boat caps, and binoculars.

"Crack the hatch," Traugott ordered.

Rittenhaus spun the hatch wheel and released the dogs. The hatch came open with ease because of the slight positive pressure in the hull, and both men were instantly met by the sound of the last few inches of retreating seawater escaping through the bridge scuppers. Within moments, they were both leaning over the railing on opposite sides of the bridge, studying the horizon and sky with their binoculars, searching for any sign of an enemy presence.

"Starboard clear, Captain," Rittenhaus announced, taking the binoculars from his face. "No visual contacts."

"Very well." Traugott had just finished his own search of the port side.

"I would have preferred better visibility," Rittenhaus commented at the low gray overcast.

Traugott's thoughts exactly. These were not ideal conditions for sitting on the surface at a dead stop for several hours.

"It cannot be helped, Number One. We must refuel if we are to keep on schedule."

The fueling stop was indeed a necessity, for *U-2553* had gotten underway from Trondheim with half-filled tanks. It was all the fuel the U-boat base could spare. All fuel had been put on rationing to support the army fighting in France and Russia. Yet another sign that the end was near.

"Now where is that milch cow, Number One?" Traugott said, placing his arms on the bridge railing.

As if on cue a tumult erupted on the surface of the water less than two thousand yards away. Slowly, but steadily, the knifing bow and barrel-like conning tower of another U-boat emerged from the depths, her hull and scuppers streaming with the frothy Atlantic. Traugott felt exhilaration as he watched the weighty U-boat rise to the surface. In spite of the dangers involved with surfacing in broad daylight, she was a friendly face in an otherwise hostile world, and it was heartening to see her.

"*U-490* is signaling, Captain," Rittenhaus reported as a rash of flashing lights emanated from the other submarine's conning tower.

"What do they say, Helmut?"

It took Rittenhaus a little longer than expected to interpret the signal. Long enough for Traugott to take notice and make a mental note to reprimand him later.

"From Captain *U-490* to Captain *U-2553*," Rittenhaus finally said. "Your U-boat is thirsty, and so are you. Request your presence aboard to share spirits."

The petty officers manning the antiaircraft turrets chuckled at the message, and Traugott decided not to spoil the mood by reprimanding the first officer in front of them.

"All right, Number One." Traugott clapped Rittenhaus on the shoulder. "Advise *U-490* that it will be my pleasure to come aboard."

"Yes, Captain." Rittenhaus's face revealed that he had trepidation over his slow interpretation of the signals. As if to make up for his fault, he now issued orders with a new alacrity, announcing to the deck below, "Man the deck to receive fuel lines!"

A flood of sailors streamed from the hatches on the side of U-2553's conning tower and began to unpack great lengths of hemp line.

"Ahead slow," Traugott spoke into the bridge intercom box. "Rudder right, fifteen degrees."

U-2553's bow came around until it pointed at the other U-boat, whose decks were already crowded with sailors laying out fuel lines. Slowly, the two U-boats moved closer to each other, seemingly taking an eternity to close the distance.

"Damn milch cow moves like an ox," a sub-lieutenant commented from the rear of the bridge.

"She may not be sleek like a hunter boat," Traugott said in a fatherly tone, "but many is the time I have welcomed the sight of one of these behemoths while trying to cross the Atlantic on a few puddles of diesel."

Traugott conned U-2553 past the other vessel and then expertly turned his submarine through 180 degrees, until U-2553 was driving parallel to her compatriot. Through a series of conn orders, Traugott brought the U-boat alongside the tanker sub, closing the distance between the two, his veteran seamanship making up for the poor maneuverability of the other boat.

He allowed Rittenhaus a few seconds but then was forced to give the expected order himself. "Lines over!"

The men on deck responded, throwing their lead

lines across the small space of water to the waiting hands on the other sub's deck.

Traugott was annoyed. The line orders were normally issued by the first officer, since the first officer was technically in charge of the deck crew during such maneuvers. It prompted Traugott to once again question the competence, or at least the wherewithal, of his new first lieutenant. It was simply another incident in a chain of events that had occurred over the past week at sea. It was as if Rittenhaus were not all there, as if he had left his experience and all his skills back on that U-boat now lying on the bottom of the Mediterranean.

"I'll go down on deck and tend to the line-handling party, sir," Rittenhaus said complacently, evidently detecting his error and wanting to get away from Traugott before his captain's wrath came down on him.

"Very well," Traugott said, eyeing his first officer harshly.

Rittenhaus avoided his gaze, quickly threw a leg over the bridge railing, and descended the outboard conning tower ladder that led down to the main deck. Traugott watched from the bridge as his first officer strode from one cluster of sailors to another down on the main deck. He did not know what to make of this man whom he was coming to like personally, but who also seemed in a haze half of the time.

"A most curious officer," a voice said behind him. "Would you not agree, Captain?"

Traugott glanced over his shoulder to see that the SS lieutenant Odeman had appeared on the bridge beside him and was also watching Rittenhaus's every move.

Odeman was not smiling. In fact, his face appeared full of revulsion.

Traugott said nothing. *U-490* was now close enough to make out the faces on her bridge, and Traugott waved enthusiastically to his counterpart, Werner, who was doing the same. Traugott was trying his best not to get into this conversation again with Odeman, the same conversation they had had at least two times in the last week.

"Would you not agree, sir?" Odeman said again, more forcefully.

"What?"

"I asked if you would not agree that the first officer is of a most curious nature."

"In case you have not noticed, Lieutenant, I am in the process of preparing to take fuel on board. I am quite busy. You may take your commentary belowdecks."

"But should your fine first lieutenant not be able to handle this simple evolution on his own?" Odeman persisted in a somewhat mocking tone. "He is, after all, a veteran of the Mediterranean station, is he not?"

"If you are being impertinent in an effort to imply something, Odeman, it is lost on me. Now, go below before I have you thrown down the ladder!"

Odeman appeared to bite his lip, his disrespect for the naval service almost shining through. Traugott knew full well the bastard smarted at being told off by a naval officer. Eventually, Odeman regained his composure.

"Of course, I must not do that, Captain," he said with all of the graciousness he could manage. "Out of my sense of duty, I must inform you that you are jeopardizing the success of this mission and, more important, the safety of my cargo with your apparent blindness and inaction. Furthermore, it is my duty to tell you—"

"Stop, Lieutenant! Stop right there! You really are overstepping your bounds, now. This is my ship, and my crew! Rittenhaus is my first officer, and if you are somehow suggesting that his curious behavior, as you say, is in some way to be construed as anything more than a temporary lapse in effectiveness, you are sorely mistaken. He is my responsibility, as is your cargo, and I will deal with him in my own way, in my own time."

"Come now, Captain. I must, of course, write a report to my superiors. Indeed, I must. And I do not think they will be happy that you are protecting a man whose every action proclaims his true identity."

"What the devil are you saying?"

"He is a spy, Captain," Odeman said evenly. "Plain and simple. It is quite obvious. The missed reports, the botched navigation corrections, the rather peculiar accent that he hides by pretending to be shy and unsociable—it all points to one conclusion. Come now, Captain. Surely, you cannot deny this."

Traugott stared at *U-490* for a long moment, digesting what Odeman had just suggested. When laid before him, the evidence was hard to dismiss. And why had he dismissed it before? Was he letting his sympathy for a shot-up U-boat veteran get in the way of his judgment? How would he have reacted had any one of the junior officers made similar mistakes?

"Ready to receive fuel lines, Captain!" The call came

from Rittenhaus down on the main deck. He was looking back up at the bridge, waiting for Traugott's order, obviously oblivious to what Odeman was saying about him, and what Traugott was now considering as a real possibility.

"Very well, Number One!" Traugott finally answered, cupping his hands to his mouth. "Receive lines!"

Rittenhaus saluted, and soon afterward the sailors on the deck of *U-490* tossed the fuel lead lines to the sailors on *U-2553*, who received them enthusiastically.

"Hello, Wolfgang!" an amplified voice called from the other bridge. It was Werner, the captain of *U-490*, speaking through a megaphone. "Have you caught anything yet, my old friend?"

Traugott simply smiled and waved. His mind was racing too fast to even answer his cheerful classmate across the water. Despite his reluctance to believe what Odeman had just told him, there was a ring of truth to it all.

"I am glad to see that you are in agreement with me, Captain," Odeman said, like the devil on his shoulder. "It may comfort you to know that I came to that conclusion only just this morning."

Traugott glanced down at the main deck, where a dozen sailors were busy hauling fuel hoses aboard. In stark contrast, Rittenhaus stood still, hands on his hips, his face expressionless as he stared back up at the bridge. It was as if he were somehow aware of what Traugott and Odeman were discussing.

Odeman opened his coat to reveal a Walther P38 tucked into his belt.

"I am prepared to deal with the situation here and now, sir," Odeman said, almost salivating. "If I may have your permission, sir."

The sight of the sidearm quickly brought Traugott out of his trance. "What? Of course not! Are you mad? There are proper procedures for placing an officer under arrest."

"That is no officer," Odeman snarled. "It is a shit-filled, cowardly American wearing the uniform of a hero of the Reich—a hero that is most likely dead now, killed by that swine. There is only one way to deal with his kind."

Odeman began to unholster the pistol, but Traugott placed a firm hand on the lieutenant's arm. He could feel the panzer veteran's solid forearm muscles twitch beneath the jacket and shirt. Odeman really was ready to kill Rittenhaus where he stood.

"Put that away, now, Lieutenant!" Traugott commanded. "We are in the middle of transferring fuel, for God's sake!"

Odeman's face twisted with hatred as he pushed away from Traugott, completely disregarding the direct order and climbing onto the ladder that led down to the main deck.

Traugott turned to the men in the antiaircraft turrets and the junior watch officer beside him, taking a moment to judge whether it would be prudent to order them to seize the armed SS lieutenant.

It was at that moment that the world around him exploded.

CHAPTER NINETEEN

Traugott had instinctively ducked behind the bridge railing when the sea beside *U-490* erupted in a giant waterspout that rose a hundred feet in the air and then came crashing down in a great shower of salt water on the decks of both submarines. The explosion had been close aboard, off the port side—close enough to send *U-490* reeling into *U-2553*, crushing the inadequate fenders between the two vessels.

By the time Traugott got to his feet again, the submarines were coming apart. He could see that most of the men down on the main deck had been blasted over the side. One sailor had been unfortunate enough to fall in the water between the two two-thousand-ton subs. The only thing left of him was a large smear of blood at the waterlines of both vessels.

Men on both U-boats were collecting their bearings. Some were looking up and pointing into the gray haze above. Traugott had not considered an aircraft because he had heard no aircraft engines, and he certainly would have for such an accurate strike. But now he began to reconsider as a great shadow fell over both submarines, blocking out the little sunlight penetrating the haze. Something was above them. Something much larger than an aircraft. Traugott looked up to see a great whale-like shape materialize from the gray haze. It was directly above the idle U-boats and seemed to hover in midair.

"Airship!" Traugott shouted, recognizing the shape as it took form and emerged from the clouds.

The great beast of the sky was a blimp or an airship— a helium- or hydrogen-filled monster loaded with a plethora of bombs and large-caliber machine guns. The Allies had been employing them of late, now that the *Luftwaffe* had largely been driven from the coastal skies. They made little noise and could stay aloft for days, and thus were perfect for hunting submarines. What was more, the airship was a very stable platform, which gave its bombs a greater degree of accuracy than those dropped from a bomber.

"Fend off!" Traugott shouted to the remaining men on deck. He saw Werner aboard *U-490* do the same. Both captains understood the danger of their situation. Lashed together and immobilized, the U-boats presented a perfect target. They had to separate and submerge. It was their only chance to escape the airship's coming bombs.

"Rudder, left fifteen," Traugott ordered into the voice box after his men finally cast off the last lines. "Ahead flank!"

Traugott noticed that the AA turret gunners near him were preparing to open up on the blimp.

"Hold your fire!" he ordered, and they reluctantly complied.

The airship was still too high for *U-2553*'s AA guns to be effective. Traugott could see that the airship was already descending, no doubt in an effort to increase its bombing accuracy. The airship captain seemed secure in the knowledge that he had several minutes to spare before either U-boat could submerge. Traugott wanted to encourage him to descend and did not want him warded off by any hasty firing from *U-2553*'s gunners. More than likely, the airship captain had never encountered a U-boat of *U-2553*'s class before, and would not expect to face the twin twenty-millimeter AA guns. Traugott was eager to give him a lesson on the new U-boat's capabilities, but the airship's descent was ever so slow. Suddenly, the airship stopped descending and leveled off, still out of range of *U-2553*'s guns.

The two U-boats had separated by about two hundred meters when Traugott saw the small black dot drop from the airship's control car. It seemed to fall in slow motion, and Traugott felt helpless as he watched the hurtling object fall five thousand feet toward a spot off *U-2553*'s starboard beam.

"Werner," Traugott whispered to himself, as he watched the bomb strike *U-490* squarely on the stern. It penetrated the pressure hull and exploded an instant later. Smoke, debris, and spray completely obscured *U-490*. Traugott felt the blast wave hit his face and heard the sickening sound of straining steel. When the air finally cleared, *U-490* was in two pieces. The stern section had broken off at the aft hatch, and now it sat in the water tilted downward with rudder and propeller free and clear of the water. A few meters away, across a space of water covered with burning diesel fuel and motionless bodies, the forward section lay rolled on its port side with the conning tower half-submerged.

Traugott tore his face away from the horrid scene and shouted to his men on deck.

"Clear the deck! Clear the deck!"

The men scrambled for the hatches. There were far fewer men on deck than had been there initially. Many men were still missing from the initial bomb strike, including Rittenhaus and Odeman. Some were probably still alive in the water, somewhere in *U-2553*'s wake, but Traugott could not afford to turn back for them. He had to submerge his boat, and fast. The airship had turned its nose toward *U-2553* now, its roaring propellers revving up to maximum speed. *U-2553* was picking up speed as well, her twin screws turning in unison to push her along at fifteen knots and beyond. Traugott knew that the U-boat would lose the race, but he wanted to get some speed on her before he ordered the dive. He was certain the airship was equipped with depth bombs, and he wanted to get enough momentum on the sub to drive her deep quickly. He needed only a few more seconds of acceleration.

Then something happened that changed his entire plan.

"He's coming lower!" the man in the aft gun turret exclaimed in disbelief.

Traugott looked up to see that it was indeed true. The airship had pitched downward and was now descending, its nose aimed directly at the U-boat. After a moment's consideration Traugott concluded that the airship captain had performed this maneuver in order to accelerate quickly and to attack *U-2553* before she submerged. But in so doing, he had also placed his airship within the effective range of the U-boat's twenty-millimeter gun turrets.

"Fire!" Traugott commanded.

Both gun mounts rang out together, firing a long deafening salvo accentuated by the clinking of spent twenty-millimeter shell casings raining onto the deck in heaps. The tracer shells formed two irregular streams that climbed into the sky and converged on the gigantic lumbering target. The captain of the airship appeared to realize his error and began to pull up, but it was too late. The shells sliced through the rubbery skin of the dirigible one after another, cutting great gaping holes in the outer skin and perforating the great bladders within. The blimp shuddered like a giant blubbery whale being kicked in the belly repeatedly. Within moments, the airship began to lose shape, its outer skin shriveling around the one remaining bladder. Then that bladder popped like a balloon and the control car plummeted like a rock.

From the size of the cockpit, Traugott assumed it carried a crew of about ten men. Those men were now suffering a horrifying final few seconds as the cockpit fell from the sky. It finally hit the water less than a mile from *U-2553* and came apart in an unimpressive splash. None of the crew could have survived.

Everyone on the bridge breathed a sigh of relief, including Traugott, who knew that he now had time to look for German sailors in the water. He was about to order the ship turned around to commence the search when the lookout beside him shouted.

"Enemy destroyer, Captain! Four thousand meters astern and heading directly for us!"

"What the devil is it doing here?" Traugott asked no one in particular, flabbergasted that the enemy could have consolidated its forces so quickly. Either this destroyer had gotten incredibly lucky and happened to be nearby when the airship discovered the heaved-to U-boats, or—"

"They must have known we were going to rendezvous here, Captain." One of the junior officers finished his thought. The young officer looked anxious. "But how could they have known, sir, unless our communications have been compromised?"

"The airship must have been escorting the destroyer across the Atlantic," Traugott said in a calming tone. "They got lucky."

Traugott did not believe a word of his own explanation. He was inclined to agree with the young officer's line of thinking but did not want to admit it for fear of starting a panic among his men when they were about to face a charging destroyer.

He leveled the binoculars on the horizon astern of *U-2553*, sizing up the newcomer. He instantly recognized her as a British D-class destroyer. She would have guns and every variety of depth charges. She was coming on fast, with her plunging bow throwing off curtains of spray. She would easily overtake the U-boat. There was no chance of escaping on the surface.

As if to confirm this, two puffs of smoke appeared on

the destroyer's bow. Moments later, two large-caliber shells screamed overhead and hit the water no more than three hundred yards off *U-2553*'s bow, resulting in two towering geysers of white water.

"Alarm!" Traugott shouted into the voice box. "Crash dive!"

The alarm bell rang out below and the men on the bridge dashed for the hatch. They had done this many times before and slithered down the small opening in rapid succession within a matter of seconds. A jet of mist shot into the air as the ballast tank vents opened and seawater rushed in to fill the dry voids. Traugott could see the bow planes up forward extending outboard as the bow nosed under the next wave. He was the last man topside and had only seconds to scramble down the hatch before the water enveloped the bridge. He decided to peer over the bridge railing one last time, as was his custom on all dives—one final check to make sure there were no stragglers left on the main deck.

What he saw startled him and left him momentarily speechless. Not even the crash of the destroyer's second salvo could take his eyes from the spectacle he now observed.

Just below him, on the outboard ladder leading up the bridge from the main deck, were two men. One was half-unconscious and was being carried by the other in a fireman's carry up the ladder. The half-unconscious man was Odeman. He was soaking wet and bleeding from one ear. Clearly he had suffered a head injury of some sort and was moaning as his would-be rescuer struggled to climb the ladder under his weight.

"Come on!" Traugott shouted, leaning over the rail as far as he could and extending a hand to grasp Odeman's jacket and help the other man pull him up to the bridge.

It was only after they managed to get Odeman's body over the bridge railing that Traugott was able to see the other man's face, previously hidden by Odeman's bulk.

"Thank you, Captain," a wet, smiling face said. "For a minute there, I did not think we were going to make it."

Traugott hesitated for a moment and then smiled and patted him on the shoulder.

"Anytime, Number One."

Without another word, they passed Odeman down the hatch, and then both men quickly followed, pulling the hatch shut behind them as the boiling sea surged over the bridge.

CHAPTER TWENTY

HMS *Daunting*

"ASDIC holds a contact off the starboard bow, Captain. Depth is estimated at three hundred feet, sir."

"Very good, Mister Hancey. Come right five degrees. Prepare for submarine engagement, starboard side."

"Aye, aye, sir."

Captain Ethan Mackay of His Majesty's destroyer *Daunting* adjusted in his seat atop the open bridge of his warship. Satisfied that his orders were being carried out, he and the handful of men with him on the bridge continued scanning the surrounding sea for any sign of the U-boat they had just forced underwater. It could not have gone far. In the eight minutes since its conning tower had disappeared beneath the waves, the *Daunting* had charged in at a cool thirty-one knots, traversing nearly four nautical miles. By his own mental calculations Mackay had figured that the *Daunting* should be almost on top of the enemy submarine. Now the new ASDIC contact appeared to confirm those calculations.

"We are set up for our run, sir," the officer of the watch reported.

"Very good, Mister Hancey. Engage the U-boat, if you please. Full spread, starboard side, standard depth pattern."

"Aye, aye, sir."

Hancey ran through the checklist and gave the necessary helm orders to drive the *Daunting* at high speed directly for the square acre of ocean where the active sonar had detected the enemy submarine.

Mackay considered himself lucky to have an enemy U-boat under his guns, although he had to admit the circumstances surrounding this engagement were odd to say the least. Yesterday, he had received a communiqué from the Admiralty stating that he was to proceed with all dispatch to these coordinates, where he would find two enemy U-boats in the process of refueling. He was to coordinate with the air assets also given the assignment. It was a stroke of good luck to find a U-boat on the surface in his sector, let alone two U-boats. That was why he was now somewhat frustrated that his counterpart aboard the American blimp K-17 had jumped the gun, attacking without giving him time to bring his destroyer in closer. Typical of the damn Yanks to charge in and try to steal the glory. Mackay had watched helplessly from miles away as the American airship was blasted from the sky. What had once been a cakewalk ambush had now turned into a duel between two ships, albeit the destroyer had the advantage.

"Commencing attack now, Captain," Hancey reported.

"Very good."

"Starboard hedgehogs, fire!" Hancey ordered the nearby seaman wearing a headset to convey to the deck.

Moments later the starboard deck disappeared in a burst of flame and white smoke, from which emerged twenty-four spigot mortar bombs, thrown out at various distances from the ship. Different from depth charges, these bombs had contact fuses that would detonate when they came in contact with any submerged object.

"Racks, fire!" Hancey ordered.

Mackay and the rest on the bridge leaned out from the railing and looked aft as the sailors manning the depth-charge racks on *Daunting*'s stern responded to the order, rolling several depth charges off into the sea.

Mackay checked his watch and waited as the three-hundred-pound charges dropped. It did not take long, but the wait seemed like forever. Hancey had already ordered another salvo from the K-guns. The same moment that the K-guns went off again, the blue sea behind the *Daunting* turned white, then erupted in a cascade of geysers and violent bubbles. *Daunting*'s hull shook from the detonations, and Mackay could only imagine what they felt like from the U-boat's perspective.

Hancey ordered a final salvo for good measure, completing the churning quarter mile of ocean that *Daunting* left boiling in her wake.

"Right fifteen degrees rudder," Mackay ordered, after receiving a nod from Hancey that he had completed his depth-charge run.

As the *Daunting* heeled over to port, Mackay contemplated his next move. Had the U-boat survived the attack, its captain would be at this moment attempting to place as much horizontal distance between his U-boat and the spot of the last depth-charge attack. But which way would he turn? That was always the question. It was the singular question that made depth-charge attacks better executed when two or three destroyers were involved, rather than just one. When attacking in a group, one destroyer could maintain ASDIC contact on the submarine while another attacked—because it was impossible for an attacking destroyer to maintain contact while depth charges exploded all around her. This was one reason why Mackay had wished the Americans had waited for him before attacking. Sinking U-boats on the surface was no problem.

As he conned *Daunting* on a racetrack pattern to get her into position for another attack, Mackay noticed that Hancey had picked up the intercom headset and was conversing heatedly with someone on the line.

"What is it, Hancey?"

"Sir, we've lost contact on the U-boat," Hancey said with anxiety on his face. "ASDIC doesn't have it, neither does sound. No screws, no breakup noises, absolutely nothing, sir."

Mackay nodded, imagining the sailors in the *Daunting*'s sound room scratching their heads and checking their equipment for malfunctions.

"Very well, Mister Hancey. Keep me informed. In the meantime we will make a second run over the last known position. Perhaps Jerry's gone dead in the water to throw us off."

It did not take long for *Daunting* to complete the racetrack pattern and line up for her next run on the U-boat. As long as he kept his ship running along with a good amount of speed on her, and as long as he inserted a periodic change of course here and there, Mackay felt confident that the U-boat could not establish a torpedo solution on the *Daunting*, should the U-boat captain be bold enough to attempt such a thing. That was why Mackay was quite shocked when a casual sweep of his binoculars detected a creeping white finger on the surface of the water. It was just a hint of a trace of bubbles—nothing when compared to the torpedo wakes he had seen in the past—but it was there, nonetheless. And it was slowly but surely creeping up on the *Daunting*'s stern. No doubt it was one of the German electric torpedoes, which left no combustion trail on the surface. But there was something else different about this weapon. As the *Daunting* turned, the weapon turned with her. It was as if it had a mind of its own.

Mackay instantly recalled a recent briefing the last time *Daunting* was in Portsmouth. The intelligence officer presenting had spoken of a new type of torpedo the Germans had developed, an acoustic homing weapon known as the G7e.

"Hard to starboard. Stop starboard, port ahead full," Mackay desperately ordered into the voice pipe.

Daunting heeled over in response to the helm order, turning more sharply than she had ever turned during any shakedown cruise, her steel girders groaning from the strain. But the bubbly trail turned with her, eventually merging with her roiling white wake.

"All stations, brace for impact!" Mackay announced.

The sailor on the headset had hardly had time to pass the word when the torpedo struck beneath the

Daunting's stern. A great shock wave hit Mackay's face, knocking him down as the hull was picked up by the explosion and set back down in the water. As seawater rained down from the ensuing geyser, thoroughly dousing *Daunting*'s bridge and main deck, a second torpedo hit amidships, erupting in a great ball of fire that singed the eyebrows of everyone on the bridge.

When Mackay regained his senses, he found the bridge shrouded in a mixture of smoke from the fires below and belching exhaust from *Daunting*'s smokestacks. The ship was slowing to a stop. Damage reports were coming in from all decks. None of them sounded promising.

"Fires on C deck and E deck, Captain," Hancey reported apprehensively. "At least three killed. Many injuries. We have major flooding in the engine room between frames one twenty-eight and one thirty-one. We are attempting to seal the compartment."

"Use counterflooding if you have to, Mister Hancey. I'm sure she's done for. We now need to concentrate on staying afloat until help arrives. Have the depth charges disarmed before the fire gets to them."

"Aye, aye, sir."

"Look!" one of the signalmen on the bridge shouted suddenly, pointing to the sea on *Daunting*'s starboard side. "Periscope, red three zero. It's the U-boat!"

Mackay grabbed up his binoculars, preparing to search for the enemy periscope, but found that he did not have to. The sticklike object was protruding from the water, plain as day, not three hundred yards from where he stood.

"He's got us dead, for sure," one of the sailors commented.

Mackay glanced at his remaining guns on the bow, considering his options. *Daunting* was already listing heavily to starboard. His gun director would be lucky to get a shot off, much less hit anywhere near the periscope. He was also concerned about *Daunting*'s stability. If he fired a salvo from the five-inch guns, she might capsize. A good portion of his lifeboats had been destroyed in the torpedo hits. If *Daunting* sank now, dozens, perhaps a hundred of his men would drown. On the other hand, if he stopped all resistance and concentrated all efforts on damage control, the crippled destroyer might stay afloat long enough for help to arrive. Of course, that also depended on the U-boat captain going along his merry way.

"Take the men out of the gun turrets, Mister Hancey. Have them assist the damage control parties. Make all preparations to abandon ship."

"Aye, aye, sir," Hancey replied, his tone clearly indicating his disappointment. "I don't think that U-boat will be as considerate, sir."

Mackay ignored the statement, and eventually Hancey carried on with his duties. The bridge was alive with activity. Men talked over each other on the intercom, and Mackay could see more than a few men on deck casting an anxious eye to the periscope lurking to starboard. They were at the mercy of the U-boat, and they all knew it.

Mackay watched the periscope in his binoculars and could see it rotate from side to side, no doubt sizing up the damage on the destroyer. Mackay could only imagine the thoughts going through her captain's mind. Did he sink this British warship whose crew might someday man other similar vessels, or did he leave her to the mercy of the sea? Mackay wondered what he would do, had the roles been reversed.

After a few minutes, Hancey appeared at his side.

"The flooding is under control, Captain. At least, we've slowed it considerably. And the engineer reports the fires below have been contained."

"Very good, Mister Hancey," Mackay said, not taking the binoculars from his face.

Hancey wiped the sweat from his face and breathed a deep sigh. He joined his captain in observing the enemy. "Surprised he's just sitting there, sir. Wonder what he's doing. Do you think he'll send another torpedo our way?"

"No way to tell, Mister Hancey. Let's just hope he prays to the same God we do."

At that moment, while they were both watching, the periscope dropped back into the sea and disappeared. For several minutes, both men watched and waited, but it did not appear again. No bubbling wakes materialized on the surface. Nor were there any other signs of a torpedo attack. The U-boat had simply gone deep, and— Mackay surmised—was departing the area.

"I can't believe it, Captain!" a dumbfounded Hancey exclaimed.

"Nor can I, Mister Hancey. But remember this moment the next time you find yourself damning poor Jerry to hell."

CHAPTER TWENTY-ONE

Lieutenant Odeman regained consciousness with his head throbbing and his ears ringing. He was stretched out on a cot with his sergeant hovering over him with a flask of brandy and a damp cloth, which he placed across Odeman's forehead to replace the bloody one that had been there before. It was the icy coolness of the cloth that brought him to his senses.

"Where am I?" he asked the sergeant groggily.

"Officers' quarters, sir. You have been out for several hours."

Odeman gasped. He could not remember how he had gotten there. The last thing he remembered was climbing down the conning tower ladder to *U-2553*'s main deck to arrest Rittenhaus. Then a sudden explosion had shattered his eardrums. One moment he was on the rungs of the ladder, the next he was in the water, unable to move, and sinking, sinking, down into the dark abyss. He remembered fighting for breath and his lungs near to bursting. It was almost like a dream now, but it all must have happened because he could feel that his clothes were soaking wet and the room stank of seawater.

Odeman's world slowly came together, piece by piece. The hum of the electric motors and the barely perceptible roll of the deck told him that *U-2553* was now submerged. He could hear the clink of a wrench in the next compartment. He could hear the footfalls of many sailors. Not the hasty shuffle of sailors running to their battle stations, just the sound of sailors that were busy. He immediately concluded that *U-2553* must have suffered some kind of damage and that the crew was in the process of making repairs.

"What happened?" he finally asked, sitting up slowly and rubbing his head where he could feel a large bandage had been affixed.

"We were attacked, sir," the sergeant answered. "First by an airship, and then by a British destroyer."

"Is the U-boat out of danger?"

"Oh, yes, sir," the sergeant said proudly. "Captain Traugott has sent them both to Valhalla."

Odeman rubbed his eyes and shook the cobwebs out of his head, trying to make sense of what had happened.

"What happened to me?"

"You were blown overboard by the first bomb, sir. We thought we had lost you, but you were saved. We all were saved. It is the amazing valor of our U-boat men, sir. I had no idea. But I am proud to report that they are as devoted to our Reich and our great *Führer* as any of our comrades in the army, sir. Everything the *Führer* has said about them is true. I can say that now with complete confidence, sir. Now that I have been fortunate enough to witness Captain Traugott send an enemy warship to the bottom as if it were something he did every day. No, sir, they are indeed worthy of the *Führer*'s praise, and ours." The sergeant paused for a moment and looked around the compartment as if to check that no one was listening. He gave Odeman a smile and a wink, then whispered, "You will never catch me saying a disparaging word about our sailors again, sir. I can guarantee you that."

"Never mind that," Odeman snapped. He did not care what personal conclusions this fool of a sergeant had come to. "Were the artifacts damaged at all?"

"I do not think so, sir."

"You do not think so? Surely, you have inspected them by now."

"Well, not yet, sir," the sergeant said hesitantly, "but I will, just as soon as I can go up there again."

"Go, then! You do not need to nursemaid me. You never should have left the torpedo room in the first place."

"But I was ordered to leave it, sir. We all were." The sergeant appeared to recognize that Odeman's temper was about to flare and offered an explanation. "Lieutenant Rittenhaus ordered us to vacate the room, sir, until he could ascertain the damage. We did take one hell of a depth bombing."

"You left Rittenhaus in the room alone?" Odeman shouted incredulously. "Alone, with the artifacts?"

"Just for a moment, sir. The torpedo room took a pounding, and I figured I did not want any of my boys in there unless it was certified as safe. Remarkable officer, that Lieutenant Rittenhaus, sir. After the first depth bombs went off, we had leaks all over the torpedo room. Half the sailors were new men, and of course we soldiers did not know what to do. Then Lieutenant Rittenhaus showed up. He took charge as naturally as any born officer. He got us organized. Told us all what to do. He even taught a few of our soldiers how to patch a pipe. Well, in no time, we had that flooding under control and the torpedo tubes ready to fire. The captain fired two torpedoes against that destroyer. Two hit, sir. I heard them hit, myself. I'm told that they were a new type of torpedo, one that follows the sound of its prey. Imagine that, sir. You never know what our scientists are going to come up with next."

"You are an idiot!" Odeman barked, unable to hear another word of this incompetent fool's story. He got up and began to grope for the door, still quite dizzy from his concussion.

"Please, sir, you must be careful." The sergeant offered a hand to Odeman, but it was batted away. "I know what you told me about him, sir," the sergeant continued, "but the captain seems to trust him. I know I was not supposed to leave the room, but I could not much disobey a direct order from the ship's first officer. Not with you out cold, sir, and not knowing when or if you would ever come to. You understand, sir, I am just a sergeant."

"Not anymore," Odeman said disgustedly, struggling to get his feet under him.

Slowly, he groped his way forward, from one compartment to the next, past sailors repairing damage, past his own men who stood at his approach and whom he beckoned to follow him with their weapons. He groped past the mess room, where off-watch sailors dined on some foul-smelling pork. When he finally arrived at the watertight door to the torpedo room, his head was ringing like the bells of Kölner Dom.

The door was shut and dogged.

"Open it!" Odeman ordered.

Two of his men instantly set about turning each dog to unlock it. At that moment, there was a noise on the other side of the door, and the final dog turned on its own. The soldiers stood back, and the door opened. Rittenhaus's smiling face appeared in the frame. He looked once at the armed soldiers and then at Odeman.

"What have we here, gentlemen?" Rittenhaus said cheerily. "Lieutenant Odeman, I am so pleased to see that you are well, comrade. But should you not be in bed with that injury?"

Odeman fumed. His hand instantly reached for the holster at his belt, but he was surprised to discover that it was empty. He saw Rittenhaus's eyes narrow almost imperceptibly.

"Pity, comrade. It seems you lost your Walther P38 when you were blown over the side."

"Arrest this man!" Odeman snapped at the two soldiers nearest him.

"Sir?" one of them responded quizzically.

"Arrest him! This minute!"

The soldiers appeared somewhat perplexed at the order, but eventually moved to take Rittenhaus by the arms.

"What is this?" Rittenhaus appeared suddenly confused. "Surely, this is no way to treat the man who saved your life, comrade."

"What are you saying?" It was Odeman's turn to be confused.

"It is true, sir," one of the soldiers said. "Lieutenant Rittenhaus jumped in after you and brought you back aboard. He saved your life, sir. It is true."

Odeman took a few moments to register what he had just heard. Why would this damn spy risk his own neck to save his? And if Rittenhaus was a spy, why would he not just let him float away? Probably to further validate his cover. It did not matter. At the very least, Rittenhaus was suspect, and that was all he needed to take him into custody.

"Hold him here while I inspect the cargo," Odeman ordered.

"Would you care to send a man to the captain, Lieutenant?" Rittenhaus said casually. "He will certainly clear this up."

"You will demand nothing, dog!" Odeman was so full of rage at Rittenhaus's smug demeanor, he felt like pushing his head through the nearest pipe stanchion. "You will be silent or I will have you beaten!"

"You will do no such thing!" a voice boomed behind Odeman.

Odeman turned to see Traugott standing with hands on hips, wearing a severe face to match his tone.

"Release the first lieutenant immediately, Herr Odeman!"

"But he is a spy, Captain! I told you of this, and now you have allowed him access to my cargo. How could you—"

"Release him!"

The soldiers did not wait for a nod from their officer but let go of Rittenhaus and stood to one side, unwilling to face the wrath of Traugott, a man they had come to respect.

Odeman was flabbergasted. "This is mutiny—"

"Shut your mouth, Lieutenant," Traugott interrupted. "You will issue no reprisals against these men for following my orders. Is that clear?"

Odeman's face turned red, but he managed a nod. He was outnumbered and had no weapon. What else could he do?

"You have suffered a terrible injury, and you need rest," Traugott continued. "I know what you told me before, but you were wrong. And so was I. Lieutenant Rittenhaus is a valuable member of this crew. He is an excellent officer and a loyal German. This entire crew owes him a debt of gratitude for his actions during our encounter with the enemy. And you, sir, owe him an apology."

"An apology?" Odeman could barely utter the words. Not only was he being drilled down in front of his men, he was being made to look like a fool. "Captain, that is ridiculous."

"Apologize, Odeman. Do that, and I'll explain away your recent behavior as fatigue-induced paranoia brought on by a traumatic injury. I think I can make that sound believable in my report."

Odeman did not know what to think. Had this idiot gone mad? Surely he could see the truth of it.

"I'm a bit confused as to what that was all about, Lieutenant," Rittenhaus chimed in, extending a hand, "but I can assure you an apology is not necessary. You have been through a lot in the last few hours—we all have. What do you say we start anew?"

Odeman did not take the hand, nor did he respond to the peace offering. Instead he turned to Traugott.

"Please be advised that I, too, write reports, Captain."

"Apologize," Traugott said simply, seemingly unfazed by the threat.

Odeman smiled politely, and then turned to face Rittenhaus whose hand was still extended.

"You have my apologies," Odeman mumbled, forcing himself to shake the hand that was offered.

"Lieutenant Odeman," Traugott said forcefully, "you are addressing a superior officer. I suggest you set a better example for the men around you."

Odeman fought back the instant urge to slap this insolent naval officer across the face. Odeman could see that the sailors in the room, even his own men, were holding back laughter at the spectacle.

Where was this U-boat bastard when I was freezing in Leningrad? he thought to himself. *Where was he when I was navigating the minefields of Eastern Europe?*

Odeman swore to himself that they would get their due. If he had to write to *Reichsführer* Himmler himself, he would see that Captain Traugott's career was over. He would teach this bastard what happens to those who defy the SS. But for now—now he would do what any good SS officer would do. He would back down. He would play along. Let them think he had moved on. Let them think he had given up. There was a long voyage ahead. Rittenhaus was sure to slip up again. He would wait for that moment, and when it came, he would strike without mercy.

Odeman came to attention, extended his arm in the Nazi salute, and spoke loudly enough for every man in the room to hear.

"Lieutenant Rittenhaus, sir. I regret my recent behavior and any disrespect I may have demonstrated toward your person or your office. Please accept my sincerest apologies, sir."

CHAPTER TWENTY-TWO

Northwestern Mediterranean
One week later

Traugott gobbled down the last scrap of roast on his plate, as did the other officers dining at the small booth-like table. All were finishing their dinners, including Rittenhaus, seated at his right.

"They don't grow beef this fat in Regensburg," one of the young sub-lieutenants joked.

"Not unless you include your sister," another said, bringing the table to a roar.

Traugott chuckled to himself as he observed the smiles on his officers' faces. They would laugh at anything tonight. They all had voracious appetites. They all were in cheerful moods, and their feelings were mere reflections of the enthusiasm that now pervaded the hearts and minds of the crew. They were like a great line of hemp that had been stretched taut under an enormous strain, stretched near to the point of breaking, and only now, with much of the danger past, had been allowed to sag.

The tension of the previous evening had been enough to break any man, but his crew had held together as he always knew they would. Last night, *U-2553* had infiltrated the Mediterranean. She had passed through the Strait of Gibraltar, the menace of every U-boat man and the stuff of nightmares. As always, the trip through the strait had been a harrowing night of sweaty, nerve-wracking silence, during which all systems, including the fans and refrigeration plant, were shut down, turning the U-boat into a perfect sauna for those inside. The tidal current flowing from the Atlantic into the Mediterranean had conveyed *U-2553* submerged through the narrow and treacherous waterway. Perhaps it had been the imminent danger of foundering on a shoal, or the fact that the strait was laced with minefields, or the idea that the channel was completely under the control of the Allies, or the idea that no fewer than five destroyers could be vectored onto the U-boat's location the instant she was discovered—whatever served as each man's tipping point, the passage through the strait was enough to make any man break down.

But *U-2553* had made it through, by the experience and luck of their captain and with help from the Almighty. Now it was time to breathe in the fresh, clean air being sucked into the boat by the chugging diesel engines.

"Where do we go now, Captain?" one of the sub-lieutenants ventured to say. "We all know that our destination is secret, but now that we are past Gibraltar, will we not know in a few days?"

Traugott smiled. Junior officers never changed. Always

bright-eyed and inquisitive. The old sailor in him found great comfort in that.

"Our destination, Otto, will have to wait, at least for a little while. Our unfortunate mishap with the milch cow happened before we could take on any fuel, and now our tanks are almost dry." He paused, looking around the table at the smirking faces, each one anticipating what he was about to say. "I have instructed the navigator to plot a course for Toulon."

The table erupted in a great cheer that hurt even Traugott's ears. The young officers laughed and grinned, toasting the navy, their captain, and each other, overcome with joy at their good fortune.

Traugott exchanged a humorous glance with Rittenhaus, who sat calmly, sipping his coffee, reviewing some reports. They were the veterans. They knew full well that a U-boat could be bombed pierside in Toulon just as easy as it could be bombed at sea.

"How long before we get there, First Lieutenant?" one of the young officers asked excitedly.

"Two days, at this speed," Rittenhaus answered casually. "But do not expect to bed every French whore within a mile of the waterfront. Liberty will be issued very sparingly."

Several winks went around the table among the young officers, who knew they would find a way, official or otherwise, to get ashore.

"May I join you, gentlemen?" a voice came from behind the curtain surrounding the table, and Lieutenant Odeman's head suddenly appeared from the other side. It was the first time in a week that he had chosen to

dine with the ship's officers, and he seemed uncharacteristically cheerful this evening.

"Please, Lieutenant. Have a seat."

Odeman wedged in between two of the lieutenants,
and the steward appeared to take his order.

"Oh, I see that I am late for dinner. I will not have the
rest of you watching me eat. Very well, then, a bowl of
flavored gelatin, some cheese, and a glass of lemon juice."

As the steward left the room, all conversation at the
table died, and a great cloud of silence descended on
the assemblage. The presence of the SS officer had a visible effect on the countenance of the junior officers, whose
smiles had faded to a collective melancholy stare. After
the steward returned, they all sat quietly, smoking and
sipping their drinks while Odeman slurped down spoon-
fuls of red gelatin. Odeman appeared to be in a delightful
mood, and Traugott thought perhaps he might make the
first effort to include the army outcast in the group.

"Did you find everything you needed, Lieutenant
Odeman?" Traugott asked.

"Mmm?" Odeman swallowed a large bite of gelatin.
"Yes, Captain. Yes, indeed I did. I must thank you for so
generously allowing me to peruse the officers' records.
I feel as though I know every one of them now."

Traugott nodded and smiled politely. Odeman had
made the odd request two days ago, apologizing for getting off on the wrong foot and promising to make an
effort to assimilate. He had said something about having
a phobia of social situations and that he might be more
inclined to mix with the other officers socially if he knew
something about them in advance. A starting point from

which he could initiate communications. He had suggested reviewing the officers' service records, and Traugott thought the request harmless enough.

"Sub-Lieutenant Baumann," Odeman said, looking at the junior officer down the table from him. "I was thrilled to discover you are from Hamburg. Do you know that I have an aunt there?"

"No, sir. I did not."

"I used to visit her as a boy. Oh, the holidays we spent together. She lived in the Altona district. I understand that is not too far from your home."

"No more than a kilometer, sir."

"Tell me, did you ever visit the Gunstig Bakery on Hegestrasse?"

"Indeed, sir. I know it well. They have the best cakes I have ever tasted."

"Indeed." Odeman smiled, suddenly as charming as a Frenchman. He turned his attention to another junior officer across the table from him. "And you, Herr Roller, you never told me you were from Leipzig. Did you know I studied there before the war?"

"Did you, sir? No, I didn't."

"What a pleasant town."

Traugott sat back in his chair studying this new side of Odeman, not knowing quite what to make of it. He was instinctively suspicious. The change was a bit too remarkable, even for Odeman. Traugott could not help but notice Odeman's eyes glancing several times in Rittenhaus's direction, as if to check the first lieutenant's response to some of the things he was saying. But if Rittenhaus had any opinion on Odeman's behavior, he did not show it. He appeared completely absorbed in the reports on the table before him.

"You seem to have not wasted your time with the officers' records," Traugott said, sensing the overall discomfort among the young officers that an SS man had been perusing their pasts.

"No, sir. Indeed I did not."

Traugott noted another glance at the oblivious Rittenhaus.

"I could not help but hear that we are heading for Toulon, Captain," Odeman said, while producing a cigarette and tapping it on the table.

"That is correct. But do not worry. It will be just a short stay. We will take on food and provisions and be on our way within forty-eight hours. We will get your cargo to its destination as scheduled."

"I do not doubt you in the least, Captain. In fact, I'm rather glad we are putting ashore. It will allow me to tie up some loose ends of my own. I have a few communiqués to send when we get there."

Another glance at Rittenhaus.

"And Lieutenant Rittenhaus." Odeman's tone seemed to change slightly. Still polite, just not as cordial. "I was most interested in your service record."

"I'm sorry." Rittenhaus looked up from the papers as if he had not heard any of the preceding conversation. "What was that?"

"I said I found your service record most interesting." Odeman's voice was losing its charm by the syllable. "For instance, I did not realize that you were such a distinguished combat veteran."

"Veteran, or survivor, call it what you like," Ritten-haus said, turning back to his papers, apparently uninterested in what Odeman had to say.

"I am truly sorry about the crewmen you lost on *U-534*. Such a tragedy."

Rittenhaus looked up. "It was *U-634*. And, yes, it was a tragedy."

"Of course, you would correct me on the number," Odeman said wearily. "And, I suspect, if I were to ask you the names of the officers you served with on *U-634*, you would rattle them off without hesitation. Am I right?"

"I am not sure what you are getting at."

"Just that we are at a stalemate. If I ask you anything about your record, I am certain you will have a well-prepared answer and that you will be ready to engage me on any point I pursue, no matter how tangential."

Traugott sighed heavily. "Have we not been through this before, Odeman? Lieutenant Rittenhaus is not a spy. Let it rest."

"I am simply getting to know Lieutenant Rittenhaus, Captain. He sits over there secure in the knowledge that I know no more of his past than that contained in his service record." Odeman then leaned over the table in an exaggerated manner and held a hand to his face as if to whisper something to Traugott, but when he spoke it was loud enough for everyone to hear. "But Herr Rittenhaus does not know something about me, Captain. He does not know that I come from a family of mountain climbers."

Odeman then sat back in his chair, rubbing his hands

together, downing what remained of his lemon juice. Everyone at the table seemed confounded at the SS officer's inexplicable behavior, although over the past weeks they had somewhat come to expect it from him. Odeman beamed, apparently very pleased with himself, even chuckling as he proceeded to slice up his block of cheese with a twelve-inch field knife that he seemed to produce out of nowhere.

"Did I ever tell you, Sub-Lieutenant Roller," Odeman said casually, as he fed himself slices of the yellow cheese, "that I was at Stalingrad?"

"I do not believe so, sir," Roller said uncertainly.

"I was assigned to the Twenty-fourth Panzer Division, Tenth Panzer Regiment. Did you ever hear of it?"

Roller shook his head, glancing at some of the other officers, who seemed perfectly content that he was the one garnering Odeman's attention.

"Mmm. Well, you should have. The Bolsheviks certainly did. We won the Iron Cross for driving the Reds out of Kharkov. And it was well deserved, Sub-Lieutenant. Do you know why? Because the Reds fight dirty, that's why. You never know whether you are looking at a meager peasant or a lying, bloodsucking Bolshevik. Early on they made a habit of grabbing our sentries at night. The next day we would find them strung up at some intersection, mutilated." Odeman chomped on another piece of cheese. "So how do you fight such an opponent, Sub-Lieutenant? How do you fight an enemy that knows no honor, an enemy that lurks in the shadows? Do you know?"

Roller glanced around the table for some help but,

seeing none forthcoming from his compatriots, shrugged his shoulders.

"You become as evil as they are, Sub-Lieutenant. It is the only way."

"If you say so, sir," Roller said before hiding his face in a cup of coffee.

Odeman grinned widely. "I would never expect a young naval officer to understand. You will never have to deal with your enemy face-to-face, as I had to, Lieutenant. I was surrounded by dirty, stinking Bolsheviks all day long. When you live among your enemies, you must be creative. We learned to be creative very quickly." Odeman paused to study the gleaming blade in his hand. "We had this certain soldier in our regiment who came to be known as the Eunuch-Maker. I'll leave it to your imagination what he did to the insurgents we caught."

Traugott observed several of the young officers adjust in their chairs.

"He had a way of striking fear into the hearts of the enemy," Odeman continued, "in a way an army division or a fleet of bombers could not. Once word got out about our comrade, the attacks diminished by the week. Eventually, they were insignificant."

"Did the colonel of your regiment approve of this butcher's work?" Traugott asked, unimpressed with Odeman's attempt to intimidate the others.

"Indeed he did, Captain. In fact, he promoted him. And now"—Odeman raised one hand—"the Eunuch-Maker sits before you as Lieutenant Odeman."

An audible gasp emanated from the other officers,

and Traugott noticed those closest to the SS lieutenant inch ever so slightly away from him.

"Oh, do not be afraid, gentlemen. I would never use my knife on a good German. And you are all good Germans." Odeman's face then lost all of its humor and steadied on Rittenhaus, across the table. "Or, shall I say, most of you."

Rittenhaus returned the gaze for a few seconds and then made to get up, gathering his papers.

"If you will excuse me, Captain," he said to Traugott. "I find that this conversation has sunk to the level of conscripted soldiers. I must prepare for watch."

"You have not yet asked me why it is so significant that I come from a family of climbers, Herr Rittenhaus!" Odeman interjected before Rittenhaus could leave.

"I was not planning to, Herr Odeman."

"Sit down, First Lieutenant!" Odeman said in a commanding tone. His face registered his error, and he instantly continued in something more of a forced polite nature. "Please sit down and tell me about your hometown. Tell me about Sonnberg. By my watch you have at least ten minutes before you must prepare for your shift. Certainly you have enough time to chat with this old homesick German about the Fatherland."

The table remained silent. Traugott could see that the other officers were just as disgusted at Odeman's behavior as he was, but he chose to say nothing. As much as he thought Odeman was being an overbearing ass, it was time for Rittenhaus to stand up for himself. Odeman was like a schoolyard bully who sensed weakness and went after it with a bloodthirsty vigor. Such a bully would stop only if one of his victims put him in his place. He fully expected a sharp retort from Rittenhaus. After all, Rittenhaus was senior to Odeman on the officer ladder. That was why Traugott was surprised when Rittenhaus glanced at his own watch and then returned to his seat as Odeman had requested. The first lieutenant's face broke into a friendly grin.

"I would be happy to talk about home. What would you like to know, Herr Odeman?"

"Oh!" Odeman said rubbing his hands together in exaggerated excitement. "Tell us all about it."

"It is cold in the winter and hot in the summer."

"Well, how convenient."

"Yes, quite so," Rittenhaus replied, maintaining the casual smile.

"But surely you have more to tell, or are your superiors even more incompetent than I suspected?"

"My superiors?"

"Precisely, Herr Rittenhaus." Odeman dabbed his chin with a napkin and then leaned forward with both arms on the table. "Let me tell you what I know of Tamberlau. It is such an isolated village, is it not? Nestled up in the foothills of the Austrian Alps, where the folk seldom come down to mingle with city folk. I must admit, it is a perfect explanation for that odd accent of yours. And I am sure you probably never come across someone you know from home, if ever. I would venture to say that you are the only U-boat man from the village, am I correct?"

Rittenhaus smiled and nodded. "Most of our young men became mountain troops. There is not much interest in the sea there."

"Let me ask you something, Herr Rittenhaus." Odeman was fidgeting, almost as if he could not wait to get to the point at which he was driving. "Are you much of a climber, yourself?"

"Not really. I chose the sea, remember?"

"Ah, yes, but surely you dabbled in climbing as a boy. How could you not, growing up there?"

Rittenhaus nodded as he sipped from his coffee cup.

"There is a mountain near there," Odeman continued, "a peak, more precisely, called Hoher Dachstein. Do you know of it?"

"Of course. It is five kilometers from my house."

"It is just a small thing, you must admit. Two thousand, nine hundred ninety meters. No real challenge for any experienced climber, would you not agree?"

"Three thousand twenty meters."

"I'm sorry, what did you say?" Odeman held a hand to one ear.

Rittenhaus paused, and Traugott saw the grin fade from his first lieutenant's face.

"Hoher Dachstein is three thousand twenty meters," Rittenhaus replied looking right into Odeman's eyes. "You said two thousand, nine hundred ninety."

Odeman's smile faded too, being replaced by the stone face of the SS officer. He said coldly, "You are not Lieutenant Rittenhaus."

"Come now, Odeman, that really is absurd!" Rittenhaus exclaimed.

"Not again, Odeman," Traugott interjected.

"If you were indeed from Tamberlau, you would know that the Hoher Dachstein is now two thousand, nine hundred ninety meters and not three thousand twenty meters."

"I am quite certain that it is three thousand twenty meters," Rittenhaus said. "But, of course, it is a silly thing to argue over. Surely, you are not suggesting I am a spy simply because we have a different memory of the peak's height."

"You are a spy," Odeman snarled. "There is no question."

"Come now, Odeman." Traugott decided this had gone too far. "Are you truly questioning a man's identity based on his not knowing the height of a mountain?"

"Captain, this man cannot be Rittenhaus. I can prove this."

"How?"

"Because this particular mountain used to be three thousand twenty meters, as this impostor says, but two years ago, an earthquake reduced its height by thirty meters."

Traugott could hardly believe the extreme lengths to which this Nazi would go. It really was quite disturbing.

Odeman spoke again before Traugott could get in a word. "It is not an issue for you to remember, Captain, or for the rest of Germany. But I can assure you, when I was there on leave with my brother last year, the great earthquake of '42 was all anyone could talk about. The war and bombing be damned, the locals wanted to talk about nothing but the earthquake that had sunk their great peak by thirty meters. No matter which pub we entered, no matter who we encountered, this was the talk of the village. Now it is unthinkable that this man"—he gestured at Rittenhaus—"who was supposedly convalescing there not six weeks ago, would not know of such an event. It is unthinkable, unbelievable, and quite impossible, unless—unless he was never there."

Rittenhaus was smiling broadly now, and it seemed to incense Odeman even more.

"Just observe, gentlemen, his casual demeanor, even now as I accuse him. Observe how he runs through the textbook procedures of an agent whose cover has been blown."

Rittenhaus kept smiling but took an extra moment to down the remaining coffee in his cup. "Of course, the earthquake. I had forgotten." Then glancing at his watch he gathered his papers up again. "I would like to say, Lieutenant Odeman, that it was a pleasure talking about the old country, but I cannot." Rittenhaus then leaned over the table toward Odeman's scowling face and whispered loud enough for all to hear. "I do believe, sir, that you should get that contusion on your head examined the moment we touch at Toulon. Delusional fantasies are signs of several very serious conditions."

"I did not say you could leave, spy!" Odeman spat.

"Paranoia is also a sign," Rittenhaus added, pushing in his chair. "If you will excuse me, gentlemen. I must prepare for watch."

Rittenhaus then ducked out of the curtain and was gone.

CHAPTER TWENTY-THREE

"But, Captain, I have proven that our earlier suspicions were correct. He is not Herr Rittenhaus!" Odeman could see by the look on Traugott's face that he was getting nowhere.

The room was empty now. Traugott had insisted that the rest of the officers go about their duties before he gave Odeman the attention he craved. Odeman expected to have gained a convert, but when he and Traugott were finally alone, he was surprised to discover that Traugott intended to issue him a reprimand.

"I do not want to hear that kind of talk again, Lieutenant." Traugott stared him down. "I do not care whether my first lieutenant remembers the geological occurrences near his hometown. It does not matter!"

"Yes, it does, Captain." Odeman paused and looked at him. "Because there was no earthquake."

Traugott looked at him in disbelief.

"I convinced Herr Rittenhaus that such an earthquake occurred and he went along with me to protect his cover, and in so doing exposed himself. There is no question now. He is not who he says he is."

Traugott sighed, closed his eyes, and began to rub his temples. "I really have no more time for your little games, Lieutenant. This stops right here, right now. This subject is closed. It will not be broached again, do you hear? Or you will be placed under arrest."

Odeman bit his lip, fuming at Traugott's stupidity. "Yes, Captain," he managed to say under his breath.

"I have enough to worry about keeping the Allied navies off our scent and holding together a crew that has taken quite a beating. Right now I need my men focused on their tasks, not second-guessing their first officer. When we reach Toulon, you can send all the communiqués you like, but until that time, you will not so much as make eye contact with Lieutenant Rittenhaus. Understood?"

"Yes, Captain." Odeman did not know what else to say.

Traugott then left the room in a huff, leaving Odeman to fume by himself.

What did these navy fools know of the shadowy world of spies? They were simpletons and idiots, he thought. They could not see an enemy agent, even after he was exposed to them as plain as day. Odeman wondered if he was the only one who had his wits about him, the only sane man on this ship of fools.

One thing was for certain, he was the only man aboard who had an inkling as to the worth of their cargo. Or at least he was the only German aboard who knew. That bastard passing as Rittenhaus knew, too. Otherwise why would he be here? Why would he be fighting tooth and nail to get a few moments alone with the artifacts? Yes, he was most definitely a spy, no matter what these naval bumpkins thought.

Something had to be done. This went beyond command hierarchy, beyond the service. This was a moment when only a true patriot could do what had to be done. Rittenhaus was a spy. The spy was a threat, even more so now that he knew Odeman was on to him. Who knew whom the spy would contact if he was allowed to go on liberty in Toulon. And of course he would be allowed. First officer's privileges. It was all working out so nicely for the posing bastard. He even had the fool of a captain eating out of his hand. Who was he? Who was he working for? Odeman thought for a moment and concluded that Rittenhaus had to be British, because only a Brit could pull off such a deception with such poise. There was a chance that Rittenhaus might be working for the exiled French or Norwegians. The Americans he ruled out entirely. They were nothing more than a bunch of shortsighted cowboys, good for shooting up a beach with twice the artillery that was needed, but mere amateurs in the world of espionage.

Odeman looked at his watch. Rittenhaus would be finishing up his prewatch tour of the ship. It was a tour that always started forward in the torpedo room and ended all the way aft in the manual steering room. The last compartments Rittenhaus would tour would be the engine room and the motor room, where only one or two sailors would be on watch, and where the blaring diesel engines would mask any cries for help.

Odeman thumbed the pommel of the sheathed knife at his belt. Should he go forward first and get one of his men's MP 40 submachine guns before confronting the bastard? No. There was not enough time. Besides, he did not want to draw attention to himself as he traversed the length of the ship. His knife would have to suffice, and that suited Odeman perfectly.

With his mind made up, Odeman walked down the central passageway heading toward the stern of the ship. He moved quickly but not frantically, so as not to draw attention. He even stood aside for two sailors hauling a disconnected valve fitting in the other direction. He kept moving in order to catch Rittenhaus while the bastard was alone in the engine rooms. He walked past the control room, where half of the officers he had just dined with now reviewed charts and reports. Traugott was there, too, in one corner of the room, and shot him an impatient glance. Odeman ducked through the door and passed through three more compartments, each with successively fewer sailors. The noise of the diesels grew louder as he moved aft. He finally came to the watertight door to the engine room and opened it. He was greeted by the roar of the diesels, a roar that was several decibels higher than it had been when he was on the other side of the thick steel door.

At first glance, the compartment appeared to be empty. The narrow catwalk that traversed the compartment ran aft between the two rumbling engines, and then straight back to the watertight door at the back of the room. This door led to the next compartment aft—the motor room. Odeman had made it halfway down the catwalk when he noticed a sailor crawling out of a small hatchway in the catwalk grating. Odeman had been on board long enough to know that the enginemen often had to go down below to check the sumps and bilges.

"Oh, hello, sir," the grease-covered sailor said wearily. "Anything I can help you with?"

"Has the first lieutenant passed this way?"

The sailor yawned and nodded. "About five minutes ago, sir. He went aft. Should be in the motor room now."

Odeman nodded. Perfect. It was perfect, not only because Rittenhaus was in the compartment aft, but also because the engine room watchstander was in this room. That meant the next room should be empty, except for the impostor Rittenhaus.

Odeman had to admit, the man was clever. The impostor had some knowledge of U-boats, that much was obvious. Perhaps he was skilled at other things, too. The thought prompted Odeman to unstrap the knife at his belt, but he did not draw it. He did not want his prey to suspect anything. He needed to get in close before he struck.

Odeman opened the door to the next compartment, stepped in, and shut the door behind him. The room was markedly quieter than the last, because this room housed the quiet electrical motors that propelled the ship. These were laid out in a similar fashion to the engine room, with a long catwalk running aft between the two boxlike motor housings. The room appeared deserted, and Odeman suddenly felt that same feeling he had sensed so many times while patrolling the wrecked alleys of Stalingrad, where every pile of rubble had presented a possible hideout for snipers. It was the feeling that he was being watched, that he, the hunter, was now the prey. It made him draw his knife and hold it at the ready.

Then he heard something. It sounded like a scratching noise at first, but then he realized that someone was turning a wrench. The sound was coming from beneath him, from the bilges. Odeman looked past the port side motor and saw that the hatchway leading down into the bilge was open. Someone was down there.

"Hello!" Rittenhaus's voice called from below. "I heard someone come in. Is that you, Schmidt?"

Odeman said nothing. He began to move quietly toward the open hatchway.

"Schmidt, bring me a torque wrench," Rittenhaus called again. "One of your mechanics did not put this valve back together properly. Schmidt?"

Odeman descended the ladder and peered into the dank, dark space. The place smelled of oil and seawater and was only high enough for a man to walk hunched over. One step off the ladder and Odeman inadvertently plunged his foot into ten inches of murky water that had collected in the bilge.

"Schmidt? Is that you?"

Rittenhaus's voice was coming from behind the port side gearbox, a large rectangular fixture that completely hid him from view. Odeman now crept toward it. He turned the corner of the gearbox and found Rittenhaus with his back to him, on hands and knees, and only a few feet away. The unsuspecting first lieutenant was hunched over a valve of some kind and appeared to be absorbed in fixing whatever the enginemen had fouled up. Odeman smiled at his own good fortune. He knew that he would never be given such an opportunity again, and he began to inch closer to the unwary impostor. He rotated the knife in his hand until it was upside down, the killing position, the way he had learned to kill Bolsheviks. One thrust in the side of the neck, and then one quick twist would do it. It would all be over. But there was something just too clean and quick about that. After all, this arrogant bastard had embarrassed him in front of his men and in front of the other officers. He had hurt his pride, and now Odeman wanted the son of a bitch to see who was going to kill him. Odeman wanted to see the fear in the bastard's eyes. He deserved that, and he would have it.

"Schmidt? Did you bring the wrench?" Rittenhaus said, in a normal voice now, evidently aware that someone was behind him, and expecting it to be the engineman.

"It is I, comrade," Odeman said evenly, when he was only an arm's length away.

Rittenhaus bolted upright as Odeman had expected, and Odeman lunged with the knife to meet him. But then Rittenhaus did something unexpected. He rolled left with lightning speed, the speed of someone trained in hand-to-hand fighting. It was almost as if he had anticipated the knife thrust all along. Odeman's blade made contact with a protruding pipe before he could stop the thrust, and a quick kick to the legs by Rittenhaus sent him off balance, but only for a brief moment. He, too, had been trained in hand-to-hand fighting and was ready to attack again before Rittenhaus could follow up on the move. Rittenhaus managed to dodge another slash and then backed away, moving farther aft.

The bastard was quick, Odeman had to admit. Very quick. But his agility would do him little good now, for he had moved as far back as he could and was now blocked from escape by a large pump housing. Certainly Rittenhaus could get over it, but that would require climbing. If he tried that, Odeman would easily stab him several times in the back before he got over.

Odeman had cornered his prey. There was no escape, and he could see in the spy's eyes that he had come to the same conclusion. Odeman could not help but grin evilly at the look of despair on the spy's face. It was the look of fear he had hoped for, and now he could make his kill fully satisfied that Rittenhaus would go to hell knowing that he had been bested.

Then he noticed Rittenhaus's hand disappear beneath his shirt. It fumbled for a moment, and then appeared again, this time holding a Walther P38—*his Walther P38*—and it was aimed right at him.

Odeman's jaw dropped open. A chill ran through him, partly from sudden confusion and partly from the prospect of being killed by his own weapon. The bastard must have stolen it during the bomb attack and later claimed it had been lost overboard.

"I am truly sorry, comrade," Rittenhaus spoke the words emotionlessly.

The next moment the gun went off, and a single nine-millimeter bullet entered Odeman's open mouth and blew out the back of his head.

CHAPTER TWENTY-FOUR

London, England

Admiral McDonough was not a moral man by any sense of the word. He believed in the United States of America because he believed in freedom. Not necessarily equality, but freedom. Everyone ought to be able to do what he wanted without some meddling government snooping into his affairs. Perhaps that was what had attracted him to the OSS—getting to do what he wanted without anyone telling him what to do, a hard thing to pull off in the Navy, though McDonough had managed it for nearly twenty years. In McDonough's position as a naval admiral serving in the OSS, if there was any government snooping to be done, chances were he would get to do it.

But that was not the case this evening as McDonough sat on the bed in his London flat, his latest mistress snoozing beside him. He could hear the increase of activity on the street outside, far more vehicle traffic than this sleepy neighborhood was accustomed to, especially at this time of night. They were military vehicles—jeeps and trucks, by the sound of them—and there were lots of them. The window was open so they were quite loud. McDonough did not bother to go to the window but simply cast a glance at the bug device he had discovered behind the credenza more than a week ago. He had discovered the miniature microphone while sweeping his apartment for such devices, a practice those in his line of work generally made a habit of, if they didn't want to get themselves or a whole lot of other people killed.

Brakes squealed on the street outside. The vehicles were stopping in front of the apartment building.

"God, what's all that noise, Mac?" the woman in his bed asked groggily. She was young, at least by his standards.

"Nothing, love," McDonough said, patting her soft hair with his old weathered hand. "Go back to sleep. I'll call someone about it."

Boots tramped in double time on the sidewalk below, approaching the main door to the building. A heavy-handed fist banged on the door, accompanied by the bellow of a sergeant.

"Military police! Open up! Open the door, now!"

McDonough had had a feeling it would be tonight. A few indicators earlier in the day had told him that things were moving, that his opponent in this grand game of chess had decided to move his queen. Being a spy was a game of chess. A game of waiting and gathering, of sending pawns to feel out the enemy, of holding back all impulses to attack until just the right moment. When you were finally ready, you struck in one quick and devastating blow that, if you were lucky, altered the outcome of the war and the course of history.

"I will break down this door if it does not open in thirty seconds!" the sergeant outside shouted, loud enough to wake Edward III in his grave.

McDonough could hear several of the other of the building's tenants in the hallway outside, roused from their beds and probably wondering what the hell was going on. Most of them were senior military officers like him, and rightfully they were confused as to why several dozen MPs were banging down their door in the dead of night, but McDonough knew exactly whom the MPs had come for. He rose and walked to the desk where the phone was.

"Really, Mac, what's the bloody ruckus down there?" the young woman said, now sitting up in bed and finding a discarded nightie to drape across her exposed breasts.

"Admiral McDonough!" the sergeant's voice rang out, announcing that the MPs had made it into the building. Boots tramped on the stairs down the hall. McDonough could hear them getting closer.

"We're looking for Admiral McDonough, sir." The sergeant's voice was much closer now. "Please step aside, General. Thank you, sir."

Obviously some general officer had been brushed aside by the MP sergeant. McDonough smirked. He would have liked to have seen that.

"Oh my God, I think they're coming for you, Mac!" the woman said in horror. She looked terrified. McDonough knew that it was not so much from the fact that her lover was about to be arrested as that she was about to be discovered fully nude in the bed of a man who was not her English colonel husband, now deployed in North Africa.

"Easy, love," McDonough said with a reassuring grin. "I'm calling about it right now." He picked up the phone and dialed the number he had committed to memory.

"Who ya calling?"

McDonough did not answer. His face went blank as he waited for the distant end to pick up, all the while contemplating the machine he was about to set in motion with this one phone call. There was still a huge risk involved. Even now, he did not have to go through with it. The easy thing would be to hang up and simply let the MPs arrest him.

A fist banged on the door to his flat. "Admiral McDonough! Open up! Military police!" a voice yelled from the other side.

"They're coming in here!" the woman shrieked, and bolted out of bed, her pale bottom jiggling as she ran inside the water closet and shut the door.

McDonough paid her no attention but waited as the line rang again and again with no answer. What was taking so long?

A rifle butt now struck the door. Then another. The MPs were going to break the door down. He had only seconds.

"Come on," McDonough whispered impatiently as he listened to the line ring over and over. "Come on, damn it!"

Finally the line answered and a male voice said the expected words. "What did you think of the play, sir?"

McDonough answered, "Methinks the lady doth protest too much."

"Good-bye," said the voice on the other end, and then the line went dead instantly.

McDonough hung up the phone just as the door to his room burst open.

CHAPTER TWENTY-FIVE

Toulon, France

The young German army corporal, envelope in hand, walked briskly along the pier, struggling to keep his cap on in the stiff salty breeze. He was looking for someone in the bustle of activity that surrounded a sleek-looking U-boat that had just pulled in not an hour ago. A stream of flags, whipping and snapping in the wind, marked the spot where *U-2553* had moored. She was a brand-new class of U-boat, and though she appeared to have been severely handled on her last cruise, judging by the state of her hull, the corporal felt confident that she and several other new weapons like her would one day bring victory for the Reich. Repair crews were already rushing aboard her, and a long line of sailors were offloading several trucks full of stores. The U-boat men were an unshaven, haggard-looking lot, but the corporal could not imagine what kind of man it took to sail for weeks at a time, cooped up inside one of those small vessels.

The corporal noticed that each man, no matter how busy, kept a wary eye skyward, and he had been in Toulon long enough to know why. It would not be the first time that Allied bombers had appeared out of nowhere, ruining what might have otherwise been a beautiful, sunny day. Evidence of previous such attacks was visible all around. A smashed jetty here. The burned-out shell of a building there. Twisted heaps of scrap metal and rubble pushed into neat piles by the dockyard bulldozers. But perhaps the danger was most exhibited by the dozen or so antiaircraft gun emplacements scattered along the jetty and the dockyard. It was near one of these that the corporal finally found the man he was looking for. After a few inquiries, some lounging sailors had pointed the man out to him—a tall man with a scar on his face, leaning against a wall of sandbags, wearing a weathered blue naval officer's uniform with blue peaked cap, and smoking a cigarette.

"Herr Lieutenant Rittenhaus?"

Hart turned to see an army corporal approaching him. The soft-faced young man was immaculately dressed in a blue-gray uniform, with spit-shined boots. His perfectly manicured hands spoke of more time spent in clerical work than in the foxhole.

The corporal saluted him. Hart returned the salute.

"Lieutenant Rittenhaus?" The corporal smiled brightly.

"I am Lieutenant Rittenhaus," Hart replied carefully. He had never seen the young man before and was suddenly anxious that this might be someone from the real Rittenhaus's past.

"I am Corporal Bergmann, sir. May I be the first to welcome you to Toulon." He then thrust out the hand with the envelope. "I have a message for you, sir."

Hart took the envelope and glanced around in a nonchalant manner, checking to see if anyone had accompanied the corporal. "Who is this from?"

"It is from my commanding officer, sir," the young man said politely. "He instructed me to find you here and deliver it. I believe that you and he are old friends, sir."

"Who is your commanding officer?"

"I do not want to ruin the surprise, sir." The corporal grinned deceitfully, but innocently. "You must read his letter."

"I see," Hart said, not knowing what to make of it.

"Will that be all that you require, sir?"

"Yes, Corporal. Thank you."

"*Heil* Hitler," the young man said succinctly, clicking his heels together and issuing the Nazi salute.

This brought several jeers from the nearby sailors. The corporal appeared somewhat rankled but must have understood there was nothing he could do about the disrespectful sailors, and, seeing no assistance forthcoming from Hart, he turned on his heel and marched away.

"A real dandy, that one, sir," one of the sailors called.

Hart smiled and waved them away, his mind still trying to get a grasp on how he was going to deal with the letter in his hand. *U-2553* would be in port for at least two days. If he did not respond, this corporal's commanding officer might come down to the pier himself, looking for his old friend Rittenhaus, and then the jig would be up. Hart tried to appear unfazed as he collected his thoughts. He put one foot on the jetty stanchion, lit another cigarette, and tossed the match into the water below where it lapped onto the hull of *U-2553*.

Hart looked down at the battered U-boat that had carried him from the frigid waters of Norway to this warm Mediterranean port. She looked like an old trooper riding on the gentle swell, brandishing the many dents and scars she had received from her encounter with the Allied destroyer and airship. Although she was an enemy ship, Hart could not help but feel bonded to her after living for nearly three weeks inside her confined hull. It seemed like so much longer than that. It seemed like ages since that night over Norway, when he had leaped from the burning B-17 and watched helplessly as the German night fighter machine-gunned the parachutes of the other men who had jumped out with him. One by one, he saw them fall, even heard their screams as they plummeted to their deaths, trailing the remains of their stark white parachutes behind them, perfect targets against the night sky. But, of course, that was according to plan, as much as Hart hated to admit to the truth of it. Every contingency had been thought of before embarking on the mission. As a result, Hart had been given a camouflaged parachute made to blend in with the night sky when viewed from below, and with the forested hills when viewed from above. Upon seeing the white parachutes of the B-17 crew, the German fighter pilot did not look for any others. The sacrifice of the airmen had saved Hart's life and led the Germans to believe there were no survivors. Hart surmised that was the only explanation for the sparse patrols he encountered in the countryside afterward.

It was not without some difficulty, but he had managed to make his way north and eventually linked up with the Norwegian resistance on the second day. Initially, he had been somewhat skeptical about putting his faith in the resistance. The ambush in the sky had been the result of a betrayal, either by someone in England or by someone in Norway, and from his position in the Scandinavian mountains with no means of communication there was no way for Hart to determine which. But Hart no longer questioned the loyalty of the resistance fighters after they showed him the body of the real Lieutenant Rittenhaus, whom they had captured in transit days before. In fact, Hart came to question his own loyalty. The poor German officer, who was probably no more than a patriot doing his duty, had been brutalized beyond belief, in a fashion Hart would have more ascribed to the Waffen-SS than to the partisans of gentle Norway. War brought out the devil in the best of men. War, fear, or hatred, it was all the same once an occupied populace got involved. Trained soldiers by and large fought out of loyalty to their unit. Partisans, on the other hand, fought for all kinds of reasons, none rational and most self-destructive.

Ding-ding . . . ding-ding.

The bell rang out on *U-2553*. A hush descended on the jetty as a litter bearing a body draped in a white sheet crossed the gangway from the U-boat to the pier. Every sailor and soldier stood in respectful silence, with hats off, as the litter passed them by. Hart did the same. After the body had finally been conveyed away in an ambulance, the work activity on the pier returned to its former state.

Hart gazed out at the harbor, recalling the events of

the past twenty-four hours. Odeman's death had been ruled a suicide by Traugott. Traugott confided to his first officer—to Hart—that he thought Odeman had been going insane in the days leading up to his death, ever since the concussion he had suffered during the bomb attack. Traugott surmised that Odeman had some kind of brain swelling that had gone undiagnosed by the ship's medic. How else could one explain a point-blank gunshot through the mouth with Odeman's own pistol, the same one the SS officer had claimed to have lost overboard. It was even more confirmation of his madness. Traugott had found little argument from Odeman's recently demoted sergeant, who dutifully took care of his dead officer's personal effects but appeared to show little remorse over the man's death.

Hart patted the folded paper inside his uniform shirt pocket. It contained the information he had copied from the artifacts during his so-called safety inspection of the torpedo room. In spite of Odeman's obsession over the cargo, it had seemed like a collection of useless items. As instructed by McDonough prior to the mission, Hart had gone in looking for ancient artifacts, and was surprised when the only items that appeared to be ancient in origin were a few shards of broken metal, bearing markings that looked like Egyptian hieratic. Everything else—a goblet and ornate breastplate, a dagger and a sword, a few empty but exquisite boxes, all rusted beyond recognition—appeared medieval in origin. Hart had copied down every symbol and letter that could be made out, recalling the crash course on relics he had been given before departing on the mission. He then made a list of each item found in each box and carefully returned each one to its proper shipping container.

Hart remembered how unimpressed he had been upon finishing his examination of the relics. He could not imagine their significance, if they had any. Odeman seemed to think they did—enough to try to kill him. Hart had not wanted to kill Odeman, but the Nazi bastard had left him no choice. He only hoped the information he had managed to obtain was worth it.

A gust of wind came close to sucking away the envelope in Hart's hand. It brought him back to reality and his current dilemma: How should he respond to this letter from Rittenhaus's friend? Hart turned the envelope over in his hands a few times and then opened it, removing the letter inside. The letter was handwritten in a very careful style on standard stationery. But it wasn't the handwriting or the stationery that made Hart's jaw drop open.

> *Dear Lieutenant Rittenhaus, my old friend,*
> *Someone told me that your U-boat put in this morning. I would very much like to meet with you if you can spare a few moments ashore with your old schoolmate. Meet me at Le Neptunia, on Avenue République, this evening at 7 P.M. sharp.*
>
> *Your affectionate friend.*
> *Major Heinz Mueller*

Hart was shocked by the letter. Not so much for its message, but for its signatory. Major Heinz Mueller was one of the cover names often used by Ives.

Was Ives here? Could he possibly be here? Perhaps it was a Gestapo trap. Odeman's superiors would certainly respond with an investigation once they found out about his death, but Hart had fully expected to be underway with *U-2553* before the investigation had a chance to get started.

Hart had not even wanted to come ashore to begin with. He had wanted to stay aboard, assist in the repairs, and get *U-2553* back to sea again before anyone could ask any questions about Odeman's death. But his duties as first officer came first, and Traugott had ordered him to try to find some quality vegetables and fruits from one of the local markets, knowing it would be better than anything the navy would supply. Something to boost the crew's morale.

Hart folded the letter neatly, then placed it in his trousers pocket. What choice did he have? If the invitation was a trap, then he was exposed and the Gestapo or SS could easily just come down to the naval yard to apprehend him later. He had to go.

He looked at his watch and then at his uniform and decided he would at least change clothes before going to the pub this evening. If he was going to walk right into a trap, then he was going to do it looking like the proper German naval lieutenant he was impersonating.

CHAPTER TWENTY-SIX

Hart had no trouble finding the pub, Le Neptunia. It was right on the corner of two major streets, and every uniformed German within several miles seemed to be flocking there at about the same time he was. He could not help but wonder why Ives had chosen such a place for a meeting, since nearly every table, both inside and out of the German-friendly establishment, was occupied with gray- or black-clad officers of the *Wehrmacht*. Normally, Hart would not have given a second thought to approaching so many Germans. After all, the first rule in being an undercover agent was to always exude confidence. Unfortunately, the second rule was to remain anonymous, and that would be difficult in such a place—especially since the establishment was obviously an army hangout and he was the only naval uniform in the place. He stuck out like a sore thumb. For all he knew, these rip-roaring drunk men were all from the same regiment.

The place was crowded to the point of standing-room only, with a great cloud of cigar and cigarette smoke hanging in the air. It was so crowded that it took Hart several minutes just to get from one side of the pub to the other. As he moved through the crowd, scanning the room for Ives, he put on his best face and ignored the endless stream of slurs and gestures administered in his direction.

"Look, it's one of those cocksucking U-boat sailors!" one red-faced drunk jeered. "Hey, faggot, do you give it or take it in the ass?"

The veiny-faced drunk and his cohorts burst into laughter, clinking their glasses together and groping the French prostitutes who were wedged between them. Hart ignored the insults as any self-respecting U-boat officer would and continued searching the room.

As his eyes scanned the smoky space, he noticed one German officer in particular on the opposite side of the room, leaning against a post and staring at him. Hart looked away for a few seconds and then back again only to find that the officer was still staring at him. The man wore the uniform of an army captain; had a close-shaved head, almost bald; and appeared to be slightly older than Hart. Unlike the rest, this man was not drunk, and Hart suddenly felt the sense of recognition as those expressionless eyes stared back at him. The man was not Ives, but something about those eyes stirred an emotional memory that Hart could not quite place. He felt certain that he had seen this man before, and judging from the man's interest in him, the feeling was mutual.

"So glad you could make it, Helmut," a cheery voice said from somewhere near Hart's waist. Hart looked down to see that he was standing next to a small round table, and at the table sat a German major who rose to shake his hand.

It was Ives, and he wore that same feigned smile that Hart had seen so many times in the past.

"How do you do, Major?" Hart shook the hand that was offered. "It is good to see you again."

"Major?" Ives said with a side glance. "A bit formal for an old schoolfellow, aren't we?"

You son of a bitch, Hart thought.

"Of course. How foolish of me. Forgive me, Heinz, but after so many weeks at sea, it is hard for me to put aside the regimen so quickly."

Ives smiled slyly and motioned for Hart to have a seat at the table across from him.

That was it. They had established their relationship in loud voices for any casual listener who might have been curious. Now they could talk in confidence since the white noise in the room would drown out everything they said beyond six inches from their table.

As Hart sat down, he glanced one more time across the room to the post where he had seen the German officer staring back at him. But the man was gone now. He had disappeared.

"See someone you know?" Ives asked curiously.

"No. No one." Hart turned his attention back to the table.

"You must be careful in a place like this. You never can tell who is a mere soldier and who is an operative. Still, it is the best place to not draw suspicion to oneself."

"For who?" Hart said in an irritated tone. "You may not have noticed this, but I'm wearing a *Kriegsmarine* uniform. A sea officer walking into an army establishment and meeting with an army major. Not exactly inconspicuous, wouldn't you say? I'm going to have to explain this when I get back to my boat."

Ives smiled and lit a cigarette. "A common enough occurrence. I'm sure you'll think of a good excuse."

That last sounded patronizing, and it stirred Hart's blood.

"So what the hell are you doing here? And why risk meeting like this?"

Ives's expression suddenly drew grave. "Something has happened."

"What? Does it have anything to do with the fact that this mission was exposed from the start? You do know that, don't you? My flight was ambushed over Norway."

"I'm quite aware of what happened in Norway, Lieutenant." Ives addressed him by his cover rank as if it were an insult. "We have been monitoring your progress from London. That's how I knew to find you here."

"Is that also how an airship and a destroyer miraculously stumbled onto *U-2553*'s exact refueling location?" Hart said heatedly, in a tone a bit too loud. "Well, is it?"

Ives glanced casually at the nearby tables. "I suggest you lower your voice, comrade, and remember where we are. The truth is—"

"The truth is," Hart interrupted, "the crew of a B-17 is now dead. The crew of an airship is now dead. And the entire crew of a British destroyer would now be dead if I hadn't interceded with *U-2553*'s captain. And believe me, he wanted to sink that floating wreck. He's been burned many times after showing mercy to Allied crews."

"So that was your doing, was it?" Ives smiled smugly. "I thought as much. How did you pull that off?"

"I told him the destroyer was done for. It wasn't going to fight again, and if he went any further it might look bad for him after the war."

"You said all that and still maintained your cover?" Ives said suspiciously.

"Yes, don't worry. He still thinks I'm Rittenhaus," Hart said tiredly. "It may come as a surprise to you, but not everyone thinks the way you do. Not everyone is driven by some power-hungry ideal. I made an appeal to his humanity. Traugott is no murderer."

"And now you are, from what I understand."

Ives had obviously heard about Odeman's fate through his channels, but Hart resented his tone. He really hated this bastard. "Just tell me that some of the British sailors survived."

"Yes, many were saved." Ives looked down at the table. "And you are quite right. The mission was blown from the start. It seems we had a mole within our unit."

"Who?"

"I'm sorry to have to tell you this," Ives paused, tapping out some ashes into the ashtray on the table. He looked back at Hart, his eyes as placid as they were unfeeling. "Admiral McDonough has been arrested for espionage."

Hart gasped, staring into space. Ives quickly poured him a drink, and Hart gladly took it.

"I know it's a shock to you," Ives continued. "It was a shock to all of us. But the evidence was very compelling, as it was condemning."

Hart could hardly believe it. He certainly had no per-sonal affection for McDonough, but McDonough was the last one he would ever suspect of working for the other side.

"How long?" Hart finally asked.

"Months, perhaps years. There has even been some speculation that he blew the cover of your men in Spain two years ago. Perhaps that's why he was so reluctant to fight for your men's release. In any event, the bastard's going to hang now."

The memory of McDonough's cold nature throughout that whole episode was still vivid in Hart's mind, but, even so, this was beyond his wildest imagination. McDonough a double agent. That was bad enough. Now, to find out that McDonough might have been to blame for the loss of Isabelle—it was unthinkable. And what of the new infor-mation McDonough supposedly had of her whereabouts? Was that all a mere fabrication of McDonough's duplici-tous mind?

"I know how you must be feeling right now." Ives leaned forward and placed a hand on Hart's arm. The gesture was certainly meant as a sign of reassurance, but it made Hart's mental defenses go into high alert. It was unnatural and not like the Ives that Hart knew, who was cold and aloof by nature. Ives went on, "I tell you, this betrayal of McDonough's puts the entire operation in jeopardy. That's why I was sent here to contact you. As far as we can tell, the Germans don't know about you yet. It seems McDonough was feeding them only a trickle of information, a little at a time, no doubt to pad his own bank account. Now that he's been isolated, we've decided that it's best to go ahead and continue with the mission."

Hart looked into Ives's eyes and was suddenly on his guard.

"If we're continuing with the mission, as before, then why did you risk coming here to tell me this? It makes no difference, does it?"

Ives stared blankly at him for a few seconds and then broke into a small smile. "I came to make sure you're all right, comrade. People have been known to get injured or killed when destroyers drop depth charges on them." Ives paused. "I also came to warn you."

"Warn me?"

"It seems McDonough's treachery continued right up to the moment he was arrested. He managed to get off a phone call. We don't know to whom. The number he called led us to an abandoned flat in the Liverpool area. Whoever it was that he was calling was long gone by the time we got there."

"So you think this compatriot of McDonough's might get word to the Germans and blow my cover?"

"It's possible." Ives shrugged. "Or that individual—or individuals—might try to contact you and feed you false information. All I'm saying is, be vigilant."

"That's sound advice," Hart said, trying to mask his own suspicion. He downed the last of his drink before grabbing his hat from the back of the chair. "Well, I had better get going. Curfew expires soon."

"Wait, comrade," Ives said, placing a hand on Hart's arm again. There was a slight hint of desperation in his voice. "There was another reason I was sent here."

Hart felt a small sense of satisfaction. His move to leave had been a test, and Ives had fallen for it. Hart looked at his watch. "Make it quick. I've got to get back to the base before my captain, or anyone else, starts asking questions."

Ives looked at him intently. "I need to know everything you have gathered on the artifacts aboard *U-2553*."

"The artifacts?"

"Surely you got a chance to inspect them."

"Yes, I inspected them."

Ives appeared to be forcing an impatient grin. "And?"

Hart shrugged. "I'm not sure what to make of them. Most of the items were medieval in origin. A few pieces appeared to be ancient. They looked Egyptian. Judging from the hieratic script, I'd say they belonged to the beginning of the Late Period of ancient Egypt— seventh or sixth century B.C.—if I remember right from my lessons."

"And this script." Ives was talking very slowly now. "Did you write it down?"

"Of course I did."

"Then let me have them before you go," Ives said hurriedly, extending an open palm.

Hart glanced once at Ives's open hand, then looked into the man's eyes. The eyes were blank, unblinking. Hart could derive nothing from them, which meant that Ives was hiding something.

"What is the problem, comrade?" Ives said, his mouth forming into a convivial smile. "None of these idiots will suspect anything. As far as they know, you're giving me a list of the best whorehouses in town."

Hart had been acquainted with Ives for nearly five years, but in all that time he never felt that he truly knew the man. Ives was a professional. He had a different personality for every occasion, and he could assume them at will. Hart had seen it many times on previous missions. Once, Hart had seen the normally cold and stiff Ives swagger and cajole with a senior German officer he would torture and kill later that same evening. He was dangerous, and everyone in Odysseus knew it. Few knew what Ives did before coming to the organization, but rumors abounded that assassination had been his specialty.

Hart's mind reeled. Had Ives been sent here to collect the information on the artifacts, and then to eliminate him? Well, Hart was a professional, too, and he knew better than to play his high trump card too early.

"I don't have it with me," Hart lied, hoping the folded paper in his left breast pocket was not leaving a visible indenture on the outside of his uniform jacket. "I left it in my locker, aboard the U-boat."

Ives's face turned harsh, his eyes narrowing. "An unfortunate mistake," he said through gritted teeth. "An unfortunate, novice mistake. Wouldn't you agree?" It was obvious that he did not believe Hart, and thus he would now be aware that Hart did not trust him either.

"I can get it. We can meet tomorrow," Hart offered, knowing that Ives had little choice. "My sub is in port for at least two days."

Ives studied him for a few moments before agreeing. "Very well, tomorrow then. And I would advise you, Lieutenant, not to play games with me. McDonough wasn't the only one under investigation. He is thought to have had accomplices within the organization. You might be interested to know that your name came up."

"Is that a threat?"

"Play games with me, and I will make things extremely hard for you, comrade. I will meet you here tomorrow at noon. Until that time, I suggest you don't talk to anyone about what we discussed."

Hart managed to chuckle casually. "And just who would I talk to?"

Ives shot him an evil glance. "Remember what I said, and meet me here at noon tomorrow. Don't be late."

CHAPTER TWENTY-SEVEN

Hart had intentionally decided to take an alternate route back to the naval base, in case Ives or anyone else had laid a snare for him. As he strolled down the dark Toulon street, keeping a wary eye out for any of the other late-night pedestrians who might be following him, he contemplated the meeting with Ives. The bastard was hiding something, that much was certain. Ives wanted the information on the artifacts. He wanted it desperately, and when denied he had exhibited a verve that Hart was unaccustomed to.

Patting his left breast pocket, Hart felt the outline of the folded paper that contained the inscriptions from the artifacts. Undoubtedly, Ives knew that Hart was not enough of an amateur to ever let the information out of his sight, much less leave it aboard the U-boat. Ives probably suspected that Hart had the paper on him, but what could he have done about it? They were behind enemy lines, in a pub crowded with Germans. Whether Ives had believed him or not, he had had little choice but to let him go. Now Hart's present quandary was not whether Ives had believed him, but whether he should believe Ives's story about Admiral McDonough. If it was true, then what was the true purpose of this mission? Had McDonough initiated the mission for his American masters or his German ones? And why was Ives so apprehensive about it?

Hart turned a corner and headed down a long, dark street that gently descended to the waterfront. The street was lined on both sides with two- and three-story apartment buildings and business offices, but they could have been abandoned for all Hart knew. Each building stood dark and looming over the lonely street, blocking most of the noise from the rest of the city. Then Hart suddenly realized why the street was so dark. The city near the harbor was under a blackout order, to throw off any Allied bombers that might try striking the naval base. A handful of high apartment windows emanated the dull glow of candlelight, but by and large the rest of the area was in complete compliance with the blackout. Thus, as Hart made his way down the street, the world around him grew progressively darker with each step, to a point that he could not see the bricks beneath his feet. Far up ahead, the one and only streetlamp was lit and served as Hart's beacon, his only point of reference in an otherwise black void. It was not a bright lamp by any means, but it was bright enough that Hart could make out the yellow cone of light beneath it accentuated by flying insects swirling in and out of its apex.

A savage dog suddenly barked from an alley on the right. It was a loud, snarling bark, mired in saliva, and it obviously came from a dog that was quite large. Hart instantly wheeled toward the sound, holding up an arm in preparation for a set of attacking fangs, but the attack never came. Hart only breathed easier when he was finally convinced that the animal must be tied up or penned inside a nearby yard. Nevertheless, the dog had unsettled him, and it made him wish for his weapon even more. Several other dogs now barked in the distance. Hart looked down the street in both directions, hoping to see other pedestrians making their way through the darkness as well, but he could see no one. For all he knew, he was the only one on this street.

Pressing on, he quickened his pace, as if the cone of light up ahead somehow represented safety. He found that it was much farther than he had realized, and when he finally reached the small area of sidewalk illuminated by the lamp, he discovered that his chest was heaving. The weeks aboard the U-boat had not been good for his cardiovascular system. Stopping to catch his breath, Hart suddenly realized that he was not alone.

Standing beside the lamppost, with her back to him, was a young woman wearing a red dress and furs. Hart was surprised because he had not noticed her there before. She was quite dolled up and resembled one of the French prostitutes Hart had seen cavorting at the bar with the German officers. As Hart drew closer, he could see that her brown hair and red dress were a disheveled mess and that she reeked of alcohol. She must have heard Hart's footsteps and suddenly turned to face him, her expression indicating that she was just as surprised as he was. She had streaks running down her face, where earlier tears had eroded great channels in her thick coat of makeup.

"Good evening, *mademoiselle*," Hart said politely, trying his best not to alarm her.

She said nothing, but then began to dig for something in her purse. For a moment, Hart thought that she might be fishing for a gun for self-defense, but then he was relieved to see her produce a mere cigarette. Her trembling hands could hardly manage to bring it to her lips.

"Oh, *monsieur*," she said finally in broken German. "Could I trouble you for a light? Tonight has been a most cruel evening, and now I cannot even light my own cigarettes."

She had the look of a dog that had been beaten once too often, and Hart suddenly felt a twinge of pity for her. She was living a life of hell in an occupied country. She could be a mother for all he knew. Who knew what she had to do every day just to put food on the table? Who knew how the Germans treated her?

Just this once, Hart thought, he could afford to take a break from the war. He could offer this frail creature a bit of humanity in a cruel world.

He quickly fumbled in his coat pocket and found his box of matches. Then, striking one into life, he held it near her face, shielding it from the breeze with the other hand.

"Oh, thank you, sir. You are so kind."

As she held her face closer to the burning match, Hart could finally see her features more clearly. He was alarmed when he came to the realization that he had seen the face before, a little more than a month ago, in Edinburgh. She had asked him for a light then, too. At that time, she had been a redhead, not a brunette.

Hart instantly stepped away from her. She did not react. She simply stared at him, her face changing from a sniveling wreck to something very stern and collected right before his eyes.

"Who the hell are you?" Hart demanded, remembering to stay in German.

She did not answer. She only stared, but now she was staring at something just past his shoulder. Hart spun around but not quickly enough to avoid the solid object that struck him in the side of the head. He dropped to his knees, stunned. Then came another blow, and he was down on the ground senseless. Men were talking over him, and he could hear the scuffle of feet. A woman's voice very distinctly gave orders. An automobile pulled up. Hands were on him, lifting him and then dropping him onto a soft car seat that smelled like perfume. The woman said something again, and he felt the automobile accelerate. The next moment he lost all consciousness.

CHAPTER TWENTY-EIGHT

The light was blindingly bright, so bright that it was painful for Hart to open his eyes. That, coupled with the throbbing pain on the right side of his head and neck, made him want to go back to the blackness he had come from.

"I think he's coming around," a man's voice said in English, heavily laced with a French accent.

"Well, don't just stand there gawking," another voice said in English, but Hart recognized this accent as Welsh. "Go and fetch her."

Hart tried to move his arms and legs, but he could not. At first he thought the blow to his head had left him paralyzed, but then he quickly realized that his wrists and ankles were fastened to the chair in which he sat. The bindings felt like piano wire, and every time he moved it felt as though they would cut into his skin. He could not tell how long he had been out, or how long he had been sitting in the chair, but the crick in his neck told him it had been for quite some time.

A door opened and shut, and he could hear footsteps on a hardwood floor. He counted at least three people, and they were approaching him. He tried to get a look at them but was still blinded by the light in his face. He had no choice but to keep his eyes shut.

"Is this the man you saw?" a female voice said. She, too, had an English accent.

"Aye, that's him," a man's voice said. "That's Hart. I thought I recognized the bugger."

"My name is Helmut Rittenhaus," Hart mumbled in the broken English of a native Austrian. He was instantly silenced with a hard slap across the face. The blow was solid, as it was shocking. He did not see it coming or who delivered it, but he knew that it had been a man's hand and not the woman's.

"No one told you to talk, Yank!" a man snarled into his ear.

"Stop it, Petey," the woman's voice said reprovingly.

Hart felt the belligerent man back off, then heard the woman continue her conversation with the other man as though Hart were not in the room.

"Did you follow the major?" she asked.

"I lost him near La Seyne station," the voice of the man who had recognized Hart replied. "I think he boarded the train to Marseilles. He's a slippery one. It felt like he knew I was following him. He's no tenderfoot. Not like this one. This one could be taken by a schoolgirl selling lemonade. Mary and Joseph, I thought I taught him better!"

Hart winced internally at having been judged as inferior to Ives, but he said nothing and kept a confused look on his face, attempting to keep up the role of a frightened German naval lieutenant. At that moment, there was a pause in the conversation, and somehow Hart knew that everyone else in the room was staring at him, particularly the female. He knew she was standing close to him because he could smell the perfume again, the same perfume he had smelled on the prostitute under the streetlamp.

"Turn that thing off," the woman finally ordered.

The light in Hart's face switched off instantly, and his spotty world slowly came into focus. He was in a room, a rather plain room that looked like it could belong to any small house in Toulon. Judging from the noise of the early-morning traffic outside, this particular house was in the heart of the city. There was a threadbare rug on the wood floor, a fireplace and mantel on one wall, and a small wooden dining table against the other. A pot of coffee simmered on the stove in the adjoining kitchen and filled the room with its rich aroma. The place had all of the look and feel of a cozy French home. All except for one corner, where a plethora of radio equipment sat atop a small table alongside a row of German MP 40 submachine guns leaning against the wall.

One man sat at the radio, headset on, seemingly oblivious to the interrogation transpiring only a few feet away.

Another man with a beard and wearing a green, knitted sweater, was setting down the light. He had gray hair and kind eyes, and he smiled at Hart and said, *"Bonjour, monsieur."* Hart concluded that this was the Frenchman he had heard earlier.

Next to the Frenchman stood a much younger man, a man who appeared no older than nineteen. Unlike the

Frenchman, he did not smile but instead wore a harsh expression that was almost as menacing as the Browning Hi Power semiautomatic pistol in his hand, pointed directly at Hart's torso. The youth had a wild look about him that indicated to Hart he should not get too comfortable around him.

The only other man in the room was not wearing civilian clothes. He wore the uniform of a German army captain, the same uniform Hart had seen him wear at the pub last night. This was the man who had exchanged stares with Hart across the crowded room. He was now much closer, pouring himself a cup of coffee near the stove, and Hart could see his features much more clearly. The oval face, the piercing green eyes, the intense mouth that always seemed pursed as if ready to play a brass instrument—Hart recognized the man unmistakably. It was Jones, his old instructor at Camp X—the OSS spy school. The British sergeant looked much older now, thinner and slightly more haggard, if that was possible. But even now, years later, just the sight of him broached painful memories of embarrassment, failure, and final success at spy school. Jones had been one of the hard ones, the kind of instructor who thought he could save the lives of his students by making them fear him more than they did the enemy. Hart had certainly learned to fear him, and to hate him. But there was also a certain grudging admiration for this sage of the spy business whose wisdom and instruction had saved Hart's life on many occasions. Now, only a few feet away, the sage sipped at a coffee cup, smiling at Hart.

And then there was the woman. She was a young

woman, or at least she was a few years younger than Hart. Although there was no telling exactly how old she was, this chameleon who had appeared every bit the red-haired, pale Scottish housewife only a month ago now had brown hair and was tan, as if she had lived in Toulon her entire life. Whoever she really was, it was clear to Hart that she was in charge here.

"So, do you prefer brunettes or redheads?" she said with a smile, making no move to untie him but offering him a drag on her cigarette, which he accepted thankfully. "I don't know what the OSS is teaching you these days, my friend, but you Yanks still have a lot to learn about this business."

The younger man holding the pistol chuckled. "Maybe it's because they're led by a bloody lawyer."

Hart knew this was in reference to General William Donovan, the director of the OSS, who before the war had been a U.S. attorney general and a Wall Street lawyer. The British spy services had always looked down on their fledgling American counterpart. This was typical behavior Hart would expect from the Brits, but it could also be an old SS trick. The presence of Jones was compelling but not conclusive. He was, after all, still wearing a German uniform.

"I do not know what you mean," Hart said, still using the German accent as if English were trouble for him. "I am an officer in the *Kriegsmarine*."

"Cut the line, Yank," the woman said, now appearing slightly irritated. "We know who you are, I saw you in Edinburgh, and you recognized me on the street. Don't think I haven't learned to read faces after all these years."

She pulled up a chair and sat backward on it, facing him. "Your name is Hart. You are an OSS operative imbedded on the U-boat *U-2553*. Your cover is quite blown, Mister Hart. So you might as well start cooperating with us. And you can start by telling us what your business was with that man in the pub earlier this evening."

Hart stared back at her blankly, remaining silent.

"Aw, we're running out of time. Just let me pistol-whip the bastard," the young man with the Browning said enthusiastically.

The woman smiled and waved him off. "Listen, Yank, I know what you're thinking," she said, this time in a more congenial tone. "It walks like British SIS. It talks like British SIS, but bloody hell is it British SIS? You think we might be Germans, am I right? I don't blame you. God knows, the bloody bastards have done it before."

Hart kept silent.

"It's all about trust, isn't it? A woman on the street asks you for a light, and, like a bloody fool, you trust her enough to give her one. Now that I tell you we're SIS, you lose your tongue." She took another drag on the cigarette and winked at him. "Well, then, let's get off on a proper footing, shall we? My name is Esther Blackbourne, and these fellows are my team." She pointed to the man sitting at the radio set. "Over there is Michael. He doesn't say much, but he likes to listen. This chap here, holding the gun on you, is Petey." Petey nodded but still kept the Browning pointed at Hart's torso. "Jacques is our local contact. This is his house."

The Frenchman nodded politely. "You are most welcome, *monsieur*."

"And finally," she continued, motioning toward the kitchen, "there is Jones. But, of course, you and Jones know each other already, don't you."

"Aye, he knows me," Jones said. "And I know him. He was the greenest lump of shit that ever passed through Camp X." Jones paused, then added with a smile, "Smelled a little better, though, when we got through with him. Till now, I thought he was a promising bugger. You got yourself mixed up in some deep shit this time, Yank."

"We all belong to SIS counterintelligence," Esther said. "We're here in Toulon on special assignment."

Hart swallowed. There was no use in continuing his act. His cover was blown, and by all appearances these were allies.

"Counterintelligence?" Hart asked, this time in perfect English.

She smiled. "That's right, Yank, but I don't think I caught your name."

"It's Matt. Matt Hart."

"Well, Matt Hart, isn't this nice. Now we all know each other." She reached out and let him take another drag on the cigarette.

"Now that you know I'm one of the good guys," Hart said, blowing out the rich smoke, "why not cut me loose?"

"Not so fast, Yank. I asked you a question. One you still haven't answered. I want to know what you were doing with that German major."

Once again Hart clammed up and just stared back at her. The SIS might be allies in the war effort, but

Odysseus was not in the habit of sharing its operations with other organizations, no matter what their allegiance. As much as Hart distrusted Ives, he was still Odysseus, and Hart would not be the one to spill details of an operation to the Brits.

Esther shook her head, her expression showing mild disappointment. "That man you met with earlier this evening, Major Mueller. His real name is Ives. He's a captain in the U.S. Navy, currently assigned to the OSS—or more specifically, a special branch of the OSS called Odysseus. How am I doing so far?"

Hart said nothing. He was doing his best to appear unfazed at the names of Ives and Odysseus coming from the mouth of this Brit. It had always been his understanding that neither the British nor any other U.S. ally knew about the existence of Odysseus.

"Until recently," she continued, "this Odysseus was headed up by an American admiral named McDonough. I say until recently because McDonough's been arrested. Now I know you have been undercover for some time, Matt, so you probably don't know what has transpired in England over the past few days. I doubt Ives would have told you, because he's caught up in it, too. So, here it is. Odysseus has been disbanded, and your commander, Admiral McDonough, is being charged with treason."

"Treason?" Hart said with surprise, as if he had not heard such rumors from Ives already. The less she thought he knew, the better.

Esther nodded. "We're not sure what his motivations were, or exactly who he was working for. No one knew exactly what he was up to, not even his own superiors.

He always produced results, so the OSS let him run free." She shook her head. "Like I said, you Americans have a lot to learn about this business. Never trust another spy. The British government, however, has been suspicious of him for quite some time, and two months ago SIS counterintelligence was ordered to investigate him. We've been monitoring him ever since."

"So the British government has taken it upon itself to investigate the OSS?" Hart asked incredulously. "I'd say that's not being much of a team player."

"The U.S. government has assisted us in this investigation, Matt. You see, Odysseus did things without going through proper channels. It kept information from the OSS and from the U.S. government. Worse, it never bothered to let us English in on its little secrets, and that's very bad form in our business, you know. It wasn't being a team player, as you call it. In essence, Odysseus went rogue. And we believe the corruption ran much deeper than Admiral McDonough. Last week, the decision was made to dissolve Odysseus. It had become far too dangerous. My bosses and your bosses issued a joint directive ordering its elimination."

"If Odysseus has been disbanded, then why is Ives here?" Hart asked.

Esther looked at him through squinted eyes. "We were hoping you could tell us. Your man, Ives, whom we know to have been McDonough's right-hand man, left Britain before we could nab him. It didn't take us long to find out where he was going. My team and I were sent here to find him. Now we think he's got connections on the other side we didn't know about."

"Like me, for instance," Hart said.

"Come on, Matt. You're a small fry, a low-level field operative who probably never got to see or even understand the big picture."

Esther had said it condescendingly, and Hart knew that she was attempting to belittle him, trying to urge his ego to prove his worth by giving her information. It was a typical interrogation technique, but one that was useless on him.

"So," Esther said. "Can you help us, or not?"

"Like you said, Miss Blackbourne, what do I know? I'm just a small fry."

"You're a bloody impudent bastard, that's what you are," Petey said, suddenly stepping forward brandishing the butt of his pistol as if to strike Hart with it. One raised hand from Esther stopped him.

"You know what I think, Mister Hart?" she said. "I think you know exactly what I am after. I think you met with Mister Ives to discuss a certain set of artifacts being shipped aboard *U-2553*. I think you know the importance of these artifacts, too. That they hold the key to unlocking some kind of ancient superweapon—a weapon that Jerry is trying to get his hands on." Hart watched as she removed a folded paper from her cleavage. It was the paper that had been in his shirt pocket. "Now, why don't you tell me what this is?"

Hart assumed Esther had ransacked his pockets and had uncovered it. He was reluctant to discuss his mission with her, but she seemed to know more about it than he did.

"Those are inscriptions," Hart said, finally. "Copied from the items aboard *U-2553*."

"The question is," she said sincerely, looking into his eyes, "if you're working with Ives, then why didn't you give him this? Jones here was watching you the whole time. He says you never handed him anything. Is that right?"

Hart nodded.

"Good," she said triumphantly, glancing over the text on the paper. "My guess is you're on the up-and-up, and Ives is playing both sides. Once he has what he wants from you, he'll expose you to his Nazi masters and walk away a hero."

"He'll never get that chance," Hart said confidently.

"I'm afraid you are right about that, Matt," Esther said in a tone suddenly solemn. Hart watched as the smile left her face, fading into something more somber and reflective, as if she were having some kind of internal struggle.

"So what happens now?" he asked, somewhat disturbed by her sudden change in demeanor. "Am I to go back to London and prove my innocence?"

"I wish it were that simple, Matt. Orders are orders, and ours are to hunt down Odysseus and eliminate it. That means all of its operatives. That means you."

"What?" Hart exclaimed, incredulously. "But I'm not involved in whatever McDonough and Ives were plotting. I hadn't even been in contact with them until about a month ago. Don't I at least get my day in court?"

She looked at him despondently. "You can see what I have here, Matt. We're a small team. We're deep behind enemy lines. I can't afford to waste any of my men watching you, let alone to arrange transport back to London. By all appearances, Ives is on the move, and we have to stay on his tail. As much as I want to let you go back and prove your innocence, I have no mechanism to get that done. And I do have my orders."

She rose from the chair and walked over to her purse on the table. From it she produced a small mascara container, which she opened to remove a shiny black pill. She held the pill up, between her thumb and index fingers.

"You, of course, know what this is," she said.

Hart knew exactly what it was. It was the L-pill, the cyanide-packed gem, the final alternative to capture.

"Wait, Esther, I can help you!" Hart offered desperately, saying whatever he could think of to head this off. "I know Ives better than anyone. I can help you find him."

She appeared not to hear him. "I'll give you the choice of methods, Mister Hart—the pill, or Petey's Browning. It's the least I can offer to a fellow operative."

Fighting back the pounding feeling in his head, Hart tried to think quickly. Nothing made sense. A death order out for all Odysseus agents? These SIS whackos certainly believed they were doing the will of the British and U.S. governments, but Hart suspected that they themselves had been duped. Who was really behind the order? If McDonough was the mole, and he was now in custody, then who was calling the shots? Perhaps the same individual who was responsible for the ambush over Norway and the attack on *U-2553*.

"Esther, please!" Hart pleaded emphatically. "Something is going on here. Think about it. Does this order make any sense? Does it?"

Esther stood before him with the pill in her hand. She glanced uncertainly at Jones, as if to ask for advice, but the veteran agent simply shrugged. Hart could see that she was hesitant.

"Just let me contact OSS," Hart said. "You've got a radio. Surely you can get a coded message through."

"You know I can't do that, Matt," she said soberly. "In our business, orders must be followed without question. Now, which is it to be, the pill or the gun?"

Seeing that he was getting nowhere, Hart quickly checked the distance to the door and the proximity of Petey's pistol. It was no use. Petey was smart enough to stand outside the absolute limit Hart might manage to move in his bound state. Besides that, Petey appeared somewhat anxious to be the one to pull the trigger. Hart had worked with many men like Petey in the past. Every team had one, a slightly unstable type, the one who did all the dirty work. Men like Petey killed without remorse or a second thought.

"Well?" Esther asked with the slightest trace of remorse in her voice. When Hart did not answer, she shook her head in pity and then ordered Jones to bring a glass of brandy.

"Sorry, laddie," Jones said, as he forced Hart to gulp

down two glasses quickly. "I wish there were another way. Hopefully, this will take some of the edge off."

The brandy was strong, and it burned on the way down. Hart felt instantly warm. His lips were numb and his head no longer hurt. Through somewhat foggy eyes, he saw Esther approach him with the cyanide capsule. The brandy had all but done in his motor skills, and there was little he could do to resist. She would only need to hold his nose to get the pill in his mouth and shove it down his throat. He smelled her perfumed hand pass his nose and grab hold of his hair to tilt his head back. Her breasts were pressing on his shoulder, forcing his intoxicated mind to dither between hatred for and attraction to this woman who was about to make him swallow poison. Then, at that moment, she paused for some reason. Hart could see that she was not ten inches from his face and looking directly into his eyes. Even in his inebriated state, he could see that she was not a born killer. The deprogramming regimen at spy school had not failed to drive the humanity from her soul completely. In that momentary pause, he saw traces of the innocent, fun-loving girl that she was before the war, the girl who was now gone forever. For some reason, her dazzling blue eyes made him think of what a shame it was that such a creature would ever have to experience cruel war.

At that moment, there was a sudden clamor at the door. Someone outside was pounding on it, not with a fist but with something solid like a rifle butt. Someone was trying to break the door down, and Hart thought he heard German voices on the other side.

"They've found us!" Jones exclaimed, rushing toward the stack of machine guns against the wall. "Get your weapons!"

"Never mind that," Esther ordered. "Come on, Jones, help me."

She and Jones rushed to a point in the room behind Hart and out of his field of vision. Michael, the radioman, produced a hammer and began smashing his radio set to pieces with Jacques assisting. Petey pointed his pistol directly at the pounding door, which had already started to splinter.

"Hurry up!" Petey shouted a warning over his shoulder. "One more and they're through!"

"Give me just a few more seconds," Michael replied, sweating profusely as he and Jacques frantically thrust small bits of shredded paper into the fire.

But Petey did not wait. He fired his semiautomatic pistol at point-blank range into the door, emptying the entire magazine. The report of the gun was deafening in the confined space, and the room instantly filled with the acrid aroma of gunpowder. An eerie silence followed, broken only by the sound of a corpse slumping to the floor on the other side of the door. Petey had ejected the spent magazine and had already loaded a new one by the time the Germans on the other side reciprocated. The typewriter retort of a machine gun rang out and a fusillade of bullets tore gaping holes in the battered door. The deadly missiles entirely missed Petey, who had stood to the side at the last moment. A few projectiles zipped past Hart's head, but they missed him, too. Michael and Jacques, however, were not so lucky. Michael lay facedown on the floor, one arm cooking in the fireplace, his brains adorning the mantel above. Jacques stood nearby, clutching his abdomen where blood streamed between his fingers. With his face wincing from pain and shock, he managed to stumble to the far corner of the room, out of the line of fire, and collapse.

"Hold them off, Petey!" It was Esther's voice, calling from behind Hart. She and Jones were struggling with something, something very heavy judging from their grunts and groans. Try as he might, Hart could not manage to turn in the chair at all to see what they were doing.

He saw that Petey was standing to the side of the pulverized door, waiting with his Browning to dispatch the first German who came through. Hart waited anxiously, too, because he would be the first thing the Germans would see, and probably shoot, when they entered. But it was not a German that first appeared in the doorway. Instead, a small object floated through one of the gaping holes in the door, tumbling as it fell and landing on the floor in the center of the room. The wandlike object was less than ten feet away from Hart, and he instantly recognized it as a German hand grenade—or more colloquially, a potato masher. He was in the kill zone with no cover between him and the grenade. He cast a pleading glance at Petey, who seemed unconcerned about its proximity to Hart but very concerned that Esther and Jones would be in the kill zone, too. Hart saw a look of anxiety cross Petey's face, replaced by sadness, then determination, all in the blink of an eye. And then Petey did the unthinkable. Hart watched in disbelief as Petey threw his pistol away and made a flying leap across the room. He landed squarely on the sizzling grenade and instantly curled his body around it.

"Petey!" Esther shrieked.

The next moment the grenade went off.

CHAPTER TWENTY-NINE

The Austrian Alps
Forty-eight hours later

"Some more water, please, *monsieur*."

"Easy with this, Jacques," Hart said, holding the metal field cup to the wounded Frenchman's lips. "I have a feeling this will have to last us through the night."

The guns on the roof erupted again, shaking the concrete floor of their prison cell and the very teeth in Hart's skull.

Karrump! Karrump! Karumpump! The massive 128-millimeter flak guns went off in rapid succession.

"I hope your bombers blow these swine to hell, *monsieur*."

"So do I. But from the sound of it, our guys are getting the worst end of it."

The guns continued to blast away, their report almost deafening, even though they were mounted five floors up from the prison cell. Hart had seen the great gun barrels protruding from the roof of the building and sitting idle when he had entered the tower several hours ago.

Now he could only imagine what they must look like, blazing away at the night sky. The top of the tower had to resemble a giant firecracker from the vantage point of its targets.

After a few more minutes of incessant pounding, the guns fell silent, presumably while the battery crews replenished their ammunition stockpiles. In the temporary lull, Hart's ears recovered enough to make out the dull droning of several hundred aircraft engines overhead. This was the target of the German guns, an Allied bombing raid headed north from air bases in Italy to strike targets deep inside the German heartland. The noise of the plane engines was so loud it sounded as though they were directly overhead, flying at low altitude. While it was true that the Allied planes were directly overhead, only one or two thousand feet above the German flak guns that now peppered their formation, they were not in fact flying at low altitude. They were flying at twenty thousand feet, an altitude sufficient to surmount the great Alps, but not high enough to avoid the numerous flak emplacements the Germans had planted on the various peaks.

It was in one of these flak emplacements that Hart and Jacques now found themselves prisoners. Hart had heard of these giant flak towers before, but he had never seen one, much less been inside one. Each tower was more like a fortress than anything else. It was equipped with a complete battery of 128-millimeter antiaircraft guns, along with offices, storerooms, mess hall, and living quarters for the two-hundred-man garrison that served them. They were another impressive feat of German engineering, designed to knock Allied bombers out of the sky at near point-blank range as the disadvantaged formations flew over the Alps.

As the guns once again resumed their tumultuous barrage, Hart closed his eyes and tried to piece together the events of the past forty-eight hours. It seemed like so long ago that he was strapped to that chair watching helplessly as the grenade exploded, splattering the room with Petey's remains. The bloodstains were still on Hart's shirt, an unsettling reminder of the sacrifice that had saved his life. Hart's memory up to that point was clear. But what happened next was a blur. The room had gone black, and Hart temporarily lost his hearing. Perhaps the blast had extinguished the lights, or perhaps Esther and Jones had doused them. Either way, the figures that burst into the room following the explosion brought their own, shining their flashlights directly into Hart's face, blinding him. There was a scuffle of sorts as a dozen or more men dressed in the black uniforms and red armbands of the Waffen-SS secured the room and ensured that both Petey and Michael were dead by discharging several rounds into their lifeless bodies. Strangely, Hart did not hear or see Esther or Jones after the blast, but he hardly had a chance to look for them. Two burly SS sergeants untied him from the chair and brusquely rushed him out of the room. Of course, Hart tried to take advantage of the fact that he was still in the uniform of a German naval officer. He attempted to maintain his cover, playing the act of a dazed prisoner suddenly rescued. But the two sergeants ignored his futile demonstrations, pushing him into the back of a truck waiting on the street outside, where he was soon joined by a severely wounded Jacques. There both he and Jacques were clapped in irons and told to keep their mouths shut, reiterated by a rifle butt to Hart's jaw and enforced by the muzzles of two MP 40 submachine guns pointed directly at their torsos.

The truck had moved quickly through the streets of Toulon, Jacques groaning with pain at every sharp turn. The curtains were drawn across the back of the cargo area so Hart could not see where they were going; he had to use his other senses to gauge their destination. After passing through several checkpoints, they ended up on a winding country road where the steep grade forced the driver to downshift several times. As the elevation changed, so did the temperature, the back of the truck dropping near twenty degrees in the matter of an hour. All of this told Hart they were headed north, into the Alps, he assumed toward Germany. At first he thought the alpine route had been chosen to steer well clear of the Allied armies driving across northern France, but then he was surprised when the truck continued to climb up the mountainous roads where the air got thinner and the temperature much colder. They drove on for the entire day in the mountains, stopping for fuel twice, the two sergeants never once allowing Hart or Jacques even a glimpse of the outside world. They did not reach their destination until sunset, about the same time that Jacques developed a fever and started to tremble. When they were finally allowed to emerge from the truck, Hart discovered that they were in a small mountain village nestled in a green alpine valley. The village was centered around a mirrorlike lake above which stood several tall gray peaks, rising from the valley's tree-lined fringe. The peaks were so high that Hart had to crane his neck to see their snowy tops, and they seemed to peer down on the village like ancient judges that had witnessed countless generations. The truck had stopped just outside the village and they were led toward the base of a cliff only a few hundred yards away. Hart remembered seeing for the first time the tall, square concrete structure situated on the cliff above, the wide platform atop the tower, the antiaircraft guns with their long barrels protruding over the edge. The flak tower was perched nearly five hundred feet above the ground, built into the very cliff. It loomed menacingly over the quiet village like some Teutonic castle of medieval times. The SS sergeants nudged him and Jacques toward a single freight elevator, which was nothing more than an open platform connected to a winch on the tower above by long steel cables. It appeared to be the only way to get up or down the sheer cliff face.

Hart, Jacques, and their Nazi escort stepped aboard the elevator platform, which rapidly lifted them away from the valley floor. On the ascent, Hart felt somewhat queasy as the platform swayed in the high mountain winds, the rock face on one side and the plush green valley on the other. He did not know if the feeling came from his earlier blow to the head or from staring down at the village, which from the rising elevator looked like a set of tiny models. Hart had a dread of heights. It was a fear that he had had all his life, and one that had never diminished, despite the dozens of operational drops he had performed. The drops were different. He somewhat trusted parachutes. He did not necessarily trust German elevators. Throughout the ascent, the two SS sergeants had seemed unfazed by the height, staring at him beneath black polished helmets, their slung MP 40 submachine guns ready to riddle the prisoners at the first sign of resistance.

Once the elevator reached the immense flak tower, Hart got a chance to see how big it really was. Its walls were at least ten feet thick and probably could resist most aerial bombs unless struck from just the right trajectory. When the elevator finally came to a stop, one level below the platformlike roof, Hart helped Jacques step across the foot of open space from the elevator to the landing, beneath which was a five-hundred-foot drop. The sergeants then ushered them inside a steel door, but before passing through, Hart noticed a large red Nazi flag hanging from the AA platform above. The flag was immaculate, as was the dress of every regular *Luftwaffe* soldier they passed.

"You boys expecting someone special?" Hart asked.

The sergeants said nothing, but one shoved him in the back to hurry him along the corridor. After turning one corner and then another, they were met by an entourage of black-clad SS officers, in company with some *Luftwaffe* men, evidently of the local garrison. The group was proceeding along very formally, with every officer silent except for one *Luftwaffe* captain who seemed to not be able to say enough.

". . . we have added another reinforced steel section in the magazine, Herr Colonel, and our new internal ammunition lifts have increased our fire output by two hundred rounds per minute. Just last week, we shot down eight B-24s. The fire is most devastating to them."

The captain spoke nervously, and his speech was obviously prepared in advance. It was obvious that this was an inspection in progress and that the object of the captain's attentions was a slightly built SS colonel who walked with his head down and arms behind his back. The brim of the colonel's tall field hat hid his face from Hart, but Hart concluded that this colonel was the VIP the tower was dressed up for. Upon sighting their senior officer, the SS sergeants on either side of Hart promptly came to attention, and the sound of their heels clicking together made the colonel look up at them.

Even now, hours later, as Hart sat in one of the flak tower's prison cells, his head throbbing from the incessant barrage above, he felt a chill run through him at the memory of the SS colonel's face—or more appropriately, the mask over his face. The procession of officers had come to a halt while the colonel observed the sergeants and their prisoners in silence. He had seemed to stare at Hart through that cold and unfeeling mask for an interval that felt like minutes. And then, with a wave of his black-gloved hand, the colonel and his procession moved on.

Somehow Hart knew that that mask, with the searing blue eyes behind it, would haunt him to his grave.

Jacques was lying on his side in the corner getting some rest after traveling all night with his wounds untended. Hart had done his best to clean the wound and bandage the gash in the right side of Jacques's rib cage, where a bullet had torn through the flesh before emerging from the other side.

"How does it look, *monsieur*?" Jacques grunted when Hart checked the wound. "What's that awful smell?"

"It's fine. Don't worry." Hart smiled to hide the bleak prognosis. The wound was infected. Without proper medical care Jacques would be lucky to last another twenty-four hours. Hart had begged the Nazi sergeants for some fresh bandages, and they had given in only after much pleading. By the time Hart finished changing the bandage this time, Jacques had drifted to sleep. Hart placed a reassuring hand on his shoulder. "Don't worry, Jacques. We'll get you some medical attention."

"You do not want their medical attention," a voice said from the other side of the room, where there was another darkened prison cell, one that Hart had thought to be vacant until now.

Hart watched as a frail-looking man stumbled into the light near the bars. The man looked horrid. His hair was disheveled, he was shirtless, and there was blood caked on his lip and bruised face. Obviously, the man had sustained a beating recently, but even in his present state Hart knew that he had seen him before.

Hart was about to speak to him, but the door to the room opened and two people, a man and a woman, both dressed like the peasants Hart had seen in the village, entered with a cart upon which were stacked several bags of trash. These were added to the reeking pile of similar bags in the far corner of the room. Hart had deduced that this room, where the German garrison had its small prison, doubled as the tower's trash dump.

"Excuse me," Hart said in English, and then in German. "Excuse me. Could you help us, please?"

The two civilians ignored him. They did not even look in Hart's direction but continued to stack the trash bags into a giant heap.

"My friend is terribly injured," Hart pleaded. "Could you ask the commandant to send a physician? Please?"

Still no response. The peasants acted as though they were the only ones in the room as they finished unloading the cart.

"They will not help you," the man in the other cell said, bemused.

But Hart continued to plead, as the man and the woman opened a large trapdoor in the floor. The barrage had stopped again, and Hart could hear the whistle of the wind outside through the open trapdoor. So it led to the outside, but to where? For the next several minutes, the man and the burly woman lugged the trash bags to the opening in the floor and dropped the bags through the hole, one after another. Hart reckoned the fall to be a long one because he did not hear any of the bags landing. Hart concluded that the trapdoor was there to drop the trash to the valley below, in which case the drop would be nearly five hundred feet.

After finishing with the garbage, the two peasants left the room, never once looking back or yielding any indication that they had heard any of Hart's pleas.

"They are forbidden to speak to us," the man in the other cell said. "And I told you, you do not want their medical care."

Hart put his hands on the bars of his own cell where it faced the other man's cell across a few feet of open space.

"Who are they?" Hart asked.

"Civilians from the local village." The man spoke very good English but had a decided German accent. "The garrison here uses them for menial tasks."

"And who are you?" Hart asked, but he knew the answer already. The man's face had been on one of the photos in Hart's pre-mission briefing package—in the file on Sweden.

"I am Ulrich Adler."

"You're German?"

Adler did not respond but instead stared intently across the space between the two cells, as if he were struggling with the decision to let the conversation continue any further. "You are American," he finally said. It was more of a statement than a question, as if he had just discovered the answer to a riddle. "And your uniform tells me that you are not simply a downed pilot."

Hart glanced at the blood-spattered and battered naval uniform that he still wore. He then looked up at Adler to see that the German archaeologist had changed his demeanor entirely. His formerly weary face took on new life as he continued talking in an earnest whisper.

"You are OSS then?"

"No," Hart exclaimed. "I don't know what you're talking about."

Hart was not sure he could trust this man. After all, he knew from his mission files that Adler was the chief engineer in charge of the excavation at Östersund, Sweden—the same place where three OSS informants mysteriously disappeared. But if Adler was indeed on the Nazis' side, then why was he in custody, and why had he been beaten so?

"If you are not OSS, then why are you wearing that uniform?" Adler inquired, this time whispering.

"Why are you whispering?"

Adler pointed to the small hole in the ceiling, one that Hart had immediately identified after being brought here.

"They are listening to us," Adler whispered. "The place is bugged."

"Oh," Hart said, feigning ignorance, still wanting to portray himself as a downed airman. He lowered his own voice to a whisper. "Why are you here? What do they want with you?"

"You are here because you are a soldier. I am here because I am a scientist."

"Scientist of what? Rockets?"

Adler smiled. "No. Something far more important. I am an archaeologist. I am a scientist of the past, and the lessons left by our forebears. I am imprisoned here because I have seen the evil of this Reich firsthand. I am here because I have information that can stop it."

That made sense to Hart. The Nazis could preach ideology and patriotism all they wanted, but they could not strip away the conscience of their nation's intellectuals.

"So why were you brought all the way out here?"

Hart had hardly gotten the question out when the door to the room opened and a dozen men in black SS uniforms entered. There were no *Luftwaffe* men among them, but the two sergeants were in the entourage, along with the black-masked colonel. These were all SS goons, and Hart could sense the tension in the air created by their presence. A look of terror had overcome Adler's face, and he melted into the shadows of his own cell.

Most of the group of Nazis took up positions on the far side of the room, as if they were mere observers come to see a play acted out. Only the colonel approached the prison cells, the heels of his boots clicking on the concrete floor as he walked slowly to the space that separated the two cells. Hart thought he could hear Adler whimpering in the other cell, but the colonel completely ignored him and focused all of his attention on Hart. The colonel was just outside arm's reach, but close enough for Hart to see the piercing blue eyes that were studying him from behind the mask. Hart's immediate instinct was to back away from the bars, but he did not. He did not want to give this Nazi bastard the satisfaction.

The colonel observed him for at least a minute, as if Hart were a slave on the auction block. The silence was interrupted only by a sudden hacking cough that came from Jacques's huddled form. The colonel's eyes expressed annoyance at the disruption.

"He's wounded," Hart said. "He needs a doctor."

The colonel said nothing and simply stared back at Hart.

"Please, sir, could you send your physician to take a look at him?"

Again the colonel only stared back at him, and Hart was beginning to wonder if he understood English. But then the colonel suddenly raised a black-gloved hand and motioned with two fingers. Like two hounds summoned from their kennel, the two sergeants instantly stepped forward, producing a key to unlock the cell. One motioned for Hart to step back and then both entered the cell. Together, they hoisted the groaning Jacques between them and carried him out of the cell.

"Thank you, Colonel," Hart said in genuine appreciation, because it appeared that the colonel was going to grant his request. "Sir, your doctor may want to know that this man's wound is infected. Please order him to see this man immediately. There's not much time to . . ." Hart's words trailed off as he saw a tinge of amusement in the colonel's eyes. Hart then realized that the sergeants were not carrying Jacques toward the door, but rather toward the trash chute in the floor. The two sergeants chuckled as they unceremoniously dropped Jacques onto the floor beside the trapdoor and then proceeded to torment him. Both men kicked him several times until Jacques had assumed the fetal position. Then, while one sergeant hoisted open the trapdoor, the other pressed the heel of his size thirteen boot into the infected wound of the squirming Frenchman. Even from across the room Hart could see the fear in Jacques's eyes as the outside air from the open trapdoor whipped through his hair.

"No!" Hart shouted, reaching out through the bars in an attempt to grab the colonel. But the colonel simply stepped to one side and struck at Hart's arm with his eagle-tipped baton. He landed two blows that made Hart's arm scream with pain and forced Hart to step away from the bars.

The two sergeants again laughed as they kicked

Jacques in the ribs some more, inching him closer and closer to the trapdoor's edge. The Frenchman batted at their boots with a feeble hand, attempting to fight them off, but it was to no avail. Once he was close enough to the opening in the floor, both sergeants got down on their knees and rolled him over the edge like a sack of garbage. Jacques screamed as he disappeared from view, his voice instantly swallowed up by the whistling of the alpine wind.

One of the sergeants looked over the side and waved a hand after the falling man, shouting *"Auf Wiedersehen!"* through cupped hands. This produced a roar of laughter from the other goons.

Hart ran against the bars of his cell, shaking them with white-knuckled hands, enraged partly at the cold nature of the murder, but also at his own foolishness for believing that the colonel had ever intended to help.

"It is a two-hundred-meter drop," the colonel said finally, in a scratchy voice that was almost a whisper. "But I am told the village has an excellent doctor. Perhaps he can tend to your friend's injuries."

"You son of a bitch!" Hart snarled.

"Yes." The colonel nodded. "Yes, I am. But perhaps you have heard my other name. Good. I can see that you have."

"You are Sturm the murdering butcher," Hart said through gritted teeth.

"That is correct, Lieutenant Commander Hart of the OSS." Sturm paused, probably expecting Hart to be impressed, which he was. Not entirely surprised, but impressed. "Since you have heard of me, Mister Hart,

I will assume you also know my reputation. If not, I am sure that Herr Adler, here, will be glad to fill you in. Let us say that he and I have come to know each other much better in the past few days."

Adler remained in the shadows of his cell, and Hart thought he heard the beaten man talking to himself in repetitive phrases.

The colonel put his hands behind his back and began to pace up and down. "For the last several weeks, Commander Hart, you have been posing as the German naval lieutenant Helmut Rittenhaus aboard *U-2553*. You were sent there by the OSS to discover the cargo and its significance." Sturm then appeared to chuckle, but it sounded more like a cough. "It is most impressive, what you managed to accomplish. Dropping into Norway, assuming Rittenhaus's identity, playing the role of first officer, and maintaining your cover all throughout. You managed to fool every man on *U-2553*. Every man but one, that is. My man was on to you from the start, but I must admit, even I was amazed at the skillful way in which you eliminated Lieutenant Odeman. Of course, his loss will be felt by our organization, but personally I cannot say that I will miss him." Sturm came to a stop in front of Hart and tapped his eagle baton on the iron bars. "You see, I know quite a lot about Commander Matthew Hart of the OSS."

"I am an officer in the United States Navy," Hart said. "And I demand to be treated according to the laws of war." Hart did his best not to show any emotion that would confirm any of Sturm's postulations.

"You certainly had a chance to inspect the items my

unfortunate lieutenant was guarding, am I correct?" Sturm said. "I am going to assume this is the case, that you managed to copy the inscriptions from the artifacts— or at least those that you could decipher—and then you gave this information to the British agents you met with in Toulon."

"What British agents?" Hart said.

He was instantly knocked on the head by the eagle-tipped baton coming through the bars, and the blow put him on the floor, clutching his head in pain.

"That is what I am most interested in, Mister Hart." Sturm began running the baton along the bars again, speaking politely, in a casual manner, as if he had not just tried to crack Hart's head open. "I would like to know exactly what information you gave to these British agents, Commander."

So Esther and Jones must have gotten away, Hart thought to himself. Why else would Sturm want to know these things? That was, at the least, encouraging.

"You want to know what I found on your own arti-facts?" Hart finally said sarcastically.

"No!" Sturm raised his rough voice, slapping the baton into his gloved hand. "I do not give a *scheiss* what you found, or think you found, Mister Hart. You will never see the light of day again. What I want to know is precisely what you told the British."

"And why should I tell you? You've already implied that you're going to kill me."

"If you care to inspect the inner seam of your trou-sers, Mister Hart, you will find that your cyanide capsule is missing."

"I know that." Hart had noticed that the capsule was missing shortly after recovering from the grenade detonation, back in Toulon. Sturm's two sergeants must have removed it.

Sturm's mask shifted as if he were smiling underneath it. "I can assure you, Mister Hart, that should you refuse to cooperate, your departure from this life will be, shall we say"—he paused, as if searching for the words—"unbearably painful."

"You can go to hell."

"I have already been there, Mister Hart." Sturm tapped his mask with the eagle tip of his baton. "I have returned, but I assure you that you will not. Allow me, Commander, to introduce you to the men who will see you off." He motioned with two fingers again and the two sergeants stepped up front and center. "You have already met Sergeants Blücher and Friedrich, I believe. No doubt, you have already witnessed a few of their unique talents, but I assure you . . . what is it you Americans say? Ah, yes . . . You have not seen anything yet."

"So far, I've seen them push a defenseless, wounded man to his death," Hart said, trying to act as casual as he could. "Doesn't take much talent to do that."

"Believe me, Mister Hart, they have many other talents. They have ways of making a man beg for the final mercy of death. I have seen some of their victims linger for hours, sometimes days, in horrendous agony. Some were no longer men when they died, if you understand my meaning." Sturm paused as if to let Hart register that. "Now, I will ask you one final time. What information did you give to the British agents?"

Hart said nothing, and Sturm did not seem very surprised at that.

"As you wish, Commander," Sturm said with a sigh, and again he motioned with two fingers.

Hart watched as the two sergeants unbuttoned and removed their uniform blouses, revealing T-shirts and muscles. They removed Hart from the cell and tied him to a post in the center of the room. The other SS men began whispering among themselves as if to bet on how long Hart would last. Hart had been trained to withstand torture, but this was not an encouraging sign.

The first blows were to his gut with brass-knuckled fists. Hart had planned to pretend that the blows hurt much worse than they actually did, an old counter-torture technique meant to garner sympathy from the torturers, but no acting was necessary in this instance. The blows were solid and succeeded in doubling him over time after time, leaving him fighting for breath. The next series of blows were to his face. He felt an open cut on his cheek and tasted blood in his mouth mingling around a dislodged tooth.

Hart knew what he had to do. He was only hoping he could maintain his senses long enough to do it. He had to take a beating and then give in with some information, just a little, but enough to leave Sturm wanting more—enough for Sturm to want to keep him around a little bit longer.

After several more blows to his face, abdomen, and groin, Hart looked up through swollen eyes to see Sturm standing before him.

"Shall I order them to continue, Mister Hart?"

Hart's mouth and face were pulsating with every beat of his heart. He felt like throwing up from the repeated blows to his stomach. Between coughs Hart managed to mutter, "They have the paper."

"And what does that mean?"

"The paper that I used to copy down the inscriptions," Hart labored to utter. "The Brits have it."

"What were the inscriptions you copied, Commander?" Sturm prompted.

Hart struggled to hold his head up to look into Sturm's eyes. "You'll have to keep me alive if you want to know that."

"It is a pity, Mister Hart," Sturm said in his high-pitched, gravelly voice, "that you think me such a fool."

Sturm motioned with his fingers again, and, through dim eyes, Hart saw the two sergeants retrieve their SS daggers from their discarded belts. The glimmering ceremonial blades were devilish-looking things. The short stubby knives looked smaller in the large hands of the sergeants, but no less deadly. The sergeants were grinning with delight, as if cutting up Hart were the final special treat they had been waiting for. Undoubtedly, the sergeants would now carve him up in the slowest, most excruciating fashion, maximizing the pain while preserving his senses.

But Hart would never let that happen. Sturm had not bought his ploy, so there was only one thing left to do.

He had managed to stay pressed close up to the post in an effort to deceive the sergeants as to the amount of play he had in his bindings. He knew he could thrust forward at least six to ten inches. He was counting on that being enough to thrust himself onto one of the exposed blades, self-inflicting a fatal blow that would serve the function of his missing L-pill. Regardless of whether he was now serving a rogue spy agency, it was his duty to kill himself before divulging any information that might harm the Allied war effort, and he was afraid of what he might say under sodium pentothal after several hours of torture.

As the sergeants approached him with blades exposed, Hart strengthened his resolve to carry out his intentions. But before the sergeants reached him, an alarm sounded in the room. The alarm was resounding in the hall outside the room as well, and throughout the entire fortress. A moment later, a *Luftwaffe* officer poked his head in the room.

"Forgive the intrusion, Colonel," he said nervously, "but the American bombers are on the return leg. They will be overhead in three minutes."

"So order your captain to shoot them down, Lieutenant," Sturm said sternly. "Bombers returning to their airfields do not concern me."

"Forgive me, again, Herr Colonel, but sometimes they still have bombs left over and try to drop them on us as they pass overhead. This room is on the north side of the tower and is not ideally suited for a shelter. If you and your officers will come with me, I will escort you to a much safer location to ride out the bombing."

"Scheiss!" Sturm exclaimed, and appeared to be very upset at the unforeseen circumstances. Eventually, he nodded his masked head in acquiescence and motioned for his men to follow the lieutenant.

"What about him, sir?" one of the sergeants asked, thumbing a finger at Hart.

Sturm seemed to consider for a long moment before finally ordering, "Put him back in his cell. I will decide how to deal with him later."

In a violent fashion Hart was unbound, dragged across the room, and thrown into his cell before the Nazis all left the room. As he tried to get his bearings Hart heard the drone of the bombers overhead. Moments later, the 128-millimeter AA guns once again commenced a deafening barrage, shaking the cold concrete floor against his swollen cheek. He did not move. He was tired, so very tired. His head throbbed and he felt like he was spinning, about to lose consciousness.

"Are you all right, Mister Hart?" he heard a feeble voice say. It was Adler's. Now that the Nazis were gone, the German scientist was again ready to venture to the bars of his cell. Hart did not have the energy to respond to him.

"Is it true what they said about you?" Adler said, his voice agitated but eager. "Have you seen the artifacts? Mister Hart? Mister Hart?"

Adler continued calling his name amid the noise of the raging air battle outside, even after Hart had lost all consciousness.

CHAPTER THIRTY

Cartagena, Spain
1942

"But you can't go alone," Hart had said to her. "It's too dangerous."

She had tossed her blond locks to one side, flashing him one of those heart-melting smiles before resting her chin on his bare chest. She used her finger to draw circles in the hair on his chest and then made a face at him. "But I have to go, silly. That was the plan."

He ran his hands from her bare hips all the way up her spine to her neck and back down again. Her skin was silky smooth, like a flawless sculpture. It aroused him now as it had so many times over the last few hours as they had made love, lost in each other's arms and in exhilaration over the success of their mission.

She began to pull away, to get up, but he pulled her back to him. Although he was quite exhausted from the uninhibited night of sex with this goddess he worshipped, he was fully ready to stay in bed all day and celebrate some more.

"We can't stay here forever, you know," she said chidingly, her hand moving down his stomach to firmly grasp him. "The dons wouldn't like to find a bunch of American spies on their soil, now would they?"

"Who cares what the dons think?" he said dismissively. "Everyone knows which way they lean. Neutral my ass."

Isabelle chuckled, reaching for a glass of wine on the nightstand, which she offered to him before drinking the last of its stale spirits.

It had been three days since Hart's team had entered Spain from occupied France. They had escaped from the German authorities and had made it over the Pyrenees only to find themselves dogged by the so-called neutral Spanish police on the other side. But the Guardia Civil was not the Gestapo, and Hart's team had little trouble evading them and making their way to Cartagena undetected, where they had arrived only the night before. Everything had gone according to plan, and now that safety seemed just a boat ride away, Hart and Isabelle were finally taking a moment for themselves, just one moment in this heart-rending, endless war. Last night, they had unleashed the passion they felt for each other—a passion that had been held in reserve all the while they were undercover in France. They had made love, and they had celebrated.

And why not? Hart thought. Risks had been taken. Lives had been saved. They deserved to celebrate for a few hours before returning to the war and the next mission old McDonough had on his plate.

"I want to stay like this forever," Hart said to her as he stroked her hair.

"We're not on holiday, love. This is not our own personal vacation, you know. We're here for extraction." She giggled, squeezing him with her hand, and then added, "Not for insertion."

He rolled her over in bed so that now she was on her back, nestled in the crook of his arm. He looked down into her eyes and said, "I thought I was the one who could never mix business with pleasure. Now it's you who's all business."

"Not *all* business," she said, lifting her face to gently kiss his lips.

He kissed her back, moving to her cheek, neck, and collarbone. "Are you sure we can't wait a little bit longer?" he mumbled between kisses.

"Come on, mission commander," she said mockingly. "You know the schedule. I have to meet with our contact down at the harbor in less than an hour. You don't want him to leave us here, do you?"

"Why don't I go instead?" he said, his face suddenly serious.

"Don't be silly, Matt. Our contact will be looking for a woman." She paused and grabbed him once again. "And you definitely don't fit the bill."

They laughed together and embraced.

"Besides," she said after a few moments in his arms, "you have to go check on the boys. Poor guys have been penned up in that warehouse all night while we've had fun. You could have at least let them get a hotel room, too."

"It'd have been too suspicious," Hart replied. "Three young men speaking Spanish with a bad accent. That'd get locals talking and bring the Guardia Civil down on us like a squadron of Hussars."

"Doesn't it make you feel the least bit guilty?"

"Not particularly," Hart said with a laugh. "Commanding officer's privilege. Besides, how could they blame me? They know about *us*, of course."

He helped her get ready, dressing her with periodic kisses and gentle squeezes of her breasts. She was beautiful, in all ways. Every curve, every gesture, every thought in her head, everything she said. He cherished all of it.

She placed her Colt M1903 pistol inside her purse and donned a half-veiled hat. She would fit right in with the *señoritas* taking lunch near the pier. After studying her once more, Hart was suddenly jealous of their transportation contact, a man who simply went by Carlos, who would be enjoying her company for lunch.

At the door, they kissed long and passionately.

"Be careful," he said.

"Don't worry about me, love. Now go and put some clothes on, and get over to see the fellas before they decide you're not coming." She winked and gave him a final peck on the cheek with lipstick-glossed lips. "I'll see you later."

He laughed, realizing that he was standing in the hotel room doorway, still stark naked. She giggled at his expression, waved, and then quickly pranced off down the walk, Hart watching her curvy figure until she was well out of sight.

It was the last time he ever saw her.

CHAPTER THIRTY-ONE

"Mister Hart." Adler's voice rang in Hart's ears as he awoke from a deep sleep, a torturous sleep, a sleep that seemed to have lasted an age but at the same time had offered him little rest.

"Mister Hart," Adler said again. "Are you all right?"

"What time is it?" Hart mumbled. His body ached all over, and he could feel a distinct swelling on the side of his face where one of the SS sergeants had landed a solid blow with brass knuckles.

"It is morning," Adler answered. "I am not certain of the time."

Hart rolled over on the floor of his cell and saw Adler looking back at him from his own cell. "Have they returned yet?"

"No. That makes two days since we have last seen them."

"Two days? You mean I've been out that long?"

"I would not call it out exactly," Adler said, looking somewhat uncomfortable. "You have been tossing and turning in that time, sometimes half-awake and shivering, sometimes mumbling, sometimes unwakable. I have been most concerned about you. How do you feel?"

"I'll live."

"Good, Mister Hart. I am very relieved to hear that. It seems our captors lost interest in you."

"Either that or they're waiting for me to recover so they can torture me all over again. There comes a point when you're torturing someone that you have to let your victim start to care about life again."

Adler gave him an astonished look.

Hart smiled, even though it hurt to. "I'm speaking from experience, Doctor."

"I see." Adler paused, and then added in a whisper, "Is it true what they said about you? That you are OSS?"

Hart glanced up at the listening device in the ceiling, meaning to remind Adler that someone was probably listening, and then he finally nodded.

"Then you must get me out of here, Mister Hart!" Adler said agitatedly, appearing somewhat invigorated from learning Hart's identity. "I have information, valuable information, information that can be most helpful to the Allies. Colonel Sturm knows this. He has tried to pull this information from me on many occasions, but he has failed."

"You stood up to torture?" Hart said skeptically. Adler more resembled a timid choirboy than a soldier. Hart could not imagine him standing up to Sturm's intimidation, much less that of the colonel's sergeants.

"My body may be lithe and pathetic, Mister Hart, but my mind is strong. It is stronger than theirs . . . It is stronger than theirs." Adler repeated the phrase several times, as if it were the one thought he had focused on to see him through the ordeal of torture.

"It looks like we got the bad end of the bargain," Hart said, rubbing his throbbing jaw.

"If you have been aboard the U-boat with my artifacts, as Sturm said, and if you inspected them, as Sturm said you did, then I am sure you know what they want from me."

"Your artifacts?"

"I was the one who excavated them. I found them in a grave in northern Sweden."

"So that's what the Nazis were using you for?" Hart asked, knowing full well what Adler had been up to in Sweden. "To find those trinkets for them?"

Adler nodded but seemed to smart a little at Hart's debasement of the priceless objects. "You have seen them, then?" Adler asked, like a brokenhearted lover inquiring about his lost love.

"They were very impressive," Hart said, somewhat truthfully, somewhat to make up for his previous insult. "I'm certainly no expert, but I found it to be a curious collection. I did not expect to see ancient Egyptian script and pottery mixed with medieval items—Byzantine in origin, weren't they? I saw that some bore the inscription of Constantine, if I'm not mistaken."

An admiring smile crossed Adler's face, and Hart could tell that he was impressed. That was bad. Pretend to be too knowledgeable in the subject and Adler would clam up.

"Now listen, Doctor." Hart chuckled casually. "I'm no expert. I'm just a guy with a good memory. I took a crash course on medieval archaeology and symbology just before I started on this mission."

"And what have you concluded from your inspection of the artifacts?" Adler asked intently.

"Nothing. Absolutely nothing. Like I said, I'm no expert."

"Do you know who Constantine was?"

"Sure. I took a Roman history class in college. He was a Roman emperor, right? The one who converted the empire to Christianity."

"Yes and no, Mister Hart."

"And what is that supposed to mean?"

"Indeed, Mister Hart." Adler smiled somewhat smugly. "That is the mystery, is it not?"

"And the link between the Egyptian and the Byzantine items, both found in a medieval Swedish grave, that is the information Sturm is trying to get from you?"

"Heavens, no! Sturm knows the origin of the artifacts. He is the one who commissioned me to dig there in the first place. He knew exactly what I would find there."

Hart was suddenly puzzled. "Then I don't understand why—"

"I will tell you everything you need to know," Adler interrupted, "but first you must do something for me. You must get me out of this place, and you must find a way to get me to Istanbul."

Hart started to laugh but stopped short from a pain in his side where the SS man had rearranged his ribs. "I'm not sure if you've noticed, Doctor, but we're both locked in prison cells at the moment. And from my inspection earlier, these cells are completely escape-proof. Not to mention, we're in a German flak tower, six hundred feet in the air. I've been beaten to a pulp and don't even have a cyanide capsule, much less a weapon. Besides, anything I come up with, the Nazi bastard on the other end of that bug is going to hear it and have a bunch of storm troopers in here before we can say boo."

"I can assure you, Mister Hart, that your superiors will be most pleased with what I have for them, but you must first get me to Istanbul."

"Doctor," Hart said, somewhat irritated. "Have you been listening to a word I've been saying? We can't escape from here."

"I am an archaeologist," Adler said distantly. "A damn good one, as you say in America. Before the war, I was a rising star in my circle. There was nothing I could not accomplish. If you commissioned me to find the lost tomb of Antony and Cleopatra, I would do it, no matter how impossible it might seem. You are a spy, Mister Hart, a man of action and a master of espionage. But are you a good one?"

Hart felt the knife stab into his ego. "Well, yes, but—"

"Then get us out of here, Hart. Get us out of here, now. Millions of lives depend on it."

Hart nodded, suddenly considering that perhaps he was not a good spy after all. Here he was in the clutches of the enemy, so close to the objective of his mission, but unable to act. He looked around the cell and the room. There was nothing within reach that he might use to pry open the bars. The lock pick that every operative carried sewn into his sleeve was missing, just like his L-pill. His captors knew all of the tricks. He had to think of something, and fast. He and Adler had been whispering, but certainly the Nazi on the other end of the bugging device had heard something. Hart expected Sturm and his men to return at any moment and his interrogation to resume. He was quite certain he would not leave the next interrogation without disabling injuries, or worse.

Just then, the door to the room opened, and Hart breathed a sigh of relief when two peasants entered toting the same trash cart Hart had seen before. The cart was the same, but these were not the same two villagers that had dumped the trash two days ago. Both of these civilians were middle-aged men, one taller than the other. They both were hunched over, graying, and wearing dingy jackets and caps. Like the two peasants from the other day, these men completely ignored Hart and Adler and went about their business, stacking the dozen or more bags of trash near the chute in the floor.

Hart suddenly got the idea that perhaps these men would respond differently from the previous pair. It was worth a try, and what other option did he have?

"Gentlemen," Hart called in German.

The men continued what they were doing, not acknowledging him in the least.

"Please, gentlemen," Hart continued. "Do you have any food? Both of us are starving." Hart tried to sound as pathetic as he could. If he could coax one of the men into coming near the bars, within arm's reach, Hart could easily overpower him and then threaten the other one to do what he was told if he wanted his friend to live.

"Please, gentlemen, show us some mercy. They are beating us. Please, help us."

Hart knew that these peasants were probably instructed not to interact with the prisoners. That was why he was surprised when both men stopped stacking trash and began mumbling to each other. They both looked around the room, and then the shorter of the two began to approach Hart's cell.

"God bless you, sir," Hart said, watching the man's every step, thankful that it was the shorter one approaching. He would be easier to overpower than would the taller man. Hart took a firm hold of an iron bar with one hand, and prepared to lunge out with the other. The man was just about to come within arm's reach when he abruptly stopped just short. Hart was confused, then studied the man more closely, from his mud-spattered shoes up to his cherry-red face beneath the low-worn cap—a face that was now grinning from ear to ear.

"The trouble with you Yanks is," the man said in a decided English accent, "you never know when to shut up."

In his mind's eye, Hart removed the dingy cap and the bushy gray sideburns, eyebrows, and mustache, and found that he was looking directly into the smiling face of Lord Holmhurst.

CHAPTER THIRTY-TWO

"What the hell are you doing here?" Hart asked as Holmhurst used a key to unlock the cell.

"I should think that was obvious, old boy," Holmhurst replied. "Admiral McDonough sends his compliments."

"McDonough?" Hart said in disbelief. "I don't understand."

"Don't really have time to discuss it now, old boy. We have only a few minutes." Holmhurst gestured at the larger man, who was obviously also in disguise. "Hart, please allow me to introduce my right-hand man. This is Patrick. He's been with me since as long as I can remember."

"Hallo," the big man said with a crooked-toothed grin. He then opened one of the trash bags, producing the uniform of a *Luftwaffe* corporal.

"You can trust him, Hart," Holmhurst added, "as you trust me."

Hart glanced at Holmhurst skeptically. "Are you serious?"

"Now is that any way to treat someone who has risked life and limb to save your stiff-necked carcass?" Holmhurst took the German uniform from Patrick and handed it to Hart. "We have to hurry, so I'll help you put this on, but don't expect our relationship to go any further, old boy."

"Wait a minute, Holmhurst," Hart interjected. Rightfully, he was suspicious of these two English criminals who had appeared seemingly out of thin air. "Just who the hell are you working for? What is this all about?"

"Listen, Hart, I'd love to sit here and explain it all over a cup of tea, but we're a bit pressed for time right now." Holmhurst then helped him get into the uniform.

"What about him?" Patrick said, jerking a thumb toward Adler, still locked in his cell.

Adler stared at Hart with pleading eyes. "Please, Mister Hart."

"We need him, too," Hart said, wincing as he pulled on the *Luftwaffe* jacket. "Release him."

"Now, just a minute, Hart. Patrick and I are here to rescue you, not to take orders from you, and I was never told anything about this gentleman. We came for you, and you alone."

"He comes with us, Holmhurst!" Hart said emphatically. "It does no good to spring me unless you spring him, too. We may need him."

"Suit yourself, Yank." Holmhurst shrugged. "Get him out of there, Patrick. We don't have a uniform for him, but maybe you can stick him in one of those trash bags. He's small enough. Maybe the Jerries will buy it."

"And if they don't?" Patrick asked.

"Ask Hart. He seems to think he's in charge."

"Shit!" Hart suddenly exclaimed. In the hustle of the moment, he had forgotten all about the listening device in the ceiling. He quickly got Holmhurst's attention and pointed at the hole concealing the device.

"What, the bug?" Holmhurst said loudly. "Don't worry about that, old boy. There's nothing but a dead Jerry on the other end of that line. Our partner has seen to that."

"Your partner? You mean there are more of you?"

"That's right, Yank. And if we don't get moving, we'll miss our rendezvous. Now let's go!"

"You will be careful with me, won't you?" Adler asked as he wriggled his thin form into an empty bag inside the cart.

"Careful as you like," Patrick answered succinctly, shoving Adler's head down into the bag and pulling the drawstring tight to seal the nervous scientist inside. "Now keep your trap shut until we say it's okay!"

The group then approached the door to the room, with Patrick pushing the cart that contained Adler. Holmhurst and Patrick resumed their peasant appearance, and Hart was now dressed like an unshaven German airman who had been in a barroom brawl the night before.

"Won't there be a guard on the other side?" Hart asked cautiously, a bit concerned that these amateurs had not considered all contingencies.

"Patrick took care of him," Holmhurst replied, pointing to one of the discarded trash bags on the floor, one that had a large misshapen object in it and a large dark red stain seeping through to the outside.

They left the room through the door and entered the main passage. The passage was not as busy as Hart had expected, but Hart still made sure that he walked behind Patrick so that the big man would hide his unfamiliar face from the garrison men. They encountered only two low-ranking *Luftwaffe* men, neither one giving them so much as a second glance. This was the bottom floor of the tower and obviously contained storerooms, generators, and other infrequently inhabited rooms, so the foot traffic would be light.

They turned down one passage, then another, and finally reached a service elevator.

"Well, so far so good," Hart said, as they rode the elevator up.

"That was nothing," Holmhurst said. "The real challenge will be on the main level, where the landing is for the lift that will take us down to the valley floor. The main level is crowded and the Jerries guard the lift like mastiffs. But in your condition, it's the only way in or out of this place."

"So what's your plan?"

Holmhurst glanced at him with a grin. "I'll let you know when it comes to me, old boy. Every situation is different. I like to improvise. Besides, the bastards didn't challenge us on the way up. Why should they on the way down?"

"Because now you're taking a bunch of trash bags down the lift instead of tossing them down the trash chute," Hart said impatiently. "A bit suspicious, don't you think?"

"It was your idea to bring that Jerry with us." Holmhurst poked a finger into the bag containing Adler, invoking a yelp from the scientist. "So don't blame me, old boy."

The elevator reached the main level and they all fell silent once again. This level had much more activity than the last. They walked down the passage in the same order as before, with Holmhurst in the lead, Patrick pushing the cart behind him, and Hart close on Patrick's heels. Hart could see barracks rooms with doors open on either side of the passage. Inside each room he saw *Luftwaffe* men lounging, cavorting, and joking, as one would see in any army barracks. Once past the barracks rooms, the procession passed a large set of double doors on the right. These doors were propped open, too, and Hart could see a great mess hall inside, where dozens of airmen enjoying their breakfasts were crowded around long tables.

So far, no one had even looked twice at the two peasants with the cart, and Hart concluded that civilian workers must be a common sight in the tower. They had almost passed by the mess hall when they were suddenly stopped by a *Luftwaffe* sergeant.

"You!" the sergeant said forcefully in German. "Stop where you are!"

Hart had the brim to his uniform cap pulled down, but he raised it to sneak a peek at the sergeant who now was approaching them. The sergeant stopped in front of Holmhurst.

"Yes, sir?" Holmhurst replied meekly in German.

The sergeant looked past Holmhurst, his eyes examining the cart. One of Patrick's hands was hidden partially by an empty trash bag draped across the side of the cart. From Hart's vantage point, he could see that the big man's hand was clutching a black metal object underneath. It was a gun of some kind, entirely concealed from the sergeant, but pointed directly at him. Hart knew that if the sergeant took one step toward the cart, Patrick would be forced to shoot him, and total mayhem would ensue. They would have to fight their way out amid a horde of startled soldiers, and the prospect of doing that successfully was very slim.

"You," the sergeant said again to Holmhurst. "You have more room on your cart. Empty those cans."

The sergeant pointed to several large cans just inside the mess hall where soldiers who were finished eating scraped off their plates.

Holmhurst smiled obediently. "Yes, sir."

Hart saw Patrick loosen his grip on the weapon, and then they all waited patiently as Holmhurst retrieved the dripping, loathsome bags from each one of the cans and tossed the reeking bundles into the cart, right on top of the bag containing Adler.

"Are you escorting them?" The sergeant directed his attention at Hart, the sergeant's face registering that he did not recognize Hart.

"Yes, Sergeant," Hart answered in the best German he could muster.

The sergeant appeared somewhat confused and looked as though he was about to question Hart further, but his thoughts were interrupted by Holmhurst, who suddenly appeared at his side wiping his hands on a towel.

"That is all of them, sir. Will there be anything else?"

The sergeant shook his head and then went back to the mess hall without so much as a thank-you.

Hart breathed a sigh of relief, as did all of them, before continuing down the passage. Another turn led them down a passageway that ended at a series of steel blast doors. These doors were propped open to let in the fresh outside air, and once the group passed through them, they were met with a stiff alpine breeze and a blinding sun. They were now outside the tower, on the landing, and looking down into the plush, green valley six hundred feet below.

Hart could see that the lift was currently up at the top level—the platform containing the 128-millimeter guns—and so he and the rest of the group casually waited. Two *Luftwaffe* privates were also waiting for the lift. They each cast curious glances at Hart but did not care enough to inquire as to who he was. They continued their conversation, leaning against the guardrail and smoking cigarettes. Both men were unarmed and had every appearance of soldiers on their way to a few hours' liberty in the village. They were probably too low in rank to care who he was, but Hart made sure he waited on the opposite side of the landing, so as to not get drawn into a conversation with them.

Hart peered over the edge of the platform and looked down the sharp cliff at the valley floor below. He could see a few fresh craters in the green foliage at the base of the cliff, no doubt left there by the bomb attack of a few nights ago. From all appearances the flak tower had suffered no damage.

The dangling steel cables jiggled, and Hart looked up to see that the lift was now descending to their level. He glanced at Holmhurst and Patrick, standing only a few feet away. This was it. A quick ride down on the lift and they would make their escape. Once in the village, they could easily disappear. Hart was contemplating the grilling he would later give Holmhurst when the lift finally reached the landing and Hart found himself face-to-face with two fully armed soldiers who were evidently riding the lift as guards.

When the lift finally came to a stop, the two airmen presented liberty cards to the guards and were permitted to step aboard. Likewise, Holmhurst and Patrick were allowed on with the trash cart, the guards not even challenging them and apparently unconcerned that the two civilians were using the lift to ferry trash. This was probably because both guards were focusing their attention on Hart. From their expressions, it was apparent that their suspicions were aroused, either because they did not recognize him or because his face looked like a punching bag.

Hart cursed inwardly. What was he to say to them? He had no liberty pass, and certainly no viable reason for leaving the tower. They would question him, and then what? He suddenly wanted to wring Holmhurst's neck for not planning this better.

"Stop!" One of the guards challenged him as he moved to step aboard. "Pass, please."

"I am escorting these men," Hart said. He had no choice but to look up from beneath the brim of his cap and reveal his face to the guard. He saw the horrid state of his swollen jaw and eyes register on the guard's face. But what had initially been an expression of shock and surprise quickly turned into suspicion. The guard immediately brought his rifle around but was at the same moment distracted by Holmhurst's finger tapping on his shoulder.

"Did I mention that this gentleman is with us?" Holmhurst said in the king's English.

The guard turned around, momentarily confused, but long enough for Hart to take advantage of the opportunity. While the guard was turned toward Holmhurst, Hart wrapped an arm around his neck in one fluid movement, placing him in a choke hold. Seeing his comrade in trouble, the other guard advanced, intent on smashing Hart's head with the butt of his rifle, but the rattle of a machine gun suddenly rang out, echoing off the cliff walls. The advancing guard spun around, shrouded by a red mist as bullet after bullet passed through his body at near point-blank range. Patrick now held the MP 40 submachine gun in clear view and continued firing until the riddled guard fell over the side. With one guard falling to the valley floor, Hart wrestled the other guard around so that he was facing Holmhurst. Hart expected Holmhurst to quickly dispatch him, but the Englishman just stood there as if he was baffled as to what to do next.

"Kill him!" Hart shouted.

But Holmhurst did nothing more than knock the

rifle out of the struggling guard's hands. The weapon bounced once on the steel grating but did not fall over the side. Patrick quickly turned his gun on the two airmen, but the gun jammed. Before Patrick could get a new magazine loaded, the airmen were rushing him. Hand-to-hand combat was definitely not their strength, because they came at Patrick one at a time, allowing him to knock each one back by swinging his gun like a bat.

The two airmen regrouped, and Hart saw them look at each other in the realization that they must charge together in order to overpower Patrick. Hart had only moments to act. Holmhurst was standing there, useless as Adler, who was still cowering inside the trash cart. Patrick was still fumbling with the weapon, but it appeared the *Luftwaffe* men would be on him by the time he was ready to fire. Hart had no choice. He did not want to let the guard go. He was not in a good enough position to break the man's neck, but he was in a position to steer him in any direction he wanted. With one final squeeze to the guard's neck, a squeeze that made him struggle to get Hart's arm loose, Hart thrust him forward, sending the guard careening across the lift and into the two onrushing airmen. The three Germans fell back against the guardrail but quickly regained their balance. The guard produced a ten-inch bayonet from a sheath in his boot and brandished the weapon with an evil grin. But his grin quickly faded and all three Germans froze when a click from Patrick's MP 40 indicated that the big Englishman had successfully loaded the new magazine and chambered a round.

The guard dropped the knife and the three Germans raised their hands in surrender.

"Good show, Patrick," Holmhurst said, stepping forward to address the Germans. "Now, gentlemen, if you will place your hands on your heads—"

Holmhurst was cut off by the loud report of the MP 40 as Patrick discharged a full magazine into the three Germans. The point-blank shots knocked all three Germans backward and over the rail. At least one was still alive when he went over the rail because his screams filled the echoing valley for the entire duration of the six-hundred-foot drop, falling silent only when he and his comrades were smashed on the rocks below.

"Bloody Nazi bastards!" Patrick said, staring over the side after them. He then turned to Holmhurst, who was staring at him with displeasure, and said, "Sorry, boss."

Hart did not understand this at all. As brutal as it was, Hart knew that Patrick's solution was the only one that made sense. There was no way they could make their escape while watching three prisoners. But then an alarm rang out in the tower, and Hart could hear voices in the passage rapidly approaching the tower's exit. Several heads were now poking over the sides of the AA platform above. Hart suddenly realized the logic of Holmhurst's intentions. It might have been a good idea to use those three Germans as human shields.

Hart picked up the rifle from the lift's floor and fired off several rounds to drive back the heads peering over the platform's edge. That would buy them a few seconds.

"Get this thing moving!" he said to Patrick urgently.

But the big man was intently watching the tower's exit, where troops would no doubt appear any second. Suddenly Patrick leaped onto the landing and darted for the big double blast doors, evidently to shut and bolt them. Hart thought it a good idea, and so he waited patiently for him to return, all the while keeping an eye out for Germans on the platform above them.

"Why the hell didn't you kill that guard when I gave you the chance?" Hart asked Holmhurst as they waited.

"Not my style," Holmhurst said as he grabbed the boxlike lift control pad that was connected to the winch assembly above by a long cable and had buttons for up and down. "I have a personal rule against killing my fellow man."

"So you let Patrick do it for you? That's absurd."

"To each his own, Hart. And just between you and me, sometimes I think Patrick rather enjoys it." Holmhurst then looked past Hart at Patrick on the landing. "Bloody hell, what's he doing now?"

Hart turned to see that Patrick had closed the blast doors and had used a nearby broom in the door handles to hold them shut. Of course, that would not hold very long if a half-dozen men were pushing from the other side, so now Patrick was working on his backup plan. He intricately placed two grenades at the base of each of the double doors, pulling the pins on both and situating the deadly devices such that the doors were holding the striker lever in place. The grenades would arm the moment the doors were forced open, giving the first Germans to exit the tower a real surprise.

"Come on, you fool!" Holmhurst shouted.

Patrick had completed his task, just as the doors began to be forced from the other side. There were lots of German voices on the other side, and they all must have been pushing because the broom handle began to splinter almost immediately. By that time, Patrick had made it back onto the lift, and Holmhurst had activated the winch to start the descent to the valley floor.

A head appeared above them, looking over the edge of the AA platform. Hart fired the rifle at it and heard a *"Scheiss!"* as the German above drew back to avoid being hit.

"What is going on?" Adler's muffled voice came from the cart.

"Don't worry about it," Patrick said, after letting off a burst from his MP 40 at another group of heads that appeared on the platform above.

The lift was descending rapidly, but to Hart it seemed like a snail's pace. The small rectangular lift was wide open with no roof and therefore offered them no protection. Any soldier with a rifle could lean over the edge of the landing or platform above and get a clear shot at them. Hart assumed that the only reason they were not under fire at this very moment was that the men of the garrison were normally unarmed, since a man did not need to carry a weapon if his sole purpose was to service a 128-millimeter gun. It would take them at least a few minutes to get to the armory and issue weapons. Then there were the two SS sergeants, who always seemed to be armed. Hart fully expected to see one of their faces appear above, along with the muzzle of an MP 40 submachine gun.

Kabamm! Kabamm!

Two explosions thundered overhead, indicating that the Germans had broken through the blast doors and set off Patrick's grenades. That would slow the others down as they picked through the now killed and maimed who had passed through the door first.

At that moment, the elevator came to an abrupt stop. Hart looked up at the winch, just visible through a hole in the bottom of the AA platform. "They've engaged the override!" he announced. "What now?"

Hart did not get an answer. He looked to see that Holmhurst and Patrick were busy unpacking some of the other bags in the cart. And Hart was surprised to see that these had contained several lengths of climbing rope. Holmhurst and Patrick tied one end of each rope to the platform and threw the slack over the side.

"I sincerely hope you're not afraid of heights," Holmhurst said as he now helped Adler out of the trash bag and began fitting him with a rappelling belt. "Ever gone down a rope before?"

"Once," Adler replied, his eyes wide with terror at what Holmhurst was implying. "On a dig in Egypt."

"First class! Then you know there's nothing to it. Just put this hand behind you, keep hold of the rope, and squeeze to brake. Now, out you go." With no more warning, Holmhurst pushed Adler out over the side, and the scientist disappeared from view.

Adler screamed briefly at the initial shock but then

apparently remembered what to do, because he had the wherewithal to yell back that he was upside down and going nowhere.

"Don't wrap your legs, you bloody fool!" Holmhurst called after him, then, apparently satisfied that the doctor would make it, turned to Hart. "I suppose you've done this before."

Hart nodded, deciding not to mention his fear of heights.

"I know you're injured, Hart," Holmhurst said, this time in a more nurturing tone. "Can you make it by yourself?"

"Don't worry about me."

"Good." Holmhurst smiled. "Here's a belt. I'll let you help yourself over the side. Come on, Patrick."

With that, Patrick slung his weapon and joined Holmhurst, and the two Englishmen descended on two other lines. Hart latched onto the remaining cord. His ribs ached at every exertion, but he ignored the pain, threw his legs over the rail, and pushed off. He found that braking hurt, so he did it as little as possible, rapidly descending the line and passing Adler, who was struggling foot by foot down his own rope. Hart stopped long enough to coach the inexperienced scientist back into the proper form to get him moving again.

They were dropping fast now, braking only when they reached dangerous descent speeds. Adler was far behind the rest, far enough that Hart could do little to help him. To make matters worse, the Germans had evidently managed to hot-wire the winch circuitry, because the lift started to ascend. Now they were rappelling down an ascending rope. Hart only hoped Holmhurst and Patrick had packed long enough rope.

A few shots rang out overhead. Hart looked up, but the lift was hiding the shooters from view, and likewise it was hiding Hart and the others from the shooters. Hart could hear the bullets clanging off the steel lift above him like hail on a tin roof.

"They're trying to shoot our ropes!" Hart called to the others. "Hurry! Adler, hurry up!"

Shots zipped past Hart and thudded into the earth below. Holmhurst and Patrick reached the ground at the same time. Hart followed a few seconds later. But Adler was still far behind.

Hart glanced at the slack of Adler's rope lying in a clump on the ground. There were about seventy or eighty feet of slack, but the slack was quickly being taken up by the rising lift. At Adler's current rate of descent the rope's end would be several feet above the ground before he ever reached it. There was only one choice. Hart quickly grabbed the end of Adler's rope.

"Adler!" Hart shouted up at the scientist. "Let go with your braking hand!"

Adler froze fifty feet above him, obviously hesitant about letting himself fall.

"Adler!" Hart yelled again, this time with more vigor. "Do it or you're a dead man!"

There was a pause while Adler summoned the courage to obey. Then Hart saw Adler close his eyes and open his braking hand. His spindly form instantly dropped down the rope, but Hart had the bitter end of the rope firmly in his hands and was already running as fast as he could away from the spot beneath Adler. This was done not to get out of the way of the falling man, but to create an angle in the rope, a slope that slowed Adler's descent just enough so that when he finally hit the ground—and Hart—the impact was only painful, not fatal. No sooner had the two fallen to the ground in a heap than the rising lift jerked the rope free from Hart's hands and Adler's belt.

Patrick and Holmhurst helped the stunned men to their feet.

"Let's move!" Patrick shouted, motioning toward the nearest building, a small barn bordering a wheat field.

They all made their way to the barn, dogged by bullets kicking up the turf near their heels. Once inside the structure they took a moment to catch their breath, but the moment did not last long. The Germans on the tower high above had abandoned their infantry rifles— which were outside the effective range—and were now shooting down the cliff with an MG 42 machine gun. The 7.92-millimeter projectiles began to cut into the barn's thin roof like it was paper.

"We can't stay here," Patrick said, peering out a window at the nearest buildings of the village, still several hundred yards away.

"I am in great pain," Adler groaned on the floor. "I think my knee is twisted. I can't walk."

"You're going to have to," Holmhurst said. "We can't stay here. We have to get farther away from that tower, and fast. We've got to make a break for the village. It's our only chance."

Hart began helping the injured Adler to his feet and said to Holmhurst, "I don't think he can make it. Won't there be Germans in the village?"

"There were only three," Holmhurst replied. "And our partner took care of them."

"You're sure?"

"Bloody sure, Yank. Now I hate to be a bother but we have to get out of this place now, or we're all dead men. We have to get to the village!"

"Adler can't make it that far," Hart protested. "That MG 42 will chop him to pieces."

"Didn't you hear me, Yank—" Holmhurst started, but was interrupted by Patrick, who was still at the window.

"What about that rock wall?" Patrick pointed across the field to a low rock wall about one hundred yards away, between the barn and the village. "We can make it there. The bastard can ride on my back!"

Holmhurst seemed reluctant but eventually nodded. "I don't know if it'll be enough, but we have little choice, don't we? Let's hope the Jerries can't shoot. All right, to the wall, let's move! Now, if you please, gentlemen!"

Hart and Holmhurst helped Patrick get Adler up into a fireman's carry. After waiting for a lull in the firing, during which they assumed the MG 42 was reloading, they each bolted out the door and darted across the field, spreading out as far as they could while still running for the rock wall. They had run about fifty yards before the shots rang out from above again. Bullets pelted the soft dirt at their heels, but they seemed to remain one step ahead of the shooters, who were at a severe disadvantage being more than six hundred feet above them and having to judge the fall of their bullets. Hart, despite his injuries, moved quickly, as did Holmhurst, and both made it behind the wall uninjured. Patrick, however, slowed by the encumbrance of the German scientist, was struck in the leg as he tumbled over the wall, tossing Adler to the ground.

"Bloody hell!" the big Englishman shouted, partly from pain, partly from frustration at being hit. He reached out with a long arm and yanked the moaning Adler under the scant cover of the wall, just as another burst from the MG 42 peppered the rocks, filling the air with deadly ricochets and a white cloud of chalky dust.

"Not the best of shots, are they?" Holmhurst said. "There's a reason those chaps are in the *Luftwaffe* and not the infantry."

"Bloody bastards!" was all Patrick could say, and he produced a handkerchief from the civilian jacket and began tying it onto his bleeding calf, where an MG 42 round had cut a long gash as it had grazed him.

As they caught their breath the firing seemed to intensify, the impacts of the bullets shattering several stones atop the low wall. Hart sneaked a peek over the wall to look up at the flak tower. He could see flashes now from two MG 42s. Both were mounted on the edge of the AA platform.

"There are two of them," Hart announced. "They've got our position zeroed in, and now one can fire while the other reloads. If we make another break like that, at least one of us dies. Plain and simple."

Holmhurst seemed unconcerned by the news, and Hart saw him checking his watch.

"I wouldn't worry so much about them, old boy," he said. "But I would advise you to find the nearest hole and crawl into it in the next ten seconds."

Hart looked at him curiously. "Why—"

Hart had hardly gotten the word out when a great rumbling resounded across the valley. The noise came from above. It came from the flak tower. The sound was muffled at first, like the distant stampede of a buffalo herd, but then it rapidly grew into a crescendo of successive explosions. Hart risked a look over the wall and was shocked to see the flak tower visibly shudder on its high rock perch. Every opening in the concrete structure spewed forth black smoke that bubbled into the air and was carried away by the high-altitude wind. Then, like an erupting volcano, the top platform blew off into several pieces, its long-barreled, thirty-seven-thousand-pound 128-millimeter guns twirling in the air like toys and falling the long way down the cliff to be smashed on the rocks below. Bodies tumbled in the air, too, mixed with the raining debris, some falling to the rocks beneath the cliff, some ejected far enough to land in the field near the rock wall. Finally, the fire in the tower reached the magazine and the rest of the fortress came apart, detonation after detonation knocking great concrete sections away as if they were papier-mâché. A white cloud of dust and soot gathered at the base of the cliff, filling the valley, forcing Hart and the others to cover their faces to keep from breathing the chalky powder. A loud crunch announced the obliteration of the barn they had been hiding in moments before.

When the explosions finally abated and the dust cleared, Hart looked up and saw that there was nothing left atop the cliff except for a single jagged corner of the flak tower. It resembled nothing of its previous form and from this distance could have been the crumbling remnants of a medieval castle.

Several shouts came from the direction of the village, and Hart could see several of the villagers abandoning their homes in terror and running away.

Adler coughed as Holmhurst examined his injury. "I can't tell if it's fractured unless you hold bloody still."

"I'm sorry," Adler said, appreciatively. "I will try. I wish to thank you, sir. I wish to thank you, and your friend, for saving me."

"We didn't come for you, old boy. But, you're welcome, all the same." Holmhurst cast a snide glance at Hart. "At least someone around here knows how to express his gratitude."

Hart allowed a small grin, then gazed again on the smoldering carnage at the base of the cliff. "You never told me you were an explosives expert, Holmhurst."

"I'm not. That bit of handiwork was our partner's doing."

"Your partner? I keep hearing about this partner of yours. Where the hell is he?"

Holmhurst looked at Hart with a sly smile. "I'm sure he'll be along any minute now. He planned this whole thing." At that moment something past Hart's shoulder caught Holmhurst's attention, and Holmhurst gestured for Hart to turn around. "I believe that's him now."

Holmhurst was pointing to the top of a cliff, one that was somewhat removed from the smoking remnants of the flak tower. Hart could make out a lone figure running along its edge. The individual was dressed entirely in black, including a black ski mask. Hart concluded that whoever this was, he had to be a seasoned climber to reach such a spot. As Hart watched, the figure tossed out a great bundle of rope that uncoiled as it fell down the cliff face. The next moment the figure was pushing off from the rock, rappelling down the cliff face, descending rapidly in great bounds. Within a few seconds he had reached the bottom, removed his climbing gear, slung a machine gun onto his back, and begun running at a steady pace toward Hart and the others.

Hart watched as the individual rapidly approached, half-expecting it to be Ives, or perhaps even Jones, the SIS sergeant. But when the approaching figure finally slowed to a walk and assumed a sauntering gait that neither man could have managed, when the black pants and sweater revealed curves where Hart had expected to see straight lines, and when a gloved hand reached up and removed the ski mask allowing locks of golden hair to fall to their full length and shimmer in the sun, Hart suddenly forgot about his throbbing head and the pain in his side. Long-sequestered feelings churned to the surface as he gazed into the smiling face—a face etched into the recesses of his mind, never to be erased.

"Hello, darling," a familiar voice said.

The next moment she was in his arms, fitting into the nook that had been hers for so long, like the missing piece of a puzzle.

Hart could not speak. He just held her, burying his face in the golden hair of the woman who made the very earth move beneath his feet.

Isabelle had returned.

CHAPTER THIRTY-THREE

"You see, Admiral McDonough made me an offer back in that row house in Edinburgh all those weeks ago," Holmhurst said, sipping at a steaming mug of coffee. "After you and your compatriots left the room and he and I were alone, he promised to give me my freedom and a new identity in America if I helped him."

"Helped him?" Hart asked.

"He wanted me to be ready to support him, in the event that something happened. I accepted, and here I am."

"And why would he put his trust in you," Hart asked skeptically, "a known criminal with questionable allegiances?"

Holmhurst looked genuinely hurt. "I resent that, Hart. I'm for king and country, always have been. You can't call me a traitor for making a few pounds on the side."

"Why would he trust you?" Hart asked again, more forcefully.

"Because he didn't trust any of his own bloody people," Holmhurst said ardently, still smarting at Hart's last remark.

Hart got up from the lounge chair and walked across the sitting room to the rain-spattered window. He drew back the curtain to look down on the busy street below, where a great throng of local Viennese moved in all directions. It was not too unlike the prewar Vienna Hart remembered, if one overlooked the piles of rubble here and there. It always amazed Hart how a civilian populace could adjust to any situation, be it disease, privation, or war. On this rainy afternoon, the citizens of Vienna were going about their daily errands, as they would on any given Sunday, but with a little extra urgency in their step. Despite their outward resilience, they all knew that in a few hours night would come, and the bombs with it.

Isabelle was down there somewhere, filing through that mass of people. She and Patrick had left the safe house to procure some food and supplies. Hart was still shocked at her return from the dead, not to mention the revelation that McDonough had set Holmhurst up as a mercenary agent.

A groan came from the adjacent bedroom, and Holmhurst ducked inside to check on the sound. He appeared again moments later.

"Poor bastard," he said.

"Is he dreaming again?" Hart asked.

Holmhurst nodded. "It's been almost twelve hours

and he's still asleep. I don't envy him for the nightmares he's having."

"Let him sleep," Hart said distantly. "He's been through a lot."

Holmhurst picked up his coffee cup from the table and joined Hart by the window. "Listen, Hart, about that doctor of yours in there," he spoke in almost a whisper, even though he had just confirmed that Adler was asleep. "Can he be trusted?"

"As much as a former smuggler I once knew."

Holmhurst looked at him. "Touché, old boy. But what I mean is, I don't know anything about him. The admiral really sent me here to find you. That's it. He didn't mention anything about this Nazi."

"He's not a Nazi. He's a scientist. And he's got information that we need."

"Whatever you say, Hart," the Englishman said without much conviction. "But if it's all the same to you, I'll keep an eye on him."

"And I'll keep an eye on you."

"Fair enough."

"You were telling me about how the admiral recruited you," Hart said. He was not sure just how much of the mission Holmhurst was apprised of, and so he wanted to steer the conversation away from Adler.

"Yes," Holmhurst replied slowly, apparently sensing that Hart was being evasive. "Well, McDonough said he felt he could trust me and that he wanted me to stand by to assist you in the event that he was incapacitated or killed. Per my request, he had Patrick released—how he managed that, I don't know—and then he put the two of us up in an apartment in Liverpool, kept us up to date on your progress, and instructed us to do nothing else but wait for his signal. Patrick and I waited for weeks in that wretched flat, and were just about to think prison a better alternative when, one night, the phone rang, and McDonough gave me the signal."

"The signal?"

"Uh, the code word. You know. Some benign phrase worked out between us to throw off any eavesdroppers."

Hart remembered Ives's casual remark at the bar in Toulon. McDonough had an accomplice, whom he called before he was arrested, but the trace turned up a dead end. It had to have been Holmhurst on the other end of that line.

Hart chuckled and shook his head. "I'm still having trouble believing that the admiral would entrust the entire success of this mission to you and your big friend."

"Don't be insulting, Hart. I have my uses. I may not be a spy, but I've got contacts in places you wouldn't believe."

"So what were your exact orders upon receiving the code word?" Hart asked.

"That I was to find a way into France. That I was to make contact with McDonough's agent there, and that I was to assist you in any way I could. I was not to try to contact him in any way." Holmhurst paused. "I guess he figured whoever was after him would also come after you."

"And Isabelle," Hart said disbelievingly, "she was McDonough's agent in France?"

"Precisely. He said, aside from you, she was the only one in Odysseus he could trust."

Could it be true? Hart thought. Had Odysseus's ranks been infiltrated to the point that McDonough had to pluck an agent from a prison camp in Arizona, not to mention recruit a common smuggler, in order to find someone he could trust? It would explain a great many things. The bomber ambush over Norway. The attack on *U-2553*. Ives mysteriously showing up in Toulon. No doubt Ives had gone over to the other side and had gone to Toulon in an attempt to reach Hart before any of the admiral's still-loyal agents did. And Ives had reached him. But why did he put on such a ruse? Why didn't Ives simply kill him or have the Germans arrest him on the spot? Why the cat-and-mouse game?

And what about Isabelle?

Hart saw Holmhurst's face assume an uneasy expression.

"What is it?" Hart asked.

"There's something else the admiral wanted me to tell you, Hart. It might be hard for you to hear."

Before Holmhurst could say any more, the door opened downstairs and two pairs of footfalls on the stairs announced Isabelle and Patrick's return.

"It's a bloody circus out there," Patrick said disgustedly. "Bloody krauts fighting for a loaf of bread like it's the crown jewels. You'd think they were on rations."

"They are," Isabelle said, placing a bag of groceries on the kitchen table. "The soldiers on the Eastern Front get priority in the Reich. They get the food, and these people get the scraps."

She flashed a warm smile across the room at Hart, and he took her in with his eyes. Since they had arrived in Vienna, she had completely changed her appearance. She no longer resembled a special operations commando. Now she wore a floral patterned dress and had all the appearances of a proper Austrian *Frau*. She was even more ravishing than he had remembered.

"You seem a wealth of information, love," Holmhurst commented with a wink.

"It's Isabelle to you, *love*," she said, somewhat austerely. "And don't think you're in my good graces just because Matt's been rescued. You and this galoot"—she gestured at Patrick—"almost blew the whole thing."

"We're new to the spy business, remember?" Holmhurst replied. "Been in the lady business for some time, though. You might say I know ladies like I know smuggling. But even with all of my experience, I can't seem to figure you out."

"Then stop trying," she said succinctly. "Now why don't you and your goon here fix us something to eat while I talk to Matt for a few minutes."

"Sure thing, love."

Isabelle shot him a fierce look that sent the English lord scurrying into the kitchen. When he had left the room, she sighed, smiled, and walked over to Hart. She placed her soft hands on his.

"Matt. My dear, sweet Matt. I suppose right now your whole world seems turned on end."

"Something like that," Hart said, but before he could continue, she placed a perfumed finger to his lips.

"Not now," she said softly, motioning with her eyes to the two Englishmen in the kitchen. "Not here. But we do need to get caught up, you and I. I know a little café down on the corner. They don't have any cream, but they serve a mean cup of coffee."

Hart smiled but was still feeling uncomfortable around her. Two years was a long time. He did not know what to feel. Gratitude? Anger? Suspicion? Betrayal?

"I know that look, Matt Hart. You've got a lot to unload on me." Her hand ran from his hair to his newly shaven cheek, as she looked into his eyes. "I probably deserve most of it. I just ask that you please hear me out. Do you promise to do that?"

"Yes, as long as you promise to be on the level with me."

Her eyes began to tear, and then she wrapped her arms around him in a tight embrace, placing her face against his chest. "Oh, I do. I do promise, Matt. I do."

CHAPTER THIRTY-FOUR

Vienna's Stadtpark, where they had once strolled together before the war, no longer resembled the warm, green park where they had basked in the sun atop a picnic blanket while Austrian families and smiling children frolicked on the gentle green slopes around them. Now the park was nearly deserted, with only a few casual pedestrians to dot its bleak untended landscape. An antiaircraft battery had been constructed at one end, serving as a constant reminder to the local population of their dire circumstances, the circumstances of a people in the process of losing a war and being conquered by enemies from all sides. The anxiety was visible on the faces of the few people Hart and Isabelle encountered as they walked through the constant drizzle, huddled beneath an umbrella. This plaza, where only a few short years ago thousands celebrated the Reich's innumerable victories over Holland, France, Norway, Africa, Yugoslavia, Greece, and Russia, now sat stark and bare, with a cloud of despair hanging over the heads of the passersby.

But Hart and Isabelle did not bother to even

comment on the changes to Vienna, changes that some-how paralleled the changes to their relationship. They had strolled along the Ringstrasse, got coffee at the Schwarzenberg café, and now walked on a winding side-walk through the park, her arm in his, both talking in fluent German so as not to arouse any suspicion from the few passersby.

"We've been walking for over an hour, Matt," she said, looking up at him, "and you still have that solemn look about you. You're all business. You haven't changed a bit."

"And you are still an enigma to me, just as you always have been," he said carefully. He still felt uncomfortable at her sudden return from the dead.

"That's not fair, Matt."

He stopped and turned her bodily to face him. "Then tell me, Iz. Tell me what happened to you. You've been avoiding my questions all afternoon."

He looked into her eyes. Tears were forming there. Before his eyes her face was melting from the playful strumpet to the sniveling wreck. She buried her face in his chest, embracing him closely. For some reason, Hart found it hard to reciprocate, and this she evidently detected. She pushed away from him, avoiding his gaze, her eyes distant now and red from crying. She began walking again, leaving Hart and the umbrella behind.

"Come on, Iz," he called after her. "Don't ask me to just pick up where we left off. You owe me an explanation."

She stopped, stood with her back to him for several seconds, and then finally turned around and walked back wearing a resolved expression.

"All right, Commander Hart. You want the truth? Then you'll get the truth. I don't think you will be satisfied once you know it, but if it will satisfy the demands of your own self-pity, then I will give it to you."

Hart responded to this jab more with anger than with regret and remorsefulness. "Isabelle, I have spent the last two years in a half-dozen POW camps, getting beaten by illiterate prison guards in order to get German U-boat sailors to confide in me. I took the job because I blamed myself for losing my team in Spain. It was my penitence. I blamed myself for losing you. I was your commander."

"You were more than that."

"I know, Isabelle. I know. I've languished, blaming myself every single day for losing the one person I ever truly loved. For the last two years I was certain that you were dead. I waited, expecting each day to hear confirmation of my worst fears. It ate me up inside. I didn't know what to do with myself. You walked out of that room in Cartagena and a part of me was suddenly gone— I thought, forever. Now, you're here. You're alive and well. You're in touch with Odysseus, and the admiral, and I have to ask myself, how could this be? How could McDonough—how could you—betray me in such a way? To not even tell me you were alive. To not even try to contact me, not even once. To let me endure that. How could you—"

"Oh, Matt, I'm so sorry. I know you've suffered. I didn't mean to make light of it." She reached out for his hand and brought it to her face. "Please understand. I couldn't tell you. Please believe me when I tell you that."

"Well, I'm listening," he said steadfastly, regaining

his composure. "I asked you for the whole story. I want to know it. I need to know it."

She kissed his hand and then put her arm in his, and they resumed their stroll. For several minutes she said nothing, staring off across the damp lawn as if deep in thought. When she finally spoke, she sounded detached, as if she were reading a post-mission report.

"When I left you that day, I went to the docks and met our contact just as we had planned. We had lunch and discussed the extraction. I didn't suspect anything, since he matched the description I had been given and he answered correctly to all of the code words. But then I started to feel drowsy and knew that I had been drugged. The next thing I remember is waking up in the hands of the Gestapo. It turns out our contact was working for whoever was the highest bidder. He sold me to a Gestapo unit that was in Cartagena at the time, tasked with finding our team. They locked me up in a rat-infested basement, took away all of my clothes, and left me with nothing but a dirty bucket of water and a cupful of soup a day to sustain me." Her voice began to tremble. "They kept me there for eight weeks, Matt. Each day I got a visit from their leader and one or two of his men. They subjected me to hours of interrogation. Whenever they were unsatisfied with my answers, or whenever they got bored, they beat me, they shocked me with electrodes, and they raped me. They tied me up for hours on end and used me in every way their depraved minds could imagine."

Hart could not resist reaching for her and pulling her close. His heart felt for her, and he suddenly hated himself for forcing her to bring these painful memories to the surface.

"Isabelle, I . . . I'm so sorry."

"I know what you're thinking," she said between sniffles. "I know how you think, Matthew Hart. You say you're sorry, but what you're really wondering is what did I tell them. Am I right? You're thinking I told them where our team was hiding. That I gave them up under torture."

"Of course not," Hart said as convincingly as he could manage.

"The truth is, Matt, I don't know. I don't know what I might have told them. The whole nightmare is just one big blur to me. Eventually they moved me to Paris, and by that time I was somewhat coherent again. That's where I heard that our friends had been put on trial and hanged by the Spanish government. I almost broke down." She looked up at him. "I know that must have been a tough time for you, too."

"How did you escape?"

"I did what I was trained to do. What every female spy is trained to do. I submitted. I served their every whim. I let them think they had broken me, and I waited. Eventually, the men of the unit started to fight over me. Apparently, I was a big secret they were keeping from their bosses. I guess their lust won out over their call to duty. Some of them wanted to turn me over to the SS; the others wanted to keep me for their own personal entertainment. It got to a point where they felt comfortable enough to leave only one man awake at night to watch me. I waited, and when the time was right, I struck."

"You killed the one on watch?"

Her eyes narrowed, and for the first time since their reunion Hart saw the cold creature the OSS had turned her into.

"I killed all of them," she said succinctly, and then paused as if to relish the memory.

Hart did not press the issue, nor did he ask how she had managed to kill them. He knew that Isabelle had been trained to kill in all of the ways in the OSS and SIS handbooks. He could only imagine how she suckered the unwary guard into thinking he was going to get lucky that night only to end his fantasy abruptly with a hairpin, a fork, a bedspring, or any of a dozen different household items thrust into his brain. The others would have been at her mercy after that. Who knows by which devilish means she chose to dispatch them.

"Men often do underestimate women. Wouldn't you agree, Matt?"

He felt an accusation in the stare that followed, and he quickly moved to change the subject.

"If you escaped, then why didn't you get out of Europe?"

"It wasn't my choice. I contacted Odysseus through an agent in Paris, and Admiral McDonough told me to stay put. I guess he thought I would be better use to him behind the lines, so here I am, and here I have been, at the admiral's beck and call all this time."

"You've been in occupied territory for the past two years?"

She nodded. "I'm sorry the admiral didn't tell you. I wanted to. God knows I wanted to so many times. I thought of trying on several occasions, but"—she looked up at him and smiled—"I had a good commander who taught me duty always comes first."

Hart inwardly cursed McDonough. The self-serving bastard more than likely kept her in Europe to avoid the political fallout of the foul-up in Spain. No agent to testify, no court of inquiry.

"What were you doing for McDonough all this time?"

"Small things." She shrugged. "Odd jobs, like this one."

"So McDonough ordered you to rescue me?"

"In so many words. He sent those two British idiots to find me."

"How did McDonough know where I was?"

"He didn't. He knew your U-boat was headed to Toulon, and that Ives would try to intercept you there. Holmhurst and his chum and I were supposed to get to you first. Obviously, we were late."

Hart wondered if Isabelle had any idea about the scope of his mission. He assumed not, since McDonough liked to keep as many agents as possible in the dark. "Did you speak to McDonough directly?"

"No, but I did get a message from him a few weeks ago. It was very strange. In it he told me that Odysseus had been compromised and that I was to trust no one, especially Ives. I guess that's why he sent those two Brits to find me. They are too far removed from the organization to be in bed with anyone."

"Wait a minute," he said, suddenly hostile. "You mean that Ives knew you were alive?"

"Easy, Matt. He was McDonough's right hand. He

knew everything the admiral did." She let that sink in before continuing. "Anyway, the admiral's letter said that you were on an important mission—I think *vital to the outcome of the war* was the phrase he used—and that you were in danger, and that I was to be ready to assist you. You can only imagine how excited I was at the prospect of seeing you again. But then I heard nothing. For three weeks, nothing. No radio messages, no couriers, nothing. Then two days ago, those two Brits show up in Vienna, give me all the right credentials and another message from McDonough. That's how I learned of your arrival in Toulon. I only wish they had reached me before Ives got to you—before those bastards got their hands on you."

"Ives may not have had anything to do with my capture, Iz," Hart said, testing the waters, seeing the extent of her knowledge. "He could have had me arrested, and he didn't. In fact, I'm not sure I would have been captured if that SIS team hadn't jumped me."

Isabelle gave him a puzzled look. "The admiral didn't mention anything about an SIS contact."

"They were the ones who nabbed me. They took me to their safe house and started to question me. That's when the SS broke down the door and I was whisked away to that fortress in the Alps. An SS colonel named Sturm was in charge there, and he seemed to know all about my mission. I don't know if Ives was in on it, or if this SS colonel was acting alone. He's one hell of an evil bastard. I only hope he was in that flak tower when you blew it up."

Isabelle had a look of concern. "The admiral did tell

me that we were not to share any information about the
mission, even with our allies. I'm worried that the so-
called SIS team was really working for Ives."

Hart shook his head. "Not possible."

"Why?"

"Because one of them was my instructor at Camp X.
I don't know about the others, but I know *he* would not
be associated with Ives."

"So what did you tell that SIS team while they were
interrogating you?" she asked.

Hart shot a glance at Isabelle, but she was still gazing
at the sidewalk in front of them.

"Iz," he said hesitantly, "I'm not sure I can trust you
either. I don't know how much the admiral told you
about this mission. Now I don't know if McDonough's
the real deal, but I know this mission is. Something is
happening. Something has been found, something very
deadly, and the Nazis are going to any lengths to get
their hands on it—even to the point of torturing their
own."

"Adler?" she asked.

Hart nodded.

"Who is he?"

"An archaeologist. An expert on medieval and classics
studies." Hart paused and looked her in the eye. "We
have to get him to Istanbul, Iz. I can't explain why. I'm
not even sure I know why, but it's imperative that we get
him there, and fast. I can't tell you any more. I'm sorry."

"Sure, no problem," she said evenly. "But are you sure
we need to rush? It would be best if we laid low here for
a few days."

"Iz, right now there's a U-boat, loaded with the makings of some kind of catastrophic weapon, on its way to rendezvous with the German scientists who know how to put it together. We don't have time to lay low. We have to leave tonight, if not sooner."

She nodded. "I've got the uniforms and passes we need to get us around without arousing suspicion. And I can arrange transportation to the Yugoslav border on such short notice, no problem. But beyond that, it would normally take some prior coordination. Usually several days. I'm not so tight with Tito's partisans."

"I know someone who might be," Hart said with a reluctant grin.

"Let me guess. Holmhurst?"

Hart nodded.

"So I suppose we'll have to take those two Brits with us?" she asked, with uneasiness in her tone.

"I'm afraid so, Iz. The admiral trusted Holmhurst for some reason. McDonough may be an old, self-serving son of a bitch, but he was always good at sizing people up. We're going to have to take a leap of faith here and trust his judgment." Hart could hardly believe the words coming from his own mouth, and then added, "At least for a while."

PART FOUR

Constantinople
May 29, 1453

The great walls stood defiantly outside the great city of Constantine, their long war-torn history evident by their appearance. They were actually a series of walls, built in A.D. 408. For a thousand years, they had kept out the enemies of Rome, even turning back the army of Attila the Hun. They predated the time of Islam and were built by a Roman emperor who was devoutly orthodox Christian, but today they had become the front line in the long war between Christ and Muhammad. After a forty-seven-day siege, an army of Ottoman Muslims was now attempting to breach the Christian bastion of Constantinople that had stood for a thousand years.

At this moment, during an uncharacteristic lull in the fighting, a litter moved slowly through the battle-scarred assemblage of soldiers and knights manning the battlements. The flickering torches revealed forlorn faces as each man watched the broken body of their gallant captain passing by. Some even reached out to touch his prostrate form, as if to confirm that he had actually fallen and was now being conveyed away from the walls he had so skillfully defended for so long.

Giovanni Guistiniani Longo had spent the last six weeks coordinating the defense of the city and had successfully fought off the Ottomans and their allies with the zeal of an Old Testament prophet. And now, after forty-seven days of fighting, he had finally been brought down by an Ottoman crossbow bolt. Through countless attempts at escalade, through fleet assaults on the seaward walls, through thunderous barrages from cannons larger than any ever seen by the Western world, Guistiniani had led a mixed handful of Greek and Italian defenders—only eight thousand in total—in holding off an army ten times that size. The odds had been enormously against them, but Guistiniani, a professional soldier from Genoa and one of the few nobles of Christian Europe to answer the call of the beleaguered Byzantine emperor, had inspired them to achieve victory after victory. Earthquakes and unseasonable storms had stifled the Ottomans and confirmed to the outnumbered defenders that God was indeed on their side and that a successful defense was ultimately achievable.

Now that Guistiniani had fallen, everything had changed. The Genoese captain who had been their motivation, their beacon of hope in the night, the one inspirational voice that stood out during those terrifying assaults, when innumerable Muslim warriors shouted *"Allahu Akbar!"* in their ears. Their brave captain was gone, struck down while directing the defense from atop the walls, and the faith of his men had been struck down with him. It was apparent on every face watching that litter pass by. Already the men atop the walls were announcing the approach of a fresh Ottoman assault, a vast horde of Muslims advancing on the walls from the darkness beyond.

One particular man—a man wearing a glimmering suit of armor and a gold-laced purple robe, and who had also been watching the body of Guistiniani being carried away—now clasped his hands together in prayer. Two priests stood beside him, along with a cluster of colorful knights.

"May Our Holy Father bless him for his sacrifice," one of the priests said, moving his hands in a blessing in the direction of Guistiniani's litter.

"Amen," said the grandly adorned man who had been praying.

"Your Holiness," the priest said, his tone revealing his anxiety. "Forgive me, but the reports are that this new assault is much larger than the last. You see the looks on the faces all about you. These men will not hold without Guistiniani to lead them. The city will fall tonight!"

"God forgive me, brother," the man in the purple robe replied with tears in his eyes, "but I fear you are right. I am the emperor, but I am not foolish enough to believe that I could ever replace Guistiniani. It is the end."

"Forgive me, Your Grace," the priest said apologetically, but curtly. "We must act now. There is not much time."

"Of course, you are right. Not much time. The city must be saved. God's people must be saved."

The priest glanced once at his colleague and then

back to the emperor. "Then are we to proceed as Your Grace has previously commanded?"

"Yes," the emperor said resolutely, wiping his face and assuming a visage more fitting to his royal personage. He held a hand out, and both priests kissed it. "Now go, my brothers. Make haste, and God be with you."

"And also with you, Your Holiness," they responded in unison. They both bowed, took up the long skirts of their robes in their arms, and then ran off into the night.

"Where are they off to, Your Holiness?" one of the low-ranked captains on the wall above shouted out in frustration. "They should stay and bless these men before the next fight."

"They do God's service, brother," the emperor called up to the restive soldier. "And they have my blessing, as do you and all of these men."

A feeble cheer arose from the few soldiers who still had the energy for it. But any cheers were soon swallowed up by a great clamor erupting from the other side of the wall. The deafening roar of several thousand Muslims shouting in their unholy language echoed off the stone ramparts, filling every Christian heart with terror. The emperor and his entourage looked up to see Ottoman troops appear atop the walls in several places, leaping from their ladders and hacking their way over the battlements. The emperor's troops put up a spirited defense, but without Guistiniani, their efforts were disjointed and ineffectual.

"Father in Heaven, help us!" one of the knights next to the emperor exclaimed. "Janissaries!"

The knight pointed to a place on the wall where at

least three enemy ladders were conveying white-clad warriors over the top. The warriors wore conical white hats and came onto the battlements in a steady inexorable stream of thrusting and slashing scimitars. These were the enemy's shock troops, former Christians captured as youths and raised as Muslims to be lifelong berserker warriors, fervently loyal only to the Ottoman sultan. The fact that the sultan had committed these troops was even more of an affirmation that this was to be the final assault.

The emperor and the knights around him watched helplessly from the ground as the Janissaries established a solid foothold atop the wall and began attacking the defenders from the flanks. Faced with attacks from two sides, the Christian troops began to desert their posts in droves. They streamed the battlements, all discipline lost, running into the city as if it might somehow offer them safety from the advancing horde. Few, if any, had the wherewithal to even pause as they ran past the emperor.

The emperor turned and faced the handful of knights around him. They were all handpicked—each man chosen because he could be trusted to stand by his emperor to his dying breath.

"God in heaven has shown us the way, my brothers," the emperor said as he drew out his gold-hilted sword from its elaborate scabbard. "You all know what to do."

The knights nodded, drawing their swords as well.

The Janissaries were filing down the battlements now, pursuing the remaining defenders, cutting the Christian troops down from behind as their legs failed them from fear. Any who turned to fight were instantly swallowed up by a glimmering maelstrom of curved blades hacking in the torchlight.

The emperor felt a surge of despair as he stared into the approaching white wave of Muslim warriors. He felt his heart pumping with apprehension, his knees buckling at the thought of what he must do to save his countrymen.

For a brief moment, he thought it oddly amusing how Rome in the West had started and ended under leaders named Romulus, and now the rise and fall of Constantinople would have a similar distinction. But the time had come, and now he must be an emperor worthy of his predecessors.

"God be with you, my brothers!"

The emperor then raised his sword aloft and ran toward the oncoming Janissaries. His knights did the same, following their leader into the wall of chanting attackers. Within seconds, the emperor and all of his knights disappeared inside the slashing mass of the enemy.

And Constantine Dragasēs Palaiologos, Constantine XI, the last emperor of Rome, was never seen or heard from again.

CHAPTER THIRTY-FIVE

Istanbul, Turkey

Hart tried not to breathe the repugnant exhaust belching from the ferry's single smokestack. The crowded two-decker slowly rocked to and fro as it plied the waters of the Bosporus loaded down with several hundred passengers crossing from the Asian side of Istanbul to the European side. It was a short trip, only one mile, but Hart wished it could be longer. He always felt somewhat at home whenever he was at sea. The fresh sea air, the wind and sun on his face, the rocking deck all converged to inspire the true Homer within him.

He glanced at Adler and then at Isabelle. Both were beside him, leaning on the upper-deck rail and gazing out at the city that now lay across the ferry's bows. Both appeared absorbed in the majesty of the spires and parapets that poked above the ancient walls. They were truly breathtaking and spoke of centuries of conflict and intrigue. The location of Istanbul, formerly Constantinople, formerly Byzantium, was just as strategic today as it had been during the Persian invasions under Darius and Xerxes. It was the gateway, the intersect, the impregnable bastion that guarded the narrow waterway running between empires, cultures, and religions. Now, in 1944, Istanbul belonged to Turkey, and thus it was a neutral city—a neutral city on the edge of a world at war. Being neutral, Istanbul lacked the spattering of military hardware and antiaircraft emplacements that now adorned every other major city in Europe, allowing Hart, Adler, and Isabelle to see the ancient city in all of its historical glory. The walls that had protected the city from a seaside attack in medieval times still stood in many places but were crumbling and in disrepair. The advent of gunpowder had made them obsolete. The domes of the city's many cathedrals still looked much as they must have to the crusaders who stopped here on their way to the Holy Land. The minarets of mosques also stood tall above the skyline—the results of the Ottoman conquest. It was as if time had no meaning in this place—much as the last five days had been for Hart and the others.

It had taken them seven days of whirlwind travel across occupied Eastern Europe to get here, and perhaps that was why all three retreated into their inner selves as they watched their final destination approach.

Hart watched Isabelle's golden hair blowing in the wind. The few strands that had escaped her head scarf glimmered in long streams across her shoulders. She had been every bit the professional over the past days. He had felt the fires of the past trying to ignite within him again and wondered if they could ever be rekindled. Her willing acceptance was the fuel they would need to keep burning—that, and a measure of trust he was not sure he could manage.

She caught him staring at her and gave him a smile that was more courteous than affectionate. It left Hart feeling embarrassed and somewhat uncomfortable. He suddenly felt like a love-struck schoolboy still infatuated with his childhood sweetheart.

"I hope the Germans haven't taken to searching ferries," Hart said, pointing out two German E-boats sitting in the narrow inlet to the Golden Horn, a narrow waterway that formed the city's harbor. He was trying to pretend that he had not been staring at her.

Isabelle seemed to accept that and looked out at the enemy vessels. The low and slender German E-boat was the rough equivalent to the American PT boat. Small, fast, and highly maneuverable, it was perfect for patrolling coastal areas, and undoubtedly this was the way in which the Germans were now employing them here in the Bosporus. The narrow strait was the only way for ships to travel between the Black Sea and the Mediterranean. It was an obvious supply line between the Western nations and their Russian allies. The Germans, of course, knew this, and their E-boats now stood ready with torpedoes to sink any Allied ship that attempted its passage.

"They won't board us," Isabelle said assuredly. "The Germans have enough problems right now. They don't need to provoke the Turkish government."

"I would not underestimate the men we are dealing with," Adler said. "Sturm may have issued orders for these boats to search all ferries in an effort to find us."

"If he is even alive," exclaimed Hart. "But even if he is, I thought you said you were the only one who knew the connection between Constantine and Sweden."

"I never said that, Mister Hart. I said I was the only one who could find the last piece of the puzzle—the item that will allow the Nazis to change the face of the world forever."

Hart must have looked somewhat perplexed just then because Isabelle suddenly laughed at him. It was the first time Hart had seen her smile in days.

"I told you we might still need His Lordship," she said. "Pity you decided to leave him back in Yugoslavia. I have the feeling he could have gotten us into the city without much problem."

"Holmhurst and his man had fulfilled their purpose," Hart answered somewhat defensively. "They did the job McDonough sent them to do. I saw no reason to risk having two individuals of questionable loyalties around while we hunt down a weapon that could be worth hundreds of millions on the black market."

"Still, they *were* handy."

"And wouldn't we have been a sight to see? Four pale white men and a blonde walking the streets of Istanbul. We might as well have carried a sign around. Besides, Holmhurst is an amateur, and we don't need amateurs on this mission. He was eager to stay with the partisans, anyway. Said he wanted to stick around to meet with Tito, remember? I imagine he's shoring up his smuggling operation as we speak. He'll be back in business in no time."

"Whatever you say, *Commander*," Isabelle said in a

tone that adequately conveyed her disapproval of his decision. It bordered on condescending, as if he were the amateur in this business and she the true professional.

It was simply another in a long string of unpleasant moments they had shared in the long trip from Vienna, during which she had all but asserted her supremacy over him in this world of espionage, a world that Hart had been absent from for so long.

Seven days ago, they had left Vienna on a cold, foggy morning. They had reached Yugoslavia without problem. With the aid of German uniforms and forged papers Isabelle had provided, along with a truck she had procured loaded with medical supplies, they made it through all of the checkpoints. It was made easier by the fact that most of the traffic encountered was flowing into Germany and consisted of broken and decimated divisions of the *Wehrmacht*, defeated by the rapidly advancing Soviet forces. Once in Yugoslavia, they had quickly linked up with Tito's partisans, thanks to Holmhurst and his connections. After a four-day journey across the Dinaric Alps, in which they traveled aboard every means of ground transport conceivable, including oxcarts and mules, and in which they were, in essence, forced into assisting the partisans in ambushing a German supply column, they eventually reached Bulgaria and the coast. There, they boarded a ship full of refugees fleeing the Soviet offensive to the north. After an uncomfortable, but otherwise uneventful trip across the Black Sea, they landed in Kozlu on the Asian side of Turkey. Once in that neutral country, they had breathed a little easier, but still kept a wary eye out for Nazi agents. It took no time at all to reach Istanbul, where they had boarded the ferry that now carried them back to the European continent and the old city, where Adler claimed the secret that they and the Nazis so desperately searched for resided.

The German E-boats did not change position as the lumbering ferry made its way into the crowded dockyard near the city's ancient walls. Now that he was closer, Hart could see that the two German craft were moored together and their crews appeared to be fishing on deck. The German sailors were undoubtedly off duty at the moment, and the arrival of the ferry seemed to be the last thing on their minds. Hart could hear excited German voices across the water cheering as one of their comrades came up with a large fish twitching on the end of his line.

Adler audibly breathed a sigh of relief, then resumed his study of the ancient walls. For some reason, the dismissive air the scientist had taken on since his rescue was starting to rub Hart the wrong way. Adler seemed to have attached some importance to himself over the past days as he realized how essential he was to the Allied cause. He was reluctant to share information with Hart, even after they reached neutral Turkey, and Hart was not sure if it was out of distrust or out of a desire to retain his trump card over his OSS escorts. Adler had hardly said two words about the object they were now, supposedly, moments away from discovering. Hart had tried to glean information from him, but Adler had been as stalwart toward Hart as he had been to Sturm and his sergeants back in that alpine prison cell. He had simply refused to talk about it until he reached the city that now lay before them. Now that they were within a few boat lengths of the old city, Hart had had enough.

"All right, Dr. Adler," Hart said sternly. "It is time you start sharing some information with us."

"What?" Adler said, appearing somewhat startled by Hart's harsh tone, after so many days of unfettered accommodation.

"We have gone to great lengths, and great risk, to get you here. I've asked you several times but you have refused to answer. Now you will tell us, or Isabelle and I will leave you right here and take the next ferry back. You'll be on your own against whatever awaits you in Istanbul, and if Sturm knows what you say he knows, then I'm sure there will be some Nazi agents around before long. Hell, they might already be there, waiting for you. I want to know about those artifacts on the U-boat. I want to know the connection between the grave in Sweden and Constantine. And most of all, I want to know what the hell we're doing in Istanbul. I want to know it right now!"

"Please, Mister Hart. It is for your own good that I do not tell you. For the good of mankind. Please believe me. You do not want to know what I know."

"Okay, I believe you. But that's not good enough. It's my mission to know. It's my mission to find out what the Nazis are after and what they're up to, no matter how far-reaching or devastating it is. You must tell me."

Adler attempted a defiant look, but it was no use. Hart could tell that the German scientist was somewhat afraid of him and that he did not fully trust him. He saw Adler's eyes stray to the lump in Hart's jacket marking the holstered Colt .45 beneath Hart's left arm. Hart had procured the semiautomatic weapon back in Yugoslavia from the partisans' ample stores.

"Do you remember what I told you in Austria, about the Byzantine-era symbols you saw on the artifacts?" Adler said after a sigh of capitulation.

"Yes, they were inscribed with a double-headed eagle symbol."

"And what did I tell you about that?"

"That it was the symbol of Constantine the Great." Hart felt like a schoolboy in front of his teacher.

"Not of Constantine, Mister Hart, but of the Roman Empire. In A.D. 330, Constantine the Great shifted his capital from Rome in Italy to Constantinople—now the city of Istanbul that lies before you. Constantine began a new dynasty that would continue after Rome in the West fell. For a thousand years after the fall of Rome, Constantinople survived as the shadow of Rome. Of course, we call them the Byzantines, but the people living here called themselves Rhomaioi—or Romans. They had Roman institutions, a Roman-style government, and even seven hills, like Rome."

"I know this story, professor," Hart said tiredly. "From my ancient history class in college. Rome in the East and Rome in the West, right? Each under a different emperor. The one in the west fell to the barbarians, and the one in the east kept going. But what does that have to do with the eagle symbol?"

"The double-headed eagle was the symbol of the Byzantines, Mister Hart. It was, and still is by most, thought to represent the dual sovereignty of the emperor in

Constantinople over both the eastern and western portions of the empire. It was the symbol of the last ruling Byzantine family—the Palaiologos dynasty. But the symbol dates back far beyond the Byzantines—indeed, even further back than the Romans. It has been seen in much earlier civilizations, including the Sumerian and Hittite civilizations. It dates back as far as the twentieth century B.C." Adler's voice trailed off as he gazed at the weather-beaten walls near the dockyard. "It was also used by a few ancient cults."

Hart could see that Isabelle was listening more intently than he was. She was hanging on Adler's every word, but Hart could see little value in them.

"This is all very interesting," Hart said. "But I don't see what it has to do with the grave in Sweden."

"It has everything to do with it," Adler said succinctly. "The grave in Östersund was Constantine's."

"You're telling me that Constantine the Great, the emperor of Rome during the fourth century, was buried in northern Europe?"

"Heavens, no! Of course not. Not Constantine the Great."

"Then who?" Hart was getting irritated at Adler's evasive talk.

"It was the grave of Constantine the Eleventh, Mister Hart, from the house of Palaiologos, the last ruler of the Byzantine Empire, the emperor at the time of the city's fall in 1453, when the Ottomans took the city."

Isabelle appeared puzzled. Hart felt the same way, and his face must have shown it, because Adler sighed as if he were dealing with college freshmen.

"In 1453, Constantinople—this city—fell to the Ottomans after a long siege. According to your history books, Miss Sevilla and Mister Hart, Constantine the Eleventh was killed on the last day of the siege. It is said that he was last seen charging into the attacking army after it had breached the walls of the city. It is believed by most that he was killed shortly thereafter."

"You say, 'believed by most,'" Hart said. "Why is that?" Hart knew when Constantinople fell to the Ottomans, but that was the limit of his knowledge on the subject.

"Because his body was never found, Mister Hart."

"So somebody found his body and sent it to Sweden to be buried?"

"Not just his body, Mister Hart, but him, the live person Constantine himself. He lived in Sweden for quite some time after Constantinople fell. He lived there in obscurity and anonymity and died at a ripe old age. He maintained secret contact with the bishop of Constantinople until his dying day."

"How do you know all of this?" Isabelle asked suddenly. To Hart she appeared somewhat agitated.

"I have done extensive research, found copies of letters exchanged between an Orthodox priest who remained behind in occupied Constantinople and someone calling himself Ragnvaldr living near Östersund. The letters are carefully crafted, but they are quite conclusive. The man calling himself Ragnvaldr could only have been Constantine."

"So he survived the battle. Great," Hart said, still not

seeing where this was going. "Why did he go to Sweden, and why do the Nazis care about it?"

"Have you ever heard of the Varangian Guard, Mister Hart?"

"No."

"The Varangian Guard was the personal bodyguard to the Byzantine emperors. They were steadfastly loyal to the emperor and would readily die for him. Can either of you guess where the Varangians came from?"

Hart shook his head. Isabelle remained silent but attentive.

"They were Norsemen."

"Vikings?" Hart asked.

"Yes, or Rüs, to be more precise. The Byzantine emperors were guarded by not Greeks, not Romans, but Vikings. They were Norsemen from Scandinavia who had made their way down the Volkhov and Dnieper Rivers to the Black Sea, raiding and trading with several places along the way. They once were enemies of the Byzantines but eventually became some of the empire's fiercest warriors." Adler paused. "The Varangians disappear from the history books in the thirteenth century, but I believe the imperial family kept contacts with their old protectors and that Constantine took refuge with some of the descendants of the Varangians in Sweden. They were people he could trust to protect him and to not reveal his identity."

"But the Ottomans never reached northern Europe," Hart said. "They could not have touched him there. Why would he need to keep his identity a secret?"

"Yes, Mister Hart. That is the great mystery we must unravel." Adler smiled and then gazed at the city. "That is why we are here. The answer lies in there, and, if my suspicions are correct, the remains of a great weapon is there, too—a weapon of the past that could be unleashed upon the present with devastating results."

"And, you say, the Nazis know of this connection?"

Adler nodded. "A little over a year ago, agents belonging to Colonel Sturm contacted me and presented me with a document they claimed to have obtained in Istanbul. They had heard of my reputation in the archaeology field and wanted me to look over the document and tell them if it had any historical significance, particularly regarding the Anok Sabe myth."

"Anok Sabe?" Hart asked. He had never heard of it before.

Adler smiled. "It is one of those thousands of myths that have floated through the classics community over the ages—like the story of Troy. It sounds good. It has some historical believability, but no one can ever really prove that it happened."

"And what is the myth about?"

"It is about an Egyptian priest of the seventh century who had gone to Jerusalem for one reason or another, and who walked out of the desert carrying a canopic jar in which he claimed to have harnessed the power of the Hebrew God. A cult in Egypt was soon established around this priest, and that cult, like so many others, eventually merged into the cult of Serapis. The cult of Serapis became the guardian of the power and threatened to use it to avenge any affront committed against their god."

Hart immediately thought of the canopic jar he had examined aboard the U-boat, the one containing the small gold nuggets.

"I see from your expression, Mister Hart, that you have seen the jar we pulled from Constantine's grave. I must confess, finding it gave me quite a rush of adrenaline, but after some further inspection I dated the object to somewhere around the second century. It is not the jar carried by the mythological priest, but perhaps it is a replica of the earlier object. Did you, by chance, open it?"

"Yes, but I couldn't make anything of it. It was full of gold nuggets shaped like teeth."

"Those were not nuggets, Mister Hart. They *were* human teeth, encased in gold."

"Human teeth? What on earth for?"

"Perhaps I should first tell you about the document Colonel Sturm's men had me examine, and how it related to the Anok Sabe myth. The document was a personal journal—a memoir—of the Ottoman sultan Mehmet the Second, the sultan who conquered Constantinople in 1453."

Hart reflected on the intelligence Odysseus had received about the rare arts dealer in Istanbul—the one who ended up as a battered corpse floating in the Bosporus, compliments of Colonel Sturm. Hart wondered if Adler knew the bloody past of the document. Judging from Adler's present demeanor, Hart surmised that he knew nothing of the gruesome murder.

"So, what was it in this memoir that led you to dig in Sweden?"

"The document was obviously meant to be buried with the sultan and to never be revealed, but we must assume that either his scribe or someone else close to the sultan kept a copy for himself. In it, the last days of the siege were described. Mehmet claimed that Constantine was captured on the last day and brought before him. In spite of his wounds, the Byzantine emperor issued a careful threat to the sultan. Stop the rape and pillage of his holy city, or he would unleash the power of God on the sultan's army. He made reference to the curse of Anok Sabe, a story that either the sultan or one of his advisers must have been familiar with. If Mehmet did not comply with Constantine's wishes, Constantine's agent would unleash it on the Ottoman host, bringing devastation on both the Muslims and the Christians, leaving no one alive in the city."

"A sort of murder-suicide pact, huh?"

"So to speak." Adler shrugged.

"Seems like Constantine was in a disadvantaged position."

"It would seem that way, but Constantine evidently had done his homework. Mehmet the Second was a very superstitious man—to the point that he would not get out of bed in the morning if the auguries were not right. Constantine's threat put the fear of God in him, if you will. His memoir clearly states that he called a halt to the sack of the city out of respect for Allah. He also spared Constantine's life with the provision that the emperor go into exile and never reveal his true identity to anyone. You see, it was important for the sultan to appear to have defeated the Christian ruler. Otherwise, he would not have survived very long. There were always factions ready to usurp his throne if he was ever considered weak in the eyes of his generals."

Hart glanced at Isabelle, but she simply stared out at the city as if she were only partially listening now.

"So, if this weapon is so powerful, as you say it was," Hart said. "Powerful enough to scare Mehmet. How come I've never heard of it?"

"You have," Adler said concisely. "You just don't realize it."

"Come again?"

Adler smiled. "You've read about it in the Bible, Mister Hart, in the books of Second Kings and Second Chronicles, where the Assyrian army is destroyed in the course of one night by the hand of God."

"Sennacherib's prism!" Hart gasped. Things were finally starting to come together for him. "The record on the prism. It must have been a cover story for what really happened. Then Sennacherib really did lose half his army outside Jerusalem!"

Adler nodded. "You've read about it in Herodotus's history of Egypt, where an army of fifty thousand Persians under Cambyses marches into the desert and never returns. You've read about it in Roman history, when Pope Leo the First turns back Attila the Hun after unleashing the power on a portion of Attila's army in northern Italy."

"Wait a minute," Hart said. "That's not the story I remember from history class. I thought Pope Leo met with Attila, presented him with some gold from Rome, and the barbarian king went on his merry way back to Hungary."

"Ah." Adler smiled patiently. "There are many versions of the past, Mister Hart. Our ancient sources only offer us a glimpse through a small hole. We must always remember that these surviving accounts were carefully crafted. They were allowed to be written by the reigning emperors, kings, and popes of the time. They no more tell the whole story than does, say, your *Life* magazine."

Hart chuckled at that. He had thought the same thing many times after reading the magazine.

Adler continued, "In Mehmet's record, he cited the last time the power was let loose on the city, when the emperor Justinian reigned." Adler paused. "You and I know this power as the famous Plague of Justinian—a plague that, according to the sources of the time, killed ten thousand people a day."

Hart's memory was a bit sketchy on the subject, but he seemed to recall the event from his undergraduate studies. The Plague of Justinian ravaged Constantinople in the sixth century. It was so named because Justinian was the Byzantine emperor at the time. But Hart still did not see how all of these events could be connected.

"I can see that you are having trouble connecting the dots, Mister Hart," Adler said sympathetically.

"To put it mildly," Hart admitted.

"Do not try to. I have spent a lifetime digging up these ancient civilizations and the truth came to me only a few weeks ago, when I found something in Constantine's grave—something Sturm never saw, and something he never will see. I destroyed it. That is why I was made a prisoner. That is why I was tortured."

"Do you mind shedding some light for us," Isabelle

said suddenly, a slight tinge of irritation in her tone. "Instead of this history lesson, why don't you just tell us what the hell this item was?"

Hart shot Isabelle a scornful glance to silence her. Adler was talking. That was what they wanted. Hart made sure he revived the conversation quickly.

"What did you find?" Hart asked intently.

Adler sighed. "You have brought me this far, Mister Hart; I suppose it is time to trust you. What I discovered was a parchment, a document that was much more valuable than the scroll or the canopic jar. It was an imperial record that contained the official seals of a dozen houses that ruled Rome or Byzantine at one time or another. It was a pass-down record—a turnover document of sorts, obviously overseen by the Church, and passed on to each emperor upon his succession, officially burdening him with the prodigious responsibility of Rome's great secret. It appeared that the document was crafted during the reign of Justinian, and his seal is the first and oldest that appears. It was one of the most remarkable things I have ever seen in all of my travels. A parchment that had once been held by the hand of Justinian. It was a true treasure of the past." Adler looked at his open palm as if to remember how the centuries-old leather had felt in his hand. "But I could not let Sturm or his men get their hands on it."

"Why?" Isabelle asked, somewhat more conducively, as if she had taken note of Hart's earlier hint. "What could they have done with it?"

"The document contained a short chronicle of the weapon's development and use. It tells how, in A.D. 391, the bishop of Alexandria ordered the local temple of the cult of Serapis to be burned to the ground. But before the temple was destroyed, the bishop ensured that all of its riches and secrets were plundered. Within the catacombs of the temple they found a copper scroll with demotic script on it and a canopic jar full of gold-plated teeth. The jar was capped with the double-headed eagle symbol of the Anok Sabe cult. The bishop knew of the story of Anok Sabe, and he knew exactly what these items represented. The scroll, supposedly written by Anok Sabe himself, contained a set of instructions—a recipe, if you will—for turning the pulp preserved within the teeth into a biological pestilence such as the modern world has never seen." Adler looked at both of them. "In modern terms, Anok Sabe was something of a Frederick Griffith of the ancient world. He had devised a way to combine the DNA of the virus that had killed the Assyrians outside Jerusalem in 701 B.C. with that of any live modern virus to produce one of the deadliest weapons ever known to man. The resulting virus would be so volatile, so deadly, that it could kill an entire city, or army, in a matter of hours, and then consume itself so that it did not spread to nearby population centers."

"When informed of the find, Theodosius the First ordered the scroll and jar to be locked away and kept a state secret. With barbarian tribes encroaching on the empire's borders, and the once-great legions decimated by countless civil wars, the emperor thought the weapon might be called upon someday as a last-ditch defense against the barbarians. That day arrived during the reign of his son, Honorius, who in A.D. 410 sat powerless in his capital at Ravenna while the Visigoths sacked Rome. Determined that such an outrage would never happen again, Honorius ordered the development of Anok Sabe's weapon. Collaborating with his counterpart, the emperor of the Eastern Roman Empire, Honorius gave the task to the greatest minds of the age, and thus the Neoplatonic Academy of Athens was founded as a front to cover up the research efforts. The scholars of the academy spent four decades devising the deadly potion, finishing their project in A.D. 452, just as the Huns invaded Italy. Expediently, the Huns were selected to be the first victims of the new weapon. An imperial agent mixed the potion into a well near the camp of one of the Hun hordes. Within hours, thousands of barbarians and their horses were dead. Unfortunately, the virulence of the pestilence had been underestimated by its creators and it went right on killing, spreading to a nearby Roman village. Every creature in the village died as well. The next day, Pope Leo the First met with Attila, the Hunnish king, and threatened to release the weapon on his whole army. Attila and his Huns left Italy, never to threaten Rome again."

"If what you say is true," Hart said, "then why all the cover-up? Why not let the greater barbarian world know of the weapon to ward off future invasions?"

"Roman histories contain no mention of the weapon, partly due to the carnage it wreaked on the unfortunate village, but also because both the imperial family and the Church felt that it was best for the people to believe that the hand of God had saved them—and in a sense, it did. The weapon remained a secret of the emperors and the Church through the centuries. After the fall of the Western Empire in the late fifth century, the secret lived on under the Byzantine emperors in Constantinople, with only one mishap."

"The Plague of Justinian," Isabelle said.

"Yes, Miss Sevilla," Adler said with surprise in his tone. "The record was not clear about what exactly happened. It just mentioned that the weapon was unleashed on the city in the year 541 during the reign of Justinian, and the city was devastated. If the weapon was released, I can only imagine it was due to the interfaction fighting that was rampant in the city at the time. I suspect a rogue scholar at the Platonic Academy was blamed for the disaster because shortly thereafter the academy was closed by Emperor Justinian, never to reopen again. The ancient world gave way to what we call the Middle Ages.

"So the emperors kept the secret safe until Constantine the Eleventh's reign and the capture of Constantinople?"

"Yes, Mister Hart. Ironically enough, precisely one millennium after Attila threatened Rome, another enemy was beating down the walls of Constantinople— Mehmet the Second and the Ottomans. The parchment was very detailed about this event. Mehmet was scared and agreed to stop the sack of the city. True to his word, after only a few hours in possession of the city, Mehmet ordered an end to all looting and killing. This was in sharp contrast to the customary policy of the Ottomans to allow three days of plunder as payment to the troops for storming a fortified city. Constantine made his home in Sweden, where his family still had deep-seated loyalties from the descendants of the Varangian Guard. Somehow, the scroll and the canopic jar ended up in Sweden with him. I assume they were spirited away from Constantinople by Giovanni Guistiniani, a Genoese officer who was wounded in the last hours of the siege and who escaped aboard a galley. Guistiniani died a few weeks later of his wounds, but it seems feasible that he could have ordered the items sent to the exiled emperor before his death."

"So the weapon was buried with him, and this is what the Nazis are after?" Hart asked. "And I suppose that's why those artifacts are aboard *U-2553*, and the U-boat is taking them to some hidden Nazi research facility where a bunch of German scientists stand ready to turn the items back into Constantine's weapon?"

"That is correct, Mister Hart."

"Then what the hell are we doing here? We should be after that damn U-boat!"

"Wait, Mister Hart." Adler raised a hand. "The jar and the scroll are merely the raw materials. It will take months, if not years, for Sturm's men to decipher them and make anything useful out of them. We are here to find the shortcut, if you will—the actual potion developed by the Romans."

"What?" Isabelle said, her voice somewhat quivering. "You mean it's here? After all this time?"

Adler nodded. "The final entry on the parchment led me to that conclusion. It was a riddle, and I think I have solved it."

"What was the final entry?"

"I have committed it to memory. It read, *Where the*

Blessed Mother and Saint John the Baptist gaze upon the hands of Christ, Christ's Hands reveal where the sacraments were carried."

Hart saw Isabelle look at him briefly before she asked, "And what does that mean?"

"Ah, Miss Sevilla," Adler said smugly. "I think I have told you too much already, and I still need your protection. If you want to know, and you are committed to making sure that Sturm does not get this weapon, then remain with me, and you will see."

Hart was suddenly skeptical about the whole thing. In spite of Isabelle's apparent conversion, Hart still had to consider what they were really talking about here. Everything hung on a few Egyptian artifacts, a piece of parchment, and a silly myth about a priest who walked across the desert. Everything else was hearsay. It reminded him of Coronado's search for the famed Seven Cities of Cibolo. He went to great lengths to find them, killing thousands of Native Americans in the process, but when he finally reached them, he found nothing more than a few collections of pueblo huts.

"Adler," Hart said. "Be on the level with me here. Is this all just a bunch of bullshit?"

"I believe your own mission here is evidence enough that it is not. Undoubtedly, your OSS superiors have attached some importance to it. Otherwise, why would they have sent you aboard the U-boat?"

"My mission was to infiltrate the U-boat so I could find out what you Nazis were up to." Hart shook his head in disillusionment. "Now I'm starting to get the feeling this is all nothing more than another of Hitler's delusional fantasies—like the search for the origins of the Aryan race."

"I assure you this is not a fantasy, Mister Hart. This weapon is very real. It exists there, in the heart of Istanbul, and the nation that first learns to master it will control the world."

At that moment, the ferry touched the pier, lines were thrown across, and the hundreds of passengers began filing toward the gangways to disembark.

"Well, here we are, safe and sound, Doctor," Hart said, still somewhat unsure about the whole thing. "Where to?"

Adler smiled and then looked up at the city on the sloping hill.

"There," he said simply, pointing at a set of four sharp minarets rising from a clump of trees at the top of a hill. The spires surrounded a circular cathedral-like structure. Adler sighed as if setting eyes on an old friend. "We are going to Hagia Sophia."

CHAPTER THIRTY-SIX

Hart stood mesmerized for several minutes in the courtyard of the most fabulous structure he had ever seen. The towering minarets that he had seen from the waterfront were now directly above him and reached up into the sky as if to touch heaven. They were at least 150 feet high. One appeared to be red brick, while the other three looked like white limestone. He stood before the western entrance and gazed upon a perfect harmony of windows, entrances, and rising arches, culminating in the massive dome in the center. The intricate brick- and stonework was a fascinating combination of nonuniformity and precision. No two bricks appeared to be the same, but together they made objects of perfect proportion.

He had been in Istanbul before but never had the time to see Hagia Sophia in all its glory. Hagia Sophia, the Church of the Holy Wisdom, the great temple of Justinian I, changed the history of architecture forever.

The very stones themselves, silent and powerful, seemed to stare back at the three visitors with arrogance, each stone having witnessed historical events that were now mere shadows of the imagination. Romans, Greeks, Crusaders, Ottomans, emperors, and kings had stood before them. Who were these pathetic visitors who dared stand before them now?

"Magnificent, isn't it?" Adler said, apparently pleased at the openmouthed stares of the two Americans. "It was constructed by the emperor Justinian, in the year 537, only a few years before the great plague broke out. The minarets were added later, after the Ottomans took over. For a thousand years it was the largest cathedral in the world. Now it is the focal point of our search."

For your lost city of Cibola? Hart thought.

"It is said that entire barbarian tribes converted to Christianity after visiting this place. Mehmet the Second, after taking the city, admitted its construction was inspired by God. He even turned it into a mosque instead of destroying it. Now it is a museum—a testament to man's devotion to God, sitting at the crossroads of two religions that claim Him as their own."

"It truly is amazing," Isabelle uttered in a small voice, as if speaking too loudly might offend the ancient stone.

"We are standing in the spot where some of the greatest figures of history have stood. Justinian, Belasarius, Mehmet . . ."

As Adler talked, Hart allowed himself to look away from the structure long enough to size up the other people milling about the courtyard. It was hard to believe there was a war on just three hundred miles north of here. There were about two dozen people in various-sized groups admiring the architecture just as Hart, Adler, and Isabelle were. They were the usual mixed bag of tourists one might find in a neutral city during a war. Caucasians, Asians, Arabs, some Africans. It was impossible to tell their occupations, but most had the swagger typical of diplomats and businessmen. And that made sense, for who else traveled in wartime?

Adler beckoned for Hart and Isabelle to follow him inside. Once inside, Hart was not prepared for what he was about to see. The architecture of the outside was nothing when compared to the views that met him within. Marble floors, columns, and ceilings that never seemed to end. Everywhere he stepped he was greeted by a once-in-a-lifetime vision of beauty, the natural light entering through high windows and glistening upon gold chandeliers the size of a house, mosaics that he could stare at for hours, and vast surfaces covered with marble and porphyry that changed color with the passage of the sun across the sky. But when they finally reached the nave, he could hardly speak from the splendor he beheld. He was now looking up at the underside of the central dome. It was a hundred feet above him and appeared to defy gravity with its ornately decorated ribs branching far out from the apex. The dome was ringed with dozens of windows that let the light dance on the high arches and columns, giving the place an eternal presence. Hart could not imagine how sixth-century man could have built such a thing.

"Solomon, I have outdone thee," Adler said at Hart's shoulder.

Hart realized his mouth had been hanging open. "Excuse me? What did you say?"

"It is what Justinian said upon completion of this wonder. He felt that he had built a temple that surpassed the temple of Solomon mentioned in the Bible."

"How are you certain the item is here?" Isabelle asked Adler in a businesslike whisper. The place demanded whispers since any normal voice echoed throughout the many-arched doorways and marble chambers. "How do you know the riddle has anything to do with the weapon?"

"I must confess, Miss Sevilla, it puzzled me, too, for several days after I first read the riddle. I even contacted a colleague in Stockholm about it. Of course, I did not tell him where I found the riddle, but I gave it to him word for word to see if he could make anything of it. I had low expectations that anything would come of it and had planned to take my inquiries elsewhere, when a package arrived for me at our dig site at Östersund. It was from my colleague. The package contained a magazine—the March issue of your *Metropolitan Museum Bulletin*. My colleague had marked an article about an American organization called the Byzantine Institute of America that had recently completed the restoration of several mosaics in Hagia Sophia. The article contained photos of the mosaics. My friend had circled one photo in particular. After I saw it, everything became very clear to me."

Hart and Isabelle looked at him with puzzled expressions.

"You see, there is an old legend, that when the Ottomans took the city, a mass was being held right here, where we now stand. It is said that people were cut down in the pews and aisles as they prayed." Adler paused, gesturing to the wide-open space before them. "It is hard to believe, isn't it, that such barbarism could ever occur in such a holy place? The Ottomans were such savage people!"

Hart thought about mentioning what the Germans had done to Leningrad and Stalingrad in modern times, but he decided not to bring it up.

"It is said," Adler continued, "that the priests who were presiding over the mass gathered up their implements and disappeared into the walls before the enemy could reach them." Adler placed one of his pale hands on the cold marble wall nearest to him. "The legend says that when Constantinople is once again in Christian hands, the priests will appear and continue the mass where they left off."

"And you believe these implements are the sacraments mentioned in the riddle?" Hart asked.

Adler nodded.

"Where the Blessed Mother and Saint John the Baptist gaze upon the hands of Christ . . . ," Isabelle quoted. "That's how it goes, right?"

Adler nodded again.

"You said it was a photo of a mosaic that keyed you in," Isabelle thought out loud. "John, Mary, and Christ all depicted in one mosaic. It's a Deesis! We're looking for a Deesis!"

Adler smiled brightly and clapped his hands. "Yes, yes, a Deesis. That is it, my girl."

Hart looked at Isabelle with some amazement.

"Art history was my major, Matt," she said, as if to explain. "You know that."

"You always did have a good memory."

She ignored his sarcasm and began scanning the ceiling. "So we're looking for a Deesis somewhere in this building. Help us, Matt."

"Excuse me," Hart said, feeling somewhat uninformed. "But what the hell is a Deesis?"

Isabelle did not seem to hear him and began walking around the nave with face upturned, examining the different mosaics that dotted the resplendent ceiling.

Adler seemed amused, but took a moment to fill Hart in. "A Deesis, Mister Hart, is a portrayal of Christ enthroned sitting between a supplicant John the Baptist and the Virgin Mother. Christ holds a book representing the Gospels."

"So what is she looking for?"

"You can see Islamic symbols all around you, but you will also see symbols from Christianity. This was, after all, a church for a thousand years before it became a mosque. Like all cathedrals of the time, this one contains many Christian mosaics. One of them is a Deesis."

Hart could see a few colorfully ordained figures on the ceiling, and he remembered seeing some above the entrance to the building. They all seemed faded and in disrepair.

"I don't see it," Isabelle said from the other side of the nave. "Not a Deesis, anyway."

"Wouldn't the Ottomans have destroyed any images of Christ when they turned this place into a mosque?" Hart asked.

"Close, Mister Hart. They did not destroy them. They simply covered them over with plaster."

Hart took a look at the thousands of square feet of plaster covering portions of the walls and ceiling. "Then the Deesis mosaic could be anywhere. It would take an army to find it."

"Lucky for us, Mister Hart, someone has already found it. Remember that I have seen a photo of it. As I said before, the Byzantine Institute of America has found and uncovered many mosaics over the past ten years. The Deesis was discovered in 1933."

"So, *where* is it, Adler?" Isabelle said with impatience, apparently disappointed that Adler had allowed her to look for it in vain.

Adler gave a superior smile. "In a quiet, out-of-the-way corner."

Then, seemingly satisfied that he had both Hart and Isabelle wanting to strangle him for an answer, he beckoned for them to follow him. He marched for the nearest exit from the nave and to the ramp portal that led up to the upper gallery. This was the second level of the cathedral, and it wrapped around the nave like a horseshoe. It was just as elaborately fashioned as the rest of the church, but it also offered an excellent view of the floor below. As Hart walked briskly to keep up with Adler and Isabelle, he considered that this was where he would have preferred standing had he ever attended a mass here. As Adler walked ahead, turning the corner to go walk along the north side of the gallery, his shoes clicking on the marble floor, Hart caught a glimpse of Isabelle's face.

She was watching Adler with a look that Hart had not seen for many years. It was not a look of impatience, but rather one of anger. The last time he had seen her this way, they were undercover together in France, and a drunken German colonel had forced his hand up her blouse. Oddly, the German colonel did not report for duty the next day. He was found dead in his quarters with a bayonet knife lodged in his throat. The Gestapo had launched an investigation that almost resulted in Hart's team's exposure. Hart had never asked her about the incident, but he had put her on notice not to let her short-fused temper get out of hand. Adler did not know what she was capable of. Hart sighed at the thought. Sadly, he *did* know, and the knowledge was weighing heavily on him.

Hart stepped aside for a moment, allowing Isabelle and Adler to walk ahead. He looked over the rail at the floor below. The same clumps of tourists were strolling around, and none looked suspicious. Then Hart saw a man enter the nave wearing a gray hat and a gray wool suit. The man stopped in the middle of the floor, looked around for a few seconds, and then his eyes scanned the upper gallery. When he caught sight of Hart, his eyes stopped.

Hart nodded a greeting at the man. The man nodded back, and then quickly walked out of the nave.

"Mister Hart?" Adler called from a side corner of the gallery up ahead. "Mister Hart, we've found it."

Hart glanced over the rail a final time and then walked briskly to reach Isabelle and Adler, who were

staring at something on a wall that was facing away from
Hart. When Hart got around the corner, he could see
the mosaic.

It was exactly as Adler had described. In the Byzantine style, the mosaic was predominantly inlaid with
gold-painted tiles and depicted Christ in the center and
Mary and John the Baptist on either side of Him. Hart
could not tell if Mary and John were looking at Christ's
hands or if they were looking at something in Christ's
hands, since only the upper half of the mosaic had been
fully restored and the bottom part was badly damaged.
The figures were calming, though. The face of Christ
stared back at the viewer with a soft expression that was
both warm and firm.

They all three stared at the work of art, Isabelle quot-
ing the parchment lines over and over.

*"Christ's Hands reveal where the sacraments were car-
ried . . . Christ's Hands reveal where the sacraments were
carried . . ."*

In the mosaic, one hand of Christ was probably holding the Book of the Gospels and either was lost to the
ages or had yet to be uncovered, while the visible hand
was arranged in the traditional sign of the cross, with
two fingers pointing in one direction and two fingers
pointing in another direction. Hart tried to follow both
sets of fingers to a particular spot in the room, but they
seemed to point off into space, to no place in particular.
Adler evidently came to the same conclusion, because his
face took on the dejected look of a man whose whole
purpose in life had been diminished.

"How can this be?" the German scientist said, almost

sobbing. "I have put so many lives in danger, and there is nothing here. Nothing . . . nothing . . ."

"There has to be!" Isabelle said desperately, as if she too had invested everything in this one hope of finding the secret.

Hart looked up at the eyes of Christ once again. They were penetrating, and hypnotic, but Hart managed to notice that there was something different about this mosaic from the others he had seen in the cathedral.

"Adler," he said, "were all of these created by the same artist?"

"What?" Adler was only halfway engaged and held his head in his hands.

"The mosaics. They appear to have different styles."

"Yes. Many different artists, from many different periods. But this is the only Deesis. This is the only mosaic in which Mary and John look on the Hands of Christ."

"But there is only one hand pointing in this mosaic," Hart said, gesturing to the only visible hand of Christ. "We can't see the other one from all the damage, but I can only assume it is holding the book, and is not pointing anywhere."

"Yes?" Adler said, apparently uncertain where Hart was going with this.

"Are you certain the parchment stated the *Hands* of Christ, in the plural?"

"Yes. It is specific."

Hart looked around the room. There were no other images of Christ nearby, but there were two farther toward the end of the gallery, in two mosaics on a far wall that was not quite visible from the Deesis. Hart marched toward the other mosaics with Adler and Isabelle following him.

"What is this one?" Hart asked, pointing to one of the new mosaics, which portrayed a similar image of Christ enthroned, except now the Messiah sat between a regal-looking man and woman. The man appeared to be a king, and he was holding a small sack. The woman could have been his queen, and in her hands she held a scroll with visible writing on it.

"This is called the Empress Zoe mosaic, Mister Hart."

"So, that is Empress Zoe, on the left hand of Christ?"

"Yes. She was empress of the Byzantines in the mid-eleventh century."

Hart noticed that in this image, Christ's hands were arranged in a different blessing sign, with the right ring finger and thumb together and the remaining three fingers extended. Also different in this mosaic were Christ's eyes. They did not look at the viewer at all but were looking someplace else—somewhere off to the right.

"The eyes!" Hart exclaimed. "They're looking at the Deesis. This must be the other hand of Christ referred to in the riddle."

Adler shook his head. "Impossible, Mister Hart. At the time this mosaic was crafted, the Deesis mosaic did not exist. It did not exist for another hundred years."

Hart thought for a long moment, still studying the mosaic before him. He noticed something strange about the writing on the scroll in Empress Zoe's hands.

"Could this mosaic have been altered after the other mosaic was finished?"

"I suppose it's possible, Mister Hart, but unlikely. Why would you think that?"

"Because the Greek writing on the scroll does not fit in the space provided. You can see where the artist started another line at the end and squeezed in the rest of the text, much like someone taking notes today would if they ran out of space on the page."

Adler gave a conciliatory nod, then rubbed his chin. "This scroll proclaims the donations given by the empress to the Church."

"So much for *letting thine alms be in secret*, eh?" Hart grinned.

"I can cite a hundred inscriptions with the same flaw, Mister Hart. It was a common enough error."

Hart shook his head. "I don't buy it, Adler. Would someone who made such an exquisite work of art ruin his creation with a botched line of text? Look at the eyes of Christ and the heads of the two monarchs. This thing was updated."

Upon further inspection, Adler suddenly appeared interested. He, too, now studied the mosaic more closely and seemed to shake off his melancholy mood. "Yes. It is as you say. Undoubtedly, this mosaic was altered after its creation. Very good, Mister Hart."

"Look at Christ's hands in this one," Hart continued. "The right hand of Christ has the index and middle finger together with the ring finger and thumb joined. The little finger is by itself. That's the sign for a blessing, isn't it?"

Adler nodded. "This particular hand sign indicates *IC XC*. It is an abbreviation for Iesous Christos—Jesus

Christ. It is a common enough sign in early Christian art."

"But why is the hand of Christ in the Deesis mosaic in the form of a cross?"

Adler did not respond, but he followed Hart over to the next mosaic, just to the right, on the other side of a tall arched window. In this portrait, Mary was portrayed holding Christ, as a child, in her arms. The boy Christ was also extending a blessing with his right hand.

"The sign of Jesus Christ again," Hart said, pointing to the child's right hand, which formed the same sign as the Empress Zoe mosaic. "And look at the eyes of the child Christ. They are looking directly ahead, as if to direct the viewer toward the Deesis mosaic."

Hart began marching back toward the Deesis mosaic and felt Adler and Isabelle follow him. Looking at it again, this time he saw the symbols *IC* and *XC* on either side of Christ's head.

"It's as if the other mosaics are pointing us to this one," he said. "But now we're back where we started."

This time the German scientist had nothing to offer and again took on a dejected look. Isabelle, on the other hand, had stopped short halfway between the two sets of mosaics.

"What is it?" Hart asked her.

"I'm just looking at those two mosaics from back here, both on either side of the window. Everything else in here is overdone with arches and circles, but this is too symmetric. It's too square. It doesn't fit. There has to be something to this arrangement."

Hart looked at the same thing. She was right. The mosaics seemed out of place.

"Why fill this one corner of the upper gallery with wall mosaics and leave the rest of the gallery bare?" Hart asked. "There has to be a reason for it."

"The upper gallery," Adler said suddenly. "That is it, of course! We are in the upper gallery." He walked over to join them and pointed at the tall window between the two mosaics. "The window—it is the spine. The mosaics—they are the arms."

"The spine?" Isabelle said in a puzzled tone. "The arms? Of what?"

Hart suddenly saw where Adler was going and answered for him. "Of a cross."

"This is the top of the cross the Deesis is directing us to!" Adler said excitedly, now full of energy.

"If this is the top," Isabelle said, "then the bottom must be . . ."

"On the first level!"

All three ran to the rail and peered over trying to see what landmark formed the base of the cross. They had to skirt halfway around the upper gallery until they could see what lay directly beneath the upper gallery mosaics. But when they finally reached the right vantage point, there was no doubting the place they were supposed to start their search.

On the first floor, tucked away behind a column, where they could only just see it from this angle, was a small, plain wooden door. It was in perfect alignment with the tall window on the gallery above it, forming the bottom of a perfect cross.

All three looked at each other. They had found the starting point for their search, and now they only had to go through that small door on the other side of the nave in order to find out if the covenant Constantine XI made with Mehmet II had a real threat behind it, or if the emperor Constantine was the greatest con man history had ever known.

CHAPTER THIRTY-SEVEN

They entered the low, narrow passage and were instantly met with a putrid, dank aroma. Dusty cobwebs hung everywhere, so many that it seemed one could conduct an arachnology study of the evolution of spiderwebs over a millennium from this single passage.

"It is quite possible that we are the first to enter this passage in five hundred years," Adler commented, the excitement hardly hidden from his voice.

Luckily, the keen archaeologist in Adler had directed them to purchase flashlights on the way to Hagia Sophia that morning, and now these three small lights lit the path at their feet. Even with the flashlights, they had trouble avoiding the gray stone bricks that dotted their path and jutted out from the wall, obviously left that way by one or more earthquakes in Istanbul's past. These dingy stones were in sharp contrast to the beauty of the cathedral only a few feet away.

Hart glanced back at the broken plaster and crumbling bricks where they had battered a hole in the wall of the closet—because *closet* was the only way to describe the small room they had found on the other side of that small door forming the base of the cross. From its small size, lack of windows, and close proximity to the business end of the nave, Adler had concluded that it had once been a prep room of sorts for the orthodox priests presiding over the Byzantine mass. Who knew what the Muslims had used the tiny room for? Now it was being used as a storage location for folding chairs, scaffolding pieces, and empty crates. The makeshift storage closet was so small that it had taken Adler only a few minutes to find the tunnel's entrance. Using an iron piece of scaffolding, he had tapped on the walls of the room until he found a spot that was unquestionably hollow. Then, with the help of the iron rod, they had taken turns chiseling away at the centuries-old plaster and mortar until a hole opened in the wall—a hole that led to the tunnel through which they now plodded.

They continued, slowly, cautiously. Hart thought he detected the path developing a slightly descending slope, but if they were descending deeper into the earth with every step, it was hardly noticeable. Obviously, whoever had constructed the tunnel had made it easy to traverse, probably to accommodate its use by the imperial family.

"Judging from the state of things," Adler said, pointing to a stone brick in their path that had obviously fallen from the ceiling some time in the past, "it is a miracle this tunnel has not collapsed."

"That's comforting," Hart said, looking up at the dark ominous ceiling only a few inches from his head.

They continued down the dark passage for several

more minutes. Their flashlights could not find the end of it, and it seemed to stretch off into eternal blackness.

"Where do you think this leads, Adler?" Isabelle said after coughing up some of the five-hundred-year-old layer of dust they were disturbing with every step.

"I have spent much of my life inside tunnels such as this one, but I am a terrible judge of direction. I do not know where it leads. But Constantinople was famous for its underground passages. Perhaps this tunnel once led to the imperial palace, or to the seawalls."

No sooner had Adler finished speaking than he came to an abrupt halt.

"What's this?" He shone the flashlight on something at his feet.

Hart and Isabelle directed their flashlights at the same object, and the collective beams revealed what appeared to be a heap of rusty scrap metal. It took Hart only a few more seconds of staring and a little imagination to realize that this collection of metal had once been a human being.

"He was a soldier," Adler said, kneeling and running a hand over the metal links between which white bone showed through. "Or perhaps a knight."

Adler's hand moved up the remains to a corroded metal plate that partially covered the skull, all that was left of what must have been an ornate suit of armor.

"One of Constantine's men?" Hart asked.

"Perhaps." Adler sighed. "The state of decay makes it impossible to tell in this light. But I believe this style is Byzantine, and it is of the right period."

"Whoever he was, he died guarding this passage," Isabelle said, pointing to a long rusty object lying beside the body that was easily recognizable as a sword. "That means the Ottomans made it down here."

"Not necessarily, Miss Sevilla. If the Ottomans killed him, they would not have left his body to rot away. At the very least, the sword and armor would have been taken. So, in a sense, this is a good sign." Adler paused, then shone his flashlight farther down the passage. "The question now is, what was he guarding?"

There was only one way to find out. The small group began to trudge down the tunnel once more. They turned a bend in the tunnel, and the air began to grow colder at every step. With no opening to look back on, the darkness took on a new meaning. It seemed even the beams of their flashlights were swallowed by the empty void ahead. They finally came to a heavy double door that blocked their path. The doors had obviously once been decorative but now appeared as half-rotten wood affixed to a corroded metal lattice. The air was thin in this space, and Hart assumed the lack of oxygen had helped to somewhat preserve the entranceway.

Adler pushed on the doors once and was met with a creaking resistance. He peered through the crack between them.

"It's bolted on the inside," he said. "The bolt is clearly visible from this side. Perhaps we can find something long to stick into the—"

"Stand back," Isabelle interrupted him, brandishing her Colt M1903 pistol and aiming it at the latch mechanism.

"Miss Sevilla, wait—"

Adler tried to stop her, but before he could, she had fired three quick shots into the latch, breaking the five-hundred-year-old fixture into several pieces.

Isabelle smiled as the lock fell apart and the tension was released on the doors. But her elation soon turned to a look of uncertainty when a low rumbling filled the tunnel. Several trails of dust and a few clods of dirt fell from the roof, and Hart could swear that he saw the brick above him move about an inch. Eventually, the vibration stopped and the tunnel returned to its former state.

"Please, Miss Sevilla," Adler said, breathing shortly. "Do not do that again." Adler appeared quite shaken and had apparently been in enough near cave-ins in his career to make him that way.

After Adler had collected himself, he pressed open the doors, and they all entered a small chamber. The air here was thinner than it was in the tunnel. The beams of their flashlights revealed what appeared to be a row of five crumbling church pews. They all faced an altar of equal disrepair. A solitary figure sat in the front pew, slumped over to one side. It was just a skeleton, a few bones inside a faded linen garment.

"This man was a priest," Adler remarked, looking into the face of the skeleton.

"A strange place to die," Hart said. "It looks like he keeled over during mass."

Adler appeared not to hear him. Two other sets of skeletal remains had grabbed his attention. These were lying on the steps leading up to the altar. One wore armor similar to the guard in the tunnel, and the other wore the same linen robes of the priest on the pew.

"Maybe this soldier killed the two priests," Hart remarked.

Adler shook his head. "There are no signs of violence. Both men do not appear to have fallen. Their bodies appear to be in a supplicant position. I believe they were praying before the altar when they died."

"Then what killed them?"

"I do not know," Adler said distantly as he shone his flashlight on the bodies and then ran the beam up the steps, up to the concrete altar, and up to the wall beyond it, where something sparkled.

They all gasped as the light revealed a large mosaic that stretched from floor to ceiling. It was a life-size image of Christ. The Messiah was standing in a dazzlingly simple blue robe and was extending his open hands toward the viewer.

Hart noticed the eyes. How confident and compassionate they were. They were all-knowing, all-seeing, as if the image itself could search into the very soul of the viewer. The eyes emanated a sense of ownership of this small chapel. But rather than feeling like an intruder, Hart felt as though he and the others were welcome, as if the silent mosaic had been waiting for them, even expecting them, for five hundred years.

"There is no other door out of here," Isabelle announced from the other side of the room. "It looks like this is the end of the tunnel."

The distant sound of rushing water reverberated

through the brick walls for a few seconds and then was silent.

"What was that?" Isabelle asked.

Adler shrugged. "Probably a water pipe several feet above us. Remember, Istanbul is a modern city built on top of an ancient one."

"I'll bet he could tell us what happened to those priests," Hart said, still captivated by the image of the Messiah staring back at him.

Isabelle poked around the boxes and canvas bags while Adler examined the skeletal remains.

"Nothing!" Isabelle exclaimed in frustration. "There's nothing here!"

"I cannot find anything of significance either." Adler shook his head while casually examining a gold necklace around the neck of one of the priests. "Some rather remarkable artifacts, but nothing of significance." His shoulders slumped and he sighed heavily. "This is a dead end."

"Wait a minute!" Hart said suddenly.

While the other two had been rummaging through the place, he had continued to study the mosaic. When he got past those hypnotic eyes, he had noticed something—something that he had not seen before.

"Christ's Hands reveal where the sacraments were carried . . ." Hart said to no one in particular. "Adler, look!"

Hart first shined the light onto the open hands of Christ, which could be interpreted as gesturing to something just in front of the mosaic. Then Hart moved the light down until it settled on the plain concrete altar at the top of the stairs. If the image in the mosaic was pointing to any item in the room, this was it.

Adler approached the altar, the other two following closely behind. Upon further examination, they saw that the top of the altar had seams. It was obviously a lid, and the altar itself a great concrete container. They all three took hold of the corners of the lid, heaved with all of their might, and managed to scoot the slab over about a foot.

Adler was the first to shine his light inside.

"Gott im Himmel!" he said, unable to control his excitement.

He reached inside and pulled out a bottle made of glass. The glass was foggy, but when Hart shone his light on it, he could see an oozing oily substance inside. The bottle was sealed with a glass cap and wax and contained a stamped symbol that Hart instantly recognized as a two-headed eagle. It was the symbol of Constantine XI, and now Hart knew it was the symbol of the deadly mixture inside, the ancient virus that had killed hundreds of thousands over the ages.

"Is that it?" Isabelle asked. Hart noticed that her eyes were as wide as Adler's and that she could hardly speak.

"If the weapon exists," Adler said, his voice quivering, "then this is it. We have found it."

"So what do you think Constantine's priests were going to do with that stuff?" Hart asked.

"Perhaps poison an aqueduct, or a well. Perhaps feed it to the Ottomans' cattle. I am not sure."

"Do you think it's still potent?" Isabelle asked. "After all these years?"

"I am just an archaeologist, Miss Sevilla. Not a bio-chemist. I am sure your government has someone who can find out."

"So then, you are willing to hand it over to us?" Hart asked.

"Yes, Mister Hart. Colonel Sturm and his men do not have it, and that is all I care about. I trust your government to do the right thing with it, and I will offer my services in any way I can."

"You are doing the right thing, Mister Adler." Hart shone the flashlight on his watch. "The U.S. consulate here in Istanbul is our best bet. They can arrange for its safe transport out of Turkey. We had better get going."

Hart took one last look at the mosaic, then caught a glimpse of Isabelle in the beam of his flashlight. She was watching intently as Adler carefully placed the glass bottle in the satchel on his shoulder. Her face was fixed in an apprehensive expression, as if she did not trust the experienced archaeologist to properly handle the object.

"Isabelle?" he said. "Are you all right?"

She looked at him and flashed a quick, impassive smile. "Yes. This thin air has me a bit hypertensive. I'll be okay when we get out of here."

Hart nodded, but he did not believe her. Something else was going on. "Then let's get going."

CHAPTER THIRTY-EIGHT

They left the passage and exited the closet, Adler carrying the satchel that now contained the glass jar with the substance. As they crossed the nave, walking briskly, Hart noticed that there were more tourists in the building than had been before. They had been in the tunnel for more than an hour, so he dismissed the increased activity as the museum's midday peak and kept walking.

Most of these people are probably just diplomats taking a tour on their lunch break, he kept telling himself. His adrenaline was up from the remarkable discovery, and for the first time since the start of this mission, he truly believed millions of lives were at stake.

Before they had made it halfway across the big open space, a man in a brown business suit appeared before them. The man had his back to them and he appeared to be admiring the ceiling. At first, Hart thought the man was another tourist, so Hart vectored the group to divert around him. But then, something in the way the man moved caught Hart's eye. It was a familiar move, and one that Hart could pick out of a hundred people. He had read in one of his operative training journals that the manner in which a person moves can be as unique as a fingerprint. That was certainly the case in this instance, because Hart had identified the man by the time the man turned around to face him.

"Hello, Agent Hart."

Hart found himself looking directly into the eyes of Ives. The tall spymaster was standing directly in their path, appearing calm as usual. But Hart could not fail to notice how his eyes quickly focused on the satchel at Adler's hip.

"Agent Sevilla, you're looking as ravishing as ever," Ives said in a polite tone.

"What the hell are you doing here, *Captain Ives*?" Hart said with contempt, motioning for Adler to stand behind him.

Ives looked once at Isabelle and then back at Hart. "Admiral McDonough sent me. He sent me to warn you—about Agent Sevilla."

"Bullshit!" Hart retorted. "The last time I saw you, you told me McDonough was a traitor."

"Listen to me, Matt," Ives pleaded now as if he were Hart's new best friend. "Isabelle has betrayed us all. She's working for the other side. If you let her leave this place with that"—he pointed at the satchel—"she'll kill you both, and the Nazis will have it."

"Don't listen to him, Matt," Isabelle said. "He's lying."

Hart noticed that she had drawn her OSS-issue Colt M1903 pistol and was holding it on Ives while using the flap of her jacket to keep it hidden from the nearby tourists. Ives appeared somewhat amused at the sight, but if Ives himself was armed, Hart could not see a weapon.

"Think about it, Matt," Ives said, not taking his eyes from the gun pointed at his torso. "She disappears in Spain. The next thing you know your team is captured. Then she shows up in Austria, out of the blue. Miraculously, she rescues you from a fortress crawling with the enemy. She gains your confidence as easy as teaching a dog to chase its own tail. Now you have led her here. Her Nazi masters planned it all very well. They are using your trust in her to get to you."

Isabelle had logical explanations for everything that Ives now mentioned, but Hart had not simply taken her explanations at face value as Ives now implied.

"Why didn't you or the admiral say anything to me before?"

"The admiral was going to tell you when you got back," Ives said. "He never thought you would encounter Agent Sevilla in the course of your mission. Now, circumstances have changed."

"And now he sent you all the way to Istanbul to tell me, huh?"

Isabelle gasped and looked at Hart with astonishment. "Matt, you don't believe what he's saying, do you?" Tears were forming in her eyes. "Matt, I love you. I would never betray you. Everything I said was true. You have to believe me."

"I didn't say I didn't believe you, Isabelle," Hart said. He turned to look at her, his face displaying a smile that conveyed no joy. *"And it's time you dropped the act. It's wearing thin."*

For a moment, she looked surprised. Then, almost like magic, the tears in her eyes dried up. Her face turned from sorrowful to cold, and with a fluid motion she turned the pistol on Hart.

"Quick, Hart," Ives said desperately. "Follow me with the satchel. She won't fire in here. Not with all these people around."

Ives reached for the satchel at Adler's side, but his hand was batted away by Hart.

"Don't you mean with all of these krauts around?" Hart said sardonically.

Ives looked confused. "Hart, I—"

"I see at least three bastards in this crowd who were at the flak tower with Sturm. My guess is, you brought these goons with you. So, why don't you get over there and stand with your Nazi whore."

Isabelle seemed unaffected by the insult, and Hart was not surprised. As Ives had said, the escape from the flak tower was too fantastical.

"Oh, Matt," she said with a smile. "You can be such a bore at times."

Ives broke into a grin and moved over to sidle up next to her as naturally as if they were joined at the hip. He placed an affectionate arm around her waist and leaned down to kiss her on the cheek while she held the gun on Hart.

"You're right, Matt," Ives said, chuckling now. "You were always right. It's hard to hide true love. I'm not surprised you recognized it, especially since you were once a suitor for my dear Isabelle's affection."

"Don't flatter yourselves."

Ives squeezed Isabelle and they both laughed.

"Come now, Matt," Ives said. "I'm curious. How long have you known?"

"A long time now."

"That's my Matt," Ives said. "I never had any trouble hoodwinking Admiral McDonough, but I could never get anything by you. You've always managed to impress me."

"So, the escape from the flak tower was nothing but a ploy to gain my confidence?"

"Just when I remark how much you impress me, Matt, now you let me down. The escape from the flak tower had nothing to do with you. It had everything to do with Herr Adler. It was about gaining his confidence so he would lead you to the object that is in that satchel."

"No!" Adler, who had been silent out of shock, now gasped, clutching the satchel to his chest. "No. You will not have this!"

"I am afraid you have no choice, Doctor," Isabelle said in a sinister tone. "And I'm afraid we no longer have a need for your services."

Hart watched as Ives gave Isabelle a slight squeeze. She aimed the gun at Adler and fired twice, sending two loud reports reverberating off the thousand-year-old walls and ceiling.

Hart spun around to see the doctor crumple to the floor. There were two small holes in his forehead barely an inch apart. He had died before hitting the ground.

The nave then suddenly came alive with a mass of screaming tourists scrambling for the doorways. Hart saw five men wearing brown suits emerge from the rush of people. These men were not in a panic. They were the men Hart recognized in the crowd. He had seen them before, in the flak tower, as part of Sturm's entourage. They had no-nonsense expressions and were converging on his position.

"Please move away from the doctor, Hart," Ives said. "Or my associates will force you to move."

Hart looked at the approaching men, and then at Ives and Isabelle. Isabelle was now pointing the gun at him. He was not sure why she had not just gunned him down along with Adler.

"Come now, love," she said, sarcastically. "Don't make them ruin that handsome face of yours."

Hart scanned the room. Mayhem reigned. People were running everywhere, even the museum security guards, but all seemed oblivious to the little standoff happening in the center of the nave. Then Hart found who he was looking for—the man in the gray wool suit and the hat, whom he had seen from the gallery an hour before. He had a large companion with him holding a jacket draped over one arm. Like Ives's cronies, these two men were not headed for the exits either, and they now took cover behind one of the marble columns and had been completely unnoticed by Ives and his men.

"Step away!" Ives now commanded, his earlier charm all but vanished.

"I don't think so, Ives," Hart answered. Ives's men had almost crossed the room. "Like you said, I've always impressed you. I wouldn't want to stop now." Hart then nodded to the man in the gray hat.

The man in the gray hat nodded back to him. It was Holmhurst. He disappeared behind the column again.

An instant later, the nave erupted in an earsplitting staccato report. The large man emerged from behind the column, a Thompson submachine gun blazing at his hip. It was Patrick, and he had caught Ives's men at the moment they had converged, when they were practically abreast of each other, and now the heavy forty-five-caliber bullets riddled their bodies with a brutal efficiency, slicing through necks, arms, and torsos, filling the sun-streaked air with a red mist as arteries were ripped open.

Ives and Isabelle turned in surprise, and Hart took some satisfaction that he too had played the game of deception. He had begun to suspect Isabelle from the moment they had left Austria, and as a result he had taken certain precautions. He had told Holmhurst and Patrick to shadow their every move from the moment they left Tito's partisans, and to be ready to pull them out of trouble at a moment's notice. Now his foresight was the tipping point that bought him enough time to make a dash for the nearest column. He decided to leave the satchel since there was no way he could wrest it free from the dead man before Isabelle got a shot off at him.

He ran as fast as he could, fully expecting to be shot in the back as he fled. But Ives and Isabelle were too busy scrambling for cover themselves. One of Ives's men escaped Patrick's fusillade with a grazing wound, but the rest were now twitching on the floor. Now, as Patrick reloaded his weapon, Ives, Isabelle, and their one remaining henchman took cover behind the columns on the opposite side of the nave. Hart pulled out his Colt .45 and a loud, reverberating gun battle erupted, with Hart, Holmhurst, and Patrick on one side of the nave, and Ives and his people on the other side, with the dead doctor and the satchel in the middle.

Marble chipped and tiles shattered as the two sides blasted away at each other, filling the air with dust and gun smoke. Magazine after magazine was expended. Hart had only three reloads, but he was soon joined by Holmhurst, who, not surprisingly, was unarmed.

"Good to see you again, Hart! Sorry we weren't close enough to save the poor doctor. There was nothing we could do."

"Understood. Can Patrick keep up his fire?"

"They'll run out before he does, if that's what you're asking, old boy. Here." Holmhurst handed Hart a box of forty-five-caliber ammunition. "Compliments of Patrick."

"Thanks." Hart presented Holmhurst with one of his spent magazines. "Why don't you reload this for me? Or does that vow of yours prevent you from being an accessory as well?"

"I'll make an exception," Holmhurst yelled over the report of Hart's .45. "Just this once."

The battle raged on for at least two more minutes without either side gaining ground or doing harm to the other. Then, during a moment when both Patrick and Hart were reloading, the nave fell oddly silent. Hart could hear their enemies talking to each other across the room. He looked, and then he saw Isabelle and Ives make a break for the nearest door. Hart was not ready for such a move and fired off two rounds with no results.

"They're making a run for it!" Patrick announced elatedly from behind his column.

"Not likely," Hart said, taking the reloaded magazines from Holmhurst. "They wouldn't leave the satchel in our hands. More likely, they have run out of ammo and are going to get reinforcements. They are bound to have some agents outside watching the perimeter."

"What about that other bastard?" Patrick said.

As if in response, three shots rang out from the far side of the nave, peppering the column nearest to Hart and sending him ducking for cover again.

"What now?" Holmhurst asked. "They left that bastard to make sure we don't get the satchel off the good doctor. If they come back with more men, they'll have us."

Hart nodded, trying to think. It did no good to die here, in a guns-blazing last stand from which there could only be one outcome. The weapon was lost. Ives and Isabelle would get it, one way or another. The only thing that remained was survival. Live to fight another day, when the odds were more in their favor. It was the only option. And Hart took comfort in the fact that he still had one card up his sleeve.

"Tell Patrick to get over here, fast," Hart said.

"Right," Holmhurst answered, and then skirted off from column to column to fetch his big assistant. As the two made their way back to Hart, they drew more fire from the Nazi agent, doing irreparable damage to the thousand-year-old columns but missing the two Englishmen altogether.

"Okay, listen, both of you. We have to make a break for that closet." Hart pointed to the door hiding the secret passage, not thirty feet away, but across an open space with no cover.

"Are you mad?" Patrick exclaimed. "They'll have us trapped then for sure."

"It's the only possible way out of here. What's more, it's defendable. Where we are right now isn't. Ives only needs to fetch two more of his men and we'll be outflanked. There is a tunnel in that closet. Once we're inside, we can't be flanked, and they can't rush us without getting lit up by your Tommy gun. It'll be a standoff."

"And let them just walk away with the weapon?" Holmhurst seemed astounded. "The bloody thing we've come all this way for?"

"Let them have it. We'll catch up with them later, when we have the advantage."

Holmhurst and Patrick exchanged skeptical glances but nodded their acquiescence.

Without another word, Hart plucked off Holmhurst's gray wool hat and, with one hand, nudged it out from behind the column. This was instantly answered by fire from the Nazi agent, who emptied an entire magazine, piercing the hat three times with nine-millimeter shells that almost tore the hat from Hart's hand.

"Might have asked first, old boy," Holmhurst quibbled. "I was rather fond of that hat."

"Let's go!" Hart said, ignoring Holmhurst entirely. "While he's reloading. Run!"

The three burst from the cover of the column and headed for the door to the closet. They managed to dash inside and duck their heads just as the closed door received several splintering hits from the Nazi's nine-millimeter pistol. Hart could already hear voices in the nave. Ives had returned with his reinforcements.

"Quick." Hart nudged the two Englishmen. "Through the tunnel. Hurry!"

They ran through the darkness as fast as they could, tripping several times over loose and fallen bricks on the dark path. When they finally reached a bend that would hide them from the entrance, Hart held them up.

"Wait here."

Hart felt around to check that his .45 was ready to fire, and he could hear Patrick clearing the chamber on his Thompson, after loading a fresh magazine. The air was cool, as it had been before, and all three men were breathing heavily from their exertion.

They listened carefully. Distant voices spoke in German and in English. There were many voices. Hart judged that at least ten men had entered the nave.

"Bloody hell," Patrick whispered. "You were right. They would have served us up for dinner."

Hart raised his hand in the darkness for them to be silent, while he continued to listen. He heard a woman's voice echoing in the nave. It was Isabelle's, and she was speaking in German. Hart could make out that she was directing the newcomers toward the closet. A moment later a rifle squad's worth of weaponry blasted away at the door, and Hart could tell by the sound that the door had been turned to splinters. Undoubtedly a precaution Ives's men were taking before following their prey.

Then all was silent, except for the sound of a woman's heels on the tile just outside the closet. Hart gripped the pommel of his pistol, fully prepared to kill Isabelle if she set one foot inside the tunnel. Then the footsteps stopped.

"Matt?" Isabelle's voice called. "Matt, we know you are in there. You know that you cannot escape. The tunnel is a dead end."

Hart did not respond and motioned for Holmhurst and Patrick to do likewise.

"Matt, we just want to talk to you. We could have killed you before. You know that, don't you? We could have stopped you many times." Isabelle paused, and Hart thought he heard a man talking to her in a low voice. "Matt, if you come out now, I promise no harm will come to you."

Each of Isabelle's words was spoken with the same affection and tenderness Hart had heard many times before. She could turn it on and off at will. She was a siren, a Milady de Winter of the first order, and it enraged him. "Tell that to Adler!" he shouted. "Tell that to our team in Spain, Isabelle!"

There was a pause, and Hart heard the man's voice again. He knew it was Ives feeding her every line.

"Matt, I am sorry about the way things turned out. I truly am. But we do not have to be your enemies."

"You and that Nazi bastard can go screw yourselves!" Hart yelled.

"Oh, Matt." This time it was Ives's voice. "Simple Matt. Why don't you step out of that Boy Scout uniform for once and take a look at the world around you. The world is changing, Agent Hart. It is changing faster than most people realize, including our leaders. Maps are being redrawn on a weekly basis. Fates of nations are being decided with the stroke of a pen. Those who learn to live in this new world, and to capitalize on its ever-changing nature, will be its rulers."

"The Nazis are going to fall, Ives," Hart said, mostly to keep Ives talking. He was playing dumb to get as much information as he could. "The Allies are closing in on all fronts. Hitler is finished. You are finished."

"I'm not talking about Hitler, you fool," Ives said, now sounding impatient. "Or the Nazis. I'm talking about a life outside Odysseus. A life outside the OSS. A lucrative life, where power and riches know no bounds." Ives paused, and Hart heard something that sounded like a small piece of tin hitting the marble floor. "I'm offering you this life, Matt. I will not offer it again. You and your companions must come out now, or this offer is off the table."

Hart did not respond, nor did he take one step toward the tunnel's entrance. Instead he pushed Holmhurst and Patrick farther into the tunnel and motioned for them to hurry—because he had just figured out what the sound of the tin was.

"Suit yourself, Hart," Ives said, after getting no response. "Don't ever say I didn't give you a chance, Agent Hart."

"*Auf Wiedersehen*, darling," Isabelle said.

Then Hart heard what he had expected to hear: the sound of an object hitting the side of the tunnel nearby, as if someone had thrown a rock into the tunnel as hard as he could—only this was not a rock, and Hart knew they had only seconds.

"Get down!" he shouted to Holmhurst and Patrick. They had run as far as they could and now the only thing that would save them was hugging the ground and hoping for the best. Hart only hoped the grenade had not made it to the bend in the tunnel.

The next instant, an explosion shook the brick beneath their faces, picking them up and setting them back down. Shards of metal traveling hundreds of miles an hour whipped above them and embedded into the brick on both sides of the tunnel. The air instantly filled with smoke and dust and they had to cover their faces to keep from choking on the acrid mixture.

Hart then heard a rumbling. It sounded like an earthquake, and indeed the ground beneath him was vibrating more violently with each passing second.

"Cave-in!" Hart shouted to the others. "On your feet, fast! The tunnel is collapsing!"

After a thousand years of earthquakes and sieges, the brick-lined tunnel beneath Hagia Sophia had finally had too much. The detonation of the grenade transformed the unstable structure into a death trap, and now it fell apart before Hart's eyes. Bricks fell from the ceiling, and the walls tipped inward from the point of the explosion outward, chasing the heels of the three men as they groped and clawed for a refuge.

The progressing collapse pushed the three men a

hundred feet farther into the tunnel, where they finally found sanctuary in the more stable area around the door Hart had passed through with Isabelle and Adler not an hour before. When the collapse finally stopped, there was no semblance of a tunnel behind them. The tunnel had completely caved in and was now filled with freshly churned dirt and crumbling bricks. It did not take a structural engineer to tell them that the extra brickwork around the door, which had not collapsed with the rest, had saved them from certain death. The unbreathable air now threatened to do what the collapse could not, and it drove them, hacking and coughing, through the door and into the antechamber. The air was still stagnant here, but breathable—at least, for the time being.

The three men finally sat down on the dusty floor and leaned against the cold wall to rest, too tired to care that three human skeletons shared the floor with them.

They could hear no sounds at all. It was as if the tunnel's collapse had swallowed up the world. For all they knew they could be twenty feet below ground. Patrick's flickering pocket flashlight was their only source of illumination. They had no food or water, and from every appearance, no prospect of assistance. The only people who knew about the cave were the ones who had just tried to kill them, and there was little chance of any help from them. Hart knew Ives and Isabelle would probably prefer that they share the fate of Constantine's priests and knights, for whom this small room had become a tomb.

"Are you quite certain that woman loved you once?" Holmhurst asked after catching his breath.

Hart first smiled and then laughed out loud. Patrick and Holmhurst laughed with him. They laughed for several minutes, clutching their bellies, their faces red as if they were intoxicated. It was a mad, uncaring laughter that defied their present situation but felt so natural after their close scrape with sudden death.

Hart suddenly thought about how absurd his entire infatuation with Isabelle now seemed. All of his time brooding in that prison camp in Arizona had been nothing more than a screen—a psychological barrier he had constructed, hiding the truth from his inner soul. He had known the truth ever since that day in Cartagena two years ago—that she had betrayed him, that she had betrayed his team, that his men were hanged because of her treachery. In his heart he always knew it. She had used him then, just as she had tried to use him now, and perhaps that was why he still felt responsible for the deaths of his men. He had let himself be used. He had let her deceive him, even while he knew he was being deceived. He had acted as those in love often do, holding on to that sliver of hope that all of his suspicions were wrong.

"I'm just wondering, Hart," Holmhurst said, leaning back on the floor with his hands folded behind his head. "She was a devilishly attractive little number, and I know even you aren't made of stone. Tell me you weren't tempted to march down that tunnel and accept her offer."

Hart smiled but said nothing. He laid his head back to rest, thinking more clearly than he had in a very long time. He had to think of a way out of this place, and Isabelle was no longer the distraction she had once been. The high-rent apartment she had occupied within his mind was now vacant.

He was free of her—at last.

CHAPTER THIRTY-NINE

SIS agent Esther Blackbourne stood among the crowd of spectators watching the emergency crews carry a covered body out of Hagia Sophia on a stretcher. The body was conveyed across the courtyard and into one of the three waiting ambulances parked on the street.

"How many is that?" she asked the grim-looking man with the close-cropped hair standing next to her.

"That's five," Sergeant Jones responded.

Esther and Jones were among a crowd of civilians standing across the street from Hagia Sophia. The crowd was being held back by the authorities while an unspecified emergency was handled in the evacuated cathedral.

"I'm afraid we're too late, Jones," she said, searching the crowd for any sign of Hart.

She and Jones had arrived at the cathedral just as the police began setting up rope barriers to keep the pedestrians out. So far, none of the policemen Esther had asked would share any information with her—probably since she was posing as a civilian tourist and not as an agent of the British government. Some people in the crowd were saying they heard shots fired about an hour ago, and that a great cloud of dust had risen from the structure. Some claimed it was just an earthquake.

Esther suspected otherwise.

Two days ago, she had been tipped off by a British agent in Yugoslavia. Hart and a team of people—one of them with a thick German accent—had passed through the country days ago. Other inquiries quickly located them in Turkey, and eventually she surmised they were headed for Istanbul. Local agents were put on alert, and one of them identified the American spy and his companions when they stepped off the ferry that morning. The agent had trailed them all the way to Hagia Sophia, followed them inside, and, soon after, completely lost them. It was as if they had vanished into thin air.

Esther and Jones had only just arrived in Istanbul an hour ago. They had taken a train from the airfield to the heart of Istanbul's historic district and were surprised to find seemingly every emergency vehicle in the city headed for the great cathedral at top speed, sirens blaring.

"Miller said there was a man and a woman with Hart. That's all." Jones recalled the debriefing they had received from the local agent.

"That accounts for three of the bodies," Esther said gloomily. "So, who are the other two?"

"Nazi agents?" Jones surmised, with a grim smile. "At least the laddie went down fighting. At least he remembered something I taught him."

"This isn't right, Jones." Esther sighed heavily. "I feel to blame for this. If we hadn't apprehended him in Toulon, things might be different right now."

"You called it like you saw it. And you were following orders."

"If only I had known what was going on in England at the time."

"The plight of field command, lass," Jones replied, this time more fatherly than subordinate. He had been in the service ten years longer than she had, but she was the officer and he still a sergeant, by choice.

"That's little consolation, Jones. We left him in that house with a German grenade cooking off. We might as well have handed him over to Ives ourselves."

"If you recall, ma'am, we were lucky to get out of there alive. If Petey hadn't bought us the time he did, we'd have bought the farm for sure. The punch-out door was only large enough for one to go through at a time. There was no way we could have brought Hart along with us. Besides, if you remember, at that time we were trying to kill him."

"Has the world gone insane, Jones? Do we know who the real enemy is anymore?"

"Of course, ma'am. Whoever the king says it is."

"That sounds so simple, yet every fiber of my being wants to resist it."

"Take it from one who's been there, ma'am. Just do your job the best you can with the information available." Jones paused, and then, looking down at her, he added, "And then never look back."

Some activity on the street caught their attention. The emergency crews were closing the rear doors of the ambulances. No more bodies. The ambulances then sped away, leaving only police cars and fire trucks on the street.

"I haven't seen the police bring anyone out alive," Jones commented. "I'm afraid it looks bad for our boy."

A police officer approached the crowd of civilian onlookers and made an announcement in Turkish.

"What is he saying, Jones?" Esther asked. She spoke French fluently, but not Turkish.

"He says the museum is closed for the rest of the day, and that he would like the crowd to disperse."

"So, no access to the crime scene, and no sign of— *What the bloody hell?*"

Esther's attention was immediately captured by three figures walking through the crowd. They looked like something from the crypt, all three caked in mud and dirt from head to foot. As they walked, the crowd of civilians seemed to part naturally for them with twisted faces and hands over noses. Esther saw flies buzzing around these specters, and after a sporadic breeze blew from their direction, she abruptly knew why. These men were covered in raw sewage.

If the policeman's announcement had no effect on the crowd, the march of these foul-smelling creatures did. The crowd no longer cared about the unusual events in Hagia Sophia. They now cared only about getting far away from the disgusting three men as fast as humanly possible.

Esther began to study the man in the lead. Getting past the skewed arrangement of his repulsively slick hair, and the caked mud on one side of his face, she began to see something familiar in this individual. Surprisingly enough, he seemed to recognize her, too, and flashed a white-toothed grin before beckoning the other two men to follow him over to her.

"Good afternoon, Agent Blackbourne," the filthy man said.

"Mary and bloody Joseph! Is that you, Hart?" Jones exclaimed with astonishment.

"It's good to see you, Hart," Esther said with a skeptical look, half-expecting him to attack her. "We thought you were dead." She then covered her nose with her hand. "Are you sure you're not dead? Are you not wishing you were, looking like that—smelling like that?"

"Oh, no, ma'am," Hart answered, wiping his face with a dirty sleeve. "Crawling through a thousand-year-old sewer pipe is like visiting your first whorehouse. Once you're inside, you forget all about where you are."

"You filthy, bloody Yank," she said, smiling.

"I suppose you're here because Admiral McDonough's been acquitted of all charges," Hart said, now all business, despite his despicable appearance.

Esther nodded. "How did you know?"

"Ives set him up. Made it look like McDonough was the mole, when it was him all along. Lucky for us, the admiral anticipated it and had these two gentlemen standing by to help me." Hart gestured at the dirty men behind him. "There is another Odysseus agent working with Ives. Her name is Isabelle Sevilla."

"I've never heard of her."

"She's been working under deep cover for McDonough for the last two years now. He began to suspect that she was an accomplice to Ives, and part of this operation was meant to expose her involvement."

"So this whole operation was meant to uncover Nazi moles working within Odysseus?" Esther asked.

"Partially. This goes deeper than just the Nazis. I don't have time to explain everything fully, just now. It's enough to say that there is a weapon, it is powerful enough to swing the direction of the war, and Ives now has everything he needs to make it." Hart looked once at Jones, and then back at Esther. "I need your help."

"Well, I suppose I do owe you one, Mister Hart," she said hesitantly.

"After knocking me unconscious, trying to make me swallow cyanide, and then leaving me tied to a chair in a room with a live potato masher, I would say that you do."

She smiled, then eyed him gamely. "What do you need?"

CHAPTER FORTY

"Are you sure that's it, Hart?"

Hart turned from the window of the modified Vickers Wellington medium bomber to face Holmhurst, who was looking out the next window aft. "That's the one." Hart had to shout over the noise of the two Bristol Pegasus engines. "No question."

They were looking down at a rock of an island, ten thousand feet below them. A mile-long, potato-shaped rock rising out of the glittering, moonlit Aegean.

"No lights," Holmhurst added. "Looks rather deserted."

"Our intelligence says otherwise." Hart handed Holmhurst the sheet of paper on which the SIS radioman in Athens had scrawled the final report from the low-level reconnaissance flight earlier that afternoon.

Holmhurst used a flashlight to read the paper again. "A radio tower, a small airstrip, a dozen GIs, a few U.S. Army tents, and a flagpole flying the Stars and Stripes. That's hardly enough to qualify as a research facility for developing a biological weapon."

"We checked with Allied headquarters—Mediterranean. There are no Allied outposts within two hundred miles of that island."

"I grant you that, Hart, and I agree it's suspicious. But wouldn't weapons scientists need controlled environments, labs, and the like? They'd need buildings. Not to mention housing, food, sanitation. You could be barking up the wrong tree here."

"They are down there, Holmhurst," Hart said impatiently, as he snatched the paper from the Englishman's hands. "This is the place."

Hart said it with certainty as he looked out the window again at the dark mass below. He knew this was the spot, and not because the low-level reconnaissance had reported a U.S. Army radio station where there should not be any. He had not spent his entire time aboard *U-2553* simply trying to get a glimpse of the artifacts. He had spent quite a bit of time poring over the ship's charts. Hart knew from his days in the U.S. Navy that it was common practice aboard any ship for the navigator to plot the ship's track in pencil. Then, after the voyage was over, the pencil marks were erased and the chart filed away in the ship's library for reuse. *U-2553* followed the same practice, and therefore Hart had no trouble tracing the paths taken by *U-2553* on previous cruises. He simply followed the visible depressions left on the charts by the navigator's pencil. Over the course of three weeks, Hart had gone over the Mediterranean charts one by one, until he finally found the one where all pencil marks converged. He had committed the coordinates to memory—this place, a dot of an island in the middle of the Aegean, far away from the prying eyes of either side of the war.

"Not much time left, Hart." Holmhurst tapped his watch. "We're already beyond the grace period you negotiated with Agent Blackbourne. No telling what will happen now."

Hart nodded. He was well aware of the time constraints they were under. He was the one who had made the deal with Esther. She and Jones had taken Hart, Holmhurst, and Patrick aboard their Wellington from Istanbul to the SIS command headquarters in Athens. Once there, Hart knew that he had to move fast. He did not trust the SIS any more than he trusted Odysseus. But he needed to trust Esther. He needed resources, and with Admiral McDonough still ironing things out in London, Esther was the only one who could help him. To her alone, he had divulged all he knew about the island's location and the threat posed by the biological weapon. He told her about Ives and about Isabelle, and about the contingent of Odysseus and SS agents that had joined them. Esther had taken it all in, surprised at some points, not surprised at others, but Hart could tell she was eager to inform her superiors. She had hit a gold mine in Hart. But Hart had headed that off.

"You can't tell anyone, Esther," he had said. "Not yet."

"But why not, Hart?" she had replied with surprise. "This is serious."

"They've infiltrated Odysseus, and if they've done that, then they've gotten into SIS, too. We can't trust anyone. You can't tell SIS command."

"How can I not, Hart? Millions of lives could be at

stake. We have to move quickly, before they use this thing."

"I know. I'll take care of it."

"You? By yourself?"

"With your help. I'll need a few things from you, Esther. Most of all your plane—and your promise."

"Promise?"

"That you'll give me a head start. That you won't tell SIS command for eight hours."

It was asking a lot, and if Esther had not nearly killed him two weeks ago, Hart was not sure she would have agreed. Eventually, reluctantly, she did. At Hart's request, she had ordered the low-level reconnaissance flight of earlier that afternoon, and managed to do it without telling SIS command why. And then she had lent Hart a myriad of SIS weapons and equipment, her personal aircraft, and Sergeant Jones to fly it. When she had seen them off at the airstrip in Athens, Hart had detected that she was envious. He could tell she wanted to come along, but deep down, Esther was a dutiful SIS officer, and she had decided to remain behind to brief SIS command when Hart's grace period ran out.

"Jones will take good care of you," she had said. "He's a surprisingly good pilot. Search me where he picked that up."

"From my intimate knowledge of him," Hart had said smiling. "I don't doubt it."

"It's a real mission to write home about, Hart." Her eyes had met his, and Hart was surprised to see genuine concern cross her face. It had lasted only for an instant, and then she had looked away as if embarrassed. Before closing the aircraft door, she had added in a surprisingly affectionate tone, "Take good care of yourself, Matt."

He had seen her from the aircraft window as the Wellington roared down the runway before taking to the sky. She was standing beside the jeep parked next to the airfield. She had waved once, her arm moving slowly, as if there were many good wishes with that send-off, and then Hart thought he saw her kiss her hand. Hart could not help but wonder if it had been meant for all of them, for her partner Jones, or for him.

That had been three hours ago.

Now they were up against the clock. When Esther told SIS command, any number of things could happen, none of which Hart wanted to see, and he was only thankful that he had been able to head them off for at least a few hours. Even if the SIS station in Athens did not have a mole working for Ives, a rambunctious SIS commander thinking he was doing his duty could be just as damaging. He might decide to do something rash, or too drastic, like ordering a full-scale assault on the island, or an air strike, neither of which would determine with certainty how far the weapon plot reached or how far along Ives, Isabelle, and their cronies were in the development process. The insertion of a single agent, however—the unexpected, the unlikely approach—had the best chance of discovering just that.

Hart checked his parachute and gear and then began applying the black face paint that would hide his white skin in the night. He would be making the jump as close as possible to the island's northern coast, the opposite side of the island from the so-called U.S. radio post. It would be a jump in the dead of night into uncertain surf and beach conditions, but there was little choice. The alternative would bring him too close to the enemy. If they saw his chute, the game would be over.

Holmhurst appeared before him and motioned for him to turn around. Hart was surprised when the English lord gave the chute one final check.

"Wouldn't want anything to happen to you on the way down, Hart. I'm not sure how my deal with the admiral would stand should you not make it home alive. I've half a mind to go with you."

Hart smiled. "No thanks. There is liable to be a lot of killing down there tonight, and I'm not sure you'd be much use in that department."

"Perhaps you're right, old boy. Perhaps I should simply send Patrick with you." Holmhurst glanced around the small passenger cabin. "Come to think of it, where the devil is that Irish bastard?"

"He's flying the plane," a gruff voice said from the passage leading to the cockpit, and then Sergeant Jones's muscular frame appeared. He was bedecked in black fatigues, black ski hat, and parachute gear. In one hand he held a tightly sealed black canvas bag, and in the other a pair of black fins. He also wore black face paint, behind which he shot Hart a white-toothed grin. "I'm going with you, laddie."

Hart was surprised and slightly touched by the gesture. But as much as he could use Jones's expertise on this mission, he felt he would be overstepping his bounds if he acceded to the veteran sergeant's wishes.

"I'm sorry, Jones. That's out of the question. Esther

loaned you to me as a pilot. She would never forgive me if anything happened to your ugly mug."

"I'm not asking you then, am I, laddie? Someone's got to watch over that greenhorn arse of yours." Jones shrugged and then added, "Besides, it was her idea in the first place."

Hart shook his head in disbelief, struck by how different his initial impression of Esther was from that he had now. He gave Jones a mild grin. "You've studied the intel, then?"

Jones nodded. "I know that rock like Winnie knows Clemmie's crotch. Just you follow me, sir."

CHAPTER FORTY-ONE

The man wearing the uniform of a U.S. Army corporal who now stood atop the great rocky outcropping at the south end of the island did not speak a word of English. In fact, that was why he and his cohort, Hans, were chosen for their present assignment. It was a lowly assignment and required little skill other than to stay awake and to shoot straight if called upon. They were former soldiers of the Waffen-SS and had been recruited to this new "assignment" by a sergeant who had shown up at their camp on the Russian front promising a life of intrigue if they would sign up with him. More important, the sergeant had offered better food, better living conditions, and more pay. The new assignment had sounded too good to be true, and perhaps that was why most of the men in Georg's unit had turned it down. But not Georg. For some reason he had taken the sergeant up on his offer, and soon thereafter he had learned that all of the things the sergeant promised were true. As he stood watch this night on the great cliffs of this idyllic island, the stark moonlight bathing the waters crashing against the base of the cliff below, Georg was glad that he had taken the assignment. Even the little oddities of this posting did not bother him anymore, like the fact that he had spent the last three months in the uniform of an American GI assigned to the guards tasked with watching this coastline, manning the sprinkling of AA batteries, or warding off any visitors who might come to the island. Most of all, he and his fellow recruits were ordered not to ask questions. And he did not. The food, the accommodations, and the pay were all in alignment with the sergeant's promise, and that was enough to suit Georg and his comrades. He had assumed with quiet acceptance that he was serving the Reich in some important capacity, and that whatever was going on in the underground fortress beneath him, where he had seen civilians in lab coats mulling about on their smoke breaks, he was sure it was important to the *Führer* and would eventually help drive back the advancing Allied armies.

This night had started off just like any other—quiet, serene, peaceful—that is, until this moment, when Georg suddenly saw something appear in the dark sea to the south.

"Hello, Sergeant?" Georg spoke into the field telephone. "I have sighted a flashing green light, approximately five kilometers out to sea. Shall I sound the—"

"No, Corporal." Sergeant Blücher on the other end of the line interrupted him. He was the same SS sergeant who had recruited him from the Russian front. "I will come up. Do nothing."

"Yes, Sergeant." Georg hung up the phone, somewhat perplexed. Were they expecting visitors this evening? He had seen a U-boat approach the island in this fashion on three occasions in the past, the last being only five nights ago. But it had always been the same U-boat, *U-2553*, and that U-boat now sat moored in the fortress dock. Could this be a new U-boat approaching?

Before Georg or Hans could devote any more thought to the subject, Sergeant Blücher emerged from the steel door that led down into the fortress below. The sergeant was also wearing an American uniform, but he carried no weapon other than the sheathed SS dagger he always wore on his belt. Obviously, he had come in a hurry.

"Good evening, corporals," the sergeant said hurriedly, as he strode past the two soldiers and brought a pair of binoculars to his face.

Again the green light flashed out at sea.

"Our visitors have arrived," the sergeant said to no one in particular. Then he turned to Georg and Hans. "And so has our payday, comrades."

Georg looked at Blücher uncertainly. He was not sure what the sergeant meant by that, but whatever it was, it seemed to bring the sergeant great joy, so Georg smiled, too.

Blücher then gestured to a mount shrouded in camouflaged canvas. "You know what to do, Corporal?"

"Sergeant?"

Blücher nodded. "Just like the last time. Do you remember?"

"Two short, one long, two short?"

"Excellent, Corporal," Blücher said, raising the binoculars to his face again. "Please proceed."

Somewhat confused, Georg complied, and he and Hans took the shroud off the object and began to swivel the device around to point it in the direction of the flashing light in the dark sea. Georg shot one last uncertain glance at the sergeant but was then prompted to continue by something of an impatient glare from Blücher.

Georg flicked on the switch and instantly felt the device turn warm beneath his hands. He then put a hand on the lever and did exactly what he had done when the *U-2553* had arrived earlier in the week. He operated the searchlight's shutter mechanism to send the signal.

Two short, one long, two short.

He repeated the signal several times until Blücher finally waved for him to stop. The green flashing light ceased, and the formerly placid sea was replaced by a churning mixture of white froth, from which arose a long, black object. It was a submarine, and it now began to approach the island just as Georg had seen *U-2553* do five days before.

"Our guests have arrived." Sergeant Blücher now spoke into the field phone. "Activate the navigation field."

Moments later, the sea around the cliff face was lit up by a myriad of dull red bulbs placed on various rocks and outcroppings around the southern approaches. Georg had seen this exercise enough to know that the collection of lights was used by the submarines to line up with the narrow channel, which was the only way for a ship to approach the island from the south without ending up dashed on one of the many jutting rock formations.

As the submarine entered the channel and slowly

approached the cliff face, and as the scant red lights allowed Georg a better look at the new arrival, he could not help but let out an audible gasp. It was not because the sub now approached a solid wall of rock, for he had seen this done many times before and knew there was no cause for alarm. What had him truly astonished was the emblem emblazoned on the side of the submarine's black conning tower, and he stared blankly at the vessel as it reached the designated location before the cliff and once again disappeared beneath the surface in a flurry of geysers and mist.

"As I said, comrades." The sergeant hung up the phone, smiling at Georg and his cohort. "Our payday has arrived. I am going below. Inform me if you see anything."

With that, the sergeant disappeared through the steel door, leaving Georg and Hans looking at each other in confusion and disbelief. They shook their heads at each other, still trying to process what had just happened, but then Georg had learned after three months on this island that the unexpected was just part of the normal routine.

It would have been good for Georg to have had those thoughts a few minutes earlier. Had he and his comrade returned to their posts and resumed their earlier watchful diligence the moment their sergeant left, they might have noticed the two black-clad figures creeping from rock to rock on the landward side, inching closer to them with every turn of their heads. Now these figures came out of the darkness with lightning speed.

Georg saw a black arm grab Hans by the neck, saw a

flash of steel, and heard a muffled yell as Hans fell to the ground. Georg raised his Thompson submachine gun, but a black arm came from behind him, too, and wrapped itself around his own mouth and throat, squeezing with an intensity that made him drop the weapon. Shots rang out, a short three-round burst, and he guessed that his Thompson's hair trigger had fired when it struck the rocks at his feet. Georg heard the man behind him curse, and then an instant later he felt a sharp pain drive into his lower back. He lost all sensation in his legs and then felt a similar sharp pain in his throat as his assailant's knife severed his windpipe. The black arm now let him go, and he fell to the ground, gurgling up blood and struggling for breath. Through foggy eyes, Georg saw that Hans was still wriggling beneath the weight of his assailant. He saw the knife flash again and again and heard his comrade cry out once more.

It was at that moment that the steel door flew open and the light from inside the door instantly bathed the area in a yellow hue. Georg saw Sergeant Blücher emerge from the doorway wielding his gleaming SS dagger. Blücher must have heard the shots and then rushed back up the stairs to investigate. Now the blond-haired sergeant made a dash for the black figure atop Hans. Before the black figure could spin around to prepare for the attack, Blücher was on him, driving a well-placed knee into his kidneys while stabbing down with the blade. The black figure took the stubby blade in the shoulder, buried to the hilt. The black figure spasmed in pain and clutched at the postlike hilt protruding from his shoulder, but it was no use. It must have sliced through an artery because the black figure's groping arm soon stopped moving and fell loosely to the ground, followed shortly thereafter by his limp body.

The whole scuffle had taken place in less than four seconds, and now, as the sergeant attempted to pull his dagger free from the dying man's tissue, Georg made every sputtering attempt to warn his sergeant about the other assailant, the one who had severed his windpipe, who was dashing to help his accomplice. But it was no use. He could not make a sound above the crashing waves below.

Georg knew he was quickly suffocating, and he began to feel his body shut down. The world was getting blurry as he watched his sergeant finally free the dagger and turn at the last moment to meet his attacker head-on. In his final moments of life, with his cheek against the loose rocks on the ground, and unable to feel any sensation in the rest of his body, Georg watched as the two men dueled with the drawn knives, inserting different combinations of body throws and judo chops. Both men were obviously skilled in hand-to-hand combat. Both men had been thoroughly trained for this. Even in his dying moment, the German inside Georg felt a surge of pride whenever Blücher landed a blow against his opponent, or connected with a slash of the SS blade. Perhaps it was a mercy then that Georg's eyes saw no more, and he had already passed into the next life, when Sergeant Blücher was finally tricked by a feint from his assailant. The sergeant lunged when he should not have and found himself lanced through the intestine by the commando's blade. It was a deep cut, and the assailant twisted the knife as it came out, tearing open the tissue until it would no longer hold the sergeant's intestines inside. The sergeant dropped his dagger, his face shocked at the sight of his insides falling out. As Blücher clutched his belly, holding it together, he knew that his opponent now had a free and clear chance to strike the killing blow. That was why the sergeant was surprised when the blow never came. Instead his attacker simply stood before him, the bloody knife clutched in his hand. Blücher looked into the man's face but he could not distinguish any features behind the black face paint.

"Schwein!" Blücher said in agony. "What are you waiting for? Finish the job, damn you!"

"I will finish it," the man said simply. "The same way you finished a poor wounded Frenchman in the Alps."

Blücher's eyes grew wide as the realization set in, and the black face now took on something more recognizable.

"Hart!" he gasped in disbelief.

Without another word Hart grabbed the SS sergeant by the collar and dragged him to the edge of the cliff. Blücher tried to resist, but could not because he was preoccupied with keeping his stomach together. With the surf crashing against the rocks a hundred feet below his heels, Blücher looked up from the vibrating stone to see Hart scowling at him. The American had him, and there was nothing he could do. In a last attempt at defiance, Blücher tried assembling enough saliva in his dry mouth to spit in Hart's eyes, but the American did not even give him that satisfaction.

"Auf Wiedersehen," Hart said simply, and then drove a

steel-toed boot into the bloody mess of the sergeant's stomach.

The force of the blow made Blücher lose his footing and he fell backward, his large frame falling over the edge like a rock. As he fell down the long, hundred-foot drop, he lost hold of his belly and his intestines began to roll out in great loops. He screamed in agony, cursing Hart's name the whole way down, his screams only falling silent when his body and streaming entrails reached the base of the cliff. The sergeant's pulverized body lay upon a wet formation of jagged rocks for only a few moments before the next surge of the sea carried it away.

CHAPTER FORTY-TWO

Hart tried to appear calm as he walked through the labyrinth of tunnels, a dazzling mixture of reinforced concrete supports and solid stone. The steel door atop the cliff had led down a winding stairwell that descended perhaps four stories into a virtual maze of passages and side doors. Hart quickly concluded that the island was like a small version of Gibraltar, just a large hunk of rock when viewed from without, but alive with tunnels and activity when viewed from within.

Hart had already crossed paths with several people, a few dressed as Americans, a few wearing civilian dress, but most in German SS uniforms. So far, he had drawn only casual glances from the passersby. Evidently this underground fortress contained hundreds of people, and his unrecognized face did not arouse any suspicions. But he could tell that the state of his uniform was attracting some curious glances.

A civilian man wearing a lab coat looked once at the bloodstains on Hart's shirt, and then at Hart's face. After a momentary confused expression, the man smiled politely at him and then walked on. Hart breathed a sigh of relief and decided right then and there that he had to get out of this uniform, before it was the death of him.

He had taken it off one of the two dead Germans on the cliff, shortly after he had tended to Jones's wound. The tough old English sergeant had survived the dagger wound, at least for the time being.

"You're damned lucky, Jones," Hart had said to him as he tied off the bandage compressing a damp rag to the British sergeant's wound. "I thought you were dead, for sure."

"I'm damn lucky," Jones had groaned, his eyelids droopy. "And you're damn late, laddie. You're running out of time. You have to leave me."

Hart remembered looking at the blood-spattered sergeant, unable to tell if Jones looked pale from the early-morning light or from the loss of blood. At least Jones was still talking, so Hart had concluded that no artery had been severed. But there really was no telling how bad his condition was.

"Do you hear me, laddie!" Jones had grumbled, batting Hart's hand away from the bandage. "You have no time for this. Go!"

"These uniforms are all blood-spattered." Hart had examined the uniforms of the two dead SS guards. "But certainly these guards had some kind of watch relief routine." Hart had found the field telephone, too. "Undoubtedly, they are required to check in on a set schedule. Maybe their sergeant will be along soon to check on them, and I can jump him and take his uniform."

"I think he was the bloody bastard you dropped over the edge, Hart." Jones winced. "Now stop blabbing, and get your arse in one of those other kraut-Yank uniforms. And don't forget to rub off that bloody face paint."

As filthy as it was, the uniform had served its purpose, and it had allowed him to descend into the hidden fortress and pass by others in the hallway with nothing more than a few curious glances. But now Hart began to think his number was coming up. It was only a matter of time before he ran into someone with authority— someone who would question him further and who would demand his photo identification card.

The passage led him past doors that appeared to be hermetically sealed. They looked as robust as some of the air locks Hart had seen at diving school. As he approached, two men in lab coats emerged from one door. They were carrying clipboards and did not look at all like soldiers, so Hart concluded that they must be two of the scientists recruited to work on the weapon. They were too absorbed in conversation to pay Hart any attention and simply walked on chatting in German.

Farther down the hall, Hart came to another set of doors with two guards in black SS uniforms standing just outside. Like the lab doors, these doors also appeared capable of being sealed airtight, but at the moment both doors were propped open, allowing Hart to see inside. The room was full of men in German sailor uniforms, sitting at several long tables and apparently enjoying an early breakfast. Hart could not think of why an apparent mess hall should have such robust doors. There were a few familiar faces in the room, and Hart realized this was the crew of *U-2553*. He immediately quickened his pace lest one of them catch a glimpse of him and recognize the face of their missing first officer. Around the next corner, another room also caught Hart's attention. This room too appeared to be used for dining, only it must have been reserved for officers, because Hart could see several stewards in resplendent white coats removing an ornate set of china from a side closet and using it to set a single dining table covered with a white linen tablecloth. The room was obviously being prepared for an elegant breakfast, but for whom Hart could not tell—at least, not until he reached the end passage and entered a space that took his breath away.

He was inside a vast cavern, hundreds of feet across and several stories high, where the voices of several dozen workers echoed off the rock ceiling above. A large array of powerful lights made the place daylight bright, allowing him to see the vast magnitude of the cave. But it was not the size of the cavern that had Hart dumbstruck. It was the fact that this cavern enveloped a vast pool of water, more like a lake, around which had been constructed a full-service dockyard complete with cleats, railroad tracks, and cranes. It had everything one might find at a typical U-boat base, and that was not too surprising, since Hart could see *U-2553* sitting idly at her moorings halfway down the dock. What did have Hart surprised was the lack of any visible entrance. The entire perimeter of the cavern was enclosed by solid rock, and Hart could not imagine how the U-boat had made it in here. But when Hart suddenly heard a band start playing, and when he moved to gain a better vantage point such that he could look down the entire length of the underground dock, everything suddenly made sense to him.

Another submarine had just arrived, and a small band bedecked in SS uniforms, amid a flurry of other uniforms, played to welcome its arrival. This was the same submarine Hart had seen a half hour earlier approaching the southern rock face of the island and submerging within the shallows. The maneuver had seemed like suicide, until now. The presence of that submarine inside this cavern into which there appeared to be no entrance led Hart to a single conclusion. There had to be an underground water channel, a waterway that ran beneath the mountain into this cavern. The channel would have to be deep to admit a U-boat the size of *U-2553*, but it had to be extremely deep to convey the submarine that now pushed up against the dockyard fenders. It was larger than any sub Hart had ever seen before, with a high freeboard, a large conning tower on the port side, and a long, humplike shape situated amidships extending just forward of the conning tower. The sheer size of the sub was one thing—nearly four hundred feet long—but what was even more shocking was the emblem on its conning tower. It was something Hart had not expected to see, at least not here.

The emblem was a white rectangle with a red ball directly in the center. It was the flag of Imperial Japan, and this was an I-boat—a Japanese submarine.

Though Hart had not seen a submarine of this type before, he was able to surmise what it was from his early days in Odysseus when he daily reviewed intelligence reports on Axis nation naval developments. This was a

Japanese Sen-Toku-class submarine, and Hart knew that
the hump on her back carried float planes. She was essentially a submersible aircraft carrier, with an extremely
long range and the ability to stage limited strike missions. From where he stood, Hart could make out the
number on her side—*I-403*.

But what were the Japanese doing here? Hart pon-
dered the thought as he watched the Japanese sailors on
the deck of the submarine receive and anchor a gangway
being lowered by a crane. Once the gangway was in
place, a man in a Japanese army uniform began to cross
to the pier and was saluted and greeted halfway by a
black-clad figure wearing an SS colonel's field hat and
leather trench coat.

It was Colonel Sturm.

Hart quickly studied the crowd on the pier. They
were mostly SS officers, but there were a few men in
civilian suits. Hart saw that one of these was Ives.

The Japanese officer appeared to be a general. He
now came ashore with his entourage in tow to mingle
with Sturm's, and both groups greeted each other in a
jumble of handshakes, fake smiles, and bows. The Japanese general was undoubtedly the VIP for whom the
elegant dining room was being prepared. The two
groups then began walking down the pier, in Hart's
direction, with an SS sergeant far out in front motioning
the few dockside workers out of the way.

Hart instantly recognized him as Sergeant Friedrich—
the other man who had tortured him in the flak tower—
and now the sergeant looked in his direction. They were
still at least a hundred feet apart, but apparently he had

caught the sergeant's attention. Whether it was recognition, the state of his American uniform, or the lack of recognition, Hart could not tell, but the SS sergeant raised a finger and shouted, "You!"

Hart did not wait to find out if Friedrich had truly recognized him or was simply warning him to get his filthy appearance out of the way of the distinguished guests. He instead ducked back into the passage and quickly mixed with the crowd in the hall. As far as he could tell, the sergeant did not pursue him. Hart turned a corner and was suddenly faced with an opportunity. The dining room was directly ahead, and he watched as the last of the stewards closed the china closet and left the room in preparation for the guests' arrival. He had reached the spot at the precise moment that the room was unoccupied—and now the door lay open before him.

CHAPTER FORTY-THREE

". . . that is all well and good, Colonel Sturm," General Yakamoto of the Imperial Japanese Army said as he and his staff officers were led into the plush dining room. "But before we proceed, I would like to know exactly who I am dealing with."

"That is most understandable, General," Colonel Sturm said in a raspy voice behind his acrylic mask, as he motioned with a black-gloved hand for the general to take a seat at the table. "I can see where you would have trepidations about these proceedings. This is not the most ideal of meeting places, but you understand that Allied advances across Europe have made it a necessity. We have extensive contacts within the Nazi regime, and we coerced them into building this place for us two years ago. Most of the soldiers and workers you see around here think they are working for the Reich. But we control what goes on out here."

"I will ask you again, Colonel," the general said with some measure of impatience. "Am I, or am I not, dealing with the German government? And what are these Americans doing here?" The general motioned to the two men in civilian suits, sitting on the far side of the table. One of them was Ives.

Sturm placed his elbows on the table and made a pyramid of his fingers. "Captain Ives is our lead in the American OSS. As I told you before, General, Axis and Allied nations all over the world have been infiltrated by our agents. The United States is no exception. This other gentleman is Dr. Arthur Geldenson. He is a distinguished American biochemist who has joined the research group headed up by our own Dr. Jungert, whom you met when we saw each other in Tokyo last month."

The general pursed his lips. "So you do not represent the *Führer*, as you had alleged in that meeting?"

"Is that not obvious? But why would you wish to deal with a dying regime, General? The Nazis have failed you. They are losing on all fronts. You can expect no help from them." Sturm sat back in his chair. "You know as well as I, General, that your own situation on the other side of the globe is equally perilous. The Americans are poised to take back the Philippines, and they already have the Marianas. Soon Japan will be subject to long-range bombing, day and night. Japan will fall, and you and your peers, if you survive the carnage, will be tried as war criminals and hanged."

Yakamoto said nothing, but the truth of Sturm's statement was visible on his face.

"We offer you what no one else can, General. We offer you a power greater than twenty bomber wings—a power that will bring the Allies to their knees in less than a year." Sturm reached out a gloved hand and placed it on Yakamoto's arm. "Think of it, General! In six months' time, the Americans, the British, the Chinese, and the Soviets all brought down by a weapon more powerful than any of these superbombs you keep hearing about. A host of fearful nations, including a subservient Germany, ready to bend to the will of the Japanese Empire. I see Emperor Hirohito upon his white horse, riding down a Pennsylvania Avenue lined with Nipponese soldiers shouting 'Banzai!' He claims Washington as his own. And who will he have to thank for it? You, General."

The general tried to remain stoic, but he shifted in his chair, and it was evident that Sturm was hitting all the right marks.

"Suppose I deal with you," Yakamoto finally said, quietly. "What is in it for you, Colonel Sturm?"

"Aside from the two thousand pounds of gold bullion you brought with you in your submarine?" Sturm whispered jovially.

"If Japan becomes as strong as you say"—the general looked at Sturm through squinted eyes—"what would prevent us from shutting you down?"

"We are giving you only a specific quantity of the weaponized agent, General. As much as your gold bullion will purchase. It will be enough to produce a sizable demonstration on any Allied region of your choice—Washington, D.C., for example—but you will not have enough to win the war for you." Sturm paused, and then added, "If you so choose, you may purchase additional quantities, but the secret of its production will remain safe with us."

"I am uncertain whether that will be acceptable to my government."

"That is your only choice, General," Sturm said, the first time his scratchy voice took on a firm tone. "If those terms are unacceptable, then we will consider this transaction canceled and politely see you back to your ship."

Sturm made to rise but was stopped by a sudden hand from Yakamoto. "Wait, Colonel. Perhaps we could be allowed to see what we are buying?"

Sturm looked down at him defiantly with his black-masked face, and then seemed to resume his previous demeanor. "Of course, General. Of course. I thought you might desire such a demonstration."

Sturm walked over to one side of the room, where a long curtain covered one wall. "You do, of course, remember the U-boat crew I just introduced you to—those enlisted men having breakfast in the next room?"

Yakamoto nodded uncertainly.

"The instant we left their room, my stewards replaced one of their water pitchers with one laced with our virus." Sturm looked at his watch. "Please check your watches to confirm with me, gentlemen. That was precisely eleven minutes ago. Now, observe!"

Sturm's gloved hand drew back the long curtain in a dramatic fashion, revealing a long tinted window that looked into the mess hall where the U-boat crew had been dining. Yakamoto rose abruptly from his chair and gasped. The men he had met only moments before—all sixty-three of them—who had been laughing and joking and so full of life now lay scattered in patterns of tangled bodies and twisted faces, each man either dead or in the throes of dying. All bled from the mouth and nose, some of them clawing at the sealed door, some of them clawing at the window, their silent screams muffled by the two-inch transparent barrier.

"Is something wrong, General?" Sturm asked with odd concern in his whisperlike voice. "Do not worry, sir. You are quite safe. They cannot get out of there. That door is hermetically sealed."

Yakamoto shook his head, but inside he felt somewhat nauseated. This was a deplorable sight, and though he had seen much worse in China, the cold, calculated nature of this killing made his stomach churn, especially the manner in which Sturm and his men, standing with arms crossed and smug satisfactory smiles on their faces, observed the agonizing deaths of these young men.

Within a few minutes it was all over. All sixty-three men had stopped moving.

"Mark your watches, gentlemen," Sturm said. "It has been precisely sixteen minutes, and they all appear to be dead."

Several of the SS men in the room and the two Americans began clapping, prompting General Yakamoto and his staff to reluctantly do the same.

"Now, gentlemen," Sturm continued. "Mark the time again. In precisely thirty minutes, all of us will enter the room. And do not worry, General. It will be quite safe. The virus will be quite neutralized by then."

Yakamoto swallowed hard and was about to speak when a burly SS sergeant with blond hair entered the room in a rush.

"Colonel?" he said agitatedly and out of breath.

"What is it, Friedrich?" Sturm said bitterly. "I told you, no interruptions!"

"Sir, Blücher is missing!"

"What?"

"So are two of the guards!"

"Well, sound the alarm and go look for them!"

"That's not all, sir," the sergeant said frantically. "Our agent in Naples has just reported in. Three flights of Lancaster bombers took off from Foggia Air Base two hours ago with orders to strike this island. They will be overhead any minute."

Sturm's black mask stared back at the sergeant for several seconds of silence. Whatever was going through the mind of the sadistic SS colonel, this setback was evidently something he had not anticipated.

The American named Ives was suddenly beside him.

"They will have fighters with them," he said in Sturm's ear. "No chance of escaping in the Siebel."

"And I am sure a commando force will follow shortly thereafter," Sturm said quietly, apparently to himself. He then nodded to the sergeant. "On second thought, Sergeant, do not sound the alarm. Any alarm would likely invoke a panic among these Nazi idiots. As quiet as you can, arrange for the evacuation of the artifacts, and have Dr. Jungert gather whatever he can and meet us pierside."

"Yes, Colonel." The sergeant saluted and made to leave, but Sturm called after him.

"And, Sergeant?"

Friedrich poked his head back into the room.

"Sergeant, I think it is time we make amends for poor

Lieutenant Odeman. I think it would be best if Captain Traugott and his officers never found out what happened to *U-2553*'s poor sailors. Do you understand?"

Sergeant Friedrich's blocklike face broke into a wide grin. "Perfectly, sir. I will see to it personally."

The sergeant then ducked out of the door, leaving Yakamoto wondering what that was all about. He hardly had time to contemplate it before Sturm was in his face.

"I must apologize for this unpleasant distraction, sir. Your submarine now appears to be the only means of escape."

Yakamoto stared at Sturm, uncertain of his implication.

"General Yakamoto, now that you understand the full potential of our device, I am sure you will be agreeable to my next proposal—a slight alteration of our original deal. If you and your men will accompany us, sir, we will discuss it as we walk to the dock."

Sturm and Yakamoto then walked briskly out of the room, followed by their entourages, leaving the room quite empty.

Moments later a steward entered and began tidying the room. He loaded the half-drunk cups of coffee and untouched china onto a large tray. As he was about to leave the room, he noticed that the closet door was slightly ajar. He was certain that he had closed it before the distinguished guests had arrived, and he could not think of any reason one of them would have gone searching for more china. He shrugged, ambled over to the closet, and attempted to shut it, but the door was being held ajar by something inside. He cursed that the colonel and his officers might have left his closet a shambles, and threw open the door. The next moment he was senseless, seeing stars, and falling. By the time he hit the floor he was completely unconscious.

He had not even seen the butt of the pistol that had shot out of the dark closet like a lightning bolt and struck him across the head.

CHAPTER FORTY-FOUR

"What the devil was that?" Richyar, the young sub-lieutenant, said in alarm, rising from the table where he and the other officers had been playing cards.

A dull thud had sent vibrations through the concrete walls of their quarters, and now more thuds could be heard, a great rolling thunder that grew louder and louder and shook their room until trails of dust streamed from the ceiling.

"Bombs," Traugott said succinctly. He too had risen from his chair and went over to try the door again, but it was locked from the outside, just like the last time he had checked. "The damn place is under bombardment and they have us locked in here like sardines."

"What does it mean, Captain?"

"I do not know, Richyar."

Traugott motioned for *U-2553*'s four other officers to hunch down in the corner of the room, near a concrete support that would surely be one of the last things to collapse should one of the bombs above score a direct hit on the underground fortress. As he knelt there with his officers, Traugott began to contemplate how very unusual the morning had been. *U-2553* had arrived at the fortress five days ago. Her cruise across the Mediterranean from Toulon had been a harrowing one, with much time spent ducking destroyers and a seemingly endless armada of aircraft. And if the Allied warships had not deprived Traugott of enough sleep during the voyage, the hole in the ship's organization certainly made up the rest. Lieutenant Rittenhaus had never returned from his foray ashore in Toulon. The word on the street was that the resistance had taken him. It was not an unusual occurrence in an occupied French port, especially with the Allies gaining victories and the liberation of France imminent. But very seldom was an experienced officer snatched away. Traugott would have expected a veteran like Rittenhaus to know which sections of town to avoid. Once again, Traugott was without a first officer, and the strain of carrying both jobs was weighing heavily on him. After a few days moored in the fortress—the same fortress he and *U-2553* had visited on two previous occasions—he finally got a chance to rest. His crew was allowed liberty around the island, providing they not go above ground during the day, and his officers moved off the ship and into a small bunk room—the same bunk room in which they were now locked. As on previous occasions, Traugott had met with the Nazi colonel with the black mask and had arranged for the U-boat's cargo to be unloaded. What the colonel intended to do with it, Traugott did not know or care.

Things had been proceeding as they had on both of Traugott's previous visits to this place, until yesterday afternoon, when he had taken a stroll down by the dock to inspect his boat and was surprised to see that *U-2553*'s two remaining torpedoes were being offloaded. When he had questioned the dockyard workers about it, he was told to take his questions to Colonel Sturm.

He had not been able to find Colonel Sturm that evening, and this morning, when he and his officers rose from their bunks to have their breakfasts, they were surprised to find the door to their quarters locked from the outside.

Were they under some type of arrest? Something was definitely wrong, and Traugott could only think about his enlisted sailors. What would they do without a captain to look out for them?

As the rolling bombardment moved farther away, Traugott and his officers were surprised to hear someone on the other side of their door, turning the lock. The door opened, and the big SS sergeant Traugott had seen hanging about the colonel on many occasions now entered the room, carrying a Walther P38 semiautomatic pistol. He was flanked on either side by two other SS men holding MP 40 submachine guns. All three men wore forbidding faces.

"Sergeant!" Traugott said harshly. "What is the meaning of this? I demand to know why these doors were locked last night!"

"You will be quiet, Captain!" the sergeant barked, brandishing the muzzle of the Walther and aiming it at Traugott. "You and your men will stand and line up against that wall!"

Traugott was shocked and could hardly say a word. He just stared at the menacing weapon as a thousand rumors of Nazi atrocities in the conquered lands came to the forefront of his thoughts.

"I said stand!" the sergeant screamed. "Now!"

Traugott and the officers of *U-2553* reluctantly complied. What else could they do? The MP 40 submachine gun could fire 550 rounds per minute, and two of the deadly weapons were now pointed in their direction. The officers grudgingly lined up against the wall and faced their assailants.

"What are you going to do?" Traugott said. "You cannot just shoot us like dogs! What have we done? What are the charges? Sergeant, I demand to speak with Colonel Sturm!"

"Silence!" the sergeant blared at them, and then a small smile crossed his chiseled face. "Colonel Sturm will not help you, Captain. He is the one who ordered this."

Traugott was stunned. He felt betrayed. He felt like a fool, and now the only thing he could think about was his crew. "What about my men? Please, Sergeant, tell me, what is going to happen to them?"

"They have already been taken care of, Captain."

"But what—"

"No more questions, Captain!"

At that moment the sergeant nodded to the two gunmen. Both stepped forward and braced their MP 40s with their bodies. Traugott squinted, expecting the next moment to be riddled with bullets, but was surprised when he heard two loud reports, barely a second apart, and saw both of the gunmen drop their weapons and clutch their necks, where blood now pulsated between their fingers. The men crumpled to the floor, gasping for breath. The sergeant suddenly realized what had happened and swung around to look behind him. He started to bring his pistol up, but his arm dropped when another loud report resounded in the room and the back of the sergeant's head blew out, spattering blood all over the U-boat officers. The big man dropped to the floor, allowing Traugott and the others to see the doorway beyond, where stood nothing less than a miracle.

It was Rittenhaus, wearing a bloodstained American army uniform and holding a smoking semiautomatic pistol.

CHAPTER FORTY-FIVE

"This way, Hart," Traugott said, turning down a passage, one that Hart would not have chosen.

"Are you sure, Captain?"

"I know this place well, Hart." Traugott managed something of a mad grin, despite the news of his crew's fate. "This is the quickest way to the lagoon."

Hart nodded. He did not question Traugott again. He simply followed him and the rest of *U-2553*'s officers, full well knowing that it was more than a simple feeling of betrayal that now drove the U-boat captain down one turn and then the next. Traugott was after revenge. Revenge on the men who had brought him here. Revenge on the men who had betrayed him, and revenge on the men who had murdered his crew. Hart could still see the fires that had ignited within Traugott's eyes as he told the German captain the fates of his men. Traugott had also listened patiently while Hart had told him his true identity and the purpose of his mission.

Whether Traugott had believed him, Hart did not know. But Hart assumed that he had. Why else would he now be leading the American agent on the quickest path back to the underground lagoon?

They ran through the crowd of workers and soldiers as the air raid continued to pound the rock fortress with a seemingly incessant ripple of bombs. With each impact the floor shook and the concrete supports threatened to buckle. As they ran past one tunnel, Hart saw it collapse before his eyes and saw three civilians wearing white lab coats crushed flat. Their arms had been full of papers they were trying to save, and the sudden collapse had blown several of the white sheets into the passage in front of Hart. People shouted for help. Some dutiful German soldiers stood their posts, but most ran, trying desperately to find a way out. But where could they go? To the surface, where they would face the full force of the explosions, or deeper into the mountain, where they might be sealed inside by the next collapse. So Hart was not surprised when they finally reached the lagoon and saw a great throng of people crowded on the docks.

There, he noticed Jones hunched by a pier stanchion. The wounded sergeant had undoubtedly decided to descend into the fortress when the bombing started. He was still dressed in his commando black, but it did not seem out of place and none of the frantic Germans nearby seemed to notice or care.

"Sergeant Jones, this is Captain Traugott," Hart said after steering the group over to him. "Captain Traugott, Sergeant Jones."

Traugott nodded uncomfortably, as did Jones, who still winced from the pain of the dagger wound.

"Krauts?" Jones said skeptically, raising an eyebrow.

"These are good krauts, Sergeant."

"Didn't know there were any. Pleased to meet you."

"What in the hell is that?" Traugott said as he gazed upon the Japanese I-boat down at the end of the dock.

"I've been sitting here watching," Jones said. "She's getting underway. Just took on a load of crates. I imagine they're important, because I saw a Japanese general and some Nazi fellow with a black mask board her, along with some civilians. Nothing I could do about it."

Hart nodded. Undoubtedly, the crates contained the artifacts, key lab data, and the prototype of the weapon itself—the biological agent Sturm had used on the crew of *U-2553*. He looked at the I-boat, his mind racing. The Japanese sailors were now casting off lines and shoving off from the pier. Hart could make out Sturm's masked face on the open bridge. Ives was there, too, along with the Japanese general. There were still no signs of Isabelle, but if his hunch was correct, she was aboard, too, along with the key German and American scientists.

Another close bomb hit shook the cavern, releasing giant boulders from the roof, which plunged into the lagoon in great splashes. Several of the German workers on the dock were holding their arms out to the I-boat, begging to be evacuated, but the Japanese sailors ignored them.

As Hart watched the I-boat move toward the center of the lagoon, a flash of despair crossed his mind. Not only were he and Jones trapped inside a cave about to collapse from bombardment, but their entire mission, everything they had suffered for, what so many had died for over the past days and weeks, was encapsulated in that Japanese submarine that was now getting away.

He had to act.

"Captain," he said to Traugott. "We have to stop that I-boat! The fate of both our countries depends on it. I need your help."

"You have it, Hart," Traugott said dejectedly. "But what can I do? Even if we make it through that crowd and manage to board the U-boat, what then? My crew is dead. My boat has no torpedoes. I am as powerless as you are."

Hart looked Traugott in the eyes. "Captain, you once told me that the most important things we can do as officers is to know our men and honor their memories. I know your crew is gone, sir, but you have me, you have Richyar, you have Baumann, Ludwig, and Roller. Not to mention Jones, here. I know these men, sir. I've seen them in action." He flashed a grin at the other officers. "They are the best damned U-boat officers in the fleet. I don't have to tell you that. They can do it, sir. We can do it together, but not without your leadership."

"What are you saying, Hart?" Traugott said tiredly.

"That I need you to think, sir. About your country, and your lost men. I'm just an agent. You're the professional U-boat man. You're the naval expert, and the highest-ranking officer present, not me. I need you to think of a way of stopping that black-masked bastard, and I need you to think of it now!"

At that moment, a flurry of geysers erupted in the center of the lagoon. The I-boat was diving now. Her decks were cleared and her hatches buttoned up. Hart and the others watched helplessly as she slowly disappeared into a maelstrom of bubbles and steered toward the entrance to the underground channel. Traugott smiled sadly and then glanced at the dock where a crowd stood around the moored U-boat watching pieces of the cavern come down around them. At that moment, Hart was watching the captain's face. Then, before his eyes, he saw Traugott's expression transform from one of despair to one of total resolution.

Traugott had an idea.

CHAPTER FORTY-SIX

I-403 rolled gently on the Aegean swell under a darkening blue sky. It had taken more than twelve hours of submerged cruising to reach a spot safe enough to risk surfacing. Now she was more than seventy miles south of the island fortress, and the smoke left by the massive bombing was nothing more than a mere smudge on the northern horizon.

From the bridge of *I-403*, Ives studied the western horizon and the position of the setting sun. It would be dark within two hours, and then all would be well.

A report in Japanese came over the bridge intercom speaker, and the Japanese naval officer next to him responded to it. Ives noticed that the Japanese sailors manning the spattering of antiaircraft guns appeared to breathe easier. General Yakamoto, who was also on the bridge, apparently read the confusion on the American's face and politely interpreted the report.

"The radar officer still reports no air contacts, Mister Ives," Yakamoto said, and then gestured to the activity down on the main deck. "Our aircraft should be ready in a matter of minutes."

Ives nodded politely. Like the general, he was dressed in a woolskin-lined flight suit. It was incredibly uncomfortable in this Mediterranean climate, but it would not be once they got airborne. And that would not be long, judging by the state of things on deck.

I-403 was equipped with three Aichi M6A Seiran aircraft, and right now these were being assembled in an incredibly rapid fashion. A group of Japanese sailors had slid the two-seater planes out of the watertight cylindrical hangar on the I-boat's deck and were now deploying wings and affixing flotation skids. They did it with a speed and efficiency that would impress the flight deck crew of any American carrier.

"We launch them from the catapult," Yakamoto said, apparently to pass the time. "The oil is kept warm by a heating loop that runs inside the submarine."

Ives nodded. "Thank you, General. Your men are doing an impressive job."

Yakamoto smiled with a small measure of pride and then turned his attention back to the main deck. He did not see Ives's smile fade behind him. Ives did not give a damn about how the oil was kept warm, he just wanted this overblown Japanese asshole and his men to get the damn things ready to fly.

The Seiran planes were sleek craft, some of the most elegant planes Ives had ever seen. From the general's earlier ramblings, Ives had learned that each one had a range of more than six hundred miles and could carry a payload of nearly a ton. More than enough to get them and their cargo to the Syrian coast, where the Organization had agents waiting.

As Ives watched with impatience while the aircraft payload supports were affixed with aerodynamic cargo bays and the artifacts and documents were carefully loaded into them, he could not help but wonder how the British had gotten wise to the location of the island. He suspected Hart had something to do with it. Only Hart could have interpolated the island's coordinates from reviewing *U-2553*'s charts. It was feasible that Hart could have survived the explosion beneath Hagia Sophia, and it was feasible that he had managed to contact the British. But something was gnawing at Ives, and he could not put his finger on it. He was sure that Hart had figured out the entire scheme and knew that he and Isabelle were part of an independent organization that had no allegiances. Sure, this fool Yakamoto thought they were going to help him bring down the Allies, but that was certainly not the Organization's actual plan. Yakamoto had purchased only a limited quantity of the weapon. After the Japanese used it, wherever they used it, the world would know of the weapon's existence, and the bidding war would begin. Yakamoto would try to purchase more, but Ives knew he would be outbid by the Soviets, or perhaps even the United States. One country would be played off another until a global balance of power was reached, with the Organization garnering the real control. The plan was still sound, and even though the destruction of their research lab had been a setback, the Organization had enough information to set up shop again in a new location and resume production. Perhaps this time in China. They had come so far. They had made sacrifices, had gone to infinite lengths to obtain the ancient weapon they now had in their possession. Certainly they could not be stopped. Not now. But despite his optimistic outlook, something still bothered Ives.

At that moment, Colonel Sturm ascended through the open bridge hatch. The colonel also wore a flight suit and had discarded the high field hat for a thin cloth garrison cap that sat awkwardly atop his ski mask–covered head. Drs. Jungert and Geldenson also appeared on the bridge. They were not wearing flight suits. There was not enough room aboard the aircraft for them. Only three Japanese pilots and three passengers would be able to go. The doctors would have to take their chances aboard the I-boat and meet up with the Organization whenever the submarine reached the Syrian coast.

"Is the cargo loaded, gentlemen?" Sturm asked, his hoarse voice barely audible in the wind.

Ives nodded stoically.

"What is it?" Sturm asked.

"Hart," Ives said succinctly.

"Do you think he's alive?"

Ives nodded. "I'm sure of it. But he wouldn't have let the British reduce the island to rubble. He's more efficient than that."

"Perhaps he did not have a choice," Sturm said in a jovial manner. "Even the famous Matt Hart cannot stop foolish generals from blundering."

Yakamoto heard this and shot a glance at Sturm,

smarting somewhat from the implied insult to flag rank officers. But Yakamoto was surprised to see the colonel's black-gloved hand resting in a somewhat affectionate manner on Ives's arm.

"Don't worry, Martin," Sturm said to Ives in a voice Yakamoto had not heard before, a high-pitched, smooth voice. "It will be all right. Once we reach Damascus, everything will be fine."

Ives gave a reluctant nod and patted the colonel's hand, all under Yakamoto's confused gaze.

A sailor on deck shouted up to the bridge with cupped hands, and Yakamoto was pulled away from his confusion. The submarine's captain then stood before him and reported that Plane 1 was ready for takeoff.

"The first plane is ready, Colonel," Yakamoto said.

"Thank you, General," Sturm replied in his former voice. "Perhaps Mister Ives could take this first aircraft?"

Yakamoto nodded in agreement. He was then shocked when Ives and Sturm embraced. Then the American agent threw a leg over the bridge rail and descended the ladder to the main deck. Yakamoto said nothing as he and the strange SS colonel watched Ives walk up to the forward deck and climb aboard the first aircraft, fully assembled and ready to launch, sitting on the catapult. Ives waved once to Sturm before closing the canopy, and Yakamoto saw Sturm wave back in a feminine manner.

As the aircraft's engine came to life, Yakamoto could not help but study the colonel in a whole new light. Sturm's flight suit afforded a better look at the cut of his body than did the long black trench coat he had worn every other time Yakamoto had seen him. Now he could make out a supple form beneath the woolskin leather. Long legs and hips with curves. And the hint of rise in the chest region, where the colonel strategically wore a flowing red scarf.

"Colonel," Yakamoto said, uncomfortably. "I must ask you something—"

Yakamoto's statement was cut short by a cry of alarm from one of the lookouts in the periscope shears.

"U-boat! U-boat!" the lookout shouted. "Off the port quarter!"

Yakamoto turned and gasped. Where a moment before had been a placid sea, now a great frothy disturbance appeared less than fifty yards from the I-boat's stern. Out of the bubbly white mixture rose a U-boat, the same one he had seen inside the fortress. It was moving at full speed, near twenty knots, and for a brief moment the Japanese general marveled at how it could have achieved such speeds while submerged. Within seconds it was on the surface, plowing the ocean waves before it, and heading straight for the stopped I-boat's beam.

"That son of a bitch!" Sturm shouted in alarm, the voice fully that of a female now. "He's going to ram us!"

"Commence firing! All guns!" the I-boat's captain ordered. In response, the antiaircraft gun crews all swung their weapons around and began to engage the charging U-boat.

As the guns rang out in long, point-blank bursts, the

twenty-five-millimeter shells peppered the U-boat's bow and conning tower but did nothing to stop its progress. Yakamoto saw this and rushed over to the captain.

"What are you doing, you fool? Those guns won't stop him. We have to move!" Yakamoto touched the intercom button and ordered, "Helmsman, all engines ahead full! Rudder hard to starboard!"

"No, General!" The captain tried to stop him. "I've just given the order to launch aircraft!"

But it was too late. The helmsman below had instantly responded to the general's order, and now the I-boat's 7,700-horsepower diesel engines brought her to life. She began picking up speed and heeled over to starboard as the rudder took full effect. At the same time, there was a loud whack up on the forward deck. It was the sound of the compressed-air catapult launching the plane.

"Martin!" a female voice squealed. It had come from Sturm.

Yakamoto looked up forward in time to see the plane accelerate rapidly along the catapult. By the time it reached the end of the seventy-five-foot launch skid, it was going ninety miles per hour. Under ideal conditions, when the deck was level and the plane had a few feet of freeboard, this would have been an adequate speed to get the plane airborne, allowing its fourteen-hundred-horsepower V12 engine to take over and accelerate it into a climb. But now, with *I-403*'s deck heeled over in the hard turn, the skid launched the aircraft at a skewed angle that drove the plane's right wingtip directly into the water, instantly putting the plane into a cartwheeling spin, like a loose wheel careening across the surface of the water. The plane progressively came apart at each impact with the water, until nothing was left but a twisted ball of metal. On one of the impacts, the bodies of Ives and the Japanese pilot flew free and clear of the aircraft, clearly visible from the bridge of *I-403*. They twirled one hundred feet into the air, as limp as rag dolls, and then fell into the sea with skidding impacts that were clearly not survivable.

"No!" Sturm screamed again, this time ripping and tearing at the black mask and ski hood until both came off.

Yakamoto had fully expected to see a face mangled by the dreaded flamethrower, but instead he saw the smooth face of a woman whose long, blond hair had been tightly wound in a ball on top of her head. The Japanese general was stunned, not only at the discovery that Sturm was really a woman, but also because this woman now had a look of uncontrollable hatred in her eyes—and she was looking directly at *I-403*'s captain. In an instant she produced a pistol that looked like an American Colt M1903. With a face red with anger she pointed the weapon at the unsuspecting captain, who had his back turned to her, and she fired. The bullet struck the captain in the back of the head, and the wind blew the ensuing red spray onto Yakamoto's face. The Japanese crewmen on deck, firing their AA guns did not even notice as their captain's dead body fell to the deck. They were too distracted by the onrushing U-boat.

Yakamoto reached for his own pistol, just as the crazed woman turned her weapon in his direction. But before either of them could fire, a great crash of grinding metal, louder than the firing AA guns, broke apart the air. The deck heeled to one side and Yakamoto found himself flying through the air directly toward the railing on the opposite side of the bridge.

U-2553 had captured her prey.

CHAPTER FORTY-SEVEN

Hart and the others inside *U-2553*'s control room had braced for impact at the last minute. They had been given a few seconds' warning by Captain Traugott, whose voice had sounded extremely weak over the intercom but had been enough to save most of them from any serious injury.

Hart was at the diving station, and Richyar at the helm, and now they looked at each other, neither quite believing they had managed to pull it off.

"Are you all right?" Hart asked the German naval sub-lieutenant.

Richyar rubbed his shoulder and shrugged. "I forgot about that pipe hanger, but I will live. I wonder how the men in the other compartments fared."

"You're the first officer, now, Richyar," Hart said with a grin. "I'll leave that to you."

Richyar smiled wearily. "Understood, sir."

Hart slung the British Sten submachine gun over one shoulder and started to climb the ladder to the bridge, but he was stopped short by Sergeant Jones.

"Wait, laddie." The English sergeant looked up at

him, holding a satchel. He had evidently managed the collision without any further injury, but Hart knew how painful any movement had to be to his dagger wound. "I believe you'll be needing these."

"Thanks," Hart said with a nod as he took the satchel and then headed up the ladder. When he reached the top and emerged onto the bridge, he found what he had fully expected to see. *U-2553*'s knifing bow had rammed into *I-403*'s stern on the port side. It was obvious that the I-boat had tried to turn away, but the attempt had come too late. Now her hull was smashed in on the port side and looked almost as bad as the U-boat's crushed bow. All of the Japanese guns had stopped firing, and Hart could see chaos ensuing on her deck, with sailors running to and fro, and some up forward trying to right an aircraft that had tilted onto one wing. They were dazed and confused. Now was the time to act. He did not have much time. But then, he had to find a moment to spare for the bloody and bruised body that now lay at his feet.

"Did we . . . stop them, . . . Hart?" the weak voice said through bloody lips.

Hart knelt down to cradle Captain Traugott's head in his hands.

"Yes, Captain. We stopped them."

Traugott managed a smile. He had been hit many times by splinters from the Japanese shells and Hart could see that one shell had nearly torn off his right arm. White bone was visible in the mess where a thin strand of flesh was the only thing that kept the arm attached. It was difficult for Hart to see him this way, this man who was his enemy, but whom he had grown very fond of over the weeks aboard *U-2553*. And now, Traugott was the man who had saved them all.

It had been Traugott's idea to recruit a dozen of the civilian dockyard workers from the pier of the crumbling fortress and use them to man some of *U-2553*'s less complex, but necessary positions. *U-2553*, leaving on patrol, would normally require a crew of nearly one hundred men to manage watch rotations, repair broken equipment, perform maintenance, cook meals, and a thousand other tasks that arise when deployed for weeks at sea. But to operate for only a few hours, with a handful of experienced officers to instruct and oversee, and a few unskilled workers to operate the lower-skilled stations, it was entirely possible to sail *U-2553* with only a skeleton crew. And that was exactly what Captain Traugott had done. He had worked feverishly to get the boat underway, seemingly everywhere at once as the ship was rigged for dive in record time by the handful of officers. Once he had conned her clear of the channel and into open water, he had made a calculated guess as to the direction the Japanese submarine had gone. Of course he only had to get it half right. He had Baumann manning the sound gear, listening for any sound that might indicate the Japanese submarine surfacing to charge her diesels. And that sound had come at four o'clock in the afternoon, on a bearing of one seven five, almost due south from *U-2553*'s position. Traugott had ordered the snorkel raised and demanded as much speed as the snorkel mast would allow. They had reached the unsuspecting I-boat's position just as the Japanese were preparing to launch aircraft and had wasted no time in ordering *U-2553* onto a collision course with the Japanese sub.

When *U-2553* had blown to the surface in the final meters of its high-speed sprint, Traugott had insisted on manning the bridge to conn her in personally. He had ignored the protests of Richyar and Hart, who had suggested using the periscope instead. Traugott had argued that the periscope provided a limited field of view, and if it was hit by the Japanese fire, they would be essentially blind. So, in the true fashion of a U-boat ace, Traugott had manned the bridge alone and had braved the Japanese fire as he called down rudder corrections to steer his ship directly into his prey. Hart and the others in the control room had listened to the intercom speaker with despair as Traugott's voice had grown weaker and weaker, his last course correction and warning to brace coming only seconds before the violent impact.

Now, as Hart held the dying captain, he knew that he had to get going, but he could not bring himself to leave Traugott's side.

Traugott seemed to sense this and said, "The Japs build good boats, Hart . . . she will have compartments . . . I doubt she will sink . . . you will have to do it . . ."

Hart nodded. Traugott tried to speak again, but instead coughed up a mouthful of blood.

At that moment Richyar emerged from the bridge hatch and scurried over to his captain's side.

"She is done for, Captain!" the agitated young sub-lieutenant reported, out of breath, as if his captain were not covered with blood and dying before his eyes. "We have major flooding up forward."

"I know . . . ," Traugott answered, and reached for Richyar's arm with his good hand. "Man the life rafts, my boy . . . abandon her . . . you are in command now."

"Yes, Captain." Richyar looked at his captain with tear-filled eyes. "Let me get you down to the deck, sir."

"No!" Traugott said gruffly, followed by a coughing fit of blood and mucus. "I will remain here, Richyar . . ." Traugott then managed a small smile and said softly, "You understand, my boy? I must remain here."

"Yes, Captain." Richyar issued something like a salute to his mangled captain, and then he tore his tear-streaked face away from the sight and disappeared down the hatch.

"Now . . . get going . . . Hart," Traugott uttered. "You are an old submariner . . . you know how to sink a boat . . ."

Hart nodded and placed a hand on Traugott's shoulder. "Rest easy, Captain. You've done your duty. Now I will do mine."

CHAPTER FORTY-EIGHT

Hart had descended the ladder to *U-2553*'s main deck with the Sten gun and satchel slung on his shoulders and now ran out onto the submarine's mangled bow. The Japanese AA gun crews had sought cover and were away from their mounts, but not for long. A Japanese officer was already spurring them back to their posts.

Hart had reached the spot where the two giant submarines' hulls were locked in a violent embrace. He was fortunate in the fact that *U-2553*'s high bow had collided with the I-boat's low stern, so he had a height advantage for making the leap over the deadly space where the two hulls ground together. Without pausing he got a running start and jumped off *U-2553*'s bow and landed on the sloping stern of the I-boat. When he had collected his bearings, he noticed that the Japanese gunners had regained their gun mounts, but in spite of that fact he brought the Sten gun to the firing position and began running for the aftermost fairwater leading up to the conning tower. The Japanese twenty-five-millimeter guns were imposing, but they had been designed for repelling aircraft, and Hart knew they were not capable of being depressed to shoot something aboard their own ship. The Japanese gunners were pointing in his direction, but still he did not stop. He pressed on, secure in the belief that Japanese submarine crews most likely operated similar to U.S. submarine crews, or to any other crew for that matter. The crews of most naval ships, no matter the nationality, did not carry small arms around as part of their normal dress. Most ships contained a tightly guarded weapons room, which held just enough rifles and pistols to arm the ship's guards whenever the ship was pierside. At sea, these weapons were normally locked up. Even when at battle stations, ship crews did not encumber themselves with small arms. In fact, in this day and age, only the big ships—the carriers, the battleships, and the cruisers—retained a standing contingent of marines onboard for shipboard security. A submarine's crew seldom carried small arms, and that was indeed the case with *I-403*.

As Hart made it to the first fairwater, the realization of this fact was visible in the eyes of the Japanese sailors manning the gun mount there. They were completely impotent to resist as Hart mowed them down with three long bursts from the Sten. Hart loaded a new magazine and pressed on, but the other Japanese sailors, including their officer, seemed to understand their predicament and quickly beat a retreat toward the forward end of their boat.

Up on the bridge, Hart saw two civilian men quickly disappear down the hatch.

Hart now had clear access to the bridge and quickly climbed the last ladder to reach the top. He had thought the bridge was clear but was surprised when a dazed Japanese general, bleeding from a smashed nose, came out of nowhere, blindly firing a pistol in every direction. The bullets missed Hart by several feet, and he wasn't even sure the confused general was aware of his presence, but he had no time to contemplate it. He fired a short burst, instantly transforming the general's chest into an uneven design of bleeding holes. The general, knocked back by the force of the nine-millimeter bullets, flipped over the rail and fell into the sea.

The bridge hatch lay open at Hart's feet; he could hear the agitated voices of the sailors in the submarine's control room far below, and he heard the sound of someone climbing up the ladder. When the climber reached the top and poked his head out the hatch, Hart could see it was a Japanese officer. Hart greeted the wide-eyed man with a steel-toed boot to the nose. The stunned officer lost his hold on the ladder and plummeted the twenty feet to the control room below.

Hart did not stop to think. He had to get down to that control room, and there was only one way to do it. He opened the satchel Jones had given him and produced five British Mark I Mills grenades. In slow, methodical procession, he pulled the pin on one and dropped the baritol-packed weapon down the hatch. He heard it hit the control room deck below, heard several Japanese voices cry in terror, and then heard a loud *Kawump!*

He waited several seconds for the survivors to get to their feet, and then dropped the next one, and the next, and the next until he had dropped all five grenades down the hatch and heard no more Japanese voices. Without pausing, he climbed down the ladder, through the smoky air, and quickly reached the control room, where he was greeted by a ghastly sight of carnage and death. Japanese bodies were everywhere, along with severed limbs and heads. He also saw the mangled bodies of the two civilians who had gone below.

Hart knew he had only a few seconds. The slow string of grenades would have the Japanese sailors in the adjacent compartments wondering if the explosions had ceased. It would take a few moments for them to muster the courage to try to enter the control room again. But Hart needed only a few moments. He had studied the intelligence reports on Japanese subs over the years. In operation, they were not that different from American submarines. He had even toured an I-boat before the war. Not like this one, of course, but he could tell from one glance at the diving control station that the basic makeup of the diving controls was the same. Hart found the electrical switches that lined up the trim pump, and he began pumping water into the I-boat's aft trim tanks. He also found the electrical control that operated the flood valve and used that to fill the forward trim tanks. He had only one thing left to do. He inched over to the switches that controlled the main ballast tank vents and switched all six of them to the open position. Instantly, the sound of air escaping the ballast tanks filled the room.

The Japanese in the next compartment forward obviously heard this too, and opened the watertight door to investigate. Hart beat them back into the compartment with several rounds from his Sten gun that sparked and ricocheted around the room.

Hart took one last look around the bloody control room and then finally at the depth gauge on the bulkhead. The needle had started to move. The submarine was on her way down now. There was nothing left to do. Hart darted to the ladder and began to climb. He could hear voices above and knew that the Japanese sailors still on deck must have been washed in a tumultuous spray of seawater the moment he opened the main ballast tank vents. They would be either scrambling for the open hatches or jumping over the side. When Hart finally reached the bridge again, he was surprised to see that neither was true.

I-403's decks were already awash, and she was headed down fast. Hart saw that the handful of Japanese sailors above decks had all congregated around something up forward, something that was two hundred feet forward of the bridge, and the only thing that was not sinking with the submarine. It was the last of the Japanese aircraft, and it was floating on the surface, riding on its two flotation skids. Hart concluded that the Japanese must have removed it from the hangar up forward and assembled it immediately after the collision. But then he saw something else—something that struck an emotional chord within him that sent surges of sorrow, betrayal, and rage through his veins all at once.

It was Isabelle. She was standing on the aircraft's left flotation skid kicking the faces of the Japanese sailors in the water who were desperately trying to climb aboard. One of the struggling sailors managed to get a knee up on the skid, and Hart watched as Isabelle put her M1903 to his head and blew his brains out.

"Get off!" Hart heard her shouting at them. "You will capsize this thing! Get off! Do you hear!"

She shot another and another, until the Japanese sailors finally swam away.

With no sign of Colonel Sturm, Hart finally concluded that his earlier suspicions—and those of Admiral McDonough—were true. That the Nazi colonel and Isabelle were the same person. Most likely, she had been a double agent before the war even started, and probably had as many contacts in the SS as she had in Odysseus. No doubt she had created the masked persona, Sturm, to allow her free access across the Reich and to facilitate garnering resources from the German military machine, such as the use of *U-2553* and the flak tower in the Alps. Obviously, she was the one who had betrayed the team in Spain. Hart had been blinded by his affection for her, but Admiral McDonough had suspected her treason all along. That was why, when she later contacted the admiral with the implausible story of her escape, McDonough had told her to remain in Europe. Holmhurst had told Hart all of this in Vienna, and the final stages of this mission had been to uncover how far her tentacles had stretched into the ranks of Odysseus, and McDonough's arrest in London had been staged to flush out whatever moles might remain.

"Hurry up, you idiot!" Isabelle now shouted at the Japanese pilot who was still deploying the aircraft's collapsible wings.

Hart caught sight of the cargo container affixed to

the bomb carriage beneath the aircraft and instantly assumed Isabelle had managed to load either some of the research material or the actual weaponized material itself. But he did not have time to contemplate it for very long. The sea now enveloped the I-boat's bridge and began to pour down the open bridge hatch at his feet. He cursed himself for skylarking and quickly jumped into the sea and began to swim away as fast as he could. The simple principles of buoyancy and hull compressibility were going to define what happened next, and Hart had to get away from this spot as fast as humanly possible. The I-boat would get heavier as it sank deeper into the water. The increased sea pressure would make the hull compress, reducing the amount of water displaced and thereby sending the sub down faster and faster with each passing foot. A six-thousand-ton vessel dropping so rapidly could create a powerful undertow— one that could carry a man down a hundred feet or more before he was free of it. With this in mind, Hart swam for his very life. But undertows were a lot like upside-down tornadoes. They were vortexes that could suck down every object in one square meter of ocean while leaving the next square meter untouched. Hart did not encounter the deadly suction forces where he was, but the Japanese sailors did, and he heard brief screams of terror as the few survivors in the water, not a hundred feet away from him, were sucked under and swallowed up by the sea.

The aircraft, however, appeared to be unaffected by the undertow, and Hart heard the engine turn over once as the Japanese pilot attempted to start the plane. Isabelle had been so preoccupied with keeping the Japanese sailors away that she had not even seen him. But Hart saw her as she closed the passenger side of the cockpit around her in preparation for takeoff.

Then Hart heard several men shouting, and turned around to see *U-2553*'s life rafts, full of her makeshift crewmen, floating only a few feet away. They had already paddled well clear of the sinking U-boat and were actually steering back toward the sinking ship to pick him up.

"Come on, Hart!" he heard Jones's voice calling. "Over here, laddie!"

Hart waved to them, but he did not swim in their direction. He took one look at the aircraft that was sputtering to life and knew exactly what he had to do.

Hart had been through extreme physical fitness training in spy school but had allowed himself to forget what he had learned about pushing his body beyond all limits. Now he reached back to those hard days at spy school and mustered everything he could. With mind, muscle, and form focused on one objective, he started swimming as fast as he could for the U-boat.

"Where the hell are you going, laddie?" he thought he heard Jones shout between strokes, but he did not stop. He just kept swimming as fast as he could until he reached the listing, half-awash deck of *U-2553*.

Behind him, he heard the pilot revving the aircraft's engine, turning the plane to find the direction of the wind. Hart knew he had only seconds. The plane would be airborne in a minute and Isabelle would get away. She would sell the secret of the ancient weapon that had killed millions in ancient times to the highest bidder, and it would kill again.

Hart dashed for the bridge ladder and climbed to the top in record time. On the bridge, he found Captain Traugott dead, with eyes open, staring peacefully at the sky. Hart did not have time to mourn his friend. He reached the aft twenty-millimeter gun turret, popped open the watertight ammunition box inside, and fed the belt of glimmering brass shells into the breech mechanism.

He tried to rotate the turret toward the taxiing plane—but there was a problem. *U-2553* had tilted to the point that the turret's field of fire was limited to a small sector of sea and sky just aft of the ship. There was no way to aim it at the plane!

As the plane's blaring engine reached full throttle, the plane began to pick up speed, drawing a double white line on the surface behind it. Hart suddenly realized that the plane's takeoff flight path would take it just past the U-boat's stern.

He would get only one chance at this.

As the plane sped toward the section of sky in front of his guns, he considered trying a test fire to judge the fall of the projectiles. Though he had fired other twenty-millimeter guns before, this was the first time he had ever fired this particular weapon, and he was not even sure he had prepared it correctly. He decided against a test fire, since it would certainly alert the Japanese pilot to the danger up ahead.

He would have one chance, and only one.

The plane had reached takeoff speed and had to be traveling near one hundred knots. Just as the plane began to climb, it entered the top of Hart's gun sight.

Hart briefly closed his eyes, opened them again, and then squeezed the trigger. The burst of twenty-millimeter shells, laced with tracer rounds, lasted no more than two seconds, but through the white smoke before his face Hart saw the stream of projectiles hit the plane's left side, near the engine, and tear the engine housing apart. The next instant the fuel-filled plane exploded in a brilliant ball of fire that seared across the sky in a low arc that ended in the sea. Flaming debris rained down for a few seconds afterward, and then there was nothing but a disintegrating trail of smoke to indicate that the plane had ever been there.

Hart rested his head against the cold steel and took a deep breath. It seemed like the first deep breath he had taken in hours.

"Good-bye, Isabelle," he said quietly.

He would have liked to rest there for a few minutes more, but he could not.

A furor of giant bubbles broached the surface a few yards away from the U-boat, marking the end of *I-403*. Somewhere, down there, in that deep, dark abyss, her remaining watertight compartments had imploded. Every sailor, soldier, and civilian aboard her had died in that instant.

Hart heard *U-2553*'s steel girders groaning from the strain of her list. She was on her way to join the I-boat, and Hart had to leave. He took one last look at the body of Captain Traugott and then leaped into the sea. Within minutes the life rafts were there, and the U-boat men were pulling him out of the water.

After reaching a safe distance, they all watched as the U-boat finally slipped under the waves. Some of the officers had tears in their eyes.

"Before we abandoned ship," Richyar said hesitantly to Hart, as the raft gently floated over a long swell, "your Sergeant Jones used our radio to notify Allied headquarters of our position."

Hart looked at Jones, who nodded and winked.

"Then I expect they will be along any moment now, Sub-Lieutenant."

"We will be prisoners of war," Richyar said in a shameful tone. "We will be shipped to one of your stinking, hellhole prisons."

"I wouldn't exactly call them hellholes, Sub-Lieutenant," Hart said. "I've spent some time in them myself."

"You?" Richyar eyed him skeptically.

"Let's just say I have some connections in that community." Hart then grinned and patted him on the shoulder. "Don't worry, Richyar. I'll see to it that you and your men are treated well. It's the least I could do for my old shipmates."

Richyar managed a small smile.

"Enough about hellholes and bloody prisons!" Jones exclaimed. "What I want to know, laddie, is how the bloody hell did you pull off a shot like that? You brought that bugger down with one burst. That was a one-in-a-million shot! I bloody well know I never taught you to shoot like that."

Hart smiled. "Well, Sergeant, she was making off with the Lord's weapon, and I had only one chance to stop her. At a time like that, I figured there was only one thing to do."

Jones looked at him quizzically.

"I closed my eyes, and I prayed."